Pinky Swear

A Pale Woods Mystery, Book Two

Courtnee Howell-Turner

Pale Woods Publishing

Pinky Swear

A Pale Woods Mystery

Copyright © August 2021
Copyright © September 27, 2025

Erwin, TN

by Courtnee Howell-Turner

Library of Congress Control Number: 2025918154

Paperback IBSN 979-8-9899846-9-5

E-book IBSN 979-8-9899846-7-1

Cover Design: Taylor Dawn, Sweet15 Designs, LLC

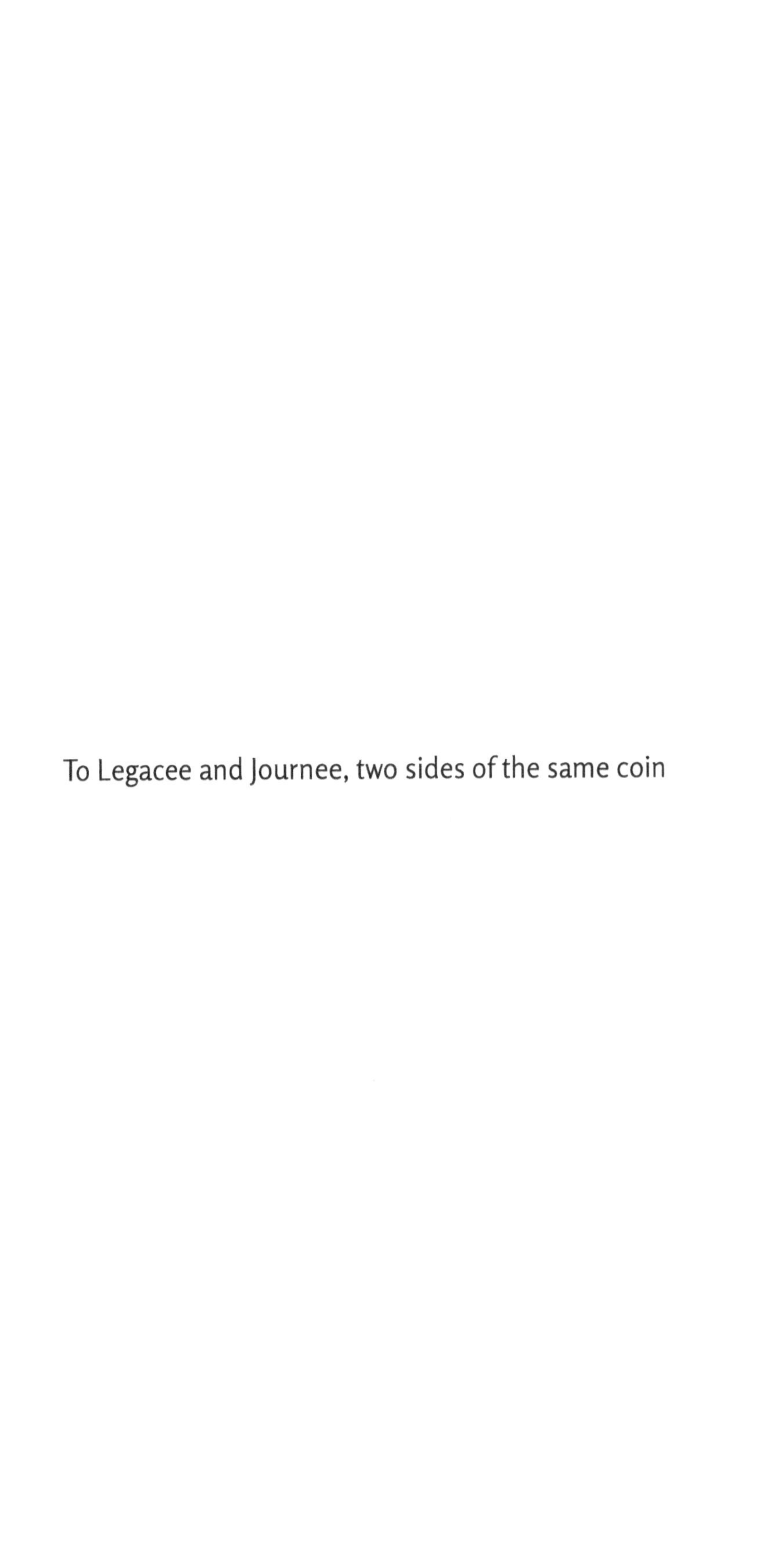

To Legacee and Journee, two sides of the same coin

A Note to Readers

Dear Friends in the Written World,

This is the second time this book has been published. I'm releasing it again with a new cover.

The publication date is significant. It marks the one-year anniversary of the flood that significantly impacted my region.

Sadly, people lost their lives that day. Many others lost their homes or were stranded.

Friday, September 27, 2024, was my preteen daughter's eleventh birthday, and the power was off and on. I took the opportunity to bake my daughter a birthday cake just before a long outage. We listened to and cheered for the helicopters that evacuated our neighbors from the hospital's roof (just five minutes from our door).

A year later, our town still isn't the same. Families are still mourning, a few people are still living in campers and tents, we haven't built an animal shelter, and we panic when we think another hurricane might make landfall near us. I mean, I thought the advantage of living in a landlocked state was freedom from the severity of hurricanes, right?

Well, what does that really have to do with this book?

I wrote Pinky Swear in 2011, and it was published with a different cover. It never seemed to fully reflect the story, though.

I never thought I'd live to see a flood like the one that destroyed a portion of my town. A two-story brick home was washed away like it was made of sticks, and asphalt ripped up and floated miles down the new path the river cut around the mountains.

I've had this book cover since before my mama passed away in August 2023. It was one of the last things she saw before she passed. I couldn't release it because part of me associated it with her death.

However, as my community rebuilds, I'll try to grow with it. The flood in my story may not be the same, but it is symbolic enough to release on the one-year anniversary.

Erwin is my home, and the people of North Carolina are my neighbors. I hope everyone who suffered from Hurricane Helene can fully recover. My love and prayers are with you every day.

With love,
Courtnee

Pinky Swear Playlist

1. "Ordinary World" by Duran Duran

2. "Lunchbox Friends" Melanie Martinez

3. "Why Can't We Be Friends?" WAR

4. "I Am the Highway" Audioslave

5. "It's a Great Day to Be Alive" Travis Tritt

6. "Thank You" Led Zeppelin

7. "Lights" Ellie Goulding (Bassnectar Remix)

8. "Bad Blood" Taylor Swift

9. "Cracks" Flux Pavilion

10. "Don't You Worry Child" Swedish House Mafia

11. "Midnight Hands" Rise Against

12. "One" Metallica

Prologue

The sky never foretold the upcoming misery. The land welcomed the light of the sun, and its heat spread over a small valley in Northeastern Tennessee. Most of Erwin's residents knew that the autumn day would reheat the icy stroke of the night air, but not a solar touch can warm everything.

The sun's rays had already soaked Pale Woods Academy when the students filed into its halls. An education enthusiast, Racer Daniels, had built the school, but he had abandoned the project when he had lost interest. Daniels had given the academy to an anonymous local woman who had seemed intelligent and kind during one of his visits, and she made certain the school continued to flourish.

The building stood on a mountainside in an area the Native American Cherokee had named Pale Woods. Daniels constructed Pale Woods Academy using an old Civil War outpost that was built from the trees cut down when they cleared the area cleared for the building and the rock from the Nolichucky River that ran parallel to Pale Woods.

Daniels designed the school to hold the brightest minds in Eastern Tennessee as they cruised from kindergarten through twelfth grade. The students were required to pay tuition. After the school almost fell into financial ruin, Daniels admitted students of average intellect so he could give some of the most intelligent members of the community scholarships to the school.

Most of the students had no problem digesting the rigorous academic curriculum, but some children, who performed very well in public schools, fell behind quickly. These students usually lasted a year or two, and their departure allowed a few new students to enter the halls of Pale Woods Academy every year.

The crisp air from the opening and closing entrances crept through the front rooms of the school, challenging the structure's outdated heating and air units. On the east side of the lower level, the eighth-grade section was busy with Monday morning activities. It was the week of the Apple Festival in Erwin, but the two-day event wouldn't take place until Friday and Saturday.

Many of the students were looking forward to a vacation from school, and they didn't want to go there at all that week. The teachers assigned projects to keep their classes busy while they prepared for the festival, because many of them had booths or worked with local organizations during the festivities.

In a town as small as Erwin, many families had a booth at the festival, a place in the pageants, or on the entertainment stage. Everyone seemed under the spell of the out-of-town revenue entering the region. It was the only event in the small town that pulled people from other parts of the country, and the Erwin residents were prepared to absorb the profits from the visitors.

The sun bathed the school and the playground, but it stopped at the woods that lined the property around the school. The warming wind rustled through the dying leaves of the Pale Woods Forest.

Some of the town's biggest secrets and deepest sadnesses whispered through the creaking branches and silent caves. One secret had learned a way to stretch beyond Pale Woods and affect the lives of the townspeople. He was delighted to ruin families and spread disease in relationships, and he was ready for the next phase of his plan. One icy finger stretched into the air, caressing the darkness just beyond the light denied to it.

"Soon," he promised. "I will have my revenge."

From deep inside her mind, Ella Miller heard him and shuddered.

Chapter One

I watched the buzzing activity from my place at the back of the room. The sun had risen high enough to light the valley below, and I could easily look out the floor-length window by my seat and see the community.

I turned my attention to the beautiful fall day. The sky was a crisp blue that promised a warm day until the sun bent its back into the mountains. I sighed and resigned myself to watching another pleasant day pass while confined to my desk. Pale Woods Academy wasn't that bad, but some days I wished to have class outdoors. It would be so much easier to think about cellular construction and algebraic expressions with a warm wind swirling through my hair and fresh mountain air feeding oxygen to my brain.

My elbow slipped, and I raised my arm in time to save my project. The assignment had been an amazingly hard task for me.

Ms. Hughes, my teacher, had given the class an assignment on our physical connection to our families. The class was studying genetics, so she thought the students could learn more by researching their own biological line.

Ms. Hughes had told us to ask our parents for a baby picture. She emphasized that she only wanted one picture, because she had received a plethora of them in past classes from proud parents.

I turned my paper from side to side. I was glad that the assignment was complete because I never wanted to ask my mother for anything from the past again.

I thought that peeling a baby picture of me from a picture album would have been a straightforward task for my mom. I didn't expect the wails of mourning and the bout of depression that followed my petition.

My mom had immediately acted upon my request by leading me upstairs to the walk-in closet off her bedroom. She solemnly collected a large, pink baby album she had stored on a white wire shelf in her closet. My mom and I blew the dust off the album, and she sat down on the bed.

I could smell dusty age in the pages of the baby book. I bounced up onto the bed so that my feet dangled casually off the side. My mother adjusted her body into a comfortable position.

At first, she smiled and giggled over my bath pictures and birthday photos. After a couple of pages, though, pictures appeared of me with other members of the family.

A picture of my brothers stabbed my eyes with unexpected moisture. Through the blur of my tears, I could make out boys with blond hair and blue eyes who smiled into the camera as they posed for a picture that made them immortal. Josh and Jerrod were holding me across their laps as I looked away from the camera and pointed at the house. I didn't fight against Josh, my favorite brother, or Jerrod, so my lower body remained still while the rest of me turned. I had been three or four, so my brothers had been in their early teens.

Unfortunately, I didn't get to enjoy the protection of Josh and Jerrod for long after the photograph. My brothers never made it out of adolescence. They had died when attempting to discover the whereabouts of our missing father.

The pictures of my father did not move me in the same way as the frozen images of my brothers. I felt empty as I looked at the photographs of him holding me at birth or tickling me as a toddler. My mom, however, broke down. She handed me the album and ran into her bathroom.

My mom's bathroom had collected the woes of most of our family. My mom tried to camouflage her cries, even though the acoustics in the room echoed them halfway down the upstairs hall. Both of my brothers had run to the room when they were frustrated or unhappy. Josh had even used the room as a gateway for his spirit after his death.

I left my mom's bedroom with my baby book after several minutes of listening to the sobs that escaped the bathroom. That room had cradled a lot of my family's pain.

I walked into my bedroom and shut the door. My younger sister, Ella, was playing video games downstairs, so I was completely alone.

It seemed like playing video games was the only normal thing Ella did, but I thought she played them to be closer to Jerrod more than for the love of the games. It was her way of remembering the sibling she had held closest to her heart.

I shared a bedroom with Ella. My brothers had been dead for almost four years, but my mother refused to move any of Josh and Jerrod's personal effects from their room. It didn't surprise me, though, because my father's razor still sat on his side of the bathroom vanity a decade after he last walked out of the front door. Orange rust ran from the razor's old blades and permanently claimed its place as it clawed onto the porcelain surface.

I flipped to a page with a border that read "Sisters". The central picture showed me sitting in a hospital chair while Josh and Jerrod flanked me. I could only see their hands in the picture, and I knew they were there to make sure that I didn't drop the newest member of our family. I was two in the picture, and I was struggling to hold a bread-shaped bundle.

Ella, firmly wrapped, did not protest my embrace. She just looked up with her baby eyes and smiled. One little hand reached up as if to touch something just above my head.

I smiled despite my ill feelings toward my sister. After all, Ella had been a baby then, and she hadn't tried to steal our mother's approval or Josh's affection yet.

I almost waited for my mom's crying fit to end so I could sneak back into her closet. I rationalized I could grab a picture from another album, but then I turned to the perfect photo for my project.

It looked like I had been just over a year old when the photograph was taken. Baby Me smiled, fully exposing gums with sporadic teeth. A large pair of pink sunglasses sat on my nose, and I held my chin high so that the glasses would not slide down my nose.

No one else was in the picture. It was a moment captured in time with me as the star.

I carefully peeled the tape that held the picture in place. I put it in my folder, and I vowed to find the perfect shade of pink construction paper to match the sunglasses I had sported.

Ms. Hughes had asked us to paste our baby pictures on large sheets of paper and try to compare our physical characteristics to those of our families. She explained some children would find physical resemblances immediately, but others might find shared features more difficult to locate. She mentioned we could write behavioral characteristics if we couldn't find anything to compare.

My project had been easy to complete. I shared my mother's long hair and olive skin tone. I thought I could be almost as tall as my father, but I compared my height to my grandfather's stature.

I wasn't ready to talk about my father. I hated hearing the whispered discussion that followed the mention of his name.

Several Christmases ago, I had learned my father had committed suicide. My mother and grandfather had kept the death a secret, since my father had no living family outside of his household and my grandfather was the Chief of Police.

I still wasn't sure how I felt about being kept in the dark for years after my father pulled the trigger on the gun that ended his life. It seemed like the world was made up of moments when you tried to rise above the mistakes of your elders.

My father wasn't the only dysfunctional part of my family. My mom lived day to day without dealing with the solid rock wall that she seemed to build in every relationship. I tried to connect with her, but she dismissed my efforts or walked away with distant eyes over a forced smile.

Ella and I lived in the same house, but we seemed to be from different planets. Ella looked like a regular teenager who dressed in tee shirts and jeans and played video games, but the video games she played made her feel like she was continuing to live a part of Jerrod's life, and the tee shirts belonged to our brothers. She wore a flannel shirt over them when my mom was home, so our mom wouldn't flip out and order her to take the shirt back to Jerrod and Josh's room.

Ella and I shared a secret when we were young, but we had grown in different directions. Ella saw dead people, and she interacted with them. I saw unexplainable things sometimes, but I was unwilling to act upon them or talk about them.

The only reprieve from the depressed madness in my house was when I spent time with my grandpa. I knew that my mom and my grandpa had experienced some tumultuous times, but I saw my grandpa's soft side and loved him for it. It probably helped that he spoiled me every second. If it weren't for my grandpa, I couldn't compete with Lydia Sneed.

Lydia was my best friend and greatest nemesis. Jerrod had once commented on our *friendship*. He said, "Only girls could be content with chit-chatting with each other and playing on the playground and then cattily comment about the cost of their pocketbooks or the number of boys swooning in their paths." Jerrod had referred to Lydia as my "best fiend" or my "frinenemy."

Lydia's parents, Bannon and Olivia Sneed, were two of the richest people in the county, but that wasn't saying a lot, since many of the families in Unicoi County were economically depressed. Bannon Sneed had worked in computer programming since its biggest rise, and he enjoyed the monetary benefits he received from the technology boom.

The Sneeds lived near Pale Woods Academy on a hill overlooking the Nolichucky River. They named their property Sterling Hills, even though their house was on only one large, raised piece of land. The Sneed's property stretched from the outskirts of Pale Woods to the waterline of the Nolichucky River. A two-lane highway between their front yard and their access to the river interrupted their stretch of land. In addition to the regular traffic, logging trucks, like the ones my father had loaded, sped down the road every day except Sunday.

Trees obscured the Sneed's mansion from April to October. During the fall and winter months, their huge log cabin-like mansion caused road travelers to do a double take. The mansion was over 7,000 square feet, and it included an indoor pool, a game room with a bowling alley, and a small putt-putt course that Bannon Sneed called his "green."

Bannon Sneed golfed in most of his free time, and Olivia Sneed expressed herself through artwork. Lydia rarely spent time alone with her parents, and when she did, they would throw money at her, so that they could continue conveying their indifference to the rest of the world.

Even though she was the wealthiest student in the school, Lydia Sneed was not a student Pale Woods Academy had admitted solely because of her parent's money. They—whoever "they" are—chose Lydia based on her high scores on state standardized tests. I found it odd that Lydia could fuss over the placement of her necklace or the contents of her purse during class and make a near-perfect grade on every test. I decided it was an anomaly, like the way some rivers flow upward.

Lydia flounced into the classroom with her project on a purple, poster-sized sheet of paper that bounced and wobbled in the air behind her. I thought briefly about the recommended size of the project, but Lydia's grade wouldn't be affected because she deviated from the directions.

Lydia spotted me and rushed over. I would have called her tall and graceful if she weren't so self-absorbed. The purple poster was folded over loosely and made gurgling sounds as it bounced in the air behind her. The bobbing creation slapped Christian Spumoni in the face. Most kids would have been beaten if they had hit his older brother, Tony, but Christian looked up and smiled at the source of his discomfort.

Christian pined for Lydia like the rest of the eighth-grade class, but he didn't have a chance. His parents were poor, so Lydia only laughed at him when he brought her wildflowers or carried her books. Lydia was nice to Christian when she wanted something, like a vote for class beauty, but she would make fun of him as soon as he turned his back to her.

I smiled at Christian. We were a lot alike.

Lydia had developed a little faster than the rest of the girls in my grade, and the boys acted like hungry dogs when she walked into a room. They practically salivated at the sight of her and would do anything for the smallest amount of attention.

Lydia brushed her long, straight-but never straight-ened-blonde-but never dyed-hair over her shoulder. Her blue eyes sparkled wickedly in the morning sun streaming through the window by her seat. She had high cheekbones, a straight nose, and a flawless complexion. She never chewed her nails, and she wasn't allowed outside in stronger temperatures for fear that she might freckle. Her parents had ordered an indoor Olympic-sized pool for her to swim in during the summer.

Lydia spotted me out of the corner of her eye. I watched her search the room for a more interesting person. She did not find a more respectable candidate, so she pranced over to my desk.

"Did you finish your project?" Lydia asked me, raising an eyebrow. "I did! Look at mine!"

Lydia held up and opened the purple paper. I noticed Lydia had not bothered to follow the teacher's instructions at all. The paper was three times the size of the construction paper Ms. Hughes had suggested that the students use for their assignment. Lydia's picture was her first modeling picture at the age of three, and there was a story about her family instead of a comparison of their characteristics.

"Brilliant job, mate," I said in a mock-Australian voice.

Lydia scrunched up her nose. Apparently, she didn't think that Australians were cool.

I broke the awkward moment by holding up my own completed assignment. Lydia took one look at the picture of Baby Me and rolled her eyes. She scanned my paper and shook her head. Lydia had a photographic memory. Or at least she said that she did.

"You look like your mom," she said. "But Ella looks more like your grandfather. I think it's her jawline," Lydia finished, stroking her face from her ear to her chin.

I thought Ella looked like our father, but I wouldn't correct Lydia. The less I spoke about the crazy side of my family, the better.

"So, you're not worried about Ms. Hughes deducting points because you didn't follow directions?" I asked.

"My parents converted all of my baby pictures to disks in their safe," Lydia explained. "It was easier for Mummy to give me a photograph from my modeling portfolio since we keep it on hand." Sometimes she talked to me like she was explaining something to a small child. "Daddy said I could write about our family, because everyone wants to know about us anyway," she added.

"Did you bring your bathing suit?" Lydia asked abruptly.

Her question reminded me of our sleepover. "I brought my bathing suit, clothes, toothbrush-"

"Good," Lydia interrupted. She bounced back to her seat with her project.

My jealousy clawed from my chest and left its mark on my face. Lydia was an only child who everyone spoiled, and she thought the earth moved around her. In fact, Lydia told our second-grade teacher that she knew that the sun revolved around the Earth because she was on the planet.

Teachers encouraged Lydia's comments to get on Bannon Sneed's good side. Mr. Sneed sent regular checks to the school, and maybe a check to a teacher's mailbox, if his daughter was treated well by that staff member.

Why did everything seem to go well for Lydia? Even the weather seemed to emphasize her beauty and potential. I could have sworn that God himself placed the sun over Lydia's seat to make the rays of the sun light her golden hair like shining threads of radiance.

Ms. Hughes breezed into the room and smiled cheerily at her students. She was probably excited about the short school week, too.

"I can see all the wonderful projects, and I can't wait to hear about them," Ms. Hughes said. Recently, she had trimmed her dark hair into a severe square cut, and her emerald green eyes scanned the room for potential rule breakers. Her height may not have been intimidating, but her voice projected fear into the most disruptive kids.

Ms. Hughes called the roll and took down the number of students who were eating school lunch. The student of the week, Donny Thomas, took the attendance and the lunch count to the office.

Donny stretched broad shoulders and muscles that he never needed to exercise. He would have been an athletic jock if it weren't for an upbringing by his kind-natured father. He was humble and shy, but he wasn't afraid to throw a shadow over a bully if he felt his friends were threatened.

He playfully pushed Christian as he walked by his seat. Christian gave him two quick punches on his thigh before Ms. Hughes noticed their roughhousing. The boys had been best friends since we had all played in my sandbox years ago.

Donny ran a hand through his lifeless brown hair as he passed Lydia's desk, and he dropped the papers he'd been carrying. Lydia laughed at him, but I bent down and helped him reorganize the pages. His small smile thanked me silently.

The class read or studied silently until Donny returned, and then Ms. Hughes asked the class who would share their project first.

Lydia's hand rose high into the air. Ms. Hughes pretended to look for other volunteers before she called on Lydia.

Lydia rushed to the front of the class and hastily explained the origin of the picture. She ended her presentation abruptly and waited expectantly. Ms. Hughes realized she wanted applause a little too late, and Lydia stomped her foot.

"Aren't you going to say anything?" she snapped at Ms. Hughes. "I didn't go shoe shopping with Mummy so I could finish this project."

Ms. Hughes became flushed, but she managed to squeak out, "We were just waiting for the story it seems you've written on your assignment."

Lydia looked inspired, and Ms. Hughes relaxed a little. She helped Lydia hold up her poster board as Lydia told her tale.

Lydia recounted the origin of her birth, even though everyone already knew the basic story. Lydia's parents had tried for years to have children. Finally, they tried in-vitro fertilization, a procedure where the woman's egg is fertilized outside of the woman's womb and then placed back inside her body to grow until the baby is ready to be born. Usually, several fertilized eggs were placed inside a woman's uterus to give her a better chance of becoming pregnant, but Lydia claimed she was the only egg put inside of her mother because she was the only child that her parents had wanted.

Most children would tease their classmates if they had admitted that their conception was less than natural. Lydia, however, was never called a "test-tube baby" or a "science experiment". Maybe the students at Pale Woods Academy were more mature than the students at public schools. Maybe Lydia was so beautiful that she could have been delivered by extraterrestrials. Or maybe people didn't talk about Lydia because her father had powerful friends.

Bannon Sneed was not an Erwin native. He was from New York, but his wife, Olivia Hensley Sneed, had spent her youth in Unicoi County. Olivia was sent to New York City to live with her aunt when her parents died. Even though Olivia no longer had immediate ties to Eastern Tennessee, she missed the community and the mountains, so she begged her husband to move to Erwin shortly after they were married. Bannon Sneed agreed to the move, and they settled in their home on the Sterling Hills Estate two years later.

The Erwinites did not greet Bannon Sneed with the respect that he felt he deserved. Bannon Sneed bandaged his injured ego by purchasing a large portion of commercial and residential real estate, and he gained a spot on the city council. Within a year after his official change of residence, he removed the people who had treated him poorly from their notable positions. The townspeople catered to him in order to keep their businesses or local titles.

It was during that time that the town circulated gossip about Olivia Sneed. There was gossip available about everyone, but the townspeople were very careful to talk quietly about Bannon Sneed's wife and her troubles.

My mother sometimes talked to her neighbors when she couldn't excuse herself politely. Mrs. Fredrickson, an elementary school teacher who lived across the street from us, tried to relate to my mother, even though they had nothing in common. Mrs. Fredrickson was married to a man who enjoyed the profession that she hated, had one living son who did not want to be around her, and loved to gossip.

My mother may not have been friends with her, but Mrs. Fredrickson was the fountain of rumors that sprayed my family if we walked too close to her. Mrs. Fredrickson told my mother that she had heard that Olivia Sneed had visited an infertility doctor. Olivia was in her thirties and Bannon was just over fifty, so everyone assumed the couple's age was hindering their fertility.

The Sneeds did not air their dirty laundry, but that didn't stop people from talking about what they thought they knew. Some rumors made it to Olivia Sneed's ears, and she erupted one day in town.

Years of childlessness had earned Bannon Sneed the nickname "Barren Seed". Poor Olivia could no longer hold her head up in town, so after her outburst, she returned to New York.

Everyone in the town expected Bannon to act more irritably in his wife's absence, but he was happier and kinder than anyone had ever seen him. The source of his newfound kindness arrived several years later.

Bannon ran an ad in the paper about his wife's return party. He wanted everyone to attend the festivities in Olivia's honor because he was going to surprise her with the number of townspeople in Erwin who loved and supported her. He promised food, drinks, and music from three in the afternoon until the party ended.

My mother, my brothers, Ella, and I had attended the party. I can't remember it, but my mom talked about the party every time I mentioned Lydia's name. My mom seemed to be pleased that she had witnessed what many people in our town considered an important event in the history of Erwin.

According to my mom, the townspeople were too scared to miss the party. Curiosity and a sense of duty led most people to drive up to the log mansion on the afternoon of the party. Some people were interested in the house because only the Sneed family and those who did maintenance on the property had ever walked freely on the grounds. Other partygoers were determined to keep themselves in Bannon Sneed's good graces.

Bannon Sneed made it his personal duty to refill champagne glasses from three in the afternoon until six in the evening. Olivia Sneed arrived in a limousine, as expected, and everyone smiled anxiously.

All the guests gathered around the limo and waited. Olivia emerged a few minutes later to applause and cheers. She seemed to blink away the shock of the party, but her face wore concern. Finally, she smiled and held up her index finger. She ducked back into the limo. Many people thought she was reaching into the vehicle to get her luggage or gifts for everyone. No one was prepared for Olivia Sneed to reveal the true reason for her lengthy stay in New York.

My mom claimed she was the first to see a small, manicured hand lifted out into the mountain air. A blonde head followed with delicate limbs behind it.

My mom remembered the people were so silent that you could hear the gurgling of the Nolichucky River. She would never have believed that so many people could hold a collective silence.

Finally, Bannon Sneed scooped up his daughter and put his arm around his wife. "I want you all to meet Lydia Constance Sneed," he declared proudly.

The town was still stunned. After a few seconds of uncomfortable silence, a man cheered, saving the Sneeds some embarrassment and sparing Erwin from Bannon Sneed's wrath.

The Sneeds had prepared for the rumors about their three-year-old miracle. Immediately, the townspeople whispered that Olivia had bought the child as they rested on the Sneed's posh furniture and drank their high-dollar champagne.

Bannon Sneed approached the microphone an hour after his wife and child made their appearance. The partygoers turned their attention to him immediately.

"I know that most of you are surprised by Lydia's sudden appearance," he began. "My wife was very upset by the terrible rumors that circulated about our childless state." Bannon's voice was unforgiving, and his stare burned the eyes of anyone who dared to look at him. "My wife left this town and went back to New York City in tears. She left me here to make the preparations to join her." Bannon's voice softened, and a light entered his eyes that had never shone. "I was about to leave you heartless people behind until I got a phone call. Olivia told me she was pregnant. It turns out that the miserable people of this town weren't completely to blame for her sensitive feelings. The pregnancy had caused her to take all of your uneducated mumblings to heart.

My mom had been upset about the slights to her family and neighbors. She hadn't participated in the gossip about the Sneeds, and she didn't appreciate the ill remarks directed at her intelligence and character. Many of the townspeople began mumbling their disapproval for the same reasons.

Bannon spread his hands in a grand show of forgiveness and proclaimed, "I have found a way for this town to redeem itself. I will forgive you if all of you treat this family with the respect we deserve. Everyone should dote upon Lydia, because I think you all will agree that she is a miracle." Bannon bent behind himself and reemerged with three-year-old Lydia.

Lydia had already adopted the haughty air of the rich, but my mom said that the young child still blushed while her father boasted. Lydia had tried to get down from the platform and run to her mother, but her father gave her a look that kept her in place. Bannon Sneed expected Lydia to act like a polished, spoiled child.

"I have finally convinced my family to return, so let's make them feel welcome!" The inflection on the last of his words gave the idea that Bannon expected applause. Cheers and loud clapping echoed off the mountain as Lydia Sneed entered the arms and gossip of Unicoi County.

Chapter Two

I stared up at the impressive log mansion. The minor details in the exterior stood out, but no one from the road would notice the intricate floral patterns in the individual logs or the perfectly polished porch furniture. Landscapers had planted flowers in places that maximized their exposure to early morning sun and the large windows allowed light to pass without inviting the intrusion of outside eyes.

Lydia bounded up the front steps and waited in front of the closed door. A local woodworker had carved the Sneed family crest skillfully into the wood of the front entrance. For a horrifying moment, I thought Lydia meant for me to open the door, but a young woman hurriedly cleared the entry and released the outer glass door.

"Miss Sneed," she said, lowering her head and her eyes. The woman had beautiful dark hair and a medium-brown complexion.

Lydia breezed past the woman without speaking. My good Southern manners would not allow me to follow Lydia's example.

"Hi," I said, extending a shaky hand. I had never introduced myself to an adult without an older family member behind me. "I'm Sydney. What's your name?"

Lydia had rounded at the sound of my voice, and she stood with her mouth open. She pointed at the young woman. "*That* is a servant," she said, as if it cleared up something I had forgotten. When she saw I wasn't moving, Lydia added, "She doesn't even speak English."

Lydia turned around and walked down a long hallway to the back of the house. She fully expected me to follow her, but I remained in the doorway with my hand out.

The servant raised her beautiful black eyes. I had heard her speak to Lydia in flawless English. "I am Beth," she said, and placed her delicate hand in mine. "My parents are from Latin America, but our family has lived in the United States for almost thirty years."

"It's nice to meet you, Beth," I said. I pumped her hand twice and released my firm grip, like my grandpa had taught me. "I better catch up to Princess Sneed before we *both* get in trouble." We shared a brief laugh before I hurried down the hall after Lydia.

I had never been inside a house so large. My steps on the green marble floor echoed against the high ceilings and silent hallways. The doors to all the rooms along the hall were closed, and the end of the hall emptied into a kitchen that was almost as large as my house. The scent of freshly baked cookies wafted through the air. I followed the smell to kitchen.

Lydia swung her feet off of a bar stool by the kitchen island and ate a chocolate chip cookie. I spotted two women near a double oven who were fussing in another language. The words were rapid, and the women were expressive. I guessed they were speaking Spanish.

The women were older than Beth, but they had the same eyes and build. I assumed the women were Beth's close relatives, possibly her mother and aunt. The women certainly fought like sisters.

Lydia had a way of blocking out anyone who could not help her achieve her self-serving ends, so it didn't surprise me when she pretended the women weren't there. She watched my eyes widen and adjust to the size of the kitchen. Lydia pulled a nearby stool out with her foot and put a cookie on the counter in front of the stove.

"Daddy likes to eat," she said, "So, our kitchen is pretty big." Lydia laughed like she'd made a joke.

I boosted myself onto the stool beside Lydia and slowly chewed my cookie. It was a warm peanut butter cookie with tiny bits of nut. I decided not to tell my mom that the cookie was better than her homemade recipe.

Lydia ate the last of her cookie and brushed her hands together. Crumbs fell from her fingers and littered the otherwise spotless floor.

I was determined to be a good example, so I jumped down from my seat, walked over to the sink, and dusted my hands over it. The two women stopped their Spanish arguing and looked at me as if I were a foreign bug.

Lydia had the door to the backyard open before I turned a darker shade of embarrassed. I had never felt ashamed of having good manners.

"Let's go to the river," Lydia commanded.

"Now, Miss Sneed," the older of the two women scolded, "you can't go out to that river. Miss Olivia will have a fit."

Lydia rolled her eyes. "That's why you're a servant. You keep your head down and your nose out of my business."

Lydia stormed off before she could hear the agitated mutterings of the two women. I ambled out of the back door, but the two women exchanged words before I was fully out of listening distance.

"Polly, how many times do I tell you that these people don't care what's best for them?" the younger woman said.

"I thank you for the work, Sissy, but I can't keep turning a blind eye to their ways."

I congratulated myself on my observation. The two women were sisters.

The woman Polly had called Sissy held her sister's hand. "We need this job," Sissy pleaded. "They pay well as long as you don't try to get in their business and you do what's expected. Mr. Sneed liked Papa, so he hires people from our family. Really, Polly, we are very lucky."

I closed the door on their voices. I felt like an intruder for listening at the eaves.

The way the Sneeds treated Beth's family outraged me, even if they paid them well. Lydia's management of them caused some of the color to drain from her beauty.

Lydia had picked up a tin bucket and was waiting for me to follow her to the river. The bucket was the oldest thing I had ever seen around Lydia. It was peeling and had rust spots.

Lydia noticed me looking at the bucket and pulled it up so that I could see the aging metal. She smiled as she held it, which I'm sure would have surprised her materialistic parents.

"My daddy had a great man working for him," she explained. "I called him Mr. Hernandez, and he took care of me. We used to take this bucket to the river all the time in the summer. I would gather rocks, and he would watch over the water."

"Watch for what?" I asked.

"Snakes and stuff, I guess," Lydia said, shrugging her shoulders.

We rounded the house, and the front yard spread out before us. I marveled at the amount of space and land money could buy. I knew a lot of families who would have loved to have half an acre of the Sneed's lovely yard or one room of Bannon Sneed's house.

I looked both ways before I crossed the road to a small piece of land by the Nolichucky River. Lydia expected traffic to stop for her, and it usually did, so she did not bother to check for vehicles.

The river was peaceful, and the afternoon sun sparkled on the water. I could smell the dusty decay of fallen leaves and the muddy scent of the silt washed up by the river. Lydia took a deep breath and let the breeze catch her golden hair.

I spotted an old building a little further down the river. "What's that?" I asked.

Lydia remembered she was not alone, and I could almost see her guard go up like a force field. Lydia straightened her posture, and aimed her nose at the sky, but her language was not as haughty.

"I used to make up stories about that place when I was little," Lydia began. "I would walk down here with Mr. Hernandez and pretend that I was a princess in a strange land. I don't remember a lot about the city now, but I was upset when Mummy and I left. I thought all the people I met here were crazy and too friendly. I didn't have anyone to play with, so I made up a story that the building was really a castle in disguise."

Lydia stared dreamily into the past. I had never heard Lydia talk about anything other than herself, but somehow her story let me see a side of my friend that I wanted to nurture and preserve.

Lydia kept talking, and her face filled with color. She may have been Princess Sneed everywhere else, but in this special spot by the river, she was simply and genuinely Lydia.

"Princesses and princes would dance all night, and they would sleep during the day, camouflaged by the shabby cover of that building. I shared my stories with Mr. Hernandez until he stopped talking. Then Mummy came down here with me a couple times until I told her one of my stories about that house."

Lydia's face darkened. I noticed the chill of the breeze for the first time, and I wondered why Mr. Hernandez had stopped talking.

"Mummy yelled at me for making up stories, and she left me here. I wasn't allowed to cross the road without a grown-up, so I had to stay here. My daddy collected me after a long time, and he was mad. I couldn't tell if he was upset with me, so I cried in my room for the rest of the day. Mummy brought me my supper that night, but she didn't apologize. She just told me to stay away from the river and the house."

I didn't understand the story, but I tried to seem sympathetic. I wanted to keep Genuine Lydia with me forever. Genuine Lydia could truly be my friend.

Lydia looked in my eyes, and I almost saw the real Lydia physically vanish. The cold, self-centered Lydia told me, "That's why you won't mention coming here today. To anyone."

Her sudden change and hardened tone didn't shock me. I was glad that I could hold on to the image of an authentic person beneath her facade.

"Okay," I agreed. I would never let Lydia rule my actions, but I could keep my mouth closed to avoid trouble.

"Let's look for rocks," Lydia suggested. She had brightened, but her feelings were blocked.

It wouldn't be very hard to fill the bucket a thousand times over. I couldn't take a step without walking on at least five medium-sized rocks. I scooped up a handful and dropped them into Lydia's bucket.

Lydia's head turned so sharply at the sound of the rocks knocking the bottom of her bucket that I thought her head would pop off. She picked up the bucket and immediately dumped the contents on the ground.

"I don't think you understand," Lydia explained. "You need to find *different* rocks. Show me stones with funny shapes or colors."

I nodded. The task made more sense; Lydia was a rock collector.

I guessed that Lydia and I had been at the river for a little under an hour when she said we needed to go back to the house. I followed my friend across the street and back to the front of the house.

Beth opened the door promptly for us. Lydia ran up the stairs, but I took off my dirty shoes before I followed Lydia's muddy prints to her bedroom.

Lydia was in her bathroom washing the rocks when I found her bedroom. She turned and motioned for me to make myself comfortable while she finished washing the rocks. I had never seen Lydia clean anything, so I was almost amused at the way she poured expensive soaps over the dirty rocks.

We had found three *different* rocks at the river. Lydia had approved only one of my choices out of the twenty rocks I had shown her. She found two rocks that looked like a car and a bird. I didn't see the shape of a muscle car and a hawk in the outline of the rocks, but Lydia said it was all about a person's perspective.

I had almost given up searching for a rock to add to Lydia's collection when I spotted a strange stone. It looked like a big heart attached to a small heart. Lydia's eyes lit up when she saw it, and she immediately added it to the bucket.

I sat on Lydia's bed while I listened to the water clean the dirt from the new pieces of Lydia's collection. The water ran smoothly, like the gentle running of the river we had just visited.

I looked around Lydia's room, and it surprised me that her room was a lot like any other teenager's bedroom. The only difference was that Lydia had the newest and best of everything.

Lydia's music board lit up when I looked in its direction. It played a song, and the screen lit up the selection: "Why Can't We Be Friends?"

Lydia popped her head into the room. "Really?" she said, nodding toward the music board.

I put my hands up. "I didn't touch it. I didn't move off the bed."

Lydia rolled her eyes. "I know you probably don't have one. I mean, why would you? Those boards are the newest thing, but haven't you read about them?"

I reluctantly shook my head. It wasn't so bad that Lydia had something my family couldn't afford, but I hated to claim ignorance about something Lydia thought should have been common knowledge.

Lydia sighed, but she did not tell me about her new musical device in a condescending tone. "It analyzes your mood by examining your heartbeat and heat signature, or something, and plays a song that best fits your mood."

I closed my mouth. Hopefully, Lydia hadn't noticed that my chin had dropped during her explanation.

"Don't act like it's so grand," Lydia said. "If you can run a device over your forehead and tell your temperature, then why can't another piece of equipment read your vitals and randomly pick a song?"

I couldn't think of a well-thought out answer. To me, the music board was magic. To Lydia, the device was just something else to litter her room with technology.

Lydia wrapped her rocks in a towel and carried them to a large chest of drawers. The chest had castles and unicorns engraved on the wood. Lydia grabbed a pearl handle and pulled out the center drawer. She removed two packs of embroidered handkerchiefs and laid them on the bed.

Lydia noticed me watching and stopped. "If you tell anyone about this, I will ruin you."

I believed her. Most of the town hated Lydia and despised her family, but the townspeople were too scared of the Sneed family to stand against them. Bannon Sneed still owned most of the business property in town, and he held a seat on the town council.

Lydia let her perfect posture drop for a moment. "I keep all my secrets in this drawer." Lydia looked so vulnerable for a moment that I almost cried. She had threatened my life and then trusted me with one of her deepest secrets. It was both confusing and endearing.

"You see, I learned a lesson that my father will never master," Lydia said. It was the first time I had ever heard Lydia call her father anything other than "Daddy".

"I learned," Lydia continued, "that all the wealth in the world is worth nothing without someone to share it with." Lydia acted like they were her own words, but I was sure the sentiment had echoed over time since fighting over material possessions began.

I bounced off Lydia's bed and slowly approached her chest of drawers. I peered in and saw a stack of papers on the left side of the drawer and piles of river rocks on the other side.

"No one ever opens this drawer," Lydia told me. "A lady from town sews our family crest on the handkerchiefs, and I get them in packs like this." Lydia held up handkerchiefs wrapped in clear plastic.

"What about the maids?" I asked. "Don't they get into that drawer to put them away after they've been washed?"

Lydia laughed so suddenly that spit flew from her mouth and rained on my face. I wiped the spittle away with a disgusted look.

"The servants throw the handkerchiefs away after I use them," Lydia explained.

Of course you can throw it away after one use, I thought. The rich could wipe their mouths with new napkins after each meal, but they would never admit their true financial situation if they thought someone was going to ask them for a donation to a local organization.

It amused Lydia that I thought she would use the handkerchiefs again. I should have known better. *When had I ever seen her wear the same outfit more than once?*

"Actually," Lydia said, "they're shredded and recycled so that no one will steal them and blow their nose on our family crest."

I wondered if Bannon Sneed suffered from paranoia. Then, our families could probably relate to each other. I had more than one paranoid loony jumping on the branches of my family tree. Oh well, at least Bannon Sneed kept a local seamstress in business.

There were two taps on the door. Lydia's eyes grew wide, and she tossed the packages of handkerchiefs into the drawer.

"I'm not decent," Lydia called as she arranged the packages to cover her secrets.

Lydia pointed a shaking finger at her bed, and I quickly and quietly raced to sit on it. Lydia carefully slid the drawer into place and walked to her bathroom. "You may enter," she said grandly.

The door opened at once, and Beth stood at its entrance with her eyes lowered and her hands folded in front of her. "Dinner is served, Miss Lydia, and your parents request the company of you and your guest."

I wondered why Lydia thought Beth didn't understand English. I decided Lydia had only said it to keep me from conversing with her.

"Dismissed," Lydia said, with a shooing gesture that Beth could not see with her eyes on the floor. Beth closed the door without looking up or turning around.

"That was close," I said, but then I realized friendly Lydia was replaced with the self-absorbed Lydia.

"Does your mother know about the rocks?" I asked.

"The only rocks Mummy knows are the ones in her glass after five o'clock," Lydia said.

Olivia Sneed's addiction to alcohol was a subject of old gossip, but I had never heard Lydia talk about it so candidly. I had always assumed that Lydia respected her parents because she spoke so highly of them. It seemed I had uncovered more than river rocks this evening.

"Wash your hands," Lydia instructed. "Get all the dirt out from under your fingernails."

I lathered my hands while Lydia changed. The warm scent of vanilla on my hands wafted up from the strong-smelling, and incredibly expensive, hand soap Lydia had poured over my hands.

I joined Lydia at her doorway with hands that smelled like fresh sugar cookies. Lydia had changed into a pink dress with fluffy pink bows.

I couldn't camouflage my amused expression. Lydia's nose climbed higher in altitude. "Mummy likes pink, girlie things."

The subject of her attire was closed, but I couldn't help smiling happily as I watched Lydia's bows bounce down the hall. No wonder Lydia had never made fun of our family's pink Ta-Ta van.

I felt way underdressed, but I was glad I wasn't required to wear a frilly ensemble. Lydia did not suggest that I change my clothes, so I guessed I looked suitable enough to dine with the prestigious Sneeds.

I let Lydia lead me into a downstairs room. Savory smells drifted out of the only open door along the hallway.

I had visited the Biltmore mansion in Asheville, North Carolina, and that building was the only structure I could compare with the Sneed's house. The ceilings weren't as high as those at Biltmore, but some rooms were just as massive as the rooms in George Vanderbilt's home.

The Sneed's dining area was as wide as the downstairs of my house, and the ceiling stretched two stories. My eyes drew upward, and my mouth hung open.

Wooden walls supported the Sneed's coats of arms and golden candle holders. Large windows carried in so much afternoon sun that it was almost unnecessary to use artificial light.

The long oak dining table could seat up to thirty people. It had places set for four, but workers placed dishes with enough protein and vegetables to serve ten people. I stood still as the sisters, Polly and Sissy, continued to lay more food on the table.

The servants stood on either side of the table and lowered their eyes. "Dinner is served," Polly announced.

Lydia walked past Polly and pulled out the chair at the right of the table's head. She motioned for me to be seated in the chair beside her.

We sat down, and the servants rushed behind us and pushed in our chairs.

"Thank you," I said to Sissy.

Sissy and Polly shared the same hair, eyes, and skin tone as Beth, but the lines around their eyes revealed their generation. Sissy had an angry red gash from her ear to her nose. The skin had healed from the wound, but the scar would never fade. Sissy would have been one of the most beautiful women I had ever met without the disfigurement.

"Don't waste good manners on the servants," Lydia remarked. "They don't understand English anyway."

It was the second time Lydia had demeaned the staff who kept her home functioning. I wondered how much spit Lydia had consumed in her food and whether it was really the fault of her alarm clock that she was always late for school.

Sissy tensed up, and the same color rose to Polly's face. Sissy placed one hand on her sister's shoulder, and Polly remembered that her family needed their jobs.

Barron and Olivia Sneed entered the open doorway. Barron Sneed strutted with his head up and hardly acknowledged his wife.

Bannon Sneed was a short, plump man, with soft pale skin, dimples, and tiny eyes. He dressed in a brown business suit with a conservative tie. Black stubble showed inside the pores of his cheeks.

Olivia Sneed was tall and willowy. She had dark blue eyes and honey-blonde hair. I had a feeling that the beauty shop in town always had that color in stock. Mrs. Sneed wore a plain gray silk dress that didn't complement her form but showed her station. Her eyes were bloodshot, and her hand shook every time she picked up her water glass.

Lydia had told me to call her mother by her first name, but she hadn't said the same about her father. I resolved I would refer to him by his first and last name since most people in the town did it, too.

Polly and Sissy pushed in the chairs of the elder Sneeds. The women served Bannon and Olivia first and the girls last. Bannon began eating immediately, but Olivia waited until the girls had been served.

The staff stood on either side of the table with their eyes lowered. Polly served the adults more food and water, and Sissy refilled the girls' plates and milk glasses.

My glass stayed full throughout my meal. Every time I took a drink, Sissy would shuffle over and pour more milk into my glass from a silver pitcher.

Bannon Sneed roughly devoured his food. He chewed the meat right off the bone and picked up green beans with his stubby fingers instead of using his fork. His family seemed to be used to his manner of eating, but it distracted me. I had assumed rich people ate delicately, but Bannon Sneed was so used to fine things he didn't stop to taste them. He lifted his head from his personal trough to ask Lydia, "How was school today?"

Lydia jumped at the attention. "They loved my project, Daddy!"

I didn't understand why Lydia was acting attention-deprived. Everyone noticed her everywhere she went.

Bannon Sneed nodded his piggy head. "I told you they'd love any information about our family."

"Maybe we could do some more research about our family tree," Lydia said timidly.

Bannon turned his attention to his only daughter. "No, I think that was enough for now. One day, when you're smarter, I'll allow a servant to go over the genealogy with you."

Bannon Sneed's insinuation shocked me. I didn't like Lydia's arrogance in class, but I knew she was one of the smartest students in our top-rated academy. I suddenly felt protective of Lydia.

"She makes the best marks in our grade," I defended.

Polly looked up and smiled. Olivia glared at me with her blood-shot eyes. You would have thought I contradicted the president's remarks about our country.

"That's just proof *that* particular academy does not encourage a higher curriculum," Bannon Sneed said without looking up.

Lydia shook her head at me. She had not wanted to be defended.

"Have you been to the range?" Olivia asked her husband. "I can smell gunpowder."

Bannon Sneed scoffed. "Now I see where Lydia gets her *brain*," he mocked. "I have been to the range, Liv, but there is not enough *gunpowder* in my bullets for you to smell it on me after I have washed." He took another bite of food and said, "Do you smell sweat on me too? I worked out in the home gym last night?"

"Daddy is an excellent marksman," Lydia bragged, hoping to discontinue the assault on her mother's intelligence. She looked over at him for an encouraging smile, but her father was more interested in his meal.

Lydia's mother had eaten two or three bites of food and sipped her water. Her presence was supposed to adorn the dining room until her husband dismissed her to her liquor cabinet.

"Who is your guest?" Olivia asked. Her voice cracked with age or from the emotion she felt from her husband's ridicule.

"It's the Miller girl I've told you about, Mummy," Lydia said. "Her name is Sydney."

"Miller?" Bannon Sneed remarked gruffly. "You mean the crazy Millers?"

I had been waiting for the slight. "Only the men in my family were crazy," I said with a chuckle.

I immediately regretted it. The joke fell flat, and I felt like I had dishonored my brothers.

Bannon Sneed stared at me like he was measuring the best way to kill an unwanted bug. "I guess it remains to be seen. Crazy is an ingredient that gets mixed into all the batter."

Most times, I barely liked Lydia, even though we told everyone that we were best friends. I had learned to deal with Lydia and her insults, but she never crossed the line into talking about my family.

Olivia had zeroed in on my hands while her husband had been bashing the Miller name. "Is that dirt under your fingernails, child?"

I was afraid that she would guess we had been at the river. I prepared to lie, but Lydia said, "Her family is from town, Mummy. Aren't you used to their hygiene, or lack of it, yet?"

I could have hit my *friend* in her perfect mouth. Instead, I revealed, "It's from the river. Lydia showed me a beautiful spot to collect rocks."

I threw my hands over my mouth too late. Lydia tensed, and Olivia jumped up from her chair. The chair clambered to the floor.

"You were at the river?" she screamed at Lydia.

Lydia glared at me. I kept my face hard and determined, but my legs turned to gelatin. It would probably be the last time they invited me to dinner.

"I was just showing off the property," Lydia lied. "We didn't even cross the street."

"You are a liar!" Olivia yelled at her daughter. "I can put up with quite a few things, but lying is not one of them. You are too much like your father."

Bannon Sneed didn't defend himself. He just motioned for the plates to be cleared.

"How many times must I explain the danger in that river?" Olivia whined. "We've had a wet year, and the water level is up. What would you do if a current drug you under?"

"I'm a great swimmer, and Daddy says the rich don't die young unless they overdose or drink themselves to death," Lydia defended.

Bannon Sneed choked on the water he had been drinking. Olivia didn't even look at her coughing husband, and raised her voice another decibel. "The river doesn't discriminate. It has claimed the lives of skilled swimmers, and it won't spit you back out just because you wear designer clothes!"

"I don't see a reason to rampage like a herd of wild boars," Bannon Sneed said. He had recovered quickly after Polly had raised his arms up to open his diaphragm.

His wife shot him a hateful glare. "You promised you would reinforce my wishes. You've always kept your promises." It was a plea for his support, despite her earlier accusation.

Bannon Sneed considered his wife's words. "You're right, Liv, I keep my promises," he said magnanimously. "Listen to Mummy, Lydia."

He meant to end the conversation and any arguments. Lydia noisily got up from her chair and ran out of the room.

I felt so awful for stirring up family trouble that I followed Lydia to comfort her. Lydia rounded on me just outside the door. "I told you I would ruin you, and I meant it!" Lydia's blue eyes shot icy daggers, making them look both beautiful and dangerous. I decided that there was nothing I could say in my defense.

I moved cautiously toward the stairs. I planned to retrieve my stuff from Lydia's room and walk home, but Beth had wisely placed my bag by the door when the arguing began. I put it over my shoulder and walked out of the front door.

Chapter Three

I was halfway to my house before I felt the cold and noticed the dark. There were only a few houses along the River Road, and most of them had a long-ago empty look. I knew my father had once lived on this road, but I couldn't remember the exact spot. A fire had consumed the house before I was old enough to remember its location, and my mom wouldn't talk about it.

I heard a break in the silence behind me, and a police cruiser rolled to a stop beside me. I continued to walk. A car door banged closed, and heavy feet thumped after my footsteps.

"I will wear you out if I have to chase you, Little Lady," a powerful male voice said.

I turned on my heel to face my grandpa. "How did you know where I'd be?"

"Lydia called your house, and your mother won't leave Ella at home alone, so she sent me looking for you. Why are you *walking* on this road?"

"I'm walking home!" I yelled. "I'm tired of being labeled as a *Crazy Miller*! Can't I move and change my last name to Murphy?"

My grandpa's hardened face softened a little at my suggestion. "I would love to share my name with you, Little Lady, but I have learned some lessons in life. One of those lessons is that you can't outrun your past. No matter what name you have, you will always be Sydney Miller, and there are people like the Sneeds who will remind you of it."

My shoulders dropped, and I started walking to the cruiser. I had pumped out most of my anger during my walk and felt emotionally exhausted. I was numb to the idea of Lydia's anger and the revenge she had promised.

My grandpa opened the door on the passenger side of the vehicle. It was much more comfortable riding beside my grandpa than behind him.

I felt like I was trapped when I rode in the back of the police car, even though I was not a criminal. The locked doors and the metal between the free world and me made me feel like a caged animal at the zoo. I was in clear view of the public, for the amusement of others, but the control I had over my life was limited and could be restricted without further warning.

I smiled involuntarily at the picture my grandpa had placed on the sun visor. A younger Sydney flashed an immortal smile as the water behind me sparkled and danced in the afternoon sun.

I wore a pair of jeans and a bathing suit top with an orange life jacket fastened around me. Water dripped off my body and out of my hair, but I was smiling. I struggled to hold up a fish a little bigger than my arm. My grandpa snapped the picture of my triumphant moment as I held up my first catch.

My grandpa and I had been fishing on Watauga Lake in a boat he brought out in the spring of every year. I had spent all morning complaining about the weather and lack of food. My grandpa was unsympathetic. He told me I'd have to catch some dinner if I wanted to eat. I walked to the far end of the boat so I wouldn't have to hear stories about Native Americans and pioneers hunting and fishing for their meat. Native Americans and pioneers had lakes, rivers, and forests. We had grocery superstores.

I had noticed that my grandpa had cast his line a great distance into the water, but I could look over the side of the boat and see fish. I had decided that my grandpa didn't know as much about fishing as he claimed, and I prepared the worm on my hook for an unfortunate demise.

I dropped my line into the water beside our boat and waited. I peered over the side of the boat and watched the fish swim. None of them looked at the wriggling food on the end of my line.

I sat down on the edge of the boat, with my feet pointing inward, and stared over the water. The soft hum of a far-away speed boat echoed off the mountains.

A sharp tug on my line brought my thoughts quickly back to my surroundings. I called for my grandpa, but another considerable tug on my line threw me off balance, and I fell into the water.

My grandpa heard the splash of the water, and he flew into action. I grabbed the life ring my grandpa had thrown overboard as soon as I surfaced. I put the ring over me with one hand, and I let my grandpa hoist me back into his boat.

Amazingly, I had held onto my fishing pole, and my grandpa and I reeled in my first fish. The catfish fought all the way into the boat, but he was still dinner in the end.

My grandpa insisted on taking a picture of me with my first catch, and I didn't mind. I was very proud of myself.

Of course, my grandpa teased me about falling out of his boat. He made comments like, 'I think there are fish out that are big enough to drag you with them,' every time we'd go out to the lake.

My thoughts turned to my mom in the time it took my grandpa to shut the door and get positioned in his seat. My mom had been against the idea of a sleepover with Lydia at her house, especially on a school night, but I had convinced her I needed a break from the silent drama in our house.

My mom probably wouldn't allow me to spend the night with anyone again, since I had walked off without calling for anyone to pick me up. Most parents would have driven another child home after he or she disagreed with their child, but somehow, I didn't believe Lydia's parents shared the same views as them.

I didn't want to face my mom. After some begging and false tears, I found myself wrapped in a blanket on my grandpa's couch. He waged the battle with my mom on the phone, and she was upset. I could hear snatches of my mom's protests, and I figured out the rest of my mom's side of the conversation from my grandpa's responses.

"She really just needs time to cool off," my grandpa spoke into his police-issued cell phone. He winked at me like he had the situation under control.

I heard my mom say, "I'm going to kill her for…" and "She can't stay hidden with you forever."

"Relax, Miranda," he countered. "It's almost nine o'clock, and you know that she's safe with me. I'll bring her home tomorrow," my grandpa said with a smile he expected to carry over the phone line.

He turned, and the sound of his daughter's voice moved with him. I watched my grandpa's face carefully. He scrunched up his face like he had swallowed something nasty.

"Why wouldn't I get her breakfast before she goes to school?" my grandpa argued. "That's not *rewarding* her. She's got to eat, doesn't she?"

I realized what my mom was doing. She seldom yelled, but she could make a person feel guilty enough to see her side of a situation. My mom was going to mention my sister and my grandpa's favoritism toward me.

"Ella can stay with me next weekend," my grandpa offered, as if on cue.

Good one, Mom, I thought. Miranda Miller had made her father feel guilty for treating me to a night of fun at his house, but my mom didn't realize that her plan would never work.

I had spent at least one night a week at my grandpa's house over the last five years, but Ella had stayed only once. Ella liked our grandpa, as far as I could tell, but she couldn't stay in his home. When I asked Ella why she didn't let our grandpa spoil her on overnight trips, Ella confided, "I can hear the dead animals."

Anyone who didn't know Ella would think she was certifiably insane. In fact, our mom only believed in Ella's ability to see the dead when it benefited the immediate family. The rest of the time, our mom wanted Ella to shove her gift into the deepest recesses of her mind. It was okay for Ella to inform us on Jerrod's condition through our deceased brother, Josh, as we raced to save him, but our mom confined Ella to her room for an entire day after she told a neighbor that his deceased wife buried money in her flower bed. The neighbor brought a portion of the money to our house to offer his thanks, but our mom denied Ella's involvement and shut the door in his face.

The emotional temperature of the house was chilly after Ella had informed our mother that her twin sons were at peace. Josh's spirit had accepted its death and had been ready to ascend to the next level of existence or non-existence, but Jerrod could not remember dying.

Jerrod spent almost a year trying to gain forgiveness for leading his twin to an untimely fate. He went through the daily routines of a living being and continued to worry about his family. I had hoped he would realize that he was dead if I ignored him, but Ella encouraged his denial.

Jerrod was Ella's favorite sibling, and it crushed her when she could not prevent his death. Ella was a genius, but she was still only a child. She wanted to keep the love and companionship of the person who she felt best understood her. Finally, Ella realized she had to let Jerrod go, and she devised a plan to put his spirit to rest.

After Jerrod accepted his death, my sister noticeably changed. Ella quit trying to share her gift with the world and turned inward. Her public shyness caused her peers to label Ella as a freak, but our mom didn't worry about that aspect of Ella's social status. Introversion was considered strange in our close-knit town, but it was not an indication of mental imbalance.

I also had a gift, but I didn't let anyone know it. Ella and I had been closer when we were younger because we would talk about and share our gifts, but I learned that my sister and I were different from other girls.

Most girls played with dolls and had tea parties, but Ella sent me telepathic messages, and I played games with our nana. The latter wouldn't have been strange if our nana had been alive. I could not see Nana, but I had other ways of interacting with her. I stopped communicating with Nana after an incident with a couple of neighborhood girls, and I shoved my gift away while Ella sought to strengthen her abilities.

Ella saw the dead and reported their wishes, and I watched as the people she helped ridiculed her. The taunts of those around her were not enough to keep Ella from trying to help the deceased. She claimed the dead were all around us and it would be impossible for her to ignore her ability to see and correspond with them.

"People wouldn't even pick their noses if they knew how close the dead are to them," Ella had once said.

Ella claimed the dead would hover around the people they had loved or the people who had wronged them in life. Some of the dead were like Jerrod—they didn't know they were dead—and others just wanted to right a wrong before they could be at peace. Sometimes Ella would help.

Our mom had been depressed for months after she learned that her sons' spirits had ascended. I was sure that my mom wanted Jerrod and Josh to be at rest, but it was hard for her to accept the finality of the situation. I wondered if my mom had sometimes felt her sons in the house during the year after their death.

Most of the time, we could function like a normal family. We dealt with our guilt in the same way. We never talked about it, but sometimes grief curled its long black fingers around my mother's heart. There were times the death of almost all the men in her life left her heartbroken, and depression caused irregular patterns in her behavior.

I was at the kitchen table doing my homework one afternoon when I heard screaming upstairs. My sister's small feet raced down the steps with my mom's thumping footfalls in pursuit. I heard my mom's usually calm voice shouting, "Tell him! Please tell him!"

I put down the pencil I had been squeezing since I first heard the disturbance. It was one of the few times I'd heard my mom yell. I walked down the hall and witnessed my mom grab my sister by the collar of her shirt and spin her around. Ella made a gurgling sound, but she didn't cry out. My mom let go of Ella and stood facing her.

I could sense the hurt and fear radiating from my sister, but the absurdity of the situation froze me. Ella looked our mom in the eyes, and spoke to her calmly, even though our mom was an emotional explosive.

"Why won't you do this for me?" our mother pleaded. "I've been a good mother and wife."

"It does not matter what you have done, Mother," Ella said evenly, "I cannot tell them if they have moved on."

Our mom cleared her emotionally-strained voice and said, "I know what you can do, okay? I'll accept it if you can just tell him."

Tears ran down Ella's cheeks, but no emotion showed in her words. "He doesn't want to communicate. His time in life is done."

Color spread from my mom's neck to her face, and she rushed Ella. My mom grabbed my sister's shoulders. "Just tell him! You do it for everyone else. Why not me?" she yelled as she shook Ella furiously.

I could feel my mom's burning red thoughts, but I knew her outburst was part of her intense grief. She didn't really want to hurt Ella.

I was scared for my sister. I don't know if it was my fear that caused my feet to move, but I ran to my mom and sister and tried to pull them apart. Ella allowed herself to be shaken, and our mom showed no signs of stopping. I dug my fingernails into my mom's skin, but she didn't seem to notice. Finally, I did the only thing I could think to do. I slapped my mom's face.

I had put all my power behind the stinging slap. It left a mark that my mom couldn't explain away. At least it had worked.

My mom stopped shaking her youngest daughter and fell onto the floor. She cried and apologized immediately, but when she moved to touch Ella, Ella silently moved away and walked upstairs to her room.

My mom's display disgusted me. I didn't want to be around her, so I called the only other family that didn't live in my house.

My grandpa answered his phone after only one ring. "Chief Conner Murphy," he said, even though he knew the number was his daughter's cell phone.

"Grandpa," I said. My voice sounded shakier than I'd expected.

"What is it, Little Lady?" he asked. I could hear papers rustling and a scanner squawking in the background.

"I think I need you to come get me," I said. "And Ella," I added after a short pause.

My grandpa did not ask for an explanation. "I'll be there in ten minutes," he told me.

My mom had pulled herself up onto the couch, and she was staring blankly into her lap. "I'm so sorry," she said without looking.

I felt a warming emotion for my mom, so I hugged her and helped her up the stairs. *Who could blame her for one outburst?* She had lost so much.

I laid my mom on her bed. I brushed the hair behind my mom's ear like she would do for me when I was feverish.

"I called Grandpa, and Ella and I are going to stay the night with him." I told her. My mother nodded absently. "We'll be back early tomorrow morning."

There was no need to waste any more words on my mom. She probably wasn't listening anyway.

I ran to the next room and flung open the door. Ella was resting on the bed in the same position as our mom.

I flew around the pink room, throwing clothes in a plastic grocery bag I found on the floor. The room was painted white, but our mom had bought pink curtains of a certain reflective material, so the outside light made the room appear pink. It was the first time it had given me a headache.

I bent down until I was eye-level with my sister. "I think Mom needs a rest. We're going to stay with Grandpa tonight."

Ella nodded. She rose from her bed and walked down the hall.

I followed my sister with the overstuffed grocery bag in my hand. Ella paused briefly at the room that once held our brothers' laughter, but she didn't linger.

I wanted to tell her how much I missed them, but I was afraid she would only give me a blank stare. She might even accuse me of lying since I had ignored Jerrod's ghost for almost a year after his death.

Our grandpa pulled into the driveway only moments after Ella and I walked down the stairs. I figured he had turned on his police lights until he got to our neighborhood because the police station was almost ten legal driving minutes away from our house.

My grandpa's heavy footfalls pounded up the steps and onto the porch. He tried the door, and when he found it locked, he rapped loudly on the wooden panels. The loud noise in the silent house startled me, and I cried out involuntarily.

"What's wrong?" my grandpa asked when I answered the door. He walked past me before I could reply and headed toward the kitchen.

"She's not back there," I called after him. He turned and looked at me expectantly.

"I think Mom needs a rest," I conceded.

My grandpa's posture dropped a little, and he brought a hand to his forehead. "I think you're right," he said, massaging his temples. "She's probably needed a rest for quite a while."

Our grandpa herded Ella and me to the cruiser. Ella climbed into the back seat, and I sat beside her with the plastic bag crinkling in my lap like a bowl of crispy cereal.

I listened to the officers and the dispatcher as they communicated in coded numbers over the police radio. It was ten minutes before I noticed Ella's expression.

Ella's face was strained and scared. She stared out of her window, but she noticed me watching her and relaxed her expression before I could voice my concern.

Our grandpa lived at the top of a hill right outside of town. He was far enough away from the downtown bustle that he could relax, but close enough to town to respond to a call if the sheriff's department needed him. I glimpsed some chain restaurants and a few other town landmarks at a distance, but I couldn't see as much of Erwin as I could see from the windows of Pale Woods Academy.

Our grandpa owned a ranch-style brick house with three bedrooms and two full bathrooms. The concrete steps echoed our footfalls as we ascended them. My grandpa's tobacco pipe was in a glass ashtray just outside of the door, and its aroma lingered lazily. The clinking of metal was the only sound as my grandpa fumbled with his house keys.

Warm, pine-scented air rushed out to welcome us as we stepped indoors. Large once-living deer heads and squirrels followed us through the living room with their dead eyes.

"I took the rest of the night off, and I don't have to be back until one o'clock tomorrow," our grandpa told us. He seemed proud of himself.

"I'll show you where you can sleep," our grandpa said.

The large man looked even bigger in the narrow hallway that led to the bedrooms and bathrooms. He motioned to the first room on the right of the hall. "This is your bathroom," he said to both of us. "You can put girl things in there."

I knew the house fairly well from my previous visits, but I listened respectfully while my grandpa gave Ella a tour. Ella seemed nervous, but she extended warm smiles to our grandpa after he explained the purpose of each room.

"This is my computer room," he said, pointing to the first room on the left. I gave the room a cursory glance. Boxes and seasonal items were stacked on the floor. A small path led to an ancient laptop. A purple bunny rested on the printer.

"This is my room and bathroom," my grandfather said, pointing to the last door on the right. "And you two can put your stuff in this room."

I walked into the room my grandfather had indicated and stepped back in time into my mother's youth. Pretty blue wallpaper was adorned with posters of once-popular teen movies and singers.

The room seemed abandoned and frozen in time. Fresh sheets were on the bed, but clothes and nail polish bottles were spread over the floor. A pink drop of nail polish was crusted on the beige carpet beside a chair. Books filled a large bookcase and overflowed onto the floor. I made a mental note to remember that the next time my mom complained about the way I treated books.

Miranda Murphy's old bedroom got the best sunlight in the house, and light was streaming through the window, even though the sun was setting. I tried to picture my mom on her bed, letting her nails dry, while she looked at teen magazines. I couldn't hold on to the image. Too much time had passed.

Ella walked over to the bookcase and pulled out a book. There was nothing extraordinary about the book, but Ella flipped straight to a page and stared into the book. I could see that something had been placed inside it.

"Well," our grandpa said, "I'll leave you to get settled."

After our grandpa walked back down the hall, I asked Ella about the book. Ella closed the book and held it to her chest.

"It is just a book I like," she said.

I raised an eyebrow. "That's an outdated nonfiction book about the menstrual cycle."

Ella looked down at the cover like she was just noticing it. Color crept into her features.

"Okay. W-Well, you can never have enough information," Ella sputtered.

"I doubt you'll be using it as a reference," I challenged.

Ella shrugged her shoulders and continued to be stubborn. I let the subject drop, but I vowed to find out what was in the book. Ella couldn't carry it forever.

I put our overnight bag on the bed. "We can probably get whatever we need from the bag," I said. "We aren't staying long enough to move around any of Mom's stuff."

Ella gently shook her head. "Grandfather needs us to move stuff around. He cannot move it himself."

I didn't question Ella. I had felt our grandpa's misery too, and I stepped over to a poster. My mom had tacked it up with four clear tacks. I carefully took out the tacks and placed them on the bedside table. They rolled onto their sides, free for the first time in almost two decades.

I rolled the poster into a tube and placed it in a corner. Ella had just finished with another poster, and she placed her tube next to mine.

We finished taking down the posters and started cleaning up the floor. I found an old grocery bag, and Ella and I tossed fingernail polish and makeup compacts into it.

Our grandpa peeked in the door just as we started going through the books. His face went from upset to accepting. Ella had been right. Someone else needed to rid the room of our mom's adolescent ghost.

"I've ordered a pizza, and I'm going into town to pick it up," he announced. "I trust that you two can take care of yourselves for twenty minutes."

We nodded our heads. Our grandpa patted the door twice and left. We heard the cruiser's tires crunch the gravel as he pulled out of the driveway. Otherwise, the car was silent.

"Do you think he's mad at us for cleaning up Mom's stuff?" I asked Ella.

"No," Ella said without pause. "He knows it is unhealthy to imagine that his daughter will rush home at any moment. I still do not think that he sees her as a grown woman."

"That explains the way he talks to her."

"But Mother allows him to make decisions for her during her most stressful times. I do not think that she realizes it, but she is feeding his protective nature," Ella mused.

"I don't see why that's bad," I said. I had found an old chocolate bar and was looking for its expiration date.

"I think Grandfather needs to feel as though he is protecting or *saving* someone from something. He feels worthless if everyone is happy and there is no injustice," Ella said, and she snatched the chocolate bar out of my hands. "And this candy expired a long time ago." She glanced at the back of the packaging to confirm her suspicion.

Ella tossed the candy bar into our trash bag and started going through the books again. "Did Mother read these books on her own or were they part of the curriculum at her school?" Ella asked after she picked up several books about physics and extra-dimensional theories.

"She read them on her own," I answered. "I see quotes from some of them floating around her head sometimes."

I had spoken without thinking. Ella smiled as if she had won the spelling bee.

"I mean, she quotes these books all the time," I backpedaled.

Ella had already heard what she wanted to hear. "How many times have I told you that you do not have to hide your talent from me?"

"I don't know what you're talking about," I lied.

I expected the subject to be dropped, and for my sister to move on to another topic of conversation. Then, a book connected with the side of my head. I smelled metal in my nose, and my vision blurred.

I turned to hit Ella or run from her, but Ella had bolted out of the room. I could hear my sister's steps echo in the hall.

I was not going to retaliate, so I held my place on the floor. Ella was acting immature, and I wouldn't encourage it.

I wiped the back of my hand under my nose and discovered a dull throb, but there was no sign of blood. I decided against looking in the mirror to see if my nose would bruise. My pride kept me in place.

I lined books on the bookcase until I heard my grandpa's cruiser pull into the driveway. I had almost forgotten about Ella's assault. I flipped through every book before I made a place for it to see if I could find something from my mom's past, but the only clue to my mom's secret was still clutched in my sister's arms. Ella had taken the book with her when she ran out of the room, so I didn't get a chance to peek at its contents.

My grandpa's keys rattle in the doorknob. He stepped into the kitchen and shouted, "Ladies! Pizza!"

I put down a book about Irish folklore and popped to my feet. My grandpa exclaimed, "What the- What are you doin' girl?"

I ran through the hall and into the living room. I followed my grandpa's wide eyes to the center of the room. Ella was shaking and pulling her hair out with one hand while the other still clutched our mom's old book.

Our grandpa seemed unsure how to handle the situation, but his eyes were clear. He had seen worse.

"Don't touch her," I said, and he nodded. I carefully walked over to my sister. "Ella," I said softly. "What's going on?"

Ella continued to shake and look straight ahead, but she answered my question. "I can hear them," she whispered.

I reached out to stroke Ella's hair, but I pulled my hand away before it made contact. "Who do you hear?"

Ella shook more violently and shouted, "I can hear them all! All the dead things! Everything and everyone he has wronged or killed is waiting for him to come through! They want me to send him to them so that they can tear him apart!"

I looked around at the once-living squirrels and deer heads. Our grandpa was a great hunter, so they were probably his most prized kills. I didn't think that my grandpa had killed anyone recently, but it was possible that he had killed a couple of criminals in the line of duty.

I tried to adjust my position so that I was in my sister's line of sight. I hadn't used my gift in a long time, but this wasn't the first time I'd had to rescue Ella from the place she went when she was assaulted by the dead. I prepared to jump inside Ella's mind, determine exactly what or who the problem was, and leave her consciousness before I became too involved in the horror of her thoughts.

Ella screamed. "Get him away from me!" she shouted. "I was rid of him! Make him leave!"

Her declaration shocked our grandfather. "I didn't think you felt that way about me," he almost whispered.

Ella may not have been talking about our grandpa, but his reaction didn't surprise me. Our grandpa was willfully blind about Ella's ability to see the dead, so he thought she was talking about him.

I got Ella under control and asked my grandpa for some orange juice. I tried to tell him that Ella had fallen asleep and reacted to a nightmare, but the hurt he felt never left his eyes.

I called my mom and asked if she was fit enough to have Ella come back. I wanted to stay the night, but every time Ella looked at the living room, her sanity threatened to crumble.

"What do you mean 'fit'?" my mom asked. "Of course I am *fit* enough to take care of my daughters!"

I reluctantly asked my grandpa to take Ella and me to our mother. He didn't look at me, but he grabbed his keys and walked out of the kitchen door.

I quickly collected our make-shift overnight bag and ushered Ella out of the door. I turned the dial on the doorknob so that it would lock and pulled the door shut. Ella was already in the cruiser's back seat. I didn't bother to ride beside her. There was nothing in the back of the cruiser my sister could use to hurt herself.

We rode in silence to the house where my mom waited. I hadn't been able to call it home since my brothers left me to move among my shattered family.

Ella waited patiently for me to open her door, and she ran to the porch steps as soon as I released the lock on her door. Ella burst through the front door and ran to the safety of our bedroom.

My grandpa got out of the car and held out the pizza box. I had forgotten about dinner. I felt empathy flood my body for my grandpa's emotional wounds and disappointment.

"You girls should have this," he said, offering the pizza over the roof of the cruiser. "I won't be eating tonight."

My heart grew heavy in my chest. Our grandpa had probably pictured a happy evening with his grandchildren, but Ella had polluted it with her episode.

"Grandpa, can I come over next weekend?" I asked. "By myself," I quickly added. My grandpa's mind had flashed to Ella's display.

The suddenness of my question brought a surprised smile to his face. "I think I could handle that."

I ran around the cruiser and hugged him. He relaxed in my embrace, and I listened to his powerful heartbeat.

"I could come in and help you if you wanted me to," my grandpa offered, and I was reminded of what Ella had said. My sister was right. Our grandpa needed someone to save.

"I think I'll be okay," I said. "I think I'll need rescuing by next weekend, though," I added after my grandpa appeared crestfallen. It worked like a charm.

"I'll see you after school on Friday," my grandpa called as he got into his cruiser. "I think I can find us something fun to do."

Chapter Four

I had been going over to my grandpa's house at least once a week since Ella's misadventure. Ella never asked to tag along, and no one pressured her. Secretly, I was glad to spend time with a normal person.

My grandpa and I fished, hunted, and camped in the woods of East Tennessee. We drove to amusement parks and museums, even though my grandpa often fell asleep on a bench while I discovered a thrilling ride or a prehistoric marvel.

I always felt full of life before a weekend with my grandpa, but the happiness would be slowly sucked out of me on the way back to my house. My grandpa always tried to cheer me up at the end of a visit by promising something new and exciting for the following weekend.

Our grandpa felt guilty about excluding Ella, so he always asked me to pick out a gift for her when he took me on a trip. Ella snubbed my choices when I presented the gifts to her, but sometimes I noticed Ella wearing the necklaces and clothes I had chosen for her.

My mom encouraged my weekend visits, but she was jealous of the time I spent with my grandpa. My mom accused her father of trying to buy the love of her children, and she found excuses for me to be grounded on the days I was supposed to spend with her father.

My mom's envy was one reason my grandpa was having a hard time convincing his daughter to let me stay the night. She seemed to have a retort for everything he said.

"It's not my fault Ella doesn't want to stay," my grandpa said. "You told me it was because she was sensitive about my hunting trophies."

Conner Murphy's jaw clenched and unclenched. He hadn't expected to defend himself. "I could take Ella somewhere away from the house."

My mom made a snotty comment in a voice she saved for irritating her father. I didn't have to hear her words to know that she was pushing her father's buttons.

My grandpa stopped trying to defend his position and told his daughter, "I'm not arguing with you, Miranda. Like it or not, Sydney is staying here tonight, and the subject is closed."

My grandpa cut my mom off in mid-sentence and placed the phone firmly on his kitchen table. He was breathing hard from his emotions, but he steeled himself and put on a fake smile before he faced me.

"Should I go to bed?" I asked. "You know, as a punishment for running off without telling anyone."

My grandpa shook his head once. He walked over to his ancient recliner and sat down. The springs screamed their resistance as he pulled the handle that lifted his legs. The leather seat made unattractive noises as its occupant adjusted his position. My grandpa flashed me a genuine smile that replaced the false one.

"Your mother has done worse," he said. "She forgets that there was a time when she broke every rule in the book."

My grandpa smiled. He remembered a time in my mom's adolescence that he didn't share with me.

He shook himself from his reverie, still smiling. "We may be able to get some ice cream in Johnson City before the shop closes. I'm not supposed to reward you, but I think you'll have earned it after you deal with your mother."

I shuffled into the cruiser with a pine-scented blanket wrapped around me. The strong aroma I associated with weekend trips to my grandpa's home was on everything he owned.

Twenty minutes later, we pulled into the parking lot outside of Johnson City's best ice cream shop. The shop was closing, and the teenager behind the counter looked a little disappointed about the interruption in his pre-closing activities. The ice cream ads boasted you could choose any of their ice creams and mix it with anything in the shop. The worker had been placing all the mix-ins, like chocolate sprinkles, strawberries, and mints, on a rolling steel cart. He wiped his hands on his apron and greeted us.

The shop was painted the color of french vanilla ice cream, and pictures hung on the walls that invited young children and teenagers to try every flavor. The ice cream freezer came up to my waist, and the glass covering it prevented me from breathing on the products as I examined the selection. I spotted the ice cream I wanted almost immediately.

"What can I get for you?" the teenager asked.

My grandpa glanced at his name tag and said, "Keller, is it?"

The teenager looked mildly surprised that my grandpa had addressed him by name. He seemed more concerned about filling our order and getting us out of the door before the shop was officially closed.

"That's a strange name for a boy," my grandpa pressed.

Keller nodded. I was ready to interject a compliment to make sure our ice cream was spit-free, but Keller responded to my grandpa's comment before I could speak.

"My mother is blind, sir," he explained. "Helen Keller was an inspiration to her."

My grandpa wasn't fond of the teenage generation. He had to deal with adolescent delinquents on almost a daily basis. He took every opportunity to humble teenagers, but my grandpa realized he was being critical for no reason. Or maybe he appreciated Keller had called him 'sir'.

My grandpa extended his hand over the ice cream freezer. "I'm sorry, son," he said. "Sometimes I say things before I think them through. I'm Connor Murphy. I'm the sheriff in Erwin."

Keller met my grandpa's eyes and firmly shook his hand. There was another point in Keller's favor. My grandpa would have torn the poor boy apart over a weak handshake.

"Little Lady," my grandpa said. "What are you having?"

I chose cheesecake ice cream mixed with graham cracker crumbs, and it was gone before we pulled back into my grandpa's driveway. I had been mostly silent on the ride back. I thought about how different my life would be if my mom were blind. She may not be as depressed from looking at the pictures of the loved ones she'd lost and watching Ella's silent stares.

I felt sleepy and sentimental. I turned my heavy-lidded eyes to my grandpa. "I'm so happy that you're in my life," I said. My grandpa was surprised by my sudden sensitivity. "I would have always wished for a normal life if I didn't have you," I finished, and left my grandpa to ponder the meaning of my words.

I let my eyes fall lazily into a blink that lasted until the next morning. I woke up in my mom's old bedroom.

The room from my mom's youth, or my weekend room, was a work in progress. I had taken down the rest of my mom's posters, but I had left all the books in the bookcase. I had tacked grinning boy bands and inspirational messages on the walls, but I had not gone through most of my mom's old clothes in her closet or in her chest of drawers. I understood I needed to add and take away from the room slowly, so I had only removed clothes from the drawer that I used during the weekends I spent with my grandpa.

I could still see the room the way my mom had seen it in her adolescence. There was something left of her, like an afterglow, that would never leave. Sometimes I could catch a smell that reminded me of my mom in some way, or I would look at a scribbled note in the margin of one of her books, and revel at the way her handwriting hadn't changed.

The air seemed still. The old house didn't creak, and I heard no traffic outside. The bedside table said that it was almost seven in the morning.

I ran around the house, readying myself for school. The ice cream still coated my stomach, so I decided to skip breakfast. I was not excited about dealing with Lydia, but I couldn't avoid school.

Possible scenarios whirled through my head as I quickly showered and brushed my teeth. I thought Lydia might get to school early and circulate a damaging rumor about me. Lydia could also say that I had shared a secret with her. I wouldn't find out about the well-placed lie until everyone started making fun of me.

I remembered when Christian had beaten Lydia in a race in third grade. Lydia had said that she had learned that he still wet the bed. She had also made some leading comments about a room monitor's hygiene when the girl wrote Lydia's name on the board for talking out of turn. I don't remember the girl's name before the class, under Lydia's direction, dubbed her "Smelly Belly".

The sound of a horn broke my thoughts. I hadn't thought to check the house for my grandpa. I couldn't believe that he trusted me enough to leave me alone in the house. My mom never left Ella and me alone after my brothers had died.

The kitchen door opened, and my grandpa called, "Let's move it, Little Lady. You better be ready for school."

I came running through the living room and kitchen. "Be careful!" my grandpa said. His tone made it seem like I was running with scissors in my hand.

I stopped quickly and walked out onto the carport. My grandpa had left the cruiser running, but the engine was almost silent.

I climbed into the passenger seat, and my grandpa shut my door. A Styrofoam cup of coffee and a white paper bag rested in the console.

"Did you get your backpack?" my grandpa asked as he climbed into the car.

I held up my backpack to affirm that I had everything I needed. "What's in the bag?" I asked.

"I picked up some doughnuts for you on my way back this morning," my grandpa said. "I had to brief my morning officers and read the reports from last night."

I reached into the bag and pulled out a beautifully glazed doughnut. "How long have you been up?" I asked through a mouthful of food.

"I've been up since around four this morning, and don't talk with anything in your mouth," my grandpa scolded. "That's one thing your mother and I agree on."

I cleared my mouth and said, "I'm sorry." I had forgotten that my grandpa was a stickler for table manners, even when we were eating away from a table. He had also saved me from a piece of turkey lodged in my windpipe on the day he had met me. I'm sure he didn't want to relive that experience.

My grandpa had been awake several hours, and he had left me alone for some of that time. I was glad that my grandpa trusted me enough to leave me alone in his house, but I also inwardly shivered when I thought about my vulnerable state.

I remembered my mother complaining that he had left her alone a lot. Maybe my grandpa just assumed that all children could care for themselves most of the time once they were old enough to pour a bowl of cereal.

My grandpa's house was closer to Pale Woods Academy than my house, so I didn't have a lot of time to finish my doughnuts before my grandpa pulled in front of the school.

My stomach dropped as I looked at the building. I would know my fate in moments. Would I be a bed wetter, a smelly girl, or would a worse "secret" be reveled?

My heart reached the speed of a racing stock car when I noticed the Sneed family limousine parked at the corner of the school. The windows were too tinted to see the forms of anyone inside.

I climbed the steps that led into Pale Woods Academy with a growing sense of dread. I really liked my school and the teachers, so I didn't want to have to transfer.

The second bell rang, and I knew I had to make a decision. Would I walk home and face my mother's wrath to put off Lydia's revenge, or would I enter the school and face my fear?

I took a deep breath and climbed the steps. The students were bustling around the halls as if this were any other morning, and I envied their innocence.

I quickened my pace so that I could be at my desk before the last bell. I wasn't going to add tardiness to Lydia's arsenal. She could use it as "proof" for any number of lies.

I walked into the classroom, and temporary relief washed over me. Lydia was not in her seat or at her locker.

The Sneeds were well known for taking spontaneous vacations. Bannon Sneed would call the school and tell the receptionist that his family was off for a week in Aspen or a long weekend in Tahiti. Perhaps Lydia's parents had decided to take a yearlong vacation. Maybe they would forget my mistake before Lydia returned to school.

My thoughts only relieved me temporarily. I still couldn't explain the presence of the Sneed limousine if Lydia and her family had decided to go on vacation.

I hurried to my seat and froze. I had turned to place my backpack over the back of my chair when I noticed a bright blond head enter the room.

Lydia Sneed and all her influence came bounding into the room with a large smile on her face. Lydia forged her emotions so often that I could no longer tell the difference between her pseudo smile and a genuine smile.

Lydia collected the books and supplies she needed for the morning. She looked around after gathering her materials, and it horrified me when her eyes fell on me.

Lydia strode over to my desk. I should have pretended everything was normal, but I couldn't stop staring at her.

My features must have been contorted in a painful, or mortified, expression because Lydia placed her hand on my shoulder. To an outsider, Lydia seemed like a concerned friend, but I could feel the lack of heat in Lydia's touch.

"What's wrong, *mate*?" Lydia asked. She had adopted the Australian accent she had told me was undesirable. Australians must have been in style today, or she was mocking me.

The question took me aback, and I didn't know how to respond. *Did Lydia bump her head and lose her memory?*

"Nothing, I guess," I said cautiously. I continued to stare into Lydia's unconvincing warmth.

The last bell rang, and Lydia glided to her seat. No one had been looking at us, but I kept glancing around to see if anyone was pointing at me and giggling.

I stared at the back of Lydia's head all morning. I couldn't concentrate on any of Ms. Hughes's lessons, and when she called for me to answer a problem, I could only stare forward dumbly. Normally, the teacher would have only had to point at me for an answer to get an immediate response.

Ms. Hughes motioned me to her desk as the rest of the class filed out of the room for lunch. "Is everything okay?" she asked with genuine concern.

Ms. Hughes knew about the death and despair that had engulfed the Miller family. She always treated me delicately, and I had the impression that she was proud of my dedication to my schoolwork.

"I'm fine," I lied, looking at the floor. Everyone who knew me well knew I was a horrible liar.

Ms. Hughes weaved her head from side to side to gain my attention. I finally looked at her.

I put on what I hoped was a bright smile and said, "May I go to lunch, Ms. Hughes?"

Adults eat up the "May I" questions. There's something about that type of question that strokes their egos effectively.

Ms. Hughes's mouth worked up on one side. I was disappointing her, but I couldn't tell her the truth. How could I say, *My friend Lydia is a self-absorbed jerk, who thinks I have wronged her, so I'm mortified about what is going to happen to me?*

Ms. Hughes could take me to a counselor, or she could get me kicked out of school for talking about the Sneed Princess. Either option was not a choice. I kept my false grin pasted to my face.

After another minute of forced eye contact, she freed me to go to lunch. I walked briskly down the hall and along the outdoor walkway to the cafeteria. I was in a hurry to get to the circular building, not because I was hungry, but because I wanted to take my seat before Lydia. I wanted to avoid the awkward moment where I would have to decide whether to sit next to Lydia or find another seat. If I sat down first, Lydia would be forced to either sit with me or to sit at another table. It would certainly help me determine where I stood with her.

I figured I had a fairly good chance of getting to my seat before Lydia sat down. She always got the best of everything and would never condescend to eat a school lunch. She usually waited near the cafeteria door for Beth to bring her a fresh plate of food from her home.

After Lydia received her food, she would parade it around the cafeteria. Everyone would admire the dish, which was the same chicken and rice combination every day, and then Lydia would plop down in the seat next to me.

Today, luck was not in my corner. Beth had already delivered her food, and Lydia was sitting at our usual table in the farthest corner of the cafeteria. Lydia said she liked the spot because her food would not be ruined by the smell of the "putrid" cafeteria food. I think she liked the table because the lunch monitors were at the front of the room, so they couldn't hear her gossip about her classmates.

I went through the lunch line mechanically, picking up a meat, vegetable, and dessert. I stopped at the beverages. I could have a milk or juice with my lunch. I decided on a juice. Milk was always nastier to throw up than juice, and regurgitation was likely with all the stress I had already experienced.

Lydia spared me an uncomfortable moment by waving her hand for me to join her. I could smell the aroma of Lydia's freshly prepared gourmet meal two tables before I reached her.

I placed my tray next to her plate and moved myself into the seat next to her. Lydia flashed her teeth in a warm gesture. God was smiling on me for a moment because chicken was lodged between two of Lydia's front teeth. I dismissed my amusement before it caused me to laugh out loud.

"That was a really hard question this morning," Lydia said. It took me a second to realize that she was referring to my blundered response to Ms. Hughes's problem.

"I guess I just wasn't paying attention," I admitted.

"We've been friends long enough for me to know when you're lying," Lydia said.

I don't know if it was the honesty of her statement or the building tension of the morning, but I had to know where I stood with Lydia. "What are you going to do to me?" I blurted.

Lydia didn't try to play innocent. She simply put down her utensils and faced me.

"Well, I was doing some thinking, and I decided to forgive you," Lydia said. *How magnanimous,* I almost said before I realized that my sarcasm would only make me feel worse than I had felt all morning. "You realize what you did was stupid and wrong?" Lydia continued. She paused to let me nod my agreement, and I did, like a good little lemming. "So, I don't expect that we will have this kind of thing happen again, right?"

I am a bad judge of character. I wish I had analyzed Lydia's intentions and decided to keep a careful watch on her while pretending that everything was okay between us. As smart as I am, though,

I can't tell when a person's words are coated with manipulation. I wanted to return to our normal relationship so badly that Lydia could have told me a leprechaun sprung up out of the river and told her to forgive me. I would have believed anything.

I finished out my day at school with relief. It was hard to stay awake during the last class of the day. My body wanted to crash after staying pumped up on adrenaline all morning, but I managed to answer Ms. Hughes's questions about our reading selection.

Ms. Hughes smiled and waved at me as I left to board my bus. She seemed to be pleased about my renewed interest in my schoolwork.

I walked down the steps, and a crisp wind pulled at my hair. The celebrations of the other students echoed off the mountains. The school day was over, and they could return to their television, smartphones, and video games.

I was in line to step onto the bus when I noticed Ella at the edge of the sidewalk. She was gazing into the woods.

I tried to see the reason she was staring so intently into the trees. There was a shimmer that almost crossed the line of the forest, and then Ella turned around to face me.

"I'm ready to get on the bus now," she said flatly.

I tried not to question Ella when she heard or saw things that no one else seemed to pick up. I was afraid of her because her "gift" threatened my way of life. I chose to be a normal Miller child, but saying *normal* and *Miller* together seemed to be an oxymoron.

Ten minutes later, Ella and I raced off the bus and into the house. We used to have a babysitter, Maria, but she had graduated from college and moved into an accounting career. Since I was thirteen, my mom didn't bother hiring another babysitter. She didn't mind if her daughters were alone during daylight hours, but she always sent a neighbor over to sit with us if she had to work into the night.

The house was quiet, and the afternoon light made the walls feel warmer and more inviting. I went to the room I shared with my sister to unload my overnight bag and start my homework.

I had completed half of my math assignment when I decided I had better start dinner. My mom would have cooked dinner when she got home, but I liked to help her by preparing our evening meal. It always made my mom's tired face shine when she saw I had given her one less worry.

It was four-thirty when I started gathering the ingredients for a chicken salad. My mom had baked Cajun-styled chicken for Ella and herself the previous night, so I tore the chicken into small pieces and placed them in the salad bowl.

My mom pulled into our driveway just after five o'clock, and I greeted her before she could make it to the door. My mom was exhausted, but she didn't seem unhappy. Hopefully, it was one of her good days.

My mom had been depressed for months after my father left, and she developed a severe case of postpartum depression after Ella's birth. She wore a cloak of sadness, but she had walked in the sunshine on more days when my brothers were alive. I tried to make her smile whenever possible, but her laughter was locked up tightly in her chest.

"I bet you can't guess what we're having," I teased.

My mom smiled with her mouth, but her eyes stayed dull. "I bet you're going to tell me."

She was right. I couldn't keep anything from her long enough to let her find out on her own.

"The chef has outdone herself this evening," I began. "Please wash your hands and join your daughters for a gourmet salad."

Ella, my mom, and I shared a somber dinner. My mom chewed her salad automatically, and Ella never spoke during the meal. All the light was sucked out of my mood, and darkness embraced me.

I picked up my plate and took it to the sink. I ran water over my dishes, and before I knew it, Ella and my mom left me alone in the kitchen. I guess I was supposed to fix dinner *and* wash the dishes.

I turned my thoughts inward and worried about things I couldn't change. I wanted my mom to be happy and wished I could block Ella's abilities. Ella had a great chance of living normal teenage years if she could focus completely on the living.

There was a knock at the door as I dried the cups. I slowly turned toward the sound, but I didn't run to the door. I was settling into the dispirited mood of the house, and my reactions had slowed.

My mom stepped into the kitchen with a strange expression. "There's a *boy* at the door," she told me.

My first response was, "Tell him we're not buying whatever he's selling." I studied my mom's face and said, "Unless it's a laptop."

My mom didn't even crack a smile at my joke. "He says that he's Christian Spumoni," my mom continued, still looking puzzled and missing my joke entirely, "but he couldn't be related to *them*, could he?"

I understood my mom's surprise. Christian had dark hair and an olive skin tone, but unlike his relatives, he had manners and an engaging disposition.

"What does he want?" I asked. I was suddenly angry, and I didn't understand the reason for my irritation.

"You," my mom said with her eyebrows raised.

I rinsed my hands and dried them. I handed a dish towel to my mom and walked down a short hallway to the living room. After my mom's display in the kitchen, I expected to see Christian standing in the open doorway, but he was relaxing on the couch smoothing nonexistent wrinkles from his jeans.

"Hi," I said lamely.

"Hey," he returned. He smiled and dropped it quickly, like his face had a twitch.

I got straight to the point. "What are you doing here, Christian?"

"I don't know," he said, and he seemed confused. "Can you take a walk with me?"

"I'll go ask my mom," I responded warily. I narrowed my eyes in his direction to let him know I thought his visit was peculiar.

I think my mom was so shocked I had a male visitor that she didn't consider all the negative things that could happen during a walk with a boy. She nodded her assent, and I grabbed my coat from the rack beside the table.

"Is everything okay?" Christian asked when I reentered the living room. He was halfway between the couch and the door. *Had he been pacing?*

"I can go for a walk," I said.

"Okay. Good," Christian said. It seemed he was talking more to himself than to me.

I thought it was strange that Christian was matching me step for step to the front door. I thought he was trying to race me, but he grabbed the door handle as I reached for it, and I realized he was trying to open the door for me.

I didn't let the shock show on my face. None of my friends had ever opened a door for me. I had a horrifying thought. *Is this a date?*

Christian blushed—almost like he could read my thoughts—and mumbled something about manners. I walked into the night without a word.

The sidewalks on the side streets of Erwin could be disastrous. Most of the sections of concrete looked as though they were tectonic plates shoved upward during an earthquake. I kept my eyes mostly on the ground so I wouldn't trip.

The night air was crisp and cold, but I barely felt the chill. I was confused about Christian's intentions, so I did what I always did when I didn't understand a situation. I made an idiot of myself.

"Why did you come to my house tonight?" I asked.

"I wanted you to come out for a walk," Christian said with a smirk.

So, he wanted to be technical? I rephrased my question. "What made you stop at my house tonight when you haven't been there in years? I didn't think you remembered where I lived."

I felt really proud of myself until he said, "First of all, I ride the same bus as you. I have seen you get off at the same stop since second grade."

Christian, one point; Sydney, zero. We had been riding the same bus since I started Pale Woods Academy.

"And I used to play with you in your sandbox when your brothers—"

"It's okay," I told him when I heard him trying to backpedal. "It's been a long time. I forgot we used to play together before we went to school," I lied.

Christian dropped his head. He was matching my slow pace. *So why was sweat forming on his head on a cold night?*

I had a sudden thought. *Is he going to ask me out?*

I thought I would feel dread, but that feeling never surfaced. I was calm and suddenly confident.

Then I noticed other little things about Christian. He was a nice-looking boy. He had glossy black hair that moved around his face with the bounce of every step. His olive skin was unblemished, and his brown eyes had a hint of gold. He wore braces, but his teeth were almost perfectly straight. He was tall, but not too tall. He certainly wasn't too tall for me to miss making the biggest mistake of my life.

Christian was bumbling through an explanation about how my house was on his usual walking path and it seemed right to stop tonight. I was thinking of stolen glances and missed cues from the past. I could remember Christian's smiling face in a lot of my memories of school. When I told Christian that I had joined the chess club, he joined the chess club. He always talked to me and saved a seat for me on the bus when Ella stayed home with her secrets.

I guess I had been so wrapped up in family concerns and keeping up with Lydia that I had missed all the things boys do to let you know they like you. I would have been more prepared for his attempts to gain my attention if I had picked up on Christian's clues. *He carried my books for me, and he usually sat at my table at lunch.*

Christian seemed flustered. I felt compassion for him well up in my chest, and I found I didn't want him to blubber through asking me to be his girlfriend. I had to make him feel comfortable.

Kissing on movies seemed easy and reciprocal, and I thought I understood the mechanics, but I was wrong. I wish I would have tripped over a crack in the pavement as I reached to turn Christian's face to mine. I wish Christian's phone would've rung before he stopped with a questioning look. I really wish a dog with rabies would have tackled me to the ground and mauled me before I rose on the tips of my toes and pressed my lips to Christian's mouth.

First of all, I pressed my mouth too tightly to Christian's lips, and it hurt him. His braces cut my lip, but I didn't notice until I got home. He pulled me back slightly, and to my amazement, he kissed me back.

For almost a minute, I thought about nothing. I took in Christian's smell without comparing it to other smells. It was blissful, and the funniest part about it was that I didn't know how much I liked him until we began our walk. As I reluctantly pulled away from him, I thought about all the times Christian had made me laugh or been a friend when Lydia had hurt my feelings. *How long had he liked me?*

It didn't matter. I opened my eyes and imagined signing *Sydney Spumoni* on our future home loan and our children's permission slips.

My vision adjusted to a different scene. Christian looked confused and troubled. *Had I moved too fast?*

"What is it?" I asked in what I hoped was a soft, concerned voice. My mouth was still tingling from our connection.

Christian's eyes darted to the side, and I felt my heart plummet into my stomach. *What had I done?*

"I think I may have given you the wrong impression," he said. He had placed his hands on my arms during our kiss. I quickly shrugged them off me.

Christian looked back at me and said, "Sydney, you are beautiful, but I don't think of you as more than a friend."

I decided to save my damaged ego. "I'm sorry," I said. I tried a careless laugh that sounded like a nervous gurgle. "I got caught up in the moonlight."

It seemed like a great thing to say, but when Christian glanced up into the lightless, cloudy night, I gave up on trying to play it cool. I started walking again.

Christian stood motionless for a moment, but then his feet jogged to catch up with me. I closed my eyes and shook my head.

The toe of my shoe caught on an elevated portion of the sidewalk, and I went forward. Christian caught up with me just in time to save me from doing a face plant on the concrete. *Where was the crack in the sidewalk a couple of minutes ago?*

I stood still to save myself from further embarrassment and listened to Christian. He chose his words carefully.

"I didn't mean for my intentions to be misinterpreted. I have always thought of us as friends. Best friends, actually." *That might have been stretching it a bit,* I thought. "But I wanted to ask you something that had been weighing on my mind for a long time now."

I couldn't stop my heart from doing a little backflip. Maybe I had acted too rashly. Perhaps he had wanted to ask me out, but I moved too quickly. A small smile pushed at the corners of my mouth. I willed it away before Christian could notice it.

"I am really confused and a little scared," Christian admitted. "I've been thinking about it for a long time, and I wanted to know your opinion."

Get to the point," I thought.

"I'm going to ask out Lydia," Christian said. He tried to focus on my face to determine my reaction.

My head did a three sixty, and the blood in my body marched through my ears. "You mean Lydia Sneed?" I asked before I could stop myself.

"You don't think it's a good idea?" he asked. The skin around his eyes crinkled up. He had been worrying for a long time.

I sighed and did what I do best. I made him happy.

"I'll talk to her for you," I responded as casually as I had to the dozens of boys who had approached me about Lydia since the third grade. "If she seems interested, I'll give you the green light."

"Really?" Christian said, grabbing my arms again in his excitement.

I moved my arms out of his grasp and said, "Yeah, I'll talk to her tomorrow morning." I felt my dinner do an uncomfortable churn in my stomach.

"You mean I could ask her out by the end of tomorrow," he said and, much to my horror, he hugged me.

I crossed my arms over my chest to ward off the embrace, but I once again was surrounded by all things Christian. I could feel and smell his hair, skin, and clothes all around me.

I carefully pulled him away from me. "I'm going back to my house, okay," I told him.

"I'll walk you," he said seriously and made a grand gesture of extending an arm with his elbow bent. I linked my arm through the bend of his elbow and walked the short distance to my house.

Christian talked rapidly all the way back to my house. Some of it I didn't mind. I loved hearing his voice, but when he talked about the way Lydia's hair sparkled in the sun and how her lips pursed together when she was thinking, I thought about vomiting in the shrubbery by my house.

I forgave Christian for misleading me into an embarrassing situation. It was adorable the way he got excited over Lydia and jumped up on his heels like he was Dick Van Dyke or Fred Astaire.

By the time we reached my door, we were relaxed in each other's company. I felt giddy, giggly, and free. Christian's easy conversation had a way of making me feel better about my confused emotions.

My mom opened the door before we got to it, and I turned on my top porch step to look at Christian. He was still standing on the walkway that led to our porch steps. I could hear a rustle of fabric as my mom crossed her arms.

"Good evening, sir," I said. I pulled the imaginary ends of my make-believe dress up into an arc in a mock curtsey. Christian bowed so low that his hair almost swept our walk. "Good night, my lady."

Christian looked up at me but stared slightly past me. He waved at my mom. "Good night, Mrs. Miller."

"Good night, Mr. Spumoni," my mom said firmly.

Christian jerked slightly out of his dreamy state and sent me a crooked smile. My stomach dropped somewhere around the Earth's core. He was still making me swoon.

I turned around and faced my arms-crossed, toe-tapping mom. She had her pajamas on, but she hadn't washed the makeup from her face. I went past her without a word.

"What's going on?" my mom asked. Her tone was the same temperature as the air outside. "Are you two dating?"

My mom followed me inside the house. She was nervous that she thought she had let me spend time alone with a potential boyfriend. I couldn't pass up the opportunity to scare her playfully.

"No, we're not going to date," I said, "but I'm three months pregnant."

I heard a small gasp, and my mom's slippered feet stopped in their tracks. I continued down the hall.

I was almost to the kitchen before I said, "Mom, we're just friends."

My mom didn't miss a beat. She followed me into the kitchen with a face of stone. She was not impressed by my humor.

My mom had finished the rest of the dishes, so I turned to go to my room. She was standing a couple of feet away. She started to say something, but squinted, and softened her voice. "What happened to your lip?"

In the time it took me to debate my answer, my mom had already figured out the way I got blood on my mouth. "He had braces, didn't he?" she concluded.

My mom swooped over and scooped up my chin. She studied my lip like it had a new rash.

"Mom, you're making me uncomfortable," I managed. "Can I at least tell you what happened?"

My mom released me. She pulled a sigh from deep inside her soul and motioned for me to sit down.

I watched her make hot cocoa out of a container that she had seldom used since my brothers died. She and Jerrod used to have long talks over hot cocoa.

A wave of relief washed over me. My mom had been depressed for so long that I wondered if she would ever return to our world. A shadow of her had moved through the house. She made the important parental decisions about the type of food we ate and our bedtimes, but she didn't play with us anymore. The child inside my mom was dead or hiding in an unreachable place.

My mom's mother had died just before my mom became a teenager. The smile on my mom's face betrayed her excitement. She thought she was finally going to have a real mother-daughter moment. I wished I had the news she expected to hear.

"Okay, you can tell me all the details," she said, smiling. "Or maybe just tell me what you feel comfortable with," she added quickly.

"Okay, Mom," I told her. I put my left hand over her arm. "I'll tell you everything, but it's not as romantic as you think."

My mom straightened a little in her chair. "First kisses are never as perfect as they seem in the movies. Boys miss your mouth or kiss you too hard." I was supposed to find her statement relatable, but I was a little nauseated at the mental picture of my mom's failed first kiss.

"Well, *my* first kiss will go into the Book of Epic Disasters," I said. "I kissed him, practically breaking his mouth, and he's going to ask out Lydia."

My mom drew back. "Was it really *that* bad?"

A surprised chuckle escaped my mouth. "No, he had intended to ask me to help him ask out Lydia. I took his nervousness the wrong way. I thought he was flustered around me because he liked me, and I kissed him." I ran through the horrifying scene in less than six seconds.

My mom didn't respond. I picked up my cup and sucked a mouthful of semi-warm liquid.

"I didn't miss his mouth," I continued, "but I kissed him too hard. At least I didn't make *his* mouth bleed."

"When did he tell you about Lydia?" my mom asked.

"After I kissed him."

"Well, I guess it could have been worse," my mom concluded with a shake of her head.

I'm glad that *she* could see the positive side.

"Yeah, at least Christian's a good guy," I conceded. "He could have really embarrassed me, but he was very mature about the whole thing." In fact, Christian's attitude was a perfect example of the advantage of hanging out with kids above normal intelligence. "He told me he thought of me as a good friend and valued my opinion."

"And you couldn't tell that he liked Lydia?" my mom asked.

"Well, all the guys like Lydia," I said. "I hadn't even thought about my feelings for Christian until he was stumbling all over himself. I got caught up in a moment that didn't really exist."

"Do you have feelings for Christian?" my mom pressed.

"No," I said with conviction. "It was just my over-active imagination."

"That sounds so much like your father that I don't know whether to smile or cry."

"Try smiling," I suggested, finishing off my cocoa. I took my cup to the sink and kissed my mom's forehead. She sat in front of her cocoa long after I left the room.

Chapter Five

E lla was already in bed when I eased into our bedroom. I could sense that she was still awake, but I pretended I thought she was asleep.

I quietly found my nightclothes in the dark. I pulled my shirt over my head and was overwhelmed with Christian's scent.

I had told my mom that I didn't really like him, but the smell on my shirt brought emotions to the surface that I had never felt. I held my shirt against my face, and an image of Christian's face came to mind.

I put my shirt back on and climbed into bed. Every inhaled breath created a small upward turn of my mouth. I was still going to help Christian tomorrow, but tonight I was going to sleep surrounded by thoughts of him.

I didn't have to wait for Lydia to come to school. She was already there, waiting for me at my seat. She was going through my stuff, but she casually tucked my papers away when she saw me enter the room.

I pulled open my locker and got out my morning books. Lydia didn't move when I approached my seat. She just sat back, drawing little circles on my desk with her fingers.

"Can I put my books down?" I asked.

Lydia looked up as if she'd just noticed me. "Sure," she said, but she didn't move out of my seat or suspend drawing her circles.

I eased my books onto the end of my desk, hoping that Lydia would take a hint, and move her hand. I had too much faith in her ability to read my not-so-subtle intentions.

"I heard you were walking with Christian last night," Lydia commented. She didn't take her eyes off my desk. *Why did I feel like she was toying with me?*

"Yes, I did. I really need to talk to you about that," I said in a rush.

Lydia stared up into my face. A slow grin spread across her mouth. "I thought you might."

I briefly wondered how Lydia had known about my walk with Christian. I hadn't seen cars go by, but I had been wrapped up in some serious emotions.

Christian came into the room holding his backpack out in front of him. He looked painfully handsome in a white button-up shirt and black pants. He had swept his hair casually to one side, and his braces actually added to his features.

I wondered if I would have thought of him in that way yesterday. I toyed with the idea and quickly dismissed it. I had been too concerned about Lydia's possible revenge.

Christian crossed the room and stopped at my desk. "Is everything okay?" he asked. I found it hard to breathe.

Lydia shot up out of my chair. "Everything's wonderful, Chrissy," she cooed. "Sydney was just filling me in about your walk last night."

Christian thought that meant that I had already talked to Lydia for him, because he beamed like he had won the prize pig at the county fair. "What do you think?" he asked Lydia.

The way she looked at him made me want to throw up. Lydia had always complained about Christian's pining over her, but she was absorbing his attention like a snake sunbathing on a rock.

Lydia led Christian toward her desk, talking to him in a sickeningly sweet voice. *Why was Lydia acting that way?* She didn't really like him. *What did she want from Christian?*

It all came crashing together for me in the next moment. Lydia looked over her shoulder at me while Christian was professing his undying admiration for her, and she smirked.

It all made sense. Lydia had heard that Christian and I were walking together last night, and she'd gotten to school early to go through my stuff. She probably thought she'd find some correspondence between Christian and me that would confirm my feelings for him. Lucky for me, I hadn't known that I liked Christian until last night.

Lydia didn't find any proof that Christian and I were interested in each other, but it had seemed like I had wanted to tell her about the feelings that I had for Christian. Poor Christian had shown up at the perfect time. Lydia did what she did best: she proved she was better than me at everything.

I vowed I would never show signs that I had feelings for a boy again. Less than twenty-four hours after I had first noticed a boy, Lydia had taken him from me. It was true Christian had never been mine, but Lydia had *thought* he and I had developed a romantic relationship.

I couldn't handle this kind of hurt more than once. No wonder my mom hadn't wanted to date anyone after my father had left. I had dipped into my emotions for only moments, but my mom had loved my father for years.

Unfortunately, I quickly forgot my promise against revealing my feelings. I let my guard down again and paid a heavy price.

Chapter Six

I was going to avoid my entire lunch period by walking very slowly to the cafeteria. I had my pace timed and walked one step every minute.

A teacher noticed the rate of my progression and signaled a hall monitor to make me speed up. I felt bad enough without a third-grade hall monitor scolding me.

"On the authority of my teacher, I have been asked to tell you to speedily proceed to your destination."

The boy's freckles, glasses, and buck teeth put him in a worse social position than me. I smiled and thanked him for his concern. He measured my words for sarcasm and carefully replied, "All in a day's work." He ran stiffly back to his post.

I tried not to look in the direction of my usual table as I filled my tray with things that I couldn't eat. I moved toward the table where I knew Lydia would be waving me down, probably already wrapped around Christian like she had been all morning. Lydia motioned for me to join her, but Christian was not at the table with her.

I sat down next to her and tried not to look directly at her face. Lydia started combing her fingers through my hair. I was upset, and it felt nice, even though she was the one who had caused me so much inner turmoil.

"Syd?"

I hadn't heard that nickname in years. Lydia called me "Syd" when she was concerned about me. "What?" I asked, almost eager to hear her words.

"I can't hide it from you." Lydia took a deep breath. She pulled her hand out of my hair and looked into her lap. I instinctively put my hand over hers. She looked up thankfully.

"Christian left lunch early because he was confused," she confessed.

I won't lie. My heart was pounding against the walls of my chest.

Lydia sighed. "I should have seen it this morning. I knew I was no match for you."

Warning bells should have been deafening me, but I didn't see through Lydia's ruse. She had a way of manipulating people that professional con artists could never master.

"Christian gave me something for you," Lydia said. She handed me a crumpled piece of paper.

I opened it. The paper had a set of directions on it, and it was in Christian's handwriting.

"He told me to tell you to meet him there at ten o'clock tonight," Lydia said. She seemed sad, but not broken. "Would you like me to send a car for you?" she offered. "I could help you. After all, you're my friend."

I stared into her deceiving eyes and felt warmth and love. I hugged Lydia and told her it would be less conspicuous if I walked to meet Christian.

"Just be careful," she told me, and hid her cruel intentions behind a façade of friendly concern.

I waited in the cold for Christian to reveal himself. It had taken me over half an hour to sneak from my room out the front door. I would have to wait until my mom was asleep before I could sneak back into the house.

I had threatened Ella with certain death if she told on me. Ella didn't even act interested as she promised not to expose me.

The instructions Christian had written were broken and hard to see in the dark, but I finally made it to the location at the end of the directions. I ended up in front of a bike shop, but it was only a few minutes away from my house, so I assumed Christian wanted to make it easier for me to get home after we talked.

I stood in front of the bike shop and stared at the wheels and spokes of the ten new bikes in the display. My mom knew the owner of the store, Mike Holder. They were both officers in the PTO.

I should have been wondering why Christian didn't talk to me on the bus or approach my front door like he had the previous night, but the potential of our meeting consumed me. *I could be Christian's girlfriend within the next few minutes!*

I waited for almost twenty more minutes. Finally, I saw headlights turn down the street. *Maybe Christian had gotten his brother, Tony, to drive him.*

I stood up straight and prepared my thoughts to stay on track. I walked to the curb with the biggest and brightest smile I could manage.

My heart dropped when I realized that the car I was walking toward was a black and white police cruiser. I knew, before the headlights washed over my guilty form, that my grandpa was the one driving the vehicle.

My father had once said that the townspeople thought that there were Crazy Millers and Dumb Millers. Guess which one I am.

Chapter Seven

I don't think I've heard so many curse words at one time. My grandpa usually never let a swear word slip before he apologized for it, but he was letting all the obscenities he had restrained himself from saying out at once. A foul word barely hit the air before another flowed off my grandpa's tongue.

Between curse words, my grandpa told me he had gotten a call from Lydia Sneed. She had told him I was planning on breaking into the bike shop to raid the cash drawer. Lydia claimed that my deviant behavior was a cry for help.

"And who should I see standing in front of the store window when I pull up?" my grandpa said.

I couldn't respond. No matter what I said, he would never believe me. I hung my head and let him continue berating me.

"All this after I went to the Sneed's mansion and threatened them in their own home? They were trying to press charges against you!" my grandpa shouted. He was so upset that droplets of spittle sprayed my arm.

Wait! He did what?

"I can't *believe* that I pulled that man out of his bed and scared poor Lydia to death. She had your best interests at heart. They tried to tell me you were out of control, but I didn't listen. I can't believe I trusted you!" He slammed a fist against the steering wheel.

I knew my grandpa would never physically hurt me, but his words stabbed my soul. I hoped for a life-altering event to happen, even if it meant my own demise, so that I wouldn't have to see the disappointment in his eyes.

I was confused and hurt. I knew Lydia was responsible for the misinterpretation of my behavior, but I couldn't believe she had focused on ruining my relationship with my grandpa instead of destroying my social image at school.

"I thought you went to a meeting at the station that morning," I said lamely.

"I went for a meeting, but I didn't go to the station," my grandpa explained through gritted teeth. "I haven't been the sheriff in this town for years without learning a few secrets. I knew how to get to Bannon Sneed, and I scared Lydia enough to get her cooperation." My grandpa snorted. "That poor girl. She tried to tell me you had blown up at her and walked out without provocation. I yelled at her and called her a liar."

My grandpa narrowed his eyes, and disgust filled his words. "You made me look like an idiot. I held you up higher than all the rest, and you used me. Just like your mother."

I was shaking so hard that I couldn't focus. Tears were streaming down my face, and I felt like all the happiness in the world had evaporated.

My grandpa slung the cruiser into my driveway and pushed open his door. My mom walked outside, and I could see her silhouette against the light from the living room. Ella moved the curtain aside in the room where I should have been sleeping.

My grandpa yanked my door open and grabbed me by the arm. His grip was firm, but not abusive. "I was wrong about her. She *is* your daughter," my grandpa spat at my mom, and he forcefully maneuvered me toward the steps.

I didn't watch my grandpa get into his car and drive away. I wrapped myself in self-pitying thoughts. *All the men in my life had left me.*

My mom didn't accost me for information as I passed her. She let me go inside without a word. Our small, newfound connection had been ruined. I wouldn't be invited for cocoa at the kitchen table anytime soon.

I opened the door to my room and hung my head as I entered. Ella's eyes drew me, and when I saw the disappointment in them, my heart broke. Ella knew the truth, and she wouldn't help me. I had burned that bridge, too.

The weight of the situation finally took its toll on my consciousness. Little black spots invaded my vision, creeping first around the outer rim of my sight, and then sucking me slowly and completely into darkness. I didn't even feel myself fade into nothingness.

I would rather have scrubbed public toilets with my tongue than go to school the next day. My mom, the ever-insistent Keeper of Family Secrets, asserted that we continue with our routines as though nothing had happened.

I think most of my family's problems hinged on our inability to talk about things that hurt us or cause us to become uncomfortable. Maybe that's why our family dinners were silent feasts. There weren't enough happy topics for a five-minute conversation.

My mom was the worst at not communicating her thoughts or feelings. She bottled up most of her emotions and lived as though we were still the picture-perfect family. My mom may have cried over my father's death and at my brothers' funeral and memorial, but my father's clothes still hung in her closet and nothing had been touched inside my brothers' room, aside from something of Josh's that I had taken.

My mom opened the blinds, and sunshine poured into the room Ella and I shared. Ella jumped off her daybed without a word.

"Good morning," my mom said. I was too tired to tell if she was being sarcastic.

I could find nothing "good" about the morning. It was the first heart-wrenching day after my betrayal.

"Your grandpa called this morning," my mom said nonchalantly.

My blood ran cold. I remembered all the events of the previous night and asked, "How did I make it to bed?"

My mom waved her hand at my question. "Ella and I took care of you. You passed out."

My mom narrowed her eyes. "You're not on drugs, are you?"

I let my mouth drop into an O of surprise. "No," I said indignantly.

No one had ever offered me a drug. I had only seen them when D.A.R.E. officers lectured about the consequences of drug use.

"It won't matter if you lie to me," my mom said. She broke her eye contact with me and added. "Your grandpa would find out anyway."

I rolled my eyes. My grandpa could have blood tested me every hour, but he knew it would be useless. My grandpa knew how a drug user acted, and he did not mention that in his tirade.

"He told me to tell you not to make plans for this weekend," my mom continued. "You're going on a road trip."

"I thought he had to stay in town for the Apple Festival?" I whined.

"He has a detective filling in for him over the weekend," my mom explained. "I wouldn't get my hopes up if I were you, though. It didn't sound like a fun trip."

I didn't think we were going to a mouse-themed theme park, I thought. "Where are we going?" I asked my mom as she walked out of the room.

"I can't tell you," my mom called down the hall, and I knew the subject was closed. I didn't have to see her snide smile to decide that I despised her for wearing it.

She mentioned nothing else about my late-night deception. I ate my breakfast, showered, and brushed my teeth. I put on a little makeup, but less than I normally used. I had a feeling that I'd be crying a lot.

My mom drove my sister and me to school in silence. I could hardly stand the indifference my mother was sending. I was used to being an obedient child. I did silly things sometimes because I didn't understand something, or I acted before I thought about what I was doing, but I had never done anything really bad.

I felt a growing sickness in my stomach when we pulled around the loop in front of the school. I longed for the time when I would be old enough to dismiss my problems as easily as my mom.

"I'm sorry if you get made fun of because of my mistake," I told Ella as we walked up the stairs to the school.

Ella didn't respond, so I put my hand on her shoulder and asked, "You're not mad at me over this, are you?"

Ella jumped so high at my touch that I thought she was going to bounce off the steps. I hadn't realized that Ella had been preoccupied.

"What?" she asked, like she was just waking from a dream.

"Do you need me?" I asked. I don't know why I rephrased my inquiry. My question felt like it fit the situation somehow, and it seemed like Ella was really considering it.

Ella finally shook her head and said, "No, I'm fine."

I watched Ella walk up the rest of the steps. I had missed something important, but I couldn't put my finger on it.

My classroom was full of its usual activity. I noticed Christian and Lydia in a corner near his desk. He had his arm around her while he talked to Donny.

Lydia made eye contact with me, but looked back at Donny quickly. I decided how to handle my predicament in that moment.

I strode over to Lydia with a purpose. "I really need to talk to you," I said, in my best friend-in-crisis tone.

Lydia looked genuinely puzzled. She broke from Christian's arm and followed me. Christian didn't look away from his conversation with Donny.

I led Lydia over to an empty corner in the room. I spoke just above a whisper, and the noise in the room covered my words.

"I hate him!" I said, and I let my eyes fill with tears.

"Who?" Lydia asked. She still didn't understand why I was talking to her.

"Christian!" I said, as if it was obvious. "He tricked me into going to the bike shop and I think he called the police station to tell my grandfather that I was out. *What did I do to him?*"

I allowed tears to spill down my cheeks. I should have signed up for drama club.

Lydia finally understood that I didn't suspect her of setting me up. I could see a plan forming in her expressions, as she put her hand on my shoulder and brought me toward her. I gave in to her embrace. A couple of kids were looking at us, but they would never say anything. If Lydia Sneed was comforting me, then whatever I was upset over was vindicated.

"I had no idea!" Lydia dulcified, pulling away with a shocked look. "I should break up with him. He came into the classroom this morning and said that he really didn't like you. He was so convincing!"

Lydia straightened her posture. "Do you want me to break up with him?" She reached into her handbag and pulled out a handkerchief with the Sneed family crest.

"No," I said. I blew my nose into the handkerchief and tried to hand it back to her.

Lydia looked rather disgusted and gave a shooing gesture. "You can keep it."

"Okay," I said and shrugged. I put the handkerchief in my pocket.

"You are my best friend," Lydia said, "and I will break up with Christian if he hurts you."

"I heard my name," Christian said as he walked up. He returned his arm to its place around Lydia's shoulders.

I mustered up my most hurt expression and told him, "We were just talking about how happy we are that you two are together."

I hoped I looked convincing. It bewildered Christian, and I wondered about his involvement. *Did he even know about Lydia's plan?*

I shrugged off the idea. He had written the directions.

I let Lydia think she was a comfort to me all morning. She even told Christian to walk ahead of us so that she could hear the details of the previous night. I left out the most hurtful things my grandpa had said to me, and I didn't mention his visit to her house. Her mock concern enraged me, but I didn't let it show.

Christian, Lydia, Donny, and I sat together at lunch. Now that Christian and Lydia were together, Christian's best friend could join us. The new couple tried to play matchmakers. Donny was nice, but he laughed like a donkey, and I think he was only invited to attend Pale Woods Academy because of his deceased mother's family's money. The school barely promoted him every year.

An idea suddenly struck Christian. "Did you get your bike fixed?" he asked Lydia.

Lydia's face drained of color, and I had my answer about Christian's involvement. Lydia finished chewing her food before she answered.

"I had it fixed," she said carefully. "Donny, what kind of restaurant did you say your dad had?"

"It's just an Italian restaurant," Donny replied. "He's thinkin' about sellin' it and going back to auto repair, though." He wasn't going to help Lydia change the subject.

"Good," Christian said, still focusing on Lydia. "I didn't know if you could read my directions. I wrote it in a hurry. Maybe we could go for a ride sometime."

"Maybe," Lydia said with a smile she quickly dropped. I could tell her mind was racing with possible explanations.

I pretended I hadn't noticed the exchange between Lydia and Christian.

"We *all* need to go out," Christian said meaningfully.

Donny was staring at his tray. He felt embarrassed about the situation, too.

"Oh! I know!" Lydia said. "We could all go to the Apple Festival this weekend!"

My heart dropped. I hadn't realized the full impact my grandpa's "road trip" during the Apple Festival would have on my teenage world. No wonder he had told my mom not to let me make any plans.

"I can't," I said. "My grandpa's taking me away for the weekend."

I phrased my words carefully to make it sound like I was excited about the trip. Lydia seemed really confused. After all, she thought she had destroyed my relationship with my grandpa.

"You're going on one of his stupid nature trips this weekend? I thought he had to patrol the festival?" Lydia asked.

"He got someone else to cover his shifts," I told her.

"Where are you going?" Christian asked.

I knew he meant well, but he was getting on my nerves. I didn't want anyone to know where I was going with my grandpa. After all, I didn't even know where we were going.

"It's a surprise," I said, trying to sound excited.

Lydia looked into Christian's eyes. "It's probably just a nature preserve," she said. "He has never taken her anywhere cool." Lydia moved her face closer to Christian's, and they rubbed noses.

I couldn't eat. Students at Pale Woods Academy were not allowed to display affection, but Lydia did not abide by the same rules, so her public display was ignored.

Christian was eating up all the attention. Lydia's family was so wealthy and powerful that the people in our small town considered her a celebrity. Other guys were giving him high-fives in the hallway, and girls who had never noticed him batted their eyes and grinned shyly in his direction.

I overheard the conversation Christian had with a high school boy that afternoon on the bus. The boy asked Christian how he had started dating a girl so far out of his league. Christian smiled sheepishly and said, "I guess I have something more to offer than all the rest of the guys in town."

I knew Christian, and he probably meant that he had more nerve than anyone else, because he had approached Lydia and asked her out. I think the high school boy took it differently, because Christian had the nickname Don Juan before he got off the bus that afternoon.

Chapter Eight

My mom woke me up at five o'clock on Friday morning. It was still dark outside, and all I wanted to do was stay warm in my bed.

"What do you want?" I grumbled.

"Your grandfather's here," my mom's voice whispered through the darkness. "He's ready to go."

"Don't I have time to brush my teeth or eat breakfast?"

"Your grandfather said that he had everything covered," my mom told me. There was a soft rustle as she left the room.

I rose from my bed and started pulling on yesterday's clothes. Ella was curled in the fetal position with her back to me.

"I am sorry about what Lydia did to you," Ella said. Her voice sounded more awake than I felt. "But you really should have known better."

"I know she's a scheming, backstabbing jerk," I said. Red-hot anger was climbing up my neck to my face. "I pretend that she's my friend so that things like this don't happen to me."

"It sounds like you should be more careful," came Ella's simple reply.

I rolled my eyes. "Next time you want to make me feel better, stay asleep instead."

"Fine," Ella returned. "But you are not blameless. You may not have meant to cause anyone harm, but you left the house without permission."

I couldn't think of a witty retort because my sister was right. I rolled my eyes again in the dark.

Ella took a deep breath. "I really am sorry about Lydia. If Grandfather becomes unbearable, just tell him you trusted the wrong people, like he did before he left the city."

Ella had given me a defense, but I did not know the best time to use it. *And what if he asked me to explain myself?*

I knew better than to ask Ella for more information, because she would remind me I didn't believe in her gift. Several years ago, I had lied to her. I swore I would tell everyone that I believed her, and then I acted like she was crazy. In the past, I had lied about my knowledge of Ella's special talent, but that was the first time that I had broken a pinky swear.

A pinky swear was sacred in our family, so Ella had made me pinky swear I would openly profess my belief in her. I went back on my word as soon as it proved inconvenient for me. Some people burn bridges, but I had destroyed the one between Ella and me with dynamite.

My mom was frightened of Ella's gift, and my grandpa wanted her to be mentally evaluated. He was afraid that she had the same condition as our father's father, "Crazy" Lyle Miller. Ella stayed away from psychiatrists because she kept to herself, and that made it easier to ignore her abnormalities.

"Sydney!" my mom called from the foot of the steps.

"Okay," I shouted back. I didn't bother to tell Ella goodbye.

My mom had already packed my bags, and my grandpa had them slung over his shoulders. I felt a sting in my heart over his continued disappointment.

"Are you ready, Sydney?" he said gruffly. He hadn't used his nickname for me since he'd picked me up in front of the bike shop.

I nodded. My mom hugged me, and to my surprised asked my grandpa, "Are you really sure about this?"

"I've never been more certain about anything," my grandpa told my mom. He added, "It's what I should have done with *you* before you pulled your little stunt."

My mom's face colored, and she said nothing else, but she waved at me from the porch. I waved back until I was sure that she couldn't see me anymore.

My grandpa had driven his old maroon SUV. He took it on the trips we made because he did not take the county police cruiser out of Unicoi County.

"Breakfast is at your feet," my grandpa said. I remembered my doughnuts from earlier in the week, and my stomach growled. I bent down to pick up the grocery bag on the floorboard. He had filled it with plain granola bars.

I was used to being spoiled by my grandpa. We would usually enjoy a big breakfast of biscuits and gravy or pancakes at a restaurant before we left on a trip. The presence of the granola bars stunned me.

My grandpa was aware of my shock and said, "Those are good for you." He chuckled. "It's better than prison food." I'm glad it was funny to him.

I didn't mind granola bars, but I had to eat four bars before my hunger abated. My grandpa reached behind my seat and retrieved a warm bottle of water to wash down my breakfast.

"Where are we going?" I asked after we had traveled for a little over an hour.

"You'll find out when we get there," my grandpa replied briskly. I hadn't expected him to tell me anyway.

We settled into a comfortable silence. I was only at ease because I knew that no matter how mad my grandpa acted, he still loved me. His temper had cooled since the incident, but he was still disappointed in me. I didn't want to hear his thoughts. They would probably break my heart again.

The radio played loudly enough to discourage conversation, so I listened to rock from the sixties and seventies. He finally turned off the interstate and navigated down several streets. All the buildings along the road were plain, and chain businesses were absent from the terrain.

I probably should have stayed awake, but I couldn't ride in a car for over an hour without falling asleep. I'm lucky to have stayed alert for three hours. I drifted off to sleep, and I didn't stop my eyes from drawing the curtains on my consciousness.

My grandpa shook me awake. "Sit up, Sydney," he said.

I blinked away sleep and struggled to right myself in my seat. I couldn't have been asleep for more than half an hour, and my body resisted wakefulness.

I stretched out my legs and took in my surroundings. I looked out the window, and my throat closed in fear.

We entered an area surrounded by a fence, barbed wire, and a surveillance system. I had never actually seen a prison, but I knew we were going into one because of all the movies I'd watched.

My grandpa pulled up to a guard in a small booth. "Conner!" the man exclaimed. "It's been a long time, but I'm glad to see you, no matter the circumstances." The guard looked down his nose at me. My grandpa had arranged to visit the prison by telling someone in charge of this prison about my supposed delinquency.

The guards patted my grandpa and me down on at least three separate occasions to check for contraband, and the man gave us badges. My pass said *guest* and had a barcode at the bottom.

Two guards with rifles met us at the metal doors and flanked us without a word. I wondered how many people in the system knew my grandpa. *How many favors had been done for Conner Murphy to bring his young granddaughter to this facility?* At thirteen, I should not have been allowed to walk inside a prison.

I tried to brush the mind of the guard next to me to find out the types of criminals I could expect to see or if he knew my grandpa. For the first time in my life, I couldn't hear anything from his mind. I looked pointedly at the guard, but he ignored my stare. *Did he know I had tried to probe his thoughts, or did he block his mind without realizing it?*

I saw another set of metal doors in the hallway, and the guards stopped to validate the sequence for opening them. We walked into the main facility, and my grandpa finally explained the reason for our visit.

"Sydney, I've always trusted that you were a bright girl—maybe a little flighty—but a *good* girl. Your family has had some illnesses in the past, but I thought you would get above all that and make me proud. I tried to raise a good girl," my grandfather continued, and I knew he was talking about my mom, "but I lost sight of her along the way. I take full responsibility for the way she turned out," he said, nodding like he agreed with himself. "I failed."

I should never have interrupted my grandpa's speech, pity party, or whatever it was, but I couldn't stop myself from defending my mom.

"She didn't turn out *bad*," I argued.

My grandpa's head snapped toward me. He talked a little lower, and the temperature of his words was colder than the bars of the prison.

"Your mother may have managed to stay married and carry a good job, but can she handle life?" he spat.

I couldn't answer.

"Has she cleaned out your brothers' room? Do your father's clothes still hang in her closet?"

Everything he said was true, but I still didn't see how death avoidance made my mom a bad person. I echoed my thoughts to my grandpa.

His eyebrows climbed halfway up his forehead. "I'll tell you why I feel that way about her. She's going to drive you and your sister crazy with her denial. Your sister already believes that she can see and talk to dead people. That must be because of your mother's refusal to accept her situation. And," he said, pointing at me, "*you* are acting out by running around at night."

I wanted to tell my grandpa that he was wrong, but his words were true. I *had* sneaked out. Even if I didn't think that I was wrong to do it, it was still a breach of trust.

We stopped in front of another metal door. The signs read "Minimum Security" and "No outside weapons beyond this point."

The guard on the left scanned his ID badge under an electronic machine. Something inside the door clicked. The other guard scanned his ID badge under an identical electronic device on our right. The door clicked again and opened.

We stepped inside the observation room. Glass lined the walls from my waist to the ceiling.

Beyond the glass, men in state-issued denim were everywhere. Some were sitting and talking at tables, others were reading, and some were working out on weight benches in the back of the room. One large window let the sun kiss the faces of the prisoners.

"Can they see us?" I whispered. I was scared the prisoners would zero in on me, like hungry dogs when they hear a rabbit, but they did not seem to notice our appearance in the observation booth.

"Yes," my grandpa confirmed. "But this glass is unbreakable."

I looked up at my grandpa questioningly. This experience was supposed to show me where bad kids go when they commit adult crimes, but I didn't understand why we couldn't just tour the county jail.

My grandpa had expected my puzzled stare. "Mike Holder owns the bike shop," he explained. "If you had robbed his cash drawer as an adult, you could have been sent here." My grandfather hammered his point home. "And *I* would have told Mike to press charges."

I looked around at all the men in the room and raised my eyebrows. My grandfather understood my unspoken inquiry.

"Female offenders are kept at another facility," he said. My grandpa took a couple of steps away from the guards, and I moved my feet next to where my grandpa stood.

"Sneaking out on Wednesday night was a minor offense," my grandpa stated. "Was it your first time?"

I nodded. It was the first time I had walked out of the house without permission—well, the first time since my brothers' spirits rested.

My grandpa shook his head like he didn't know whether to believe me. "First time or not, you broke the rules. Over there—" my grandpa said, pointing to a man with bright green eyes and a white beard. "—is Mason Kyte. He is here for robbing a bank. Robbing a bank is a federal offense. Do you think that was the first time he'd disobeyed a law?"

I was momentarily speechless as I caught the gaze of another inmate. He was tall and lean, with brown hair and blue eyes. A small, round scar glanced the underside of his cheekbone. He looked familiar, but I couldn't place him. His physical appearance placed him in his thirties, but his eyes were older. *Maybe he had been one of my dad's friends?*

My grandpa grunted for my attention, and I gave him the answer he wanted to hear. "No," I sighed.

"You're right, Sydney. He robbed several convenience stores before he hit the bank. He has quite a record, stretching back to his adolescence when he sold beer to his friends."

"Beer is legal," I said.

"Beer was legal for people eighteen and older when Mason was growing up, but fifteen-year-old children should not drink it. One young lady died from alcohol poisoning because she didn't know that liquor was stronger than beer. She just drank whatever her boyfriend poured into her cup. Don't get me wrong," my grandpa continued, "he probably just thought he'd have a better chance at getting lucky, but Mason should never have been that careless with alcohol."

"He killed his girlfriend?" I asked. I couldn't help falling for the humanity of the situation.

My grandpa nodded. "Her name was Beverly Ann Clark, but I doubt Mason even remembers her face."

I could see where this was going. There was no need to tell my grandpa that I wouldn't live a life of crime because I snuck out of the house once.

My grandpa pointed to another inmate who was doing push-ups in the back of the room. The veins in his neck stood out as he forced himself harder than our coach pushed the football team. Sweat dripped from his bald head, and the distance the other inmates gave him was not because of his smell.

"That's Garrett Hughes," my grandpa continued. "He committed thirteen counts of rape," he said with contempt. "But he was only convicted of vehicular homicide."

I looked sideways at Garrett Hughes. He seemed attractive enough to find a girlfriend. I couldn't understand his need to lay claim to unwilling participants.

My grandpa seemed to read my mind. "He was a respected member of his community. He was married and had three children while he was hurting those girls."

I looked sharply at my grandpa. "Girls?"

My grandpa nodded. "Yes, Sydney, *girls*. He lured teenage girls he met online to a secluded spot. He told them he was a good-looking teenage boy. He even used a picture of his own son to make his story more believable."

My grandpa was really emotional about the circumstances of the case we were discussing. He threw eye-daggers at Garrett Hughes. Garrett continued his exercises, but he held my grandpa's watch. It looked like they were going to stare each other down, like in old westerns, but one guard said something to the Bald Monster, and he resumed his pushups.

"People like *that*," my grandpa motioned to Garrett Hughes, "don't deserve the air they breathe. People like him are out late at night, waiting to prey upon poor, defenseless girls."

He was referring to the possible dark consequences of my unauthorized outing, but I didn't object. I respected my grandpa, and he worked to put people who committed crimes away from individuals who respected and obeyed laws.

My grandpa pointed out a few other examples in the room. He told me about all of their offenses, and I listened with interest. My grandpa seemed to know every criminal in the room. I didn't think they were all from our hometown, but I wondered how many of them had been put behind bars because of my grandpa. After all, my grandpa had worked undercover for a while before he officially moved to Erwin.

Two hours had passed before I realized it, and the prisoners were called for lunch. The window's sunlight was less direct than when I had first arrived.

The man with blue eyes stole glances in our direction every couple of moments. I looked at him, and he glanced away, but his gaze was always on me when I turned back to the place he sat.

My grandpa had not mentioned the blue-eyed prisoner when he was pointing out the adult outcomes of deviant teenage behavior. I finally asked my grandpa about the man as we were being led from the room.

My grandpa sighed with disappointment. "That's Bryan Shelton. He was my greatest success and my biggest failure."

I don't know why adults speak in riddles. My grandpa didn't explain himself, so I became more curious about Bryan Shelton than I had been about any of the other inmates. My grandpa had hinted that Bryan Shelton's offense was heinous, but he looked like the only prisoner who didn't belong in the facility.

"Have you learned anything today, Sydney?" my grandpa asked when we slid into his SUV.

I wanted to scoff at his question and reply with a sarcastic comment, like, *I won't get caught when I plan the heist of the century.*

Instead, I took a deep breath and proudly stated, "I learned you love me, and you want me to be a person you can be proud of."

I don't know how the words came out of my mouth because I don't remember thinking them before I spoke. My grandpa had to recover from his shock. It must have been the right thing to say, though, because my grandpa's eyes moistened and he reached over the console to embrace me.

I could feel my grandpa's unconditional love. "You're right," he said. "I love you so much, Little Lady."

My nickname was back.

I sent all the love I could feel back into my grandpa's arms. I looked up and hadn't realized that I'd been crying.

My grandpa wiped away my tears and said, "Enough of this stuff. Let's go get a pizza."

Chapter Nine

F ood can be delicious, and the ability to order what you want is extremely underrated. At home, I had shared food with three other siblings, so we had to eat whatever our mother fixed.

Josh and Jerrod ate anything, so I never worried about them, but my mom was allergic to seafood and Ella was allergic to nuts. My choices were limited, and there were still many foods I had not sampled.

On the rare occasions that our mother took us to a restaurant, I couldn't order fish tacos or crab cakes, because everyone shared their food. My mom picked out the peas in a casserole, since peas belonged to the nut family, and the people in our house never tried crunchy peanut butter.

I also had to worry about actually getting food. I learned to eat quickly, because even though my mom fixed me a plate, if no other food was available, other family members would pick up food from my plate. My father was the worst for stealing bites of my pancakes or pieces of bacon, and Josh and Jerrod learned from his example.

My grandpa let me order anything on the menu. I remembered the first time my grandpa took me to a restaurant. It was a pizza buffet. I spent two hours sampling different pizzas.

My mom didn't like onions, so almost every pizza I had eaten had onions. If there had been a pizza with nuts on it, I would have eaten that one, too!

I ordered a large Hawaiian pizza with a side of cheese sticks. My grandpa remarked, "Good choice," like he always did after I placed my order.

I leaned over the table and sipped my soda. When I looked up, my grandpa had his eyebrows raised.

"Pick up your cup next time," he reprimanded.

"Yes, sir."

My grandpa may have spoiled me, but he insisted on almost perfect table manners. I sat up straight, put my napkin in my lap, and decided not to disappoint him for the rest of the meal.

"I'm so glad that we learned a lesson today," he said.

We? I thought *I* was the one who had to walk into a prison full of violators and burglars and learn about the inmates' sordid pasts.

The server laid the pizza on the table in less than ten minutes. The server, a young girl whose boyfriend thought he should show his love with bruises, asked if we needed anything else. My grandpa gave her a generous tip and told her to keep our cups filled. She smiled sadly and walked away. We didn't see her for the rest of our meal.

My grandpa ate quickly, but he waited patiently for me to finish. He folded and refolded his napkin, but he was alert to the happenings in the room. My grandpa could have told me the type of pizza on every table and the subject of every conversation within twenty feet of us.

"Maybe next summer I can take you up north with me," my grandpa suggested after we checked into our hotel.

I was preparing for a shower, but his words stopped me. "You mean where Mom grew up?"

"Yeah, I think it would be a nice little trip for us," he said, smiling. "I have some things I'd like to resolve in the city, but I would sit through one of those Boardwalk plays—if it made you happy," he added quickly.

"You mean Broadway?" I corrected.

"Sure, whatever." He waved his hand dismissively. "You would have to get your mother to go along with it. She has some sort of attitude about cities now."

Some of my mom's worst memories happened in the city where she spent her younger years. She never really talked about it, so her life there must have been difficult.

"So, what's the story with Bryan Shelton?" I ventured. Once again, I didn't think about what I had asked before the words had already flown out of my mouth.

My grandpa's eyes clouded over, and he turned his face to the floor. I regretted bringing up the subject again.

To my surprise, my grandpa spoke. He chose his words carefully as he told me Bryan Shelton's story.

"Bryan Shelton was a very promising young man," my grandpa began. "His family had lived near the river for as long as anyone could remember. He wanted to break the cycle of poverty in his family, so he went through police cadet training."

All the police officers I knew had to go through training before they joined the police department. I had heard my grandpa talking about it, and I thought the training sounded like a glorified boot camp.

"Bryan was assigned to me when he graduated," my grandpa said. "He was full of life and eager to learn the law, so we got along well." My grandpa stopped and took a deep breath. I knew that if I stayed quiet, I would learn more than if I mentioned Bryan Shelton in the future.

"Bryan had a way of spotting a liar. He could tell better than a lie detector test." My grandpa drove his knuckles into the wood of the hotel room's dresser. It creaked its resistance before he released the pressure. "I guess it takes a liar to know one."

The display startled me, but he didn't direct it at me. My grandpa would never hurt me.

"Bryan lived on the river with his wife and young daughter. His family was beautiful. Bryan's wife, Nellie, was a sweet young woman, and his daughter, Lily, was the cutest tot I had seen—outside of my family." My grandpa gave me a confidential wink.

"Bryan learned the laws quickly, and I was proud of him. I'm ashamed of it now, but I treated him like my own son. We went fishing by the river, and Nellie brought us sandwiches for lunch. I can still remember little Lily toddling down to the riverbank with a pitcher of lemonade in her arms. She threw her tiny, trusting arms around me and called me 'Poppy'. Her hair smelled like freshly cut flowers." Tears formed around my grandpa's words. His eyes stayed clear, but his voice betrayed the sadness he felt.

"I gave Lily a little bunny for Christmas," he said. I hadn't heard my grandpa's voice so thick since my brother's memorial service. "It was purple, her favorite color. That little girl hugged that stuffed bunny until I thought it would burst. She named it 'Puppy'. Bryan and I used to laugh over Lily calling that bunny *Puppy*.

I could almost see my grandpa and the Shelton family. It must have helped my grandpa to share his love with them. Especially since my mom wasn't talking to him a lot at the time.

"I guess you've heard of the big winter flood?" my grandpa asked me.

"Yes, sir," I answered immediately. I wanted to keep my grandpa talking before he thought too hard about telling his young granddaughter a story about a difficult time in his life. "I heard that there was a blizzard that dumped a bunch of snow on the town, and then a week later, it rained four inches in a day."

My grandpa nodded. "The temperature got warmer, and the snow melted fast."

My grandpa took a deep breath. He looked away from me as he spoke, but I could still hear the pain in his voice.

"The river was swelling with all the melted snow, and it was getting worse with the rain. Bryan helped evacuate the people who lived closest to the river. I asked him about Nellie and Lily, and he said they had gone to Nellie's friend's house. I knew Nellie's friend, so I didn't worry about them.

"We had been evacuating and rescuing people for most of the day. I noticed Bryan was upset, but I thought he was just worried about his family.

"Bryan's cell phone rang while we were eating a quick supper, and he answered it. Nellie was shouting on the other end. I couldn't hear exactly what she was saying, but I heard him say, 'Fine! Go with her, and I don't care if you ever come back.'

"I was disappointed in him for yelling at his wife, and he knew it. He told me that Nellie's friend wanted to take her away until the floodwaters receded. Bryan didn't like the idea, and he said that he felt Nellie's friend had been driving a wedge between him and his wife.

"I gave Bryan the best advice I felt I could give him," my grandpa recounted. "'Go to your wife. Spend some time with your family and show Nellie just how much you'd miss her.'

"I let him take my cruiser, and I stayed the night helping everyone on the south end of Erwin. I was so tired by the time I got a ride back to the station that I could have probably slept on the pavement outside the door.

"I walked into the office to ask an officer for a ride home, but everyone looked at me like they expected me to explode. I asked Officer Novack if he would take me to my house.

"Novack walked me out to his cruiser, but he kept his distance, and he didn't try to strike up a conversation. That should have told me something," my grandpa informed me. "Novack is usually pretty chatty."

I pictured Officer Novack. He was always kind to me, but Ella avoided him more than the other police officers. He *was* talkative, and Ella did not like to be dragged into conversations.

"I thought he was keeping his distance because I smelled like I had been working on a pig farm," my grandpa continued, "but we hadn't been on the road more than five seconds before he said, 'I am so sorry.'

"I hadn't heard words in that tone since your grandmother's funeral, so I got defensive. I must have scared him to death.

"I wanted to know if something had happened to your mother," he remembered. "I asked him if my house was severely damaged. I asked if Bryan had made it home okay.

"When I said Bryan's name, it sparked something, and Novack pulled the cruiser over in a bank's parking lot. 'You haven't heard?' he asked me.

"'No,' I said. I wanted to add that I would strangle the life out of him if he didn't tell me what I didn't know, but that kind of talk doesn't get you anywhere when people are already scared of you.

"He braced himself for my reaction and said, 'Nellie and Lily are dead.'

"I let out something like a sob." My grandpa admitted his grief sadly and continued his story.

"I guess you've seen your father get mad, and you know how men are with their emotions," my grandpa said.

I nodded. One of my first memories was of my father lashing out at Jerrod after my mother's miscarriage.

"I got out of the car and punched the sidewalk until my knuckles bled," my grandpa admitted. "I would've probably kept hitting the ground if Novak hadn't stopped me.

"It took a long time for me to recover. I decided I needed to get myself together to help Bryan make all the arrangements. I asked Novack about him.

"I will never forget the look on Novak's face. He didn't know that he was about to double my pain.

"He said, 'Bryan's in custody, Chief.'

"I was confused about the imprisonment of a fellow officer, but I thought it was because Bryan had gone crazy after the death of his wife and child. 'Probably for the best,' I said.

"Bless Novack's soul. He saw that I still didn't understand the full situation. 'Bryan's in custody for killing his family,' he told me."

I could feel my grandpa's thoughts. He had lost his sanity for some time. There were snatches of anger where he spoke through a thin red curtain of fury. He walked into the jail and straight up to Bryan's cell. At least he didn't stop for the keys to Bryan's cell before he confronted him. Otherwise, he would never have stood trial for his crimes, and my grandpa would be the one in prison.

"You see, Little Lady," my grandpa continued, "I loved that little girl and her mama like they were you and your mama, but there was no bad water under the bridge between Nellie and Lily and me. I broke bread with that family, and they were a big part of me. I doted on Nellie and Lily when your mom wouldn't let me see any of my own grandchildren."

I was right about my grandpa's connection with Bryan, Nellie, and Lily. They almost replaced the family that seemed to have forgotten about him. I imagined my grandpa had the same blind fury when he faced Bryan Shelton that he would have had if my father had killed my mother and me.

"Bryan lied to my face about everything, my grandpa recalled. "He told me he had gone home and caught Nellie trying to leave with Lily. He admitted they had fought, but he said Lily's death was an accident, and he swore that he didn't kill Nellie.

"Novack briefed me later that day. When Bryan had left to help evacuate and rescue area residents, Nellie had decided to leave with her friend. She had every intention of returning to Erwin after the crisis was over.

"Nellie's friend said in her statement that Nellie thought it would be best to pack her things and leave before Bryan came home. Nellie rushed over to her house to gather a few things after promising her friend that she would be back in a few minutes. She took Lily with her because she wanted the girl to pack her favorite toys.

"The friend's husband was worried after Nellie and Lily had been gone for more than an hour, and he and another fellow went down to the house to see about Nellie and Lily. That's when—"

My grandpa took a great shuddering breath. I had been crying silently since I'd heard about Nellie and Lily's death. I walked up behind my grandpa and tried to comfort him. I put my hand on his shoulder. He patted my hand, but he didn't turn around.

"Novack told me that the friend's husband and the other fellow saw Bryan at the edge of the river. They said he had his hands around Nellie's throat, and he had already choked the life out of her. Lily's body was lying half in and half out of the river.

"The men tied Bryan's hands and feet, and Nellie's friend called the police. Novack was one of the responding officers. The EMT's pronounced Nellie dead on the scene, but the river had already swallowed Lily.

"He found a stuffed purple rabbit on a rock. He said it was positioned to look out on the river. It was almost like Puppy was looking for his lost friend." He took a breath to steady himself. "Novack kept it and gave it to me after I had taken out my grief and anger on the asphalt beside his cruiser." He looked at the top of his hands, but only one visible scar remained. "It still smelled like Lily."

I remembered the stuffed rabbit on my grandpa's computer. I didn't think I could bring myself to go into that room again.

"I went crazy," my grandpa admitted. "I insisted Lily was alive, and I organized search teams to scour the river and woods. Every person on the search team was instructed to report directly to me if they found Lily-or her body. After a week, my search team dwindled from fifty people to five devoted men from my department, but I couldn't accept Lily's death until I saw proof of it.

"A couple of weeks later, Novack came into my office with paperwork in his hand. He looked scared of me, and after the way I had broken down on him, I couldn't blame him. I could tell he was nervous, so I told him to tell me whatever it was and get it over with.

"I remember the entire conversation like it's playing in front of me right now," my grandpa said.

"'They found her body, Chief,' Novack told me."

I didn't have to ask whose body had been discovered. I braced myself for the inevitable result of my grandpa's search.

After a shaky breath, my grandpa said, "I told Novack that I was going to go to the morgue and make the necessary arrangements. He handed me the paperwork before I could get out of my chair.

"I read that the body had been eaten by animals. I held out a glimmer of hope that the body they had found had not been Lily's, but then I read the rest of her file. A video had been made of her remains and it had been sent to our station. Novack had taken it to Nellie's brother, and he had given a positive ID on Lily.

"Bryan and Nellie had taken Lily to regular doctor and dentist appointments, and the records matched. My little Lily was dead.

"I could have watched the tape that Nellie's brother watched, but I didn't have any fight left in me. That was the year that your mother had let me back into your lives, so I had somewhere else to focus my attention.

"I'm afraid I haven't been totally fair with you, Sydney," my grandpa confessed. I raised my eyebrows, but I didn't think that he could tell me anything worse than the story I'd just heard.

"I wish I had spoiled you simply because you are my granddaughter," he said, "but I think I doted on you because you reminded me of Lily. I gave you the love and attention that I wanted to give her."

"I thought it was because I reminded you of my mom," I whispered.

My grandpa turned to face my words. His cheeks were splotchy without a trace of tears.

"Who told you that you remind me of your mother?" my grandpa asked.

"I just kind of felt that way," I admitted. "Mom said that I looked a lot like she did when she was younger. I guess I thought that you and Mom had a better relationship when she was little and maybe you could see some of her in me." I started with confidence, but I added the last part shyly. "I also thought that maybe you felt like you were making up the time you lost with Mom by focusing your attention on me."

My grandpa walked to the window. The horizon was turning deep orange against the fading cornflower sky.

"I think that may be part of it, too," he said. "I was too hard on your mother after your grandmother died. I feel like I forced her to leave part of her childhood behind. She took over cleaning the house and cooking when she should have been playing with her friends. She tried to be caring and understanding, but I was grieving so much."

I could hear the explanation in his voice. "You didn't want to be around her because she reminded you of her mother."

My grandpa looked back at me like I had saved him from drowning. "I'm glad you understand, Little Lady."

My grandpa's heavy footfalls crossed the distance between us. I had been standing, but I suddenly felt weak. I let my grandpa's arm encircle me and leaned against his protective form.

"I may have been confused before, but I've had a lot of time to think about my feelings for my family and the people I considered my family." I listened to his voice echo in his chest. "I can honestly say," my grandpa continued, "that I love you for who you are, Little Lady," he said.

At that moment, I doubted my grandpa's words. I felt like a replacement granddaughter, even though I was his biological kin.

"I may have singled you out because you reminded me of Lily or you strongly favor your mother," he said, "but I grew to love the *real* you over time. Besides, no one else has fallen out of my fishing boat trying to reel in a fish."

We shared a laugh at that memory. I closed my eyes.

I could hear my grandpa's words clearly through one ear, and my other ear picked up the vibrations in his chest when he spoke. I nodded my head and let him slowly rock me on my feet.

I decided it was okay that my grandpa had used me as a rebound for the women he had lost in his life. I had treated him in the same way. My grandpa had taken the place of my father and my older brothers. We were codependent on each other for love and attention, but I never felt as though I had missed out on anything another grandfather and granddaughter would have shared.

I was glad we'd taken the trip. It helped mend the broken bridge between my grandpa and me, and I understood him a little better. I had been too young to really remember my father's love, and all the men in my life had left me, so it felt nice to be encircled by my grandpa's unconditional love.

His gentle sway relieved my troubles. His hold was as pure and loving as a hammock made of angels. I eased into carefree sleep, knowing that I was protected by a man who would never leave me.

Chapter Ten

I had a terrible dream that night. I woke myself screaming.

I was near the edge of the river, and I could see the dilapidated house Lydia had shown me during our doomed sleepover. I was young, and I had a little purple rabbit in my arms.

A beautiful young woman with short blond hair shook me. "I told you not to play near the river unless I was with you," she said.

I dangled my bunny over the water defiantly. The young woman crossed her arms and gave me a stern look. "If you drop him in the water, he may get sucked into the river. Mr. Rabbit may not pop up for miles. You may never see him again."

I shook my head and pressed my rabbit back to my chest. I threw my little arms around the woman's waist. "His name is Puppy," I reminded her.

"Okay, keep *Puppy* close to your heart so you won't lose him," the woman said, clearly humoring me.

"I will keep *you* close to my heart," I said, holding the woman more tightly.

An unexpected sob leaped out of the woman's mouth. Tears fell on my arms as the woman professed, "I will keep *you* close to my heart, my darling baby. I love you so much."

I let the woman rock me, even though I was getting cold. The day had been rainy and warm, but it was chilly after the sky had finally cleared.

A car squealed into the driveway, and a man charged toward us. I was nervous because he was so angry.

The young woman yelled, "I'm already packed, Bryan. You better leave before I call the cops." The woman pushed me behind her.

"I'm not leaving without my daughter," he spat, easily pushing the woman aside, and snatching me off of my feet. I dropped my rabbit, and I cried. I wriggled in the man's arms, but he held me firmly.

"You can't leave me," the man pleaded. "I love you, Nellie. I don't know if that woman's like a mother or a sister to you, but I'm your husband. We chose each other. Please choose me again." The man's voice had softened as he begged the woman to stay. I wasn't scared anymore. I just wanted Puppy.

The woman threw up her hands. "I need a break, Bryan," she cried. "I want to be with you, but we need some time apart. Our relationship is just too intense."

The man's voice elevated. "Intense?" he yelled. "I love you, Nellie! You talk about us like we fight all the time. We only fight when *she's* involved." He pointed across the road.

The woman was irritated, and her voice rose even higher. "I'm done, Bryan! I want a divorce! You aren't married to me anyway. You're married to the police station and Chief Murphy! If Lily and I are going to be alone, I'd rather us be alone without someone else in the house."

The man waved his finger in the direction of the home across the street. "That's *her* talking again! She puts these ideas in your head, and I think she has an unhealthy attachment to you."

"Don't talk about her like that!" the woman shouted, and I wailed. She tugged on my arm, but the man held me in place.

"Give me my daughter!" the woman screeched.

The woman stood on the tips of her toes and head-butted the man holding me. The man was not ready for the attack, and he dropped me. I fell, head first, onto a large rock.

My vision was blurry, but I tried to sit up. I could see little, glittery stars dance through my vision, and something sticky cascaded down my face. I touched my shaking hand to my cheek and brought it close to my eyes. My vision had taken on a black and white quality, but I knew the liquid on my fingers was blood.

The man was trying to hold the woman away from me while simultaneously attempting to check on me. It was apparent that I was dazed, but I don't think he could see the blood on my face. My bloody side was turned away from him, but they both cried out when I showed them my crimson fingers.

The man lost his hold of the woman, and she threw her head into him again. He was ready to defend himself, but he fell near the edge of the water. I briefly worried that the river's water would swell like the tide of an ocean and swallow his body before he could wake up.

The woman ran to me, and another woman's voice called, "Is everything okay?"

Three black shadows ran to the edge of the river. I lost my vision almost immediately after making out their forms.

"I'll kill him for this!" the new woman's voice said.

The woman I knew as my mother tried to lift me. I could feel the heat of her body on my arms and legs. My head was a burning river of fire.

"Don't move her," a man cautioned.

"I don't know what to do!" my mother shouted. The hysteria in her voice climbed a notch.

The man who called himself my father stirred. I let myself fade. Everyone's voices softened, and I heard my mother yell, "You killed my baby!"

As I faded out of consciousness, the man replied, "I would rather her *die* than see her with the likes of them." He was talking about the people who had come to our aid.

I was cold and sleepy, and I couldn't fight it off any longer. I let the bitter darkness swallow me.

My grandpa was gently rocking me when I awoke. I wondered why his arms were around me, but then I realized I was a sweaty mess on the floor of the hotel room.

My grandpa kept telling me, "It was just a dream," repeatedly. A note in his voice suggested that he wasn't sure how much of his own words he believed.

I let my grandpa run his fingers through my sweaty hair, even though it hurt when he tried to pull them through a tangle. His repetitive rocking brought me back to reality.

I opened my eyes. Worry lines creased on my grandpa's face as he studied my expression. "No more scary stories before bed," he joked.

I had realized something in my dream, and as badly as it scared me, I wasn't ready to pull myself from its clutches until I asked my grandpa a question. I hoped he would be as candid with me as he had been when we were discussing Bryan Shelton.

"Grandpa?" I asked. My voice sounded like the creaking of a long-forgotten trunk. The raspy quality hung in the air. I must have screamed in my dream until I was hoarse.

My grandpa stopped rocking me and gave me his full attention. I debated over the way to form my question and decided it would be best to be straightforward.

My voice grated out, "Who was Nellie's friend? You know, the one who was going to take her on a trip."

My grandpa opened his mouth to reply and snapped it shut. He shifted his focus to the window, toward the slowly opening dawn of the day. He answered me slowly, giving me the answer that I already knew. "It was Lydia's mother, Olivia Sneed."

My grandpa decided we needed a day of fun since I had "learned my lesson". I think my reaction to his story about Bryan Shelton had scared him.

I had dealt with too many paranormal situations to be too shaken by the dream I'd had the previous night. I knew I'd had a vision. I had been Lily and had witnessed her death.

I wanted to clear Bryan of the charge of murder, but I couldn't make myself feel any emotion for him. Lily's cause of death may have been accidental, but I had seen pure rage in his actions, and I was sure that he had killed Nellie.

My grandpa was tight-lipped about the murder when I asked him, but he told me Bryan's attorney had argued the charge down to manslaughter. He must have had a high-powered lawyer since the witnesses were so powerful.

The rest of our trip went by very quickly. My grandpa and I visited an amusement park, and we ate all the junk food that found us. He took me home the next day, and I was just in time to help my mom finish the dinner dishes.

"How was the trip?" my mom asked, handing me a dish. I drug it through the rinse water and placed upright in the dish drainer.

"I guess it was okay," I said. I didn't want to ruin my mom's mood. I very seldom found her in a good disposition, but I wanted to know more about the Sheltons.

"Did you know Bryan Shelton?" I asked in what I hoped was a casual tone. My voice had returned, so I didn't sound like I had tried to swallow razor blades.

My mom nearly dropped the cup she had been washing. It slipped in her soapy hands, but she caught it before it fell to the floor.

She was surprised and curious. "Where did you hear that name?"

I remained truthful. "I saw him when we were touring the prison. He kept looking at me, so I asked Grandpa his name."

My mom returned to scrubbing the cup, but she did it more slowly and deliberately. She didn't speak until she handed it to me.

"I don't think he was looking at you, dear," my mom began. I felt a lie run through her mind. "I think he was probably studying your Grandpa."

"I know they were friends," I commented. My mom shook her head.

My family shook their heads at me when I said something before I'd thought it through or stated a fact incorrectly. Most of the time, they would laugh at me over my mistake for a long time before correcting or sharing what I had missed with me.

I didn't want to be left in the dark any longer. I could find out what I wanted by probing my mother's mind, but I considered it an invasion of a person's privacy to ransack his or her brain. I tried to keep my interactions as normal as possible by placing a barrier against my ability. At times, it was extremely frustrating.

"What else?" I said unkindly.

My mom turned her offended gaze on me, and I could see any trace of her good mood had vanished. *Oh well, might as well go for broke.*

"Don't look at me like I'm stupid," I snapped. "I never knew Bryan Shelton. How can it be common knowledge if I have never heard about it?"

My mom was shocked, but she quickly recovered. She went back to washing the dishes, but there was a harsher tone in her voice.

"Bryan was like a son to your grandpa," she said briskly. "Bryan lost his parents in a car crash when he was seventeen. In any other town, Bryan would have spent the next year in a foster home, and his parent's possessions would have been liquidated and divided among their debts."

"What do you mean?" I asked. I had never learned about what happened to a person's possessions after he or she died. I just assumed they went to that person's closest relatives.

My mom took a deep breath and handed me a soapy bowl. I didn't understand why she seemed so upset. Her voice cracked, and her hands were shaking.

"Bryan's parents were poor," she continued. "but they owned a house on the river and an acre of land. They had a truck and a car. The truck was theirs—they didn't owe any money on it—but the bank had given the Sheltons a loan for the car. There was a little over five thousand dollars left on the car, so Bryan gave it to the bank before they repossessed it. It was all the money he had saved to go to college.

"Why didn't Bryan just let the bank repossess the car?" I asked.

"Pride, I guess," my mother answered. "People in town looked down on people who didn't pay their debts, especially when the loan was made at a local bank.

"Anyway, the townspeople felt so bad for Bryan that they helped him. His parents had a few other debts, and in order to keep his parent's property, Bryan had to pay seven thousand dollars."

"The town raised seven thousand dollars for him?" It seemed like an astronomical sum of money to me.

"Yes," my mother said. "We all loved Bryan. He was a good guy."

My dream had not shown him in a colorful light, but I let my mother continue. People could change, for better or worse.

"Bryan had been mowing our lawn since we moved from the city," she said. "I think my father developed an attachment to him then, but he rarely mentions that he knew Bryan before Bryan started working at the sheriff's department."

I remembered that my grandpa's story started with Bryan's academy training and his position at the county's station. My grandpa had not trusted me with *all* of Bryan Shelton's story.

"My father wanted me to end up with Bryan," my mom said, "and he would ask Bryan to take me on dates. I went out with him, and we had a great time, but something was missing. We were friends, but I wasn't attracted to Bryan.

"When Bryan's parents passed away, he came to my house in tears. I had lost my mother, and he told me I was the only one who could understand him. I felt sorry for Bryan and started dating him."

"I thought going out on dates meant you were dating," I said.

"Not exactly," my mother replied. "A person could go out on *dates* with different people, but if you said you were *dating* someone, then it made it more exclusive."

I had always thought that my mother had only dated my father. It was strange to learn that a murderer had been my mother's first boyfriend.

"Bryan was always intense," my mother recalled. "He would say something untrue and expect me to fight with him. Bryan had a temper, too. He was very jealous, like—"

My mom broke off, and I thought she might swallow her next words. She was going to say *your father*, but talking about her deceased husband would mean he had been a real part of our lives. I had a firm belief that my mom didn't discuss my father because if she recounted anything about his life, she would have to admit that my father had died.

The unspoken words made their way far enough down my mom's throat for her to continue. "Bryan would see a guy looking at me, and he would try to start a fight. He once pelted a guy with french fries because he gave me his juice at lunch. The guy was just a dorky kid whose girlfriend was in my second period class. He was just being nice.

"Anyway, the people in town wanted to help Bryan, so they got Bannon Sneed to pay off the Shelton's debts. Bryan went crazy. He walked right up to the Sneed's door and demanded to know the exact amount so that he could pay it back. The Sneeds were offended, but Bannon finally agreed to let Bryan pay him back.

"My father got Bryan a job in Johnson City on a small farm, and Bryan worked every day. Bryan had almost paid off his debt to the Sneeds when he was fired.

"My father was sympathetic to Bryan's predicament, and it made me angry," she admitted. "My father would have punished me until I was thirty if I had been fired from a job."

"Why was he fired?" I interjected.

"Oh, it was something silly," my mom said. Red hot flowers flushed her cheeks.

"I acted very resentful toward Bryan after that," my mom said hastily. It was obvious she didn't want me to think too much about Bryan's termination from his farm job. "He tried to tell me that his actions were justified, but I wouldn't listen to him.

"My father got Bryan another job in town, and he continued to work every day of the week. I hated him for staying in my father's good graces, but I cooled down after a week and forgave him. I was going to forgive him by kissing him at a special town event."

I tried not to show my disgust. Parents were not allowed to be romantic.

"Bryan and I had been dating for over a year. He was always respectful, and he never tried to do more than hold my hand. I think he may have been afraid of my father."

My mother was right. I would not have wanted to get on my grandpa's bad side.

"There was an autumn festival going on that weekend, and I asked Bryan to take me," she recounted. "He said that he would pick me up after he got off of work, but he called me that afternoon and told me he had to work late.

"I was furious! I hung up the phone without telling him goodbye, and I walked into town to the festival.

"I've told you before that I saw your father at that festival. He took my mind away from Bryan and all my other worries. I kissed him on a hayride, and the rest is history."

I had gotten increasingly upset during my mother's story. My mother had nonchalantly told me she had cheated on Bryan. *Maybe Bryan had been right to be upset about the boy who had given my mother his juice!*

"You mean you kissed my father while you were dating Bryan!" I exclaimed. I had forgotten that Bryan could have murdered my mom and me as easily as he had killed Nellie and Lily.

"Yeah, I guess I did, but I was *meant* to be with your father," my mom defended.

"That's cheating!" I accused, and I instantly regretted it.

My mom slung a glass cup into the soapy dishwater. White bubbles splashed onto our faces, barely missing my eyes.

"What business is it of yours!" my mom yelled. Ella moved around upstairs. "Besides, where would we be if I hadn't met your father?" My mom threw up her soapy hands. "I can tell you," she shouted. "You would never have been born, and I would have been the one they found drowned in the river!"

My mom stormed out of the kitchen. I picked up the closest dish towel and patted the suds off my face. I could hear them popping as I pressed the fresh linen to my cheek.

"There is more."

I turned my head at the sound of the voice, and I saw Ella in the kitchen doorway. She had on a long shirt of Jerrod's that she slept in when she knew our mom wouldn't see her. Amazingly, it still smelled like him.

"What?" I asked my sister, turning around to face her. I leaned my back against the counter.

"There is more to that story," she said. "It is in her head." Her eyebrows rose suggestively.

"Stop talking crazy," I barked, and squeezed my eyes shut.

"All you have to do is look into the minds of everyone around you. They all know the story." Ella took a couple of steps into the kitchen. Her bare feet made the only noise in the silent house. They stuck to the cold, polished floor.

"Use your gift, Sydney," Ella demanded. "Or I cannot help you anymore."

Chapter Eleven

My mom had dated Bryan, but I didn't know more of the situation than I had before I'd gotten home. I hoped the information I was gathering would somehow fit together into the full story.

I sat down on the back deck and stared into the night. The faraway sound of a train whistle echoed against the mountains, and a slight breeze ruffled the aging leaves in the trees.

I did not want to dive into people's heads. I had spent almost my whole life denying that I had a super-sensory ability, and I wasn't ruining my efforts by climbing into people's thoughts. Besides, I usually found out things I didn't want to know when I violated the minds of those around me.

There was a time when I didn't know that I was different, and I told my father that Jason, his friend, was thinking about my mom without her shirt. My father stormed out of the house and found Jason with his hand on my mom's arm. Jason may have been trying to get my mom's attention, but my father thought he was trying to kiss her. He hit Jason until I couldn't tell that it was Jason anymore.

My father never questioned me, but my mom gave me icy stares. I listened to her mind and understood that she was afraid of me. She tried to guard her mind, but I could read her most recent thoughts. My mom was always a private person, and she didn't want me to know her secrets. It scared her to think that I could invade her thoughts and memories at any time.

I stopped listening to my mom, and I told my dad that I had heard Jason say what he was thinking about my mom. I knew my dad would tell my mom, and by the following morning, my mom was treating me the same as she had before the incident.

Ella thought it was easy for me to deny my gift, but she didn't share my ability. I wanted to read *everyone's* mind! I wanted to know where I stood with every person I met. I wanted to help people solve their problems. I wanted to help prevent abuse and suicide.

Even at a young age, I knew I had a duty to my family. They sometimes made fun of me, but they still thought that I was normal. People gave Ella strange looks, and they whispered about my mom's introversion, but everyone still spoke to me and treated me warmly. I made friends easily, and I was never picked last for sports teams.

I wished that there was a way to live a happy, fruitful life and share my gift with the world. I wanted to be Lydia's friend and find a way to make her smile at me the way she had when we'd gone to the river. I wanted to look into Christian's head and find out what he liked most about Lydia so that I could copy it.

That was a crazy thought. A week ago, I didn't even know that I liked Christian. Maybe I should run through the maze of my mind before I try to analyze anyone else's thoughts.

The kitchen light turned off, and the sliver of light I'd depended on was gone. I got up quickly and opened the back door.

My mom screamed. I caught an image of my father in her thoughts before it flew out of her mind.

"You scared me," she accused.

"I didn't mean to," I said defensively. "I was just getting some fresh air before bed."

"Fine," my mom said. The good mood was gone, so I thought I'd chance one more question before I went to bed.

"Did Dad know about Bryan?"

My mom sighed noisily and looked away, but she answered my question. "Of course he did. Your grandfather never missed an opportunity to throw Bryan's achievements in his face. Your father harbored no ill will toward Bryan, but I don't think Bryan ever got over losing me to your father. It took him several years before he started dating again, and then he married Nellie before they had been together for a month."

I had agitated my mom, but I pressed on. "Did you and Grandpa quit talking to each other because he wanted you to be with Bryan?"

My mom's eyes widened. "Now that is none of your business!"

My mom stomped away from me. In the absence of a door, my mom stopped before leaving the kitchen. She opened the cabinet that held our cups wide and slammed it. The reverberation rattled the glasses and caused a few of the plastic cups to tumble over.

I had to stifle a laugh. I knew my mom was seriously angry with me, but her childish actions reminded me of a four-year-old throwing a tantrum because she couldn't have her way.

My mom walked down our short hallway to the steps and climbed them without looking at me. I could see her purposely gazing upward, with her button nose pointed toward the ceiling.

My mom didn't have to voice a response to my question. I straightened the tumblers in the cabinet and walked down the hallway to the living room.

The night was quiet after my mom's outburst. The silence was almost audible, like a buzzing only I could hear. Maybe it was my mind trying to keep out all the thoughts flying toward me. Suddenly, the idea of reaching into people's minds made me exhausted. I thought about climbing the stairs to my bedroom, but the couch welcomed me into relaxation and easy slumber.

Chapter Twelve

My mind slipped into a world where I was painting my nails a pretty pink to match my new shoes. My hand shook slightly as I painted the thumb that rested on my lap.

A loud banging on the door made me jump. My polish flew off my knee, but I caught the bottle before it made more than a couple of pink dots on the carpet.

I had been expecting a reaction, but I had thought it would be a phone call. I ran out of my bedroom and down the hall, pausing at the entrance to the living room. *He could see me if he was looking in the window from the porch.*

I moved my head around the wall and quickly drew it back into the hallway. I could see his entire body through the open blinds. He had come straight from work and still had on his blue jeans and flannel shirt. He was standing with his arms slightly out from his body, like he had a bad sunburn, even though it was almost winter. *Had he seen me?*

"Miranda?" Bryan's voice called from my porch. "Come out here and talk to me. I saw you in there!"

He knew me well. It almost seemed like he had studied me as he had befriended my father. He memorized my favorite books and shows, and he even knew what I would say before I said it.

"Don't make me involve your dad," Bryan warned. He stepped away from the window and spoke through the door. "I have his number."

I was so mad that I couldn't remember crossing the room and throwing open the door. *Who was he to threaten me with my father?*

"That's better," Bryan said.

I didn't consider him my boyfriend anymore, but I couldn't help feeling my heart skip one of its angered beats. Bryan had come straight from work, and I could smell sweat radiating from his body, but he had some of the most perfect features I had ever seen. He almost looked like a movie star with his perfectly straight teeth and long eyelashes. He wore his hair just long enough to sweep it over casually or slick it back for formal events. His blue eyes sparkled radiantly when he saw me but turned cold as he remembered the reason for his visit.

I crossed my arms and looked away. I was at fault for his confusion and anger, but I didn't want to admit it.

Bryan slowly extended his hand. I saw his hand moving toward me in my peripheral vision, and I decided what I would do when he touched me.

"Miranda," he said softly as his fingers brushed my arm. His touch was tender, but I swatted his hand away.

Bryan grabbed me so quickly that I didn't know that he was holding me up to his face by my upper arms until he started speaking. He let go of me quickly when he realized that his grip had hurt me.

"Why are you doing this?" Bryan yelled at me. He cocked his head to the side so that he could look into my eyes. A thick vein throbbed across his forehead.

"I don't know what you're talking about!" I was too scared to act in control.

"I'm talking about Johnny Miller!" Bryan screamed at me. Little drops of spittle flew onto my face.

"Why did you let him hold you and kiss you on that hayride?" Bryan was hurt, and his anger deflated a little.

I rubbed my arms and saw the beginnings of the bruises I was getting from the conversation. Bryan saw me rubbing my arms and managed a look of remorse.

"I didn't mean to grab you," he said. He walked the length of the porch and back to me. I considered running into the house and locking the door, but we'd have to have this conversation sooner or later.

"I thought we decided we would be each other's first kiss," he said softly. He looked at me with so much hurt in his eyes that I almost forgot about Johnny.

"I wanted it to be special—" I began, but Bryan stopped me by stepping toward me.

"And I guess I wasn't as special as the Crazy Miller?"

"Don't call him that!" I yelled at him. "At least he's kept all his promises to me!"

"You just started kissing him last night!" Bryan threw up his hands and matched the volume of my voice. "What promises has he kept? Oh, he probably called you today to make sure you had kicked me to the curb!"

I wanted to contradict him, but I couldn't say a word. Johnny *had* called and asked, "Was I dreaming or are you *my* girl?"

I had told Johnny I was his girl and would tie up any loose ends with Bryan. I didn't have a lot of time to finish my business with Bryan before Johnny picked me up to go riding through town.

"Look, Bryan," I said in what I hoped was a soothing tone. "We have been going in the wrong direction for a long time. You knew we weren't going to last. You even said we were arguing like your parents."

I regretted using his deceased parents as an example, but Bryan didn't criticize me for it. "My parents stayed together and worked through their problems. I would never have compared our relationship to theirs if I had thought we wouldn't last."

"I'm sorry," I said, with honey dripping from my every word. "I need a break from us for a while."

Bryan's eye twitched. He was one step away from getting uncontrollably angry. He had never hit me before, but my arms were still stinging from his hands.

"Go on, then," he said, waving a hand at my face in a shooing gesture.

I blinked. Bryan had seen my fear, and he smiled.

"Go be with the crazy Miller boy," he said mockingly. "Kiss the craziness from his lips. I'm sure it'll rub off."

Much to my horror, a blue truck pulled into my driveway behind Bryan's truck. The vehicles looked almost identical. Johnny's truck was only a few shades lighter than Bryan's old Chevrolet.

"Speaking of Mr. Wonderful," Bryan said as he bounded off my porch. His malice was so strong that it practically left a trail behind him.

Johnny got out of the truck and walked toward Bryan purposely. He was just as beautiful as Bryan; except he was clean. He wore a pair of cowboy boots with light-colored jeans and a white button-up shirt.

"I don't want to hurt you, man," Johnny said.

"It's too late for that," Bryan told him as he connected the inside of his closed fist to Johnny's face.

Johnny was left-handed, and he easily blocked the hit while sweeping his foot across Bryan's legs. Bryan was knocked off his feet, but he caught Johnny's leg and tripped him onto the ground.

"No!" I screamed, and I ran to them. I was almost to the fighting boys when I realized my mistake. *What could I do?* I was maybe a hundred pounds.

I watched as the boys fought. I noticed Bryan aimed his punches at Johnny's face while Johnny delivered blow after blow to Bryan's midsection. Finally, the boys broke free of each other. Johnny jumped to his feet, ready for the next attack. Bryan doubled over and coughed. Pink-tinged saliva ran in a string from his mouth.

Johnny dropped his fists and straightened his posture. A look of concern troubled his face.

He walked over to Bryan. "Are you okay, man?"

I saw Bryan's smile before Johnny finished his sentence. As Johnny approached him, Bryan closed both his hands together and swung them up toward Johnny's face. The hit connected with a smack, and it threw Johnny backwards.

Bryan's victory was short-lived. Johnny rose from the ground as fast as he had fallen. Every muscle seemed to be rigid, pulled taunt with anger.

Johnny bridged the distance in three long, determined strides. There was no running from Johnny's enraged retribution.

"You sucker-punched me!" he said as he grabbed Bryan by his hair.

Bryan's face contorted in pain as a section of his hair parted from his scalp. I could hear the strands of hair being ripped out from over ten feet away.

Bryan swung at Johnny, but he blocked it easily. The muscles in his jaws tensed and relaxed so fast that it looked like he had a twitch.

Johnny brought Bryan's hand around behind his back and forced Bryan to look up into the fading day. Birds circled overhead.

"I want you to apologize to Miranda," he said. "She's my girl now, and you're going to recognize that."

Johnny tightened his grip on Bryan, and Bryan almost lost consciousness, but he didn't cry out.

"Do you hear me?" Johnny shouted into Bryan's upturned face.

"That's really not necessary," I squeaked out, but one look from Johnny froze any other words I might have said.

Bryan managed to speak in a dignified voice, even though I knew he was in a lot of pain. "Miranda, you know I love you."

Bryan still held part of my heart. I tried not to think too much about it.

Johnny loosened his grip on Bryan as he continued to speak to me. By the time Bryan had finished, he had gotten to his feet and looked into my eyes.

"If you need a break from me, I understand," Bryan continued. "I know I couldn't always be there for you, but I wanted to be. It wasn't because I was with some other woman. I was working so that we could have a good life together without owing anyone. I wanted us to build a family."

Bryan spoke so low that I had to go over in my head what he'd said. If I hadn't known him so well, I probably wouldn't have made any sense of his words. "You and your dad are the only family I have left."

Bryan's last words hung in the air. He had spoken the truth, and I didn't have anything to say.

Bryan looked back at Johnny. Johnny was standing behind him, but he showed no sign of preventing his approach.

"When you're done with Mr. Wonderful—" Johnny cleared his throat and a smile played on Bryan's lips "—call me. I'll wait for you."

Bryan walked past Johnny without looking at him. Johnny watched Bryan until he got into his truck and revved the engine to life. Johnny climbed into his own truck and backed it into the road so that Bryan could pull out of my driveway.

I didn't realize that every muscle in my body was tensed until Bryan left. I had been worried that the fight was not over. I didn't know if Bryan was still angry enough to crash his truck into Johnny or to spit at him from the safety of his moving vehicle.

Bryan left with only one more look at me. The soul-crushing stare broke my heart.

The crunch of gravel broke the spell of Bryan's eyes. Johnny walked up my driveway in worse shape than he'd arrived.

His hair was disheveled, and his face was covered in blood and dirt. Bryan had torn his shirt, and it and seemed more brown than white. The knees of his jeans were caked with dirt and grass.

I ran to Johnny, and he held his arms up for me. We embraced, and I kissed him. I could taste the metallic flavor of his warrior blood. He smelled of victory, and it made me swoon. A few kisses later, I took Johnny by the hand and led him into my house.

We went through the living room and into the kitchen. I made him sit in my father's chair at the head of the table while I gathered water, washcloths, peroxide, and bandages.

Johnny's eyes grew wide as I sat my makeshift first aid kit in front of him. "I don't look that bad, do I?" he asked.

I laughed. "I just want to make sure I take care of my knight in shining armor."

Johnny's hand caressed my face. I let his fingers drift lazily down my cheek. "I'm not a knight, but I will always take care of you."

I was so caught up in the moment that I didn't hear the front door open. My father was standing in the kitchen before I realized he was home.

"Miranda?" he said.

I jumped away from Johnny's touch and stood up quickly. I knocked the table, and the bowl of water fell to the floor.

"Hey, Dad," I said lamely and hurried to the kitchen drawer that held the towels. I chose an old dish towel and began cleaning up the mess.

I looked up from my position on the floor and saw Johnny on his feet with his hand extended. "I'm John Miller, sir. Your daughter invited me in. If you would like me to wait outside, I understand."

My father didn't shake Johnny's hand. He looked from Johnny's dirty boots to his tousled hair. "You were sitting in my chair," he remarked.

"I'm sorry, sir," Johnny said, dropping his hand. "It won't happen again."

My father glared at him and chuckled. "It doesn't matter. You could never take my place."

Johnny must have assumed the battle for my father's favor was lost, and he walked toward the door. He turned to mouth that he would wait for me outside. My father had let Johnny walk away, but he wasn't done speaking to him.

"You're Crazy Lyle Miller's boy," he said matter-of-factly.

It wasn't a question, but Johnny treated it like one. He stood to his full height and firmly said my father's title.

My father turned to face the proud boy in his living room. His face gave away nothing as he waited for Johnny to speak.

"I am Lyle Miller's son," Johnny said. "My mother and father grew up in a town full of lies and rumors. Most of what you have heard about my family is probably true, but don't judge me by the things my father has or has not done."

My father considered Johnny's words. I thought he was going to invite him back to the table or at least shake his hand.

In the end, my father only had one thing to say to Johnny's request. "Okay."

Johnny nodded his head and walked out onto the porch. I was left with my father in our silent kitchen.

"Why are you being so mean?" I finally asked.

"He was sitting in my chair," my father said, as if that explained everything.

"Are you crazy?" I asked. My emotions had been on a roller coaster ride for the past half hour, and I didn't feel like entertaining my father's lack of emotion.

"Okay," my father spat. "What do you *want* me to say? Am I supposed to say how great it is to have a boy in my house when I get home with his hands all over my daughter? Should I be happy that he looks like he's crawled through the woods on his way here? Or maybe I should be thankful that he's the reason you ran off a good boy who would have loved you and taken care of you the *right* way."

"Who I date is my decision," I said. I raised my eyebrows to indicate that I felt strongly about the direction in which this conversation was going.

"You can raise your eyebrows to the moon, girl, but it won't change the fact that Bryan is the better choice. He loves you, he respects me, and he would never show up in that *condition*."

"Johnny looks like that *because* of Bryan," I shot back. "He defended himself when Bryan charged him."

"Good for Bryan," my father said. He laughed as he got a cup out of the cabinet. It dinged against the counter of our quiet house.

"Was it *good for Bryan* when he sucker-punched Johnny?" I asked. "I thought it was cowardly."

My father stopped for a moment and quickly resumed his routine. He walked to the refrigerator and took out his favorite soda.

I could tell I'd hit a nerve with my father. He only believed in fair fights.

"Bryan pretended he was hurt, and Johnny went over to help him," I continued. "Bryan sucker-punched him, and Johnny finished the fight."

I thought my story would earn Johnny some respect, but my father showed no sign of giving in. He opened the stove and checked the progress of his dinner. The casserole I made bubbled softly in the light of the oven.

"He sat in my chair," my father said, and I knew that dropping the subject was the best way I could hope to finish the conversation.

"I'll be back by eleven," I said as I walked out the door. I stopped to kiss my dad before I left. He was stubborn, but he was fair most of the time.

I heard my dad mumble something that sounded like, "Just be careful," as I opened the front door. Johnny turned his dazzling smile to me when I opened the door, and any thoughts of being careful with my feelings disappeared.

Chapter Thirteen

I woke from my dream feeling like I was not myself. My mom's emotions and mixed-up teenage thoughts had consumed me.

It was weird that my mom had kissed my father in the dream, or vision, I had experienced, but I didn't feel like it was me. I was my mom, and I was only a passenger in her mind. I was simply reliving her memories without the ability to affect them.

I stretched my legs and wiggled my toes. My body had been asleep in the same position for a long time, but my mind did not feel rested.

I had gotten a lot of answers from my dream, but I had several questions about the validity of my dreams, visions, or whatever I had experienced. *Was I really looking into the past, or were the dreams a product of my subconscious giving me visual possibilities? Where did my visions come from? Did I pick them up from the dead, the living, or were they a divine bequest? Why had I never had visions within my dreams before my trip to the prison?*

I rubbed my eyes and got out of bed. I wondered briefly how I had gotten from the living room couch to my bedroom. I assumed I had climbed the stairs and fallen into my bed during the night.

Ella had already left our room. I don't know who or what woke me, but I was glad to be awake on time. I had to prepare for another socially challenging day at school.

I made my cosmetic preparations and trudged down the steps to the kitchen. My mom had swept last night's conversation from her thoughts. Maybe she placed it somewhere near the area where she stored my father's death and the good times she'd shared with her sons.

"Did you sleep well, dear?" my mom asked.

My mom never asked about our dreams before we ate breakfast. She believed the old wife's tale that dreams would come true if you discussed them before the first meal of the day. My mom didn't know that my dream had already come true because it had been part of her life years ago.

"Yes," I said. "I don't think I even moved once I got to my bed."

My mom continued to stir our oatmeal. She opened the drawer next to the stove and noisily moved around wooden spoons and plastic spatulas before she pulled out a metal ladle.

The steam rose from my bowl as my mother carried my oatmeal to me. She balanced Ella's breakfast in her other hand, and Ella grabbed her bowl quickly.

I tried to think of some light conversation to share with my mom and sister. "How was the Apple Festival?"

Ella stared more deeply into her bowl. She wouldn't answer because something was bothering her. I guess something had been bothering her for the past five years or longer.

"I sent your sister for the presents. I didn't feel like going this year," my mom said.

Ella nodded her head and continued to look captivated by her oatmeal. She moved her spoon around, but she did not raise it to her lips.

My mom usually waited to go to the Apple Festival during the last several hours. My family walked the short distance from our home to the nucleus of the festivities around five o'clock on the last day of the festival.

My siblings and I looked through the booths and played some games while my mom took mental notes of the arts and crafts she fancied. At seven-thirty as the vendors packed up their products, my mom would swoop in and start haggling. She always told the vendors that it was better to sell her the items at half cost than to load them back into their vehicles.

Most of the time, the vendors would agree with my mom's rationale, and my mom would take a small amount of money and make it look like she had spent a large sum on Christmas presents. She distributed her gifts to our unsuspecting distant relatives and friends, who were overjoyed with the lovely and seemingly expensive gifts. I couldn't help but appreciate my mom's thrifty ways.

"So what did Ella pick up?" I asked. The sharp look my mom gave Ella made me drop the subject.

Ten minutes after breakfast, my family piled into my mom's car and began a new week. I faced forward in the passenger seat. I started sitting in the front seat after Ella had stopped holding her hand out to the back of the passenger seat in order to lock fingers with our dead brother's ghost.

"I'm so tired," my mom said. She brought her fingers to her temple and massaged a place that had a lot of tension.

I saw my mom every day, but I suddenly noticed stress lines around her eyes and an older expression on her face. I wanted to make my mom happy again, to truly see her smile, but I doubted I had the power to help her.

A solution flew into my mind. She had experienced true joy in my dream, and she had been happy with my father. My mom needed a partner so she could share her joys and they could help balance her responsibilities. Maybe I could visit a dating website and locate someone who suited my mom. I knew the characteristics she favored in a man, and who knows a mother better than her children?

I smiled to myself. Ella stared at me in the side mirror. I raised my eyebrows. *What?*

"Whatever you are thinking, do not do it," Ella cautioned.

"What's that, El?" my mom asked. Her good humor continued, and I decided I would keep a smile on her face for the rest of the morning.

"Sydney is thinking about matchmaking," Ella betrayed.

"Really?" my mom mused. "I didn't hear her say a word, but I think it's a wonderful idea. We Millers have a sixth sense about love." She winked at me confidentially.

I couldn't hide the horror I felt. *You read minds now, Little Sister?*

Ella didn't respond. She stared out her window at the trees that we saw at least ten times a week and acted as though the passing scenery was varied and original.

Maybe I *should* put pressure on my mom to get Ella's mental health evaluated.

I caught Ella's eyes in the side mirror again. She seemed like she was staring into my soul, and she didn't like what she saw.

I ignored her. I had bigger problems than my sister's gift, or curse. I had to face Lydia Sneed.

The school's activity volume had been muted over the long weekend. Students walked slowly to class without talking.

Apples lined Ms. Hughes's desk. *Did parents still believe that teachers liked apples, or did they think she needed the fiber?*

I wondered briefly what started the tradition of students presenting their teachers with apples. *Was it because teachers were exposed to small, germ-carrying humans on a regular basis?* I knew that eating an apple daily was supposed to eliminate visits to a doctor, but I thought it was because the fiber in the fruit prevented a person's intestines from becoming clogged.

I thought about my trip to the prison and the monster, Garrett Hughes. *Was it possible that he and my teacher had been related?*

I gathered my books and notebooks from my locker and sat down at my desk. Christian turned around and asked nervously, "Have you talked to Lydia?"

"I've been gone all weekend, remember?" I said, narrowing my eyes. "Did you do something to her?"

"Oh, no," Christian said hastily, but he kept bouncing his legs and turning to look at the door every six seconds. The room felt cool, but beads of sweat formed just over Christian's eyebrows.

Oh well, he wanted to be with Lydia. Now he could just suffer through the drama that followed her like a dark cloud.

The pat, pat of Lydia's expensive shoes echoed through the room before she stopped behind me and said, "I need to talk to you."

I followed my pseudo friend to the corner of the classroom. Christian watched us with his eyes, but he didn't turn his head in our direction.

"What's up?" I asked.

Lydia flung her golden tresses over her shoulder and gave me a pout. It may have worked on boys, but I was immune to her sulkiness.

"I was having the most wonderful weekend and then Christian ruined my life by calling me *Sydney*," she said, waving her hands to show the devastation of the situation.

"It was a mistake," I said. My insides bubbled at the thought of Christian thinking of me.

Lydia looked scandalized. "Of course it was a mistake! A very, very big mistake!"

Lydia crossed her arms and looked away from me. "I don't know if I can forgive such an insult."

The bubbles in my stomach popped and raging magma rushed through my veins. It forced its way to my mouth and exploded on Lydia in the form of lava-filled fury.

"An insult?" I shouted, and the class couldn't disguise their interest. "Christian and I are always hanging out together! We talk almost every day! He made an honest mistake because he is used to being around me! Besides, you should have been flattered to be called by my name." Everyone in the room stared at us with unveiled curiosity.

Ms. Hughes walked to where we stood. She seemed unsure about the best way to handle the situation. She considered how much she liked her job and Bannon Sneed's influence on it.

I continued my frenzied outburst. "It would have been an insult for *me* to be called *Lydia*!"

Lydia's face contorted from surprise to outrage. She moved her mouth, but the venomous words she wished to say did not find a way past her lips.

Since Lydia couldn't voice her distaste for my eruption, she slapped me. It was a small slap, and it barely stung, but I had balled up my fist and retaliated before I knew what I was doing.

Lydia crouched instinctively to prevent more damage to her face. She clutched her nose and looked up at me in surprise. A purplish bruise formed at the bridge of her nose between her fingers.

"Ladies!" Ms. Hughes shouted, like she was scolding a dog for peeing on the carpet.

Christian ran to kneel at Lydia's side, but she pushed him away. He backed up a couple of paces and sat on his knees watching his girlfriend.

I was still in shock. I had never hit anyone before, but Lydia had slapped me. I looked down at my hands and noticed that I still had them in fists. I relaxed them and quickly dropped them to my sides.

Suddenly, the room exploded in applause and cheers. Lydia, Christian, Ms. Hughes, and I were shocked, but the rest of the class was jubilant. Donny stood up and turned Lydia's desk over, and some of the other students tore open Lydia's locker and threw books and papers on the floor. It was almost like watching a country overthrow a tyrannical ruler.

Ms. Hughes watched numbly as her students ran about the room. She finally decided on a definite course of action.

"Sit down!" she yelled. Ms. Hughes's voice projected the authority needed to calm the class. Everyone dropped what they were doing and settled into their seats.

Lydia allowed Christian to help her onto her feet. Ms. Hughes commanded, "Not you three. You get to the principal's office immediately. I will send an Intra-Message before you get there."

Intra-Message was a web-based system the teachers used to communicate with other teachers and staff at Pale Woods Academy. The principal would know everything Ms. Hughes had witnessed by the time Lydia, Christian, and I made it to her office.

Ms. Hughes wanted to take us to the office herself, but another teacher was not available to watch her room. She could not afford to leave the chaos and risk more deviant behavior in her absence.

Five minutes later, after an uncomfortable walk down the hall, Principal Georgia Bailey looked at us through glasses that dipped to the edge of her nose. I had tried to help Christian carry Lydia, who I'm sure was overdoing her injuries, but they both pushed me away.

Lydia took the chair nearest to the door, and I sat in the other seat before Christian could be selfish or chivalrous. There were thirty seconds of uncomfortable silence that seemed to stretch on for an eternity.

"Sydney," Principal Bailey began, "I would have expected this kind of behavior from Jerrod." She paused and looked at her hands. "God rest his soul." Principal Bailey's attention returned to me. "I wouldn't have been shocked to see Ella in front of me, heaven knows she looks like silent dynamite, but I never expected *you* to be sent to my office."

Principal Bailey's short red hair drew me to her eyes. She seemed ageless to me until that moment. I noticed the deep lines that rippled down her cheeks and the worry around her lips. She had once told my mother that being around children made her feel young, and I wondered about her age. *Could she be in her late sixties or early seventies?*

"Well, what do you have to say for yourself?" Principal Bailey asked me. She tapped her pen on her desk. She probably didn't even realize she was doing it.

I tried to think of a liberating answer. I didn't want to imagine the look on my mom's face when she realized I had lost my temper over something so foolish.

"Lydia said it was an insult that her boyfriend called her by my name, and she slapped me," I explained, pretending that Lydia was not sitting six inches away from me. "I'd hit her before I knew what I was doing." It wasn't much of a defense, so I knew I would still hang for my actions.

Principal Bailey stopped tapping her pen on her desk. "So it was self-defense?" she asked. "Ms. Hughes said that you were screaming some pretty terrible things at Lydia before you hit her."

Lydia was quiet. She didn't think she would be punished. Her father contributed way too much money to Pale Woods Academy for the principal to expel the daughter of its largest benefactor.

"Will anything I say matter?" I asked abruptly. Everyone's eyes turned to me, and Lydia let out a sigh.

"What you say matters to *me*," Principal Bailey said carefully, "but I have a duty to the school and the other students to uphold the rules."

"In that case," I said, "expel Lydia *and* me. Lydia slapped me first, and I hit her back. We were both wrong to strike out physically, and I am ready to accept the consequences for my actions."

A smirk crawled across Lydia's face. Unfortunately for her, Principal Bailey could see it.

"I think you're right, Sydney," she concurred. Principal Bailey's gaze was steady, and she started clicking her pen on her desk again.

Lydia's face expressed her open-mouthed outrage. Christian braced himself for the backlash.

"I didn hit mythelf," Lydia said, holding her swollen nose. I wanted to laugh at her nasally tone, but I didn't think it would improve my case. "Mummy and Dathy will noth sthand for ith!"

That seemed to solidify Principal Bailey's decision. Her pen clicked faster in agitation.

I hid my smile with my hand and looked casually out the window. The morning was brighter, and my vision seemed clearer.

"I will notify your parents," Mrs. Bailey said. "You may wait for them to pick you up in the reception area."

Lydia jumped up from her chair and placed her hands on Principal Bailey's desk. Christian was at her side in lightning speed in case she reverted to her feeble, pre-tantrum state.

Lydia's face was as red as the apples on Ms. Hughes's desk. "I will noth be thethpended! You need to think about your pothition and rememba who you're thalking tho!"

Principal Bailey's pen was clicking at a rate that could have broken the speed barrier. I continued to sit in my chair and enjoy the show.

"You are suspended for a week, Lydia!" Principal Bailey shouted. "Given the circumstances, I am only expelling Sydney for three days."

I jerked in my chair with surprise. I had done more than accomplish my goal. I only wanted Lydia to get the same punishment as me.

Lydia's nose started to bleed again, and a drop of crimson fluid fell on Principal Bailey's desk. Christian hurriedly grabbed a tissue from a nearby box and held it out to Lydia. Lydia rewarded him by slapping his hand away. The strike echoed off the walls, and the room fell quiet.

Christian gave Lydia a dumbfounded look. The room remained silent as he turned away from her and walked out the door. The door made a stiff click as it closed on Lydia's romance.

Lydia tried to process all the bad things that had happened to her. She still believed that all the problems she was facing could be solved if her father threw around enough money. I wondered if Christian could be bought.

Principal Bailey had Lydia removed from her office, and I followed her as she kicked the school officer who held her. He looked mortified to be touching Bannon Sneed's daughter, but he was even more scared of Principal Bailey.

Lydia started crying and screaming as we waited for our parents. "It's all your fault!"

I didn't say anything in response, and that made Lydia even madder. She got up and paced the room.

The receptionist watched her like she was a loose tiger. The officer stayed in the room and moved into a corner. He didn't want to touch Lydia again.

I suddenly realized that I would be dealing with my mom's wrath soon. She would probably ground me for the rest of my life after she talked to Principal Bailey.

Olivia Sneed entered the school like a high-powered attorney. She carried a briefcase and had on a fashionable black business suit. She walked right past her hysterical daughter, rapped twice on Principal Bailey's door, and entered without an invitation.

Principal Bailey's calm voice turned hostile almost immediately. Olivia Sneed seemed to stay composed, and I could only hear the faint mumbling of her voice.

"What have you done now?"

My mom's voice startled me back into the reception area. Her face was a maze of expressions, and she looked dispirited and tired.

"I hit Lydia in the nose because she slapped me." I didn't feel like going into the details.

My mom was shocked. Her eyes drifted lazily upward as if she was trying to process the information with a weary mind.

Lydia couldn't stand to be left out of our conversation. "She hit me for no reason, Mrs. Miller!" Lydia exclaimed. "She stole my boyfriend, and then she hit me."

My mom's response honestly surprised me. I recorded it in my mind because it was one of the best things to happen to me in my life.

"Lydia," my mom said as she brought her fingers to her temple, "I really don't understand you. You have all the material possessions a child could want, and you entertain yourself by creating misery for others. I don't know who your boyfriend is, but I don't see him here. I can only assume that he has washed his hands of you, like my daughter should have done a long time ago."

Lydia was shocked into speechlessness. My mom took the silence as an opportunity to continue her Lydia roast.

"Don't you see how people react to you?" my mom asked. She pointed to the corner of the room. "The school's police officer is standing in a corner watching your every move, and the secretary hasn't answered the phone for fear of your reaction."

I had not registered the faint buzz of the ringing phone. At my mom's mention of the phone, the receptionist looked at it like she had just noticed it, too.

"I hope you get everything you deserve one day," my mom continued, pointing at Lydia. "If you were *my* daughter, I'd disown you, but it looks like you fit perfectly into your family of wealthy despots. I'm going to reward my daughter for standing up to you and forbid her to speak to you again."

Lydia's rage had boiled over and calmed, but my mom wasn't finished. My mom never moved from the seat beside me, but her words seemed to assault Lydia's ears like they had been yelled.

"Everyone can see your swollen, bloody nose, Lydia. Ask yourself why no one's tried to help you. You won't like the answer," my mom finished.

Lydia opened her mouth a couple of times, but she shut it quickly each time. She couldn't find the right mix of verbal sewage to throw at my mom.

Lydia stormed out of the reception area and out of sight. No one made a move to stop her. I could almost feel the tension in the room leave as Lydia walked out the door.

My mom patted my hand and said, "I'm really not going to reward you. And," she added, "you are not allowed to speak to Lydia again."

I nodded my assent. My mom ran one hand down my long brown hair and got to her feet.

"Now it's time to deal with your suspension," my mom said. She approached Principal Bailey's door as Olivia Sneed opened it.

Olivia Sneed's composed demeanor was slightly ruffled. She was even more upset when she realized her daughter had fled the reception area.

Principal Bailey motioned for my mom and me to enter her office. Olivia Sneed tried to follow us, but Principal Bailey prevented her entry.

"I have to discuss the situation with the Millers," she told Lydia's mother.

Olivia Sneed stretched herself to her full height and put her nose into the air. "I think I have a right to be in the room as you discuss anything pertaining to my daughter."

"You're absolutely right," Principal Sneed said. "But I'm not discussing Lydia. What I have to say is strictly for Sydney and her mother."

Principal Bailey motioned to the chairs next to the receptionist. The receptionist looked at Principal Bailey as if to say, *I really don't get paid enough to deal with this.*

"You may sit and wait for your ill-tempered daughter, or you may leave," Principal Bailey concluded.

I sat down in the same chair I had occupied when Lydia and Christian had been in the room. The drop of Lydia's blood still stood out like a crimson flower on Principal Bailey's desk.

"Your reputation precedes you, Miranda," Principal Bailey began, "so I'm going to have to ask you to leave if you interrupt me."

My mom didn't look happy with Principal Bailey's reference to her temperament, but she remained silent. She crossed her legs and directed her exhausted eyes to Principal Bailey.

"Lydia Sneed's parents donate a lot of money to this school," Mrs. Bailey sighed. "That is why it is so hard to discipline Lydia without interfering with Pale Woods Academy's balance sheet."

Principal Bailey drummed her fingers on her desk. She looked away from my mom and me and out into the sunny day.

"I need their money," Mrs. Bailey said. "I won't lie to you. If the Sneeds did not donate their money to Pale Woods, then Sydney and Ella probably couldn't go to school here."

My mom nodded her head. I already knew where this conversation was going, and it didn't make me happy.

"Olivia Sneed came here to remind me of my obligation to her family. I am so tired from arguing with her I can hardly think straight." Mrs. Bailey reached a shaky hand to her forehead. "I had to suspend Lydia's punishment."

I could feel my mom's skin emanating heat. It was like being next to a bathroom where someone had just taken a long, hot shower.

Principal Bailey spoke before my mom could erupt. "But I told Olivia that I couldn't erase this event from Lydia's file without also vanquishing it from Sydney's record."

My mouth dropped open. My mom's anger was instantly cooled.

"Tell me in detail what that means for Sydney," my mom said. She leaned forward in her seat as if she were trying to have a confidential moment with my principal.

Mrs. Bailey stretched in her chair. She was just over five feet and weighed maybe a hundred pounds, but her chair squeaked from years of use.

Principal Bailey paused and hit me with a stern stare. "You should have hit her in her spoiled mouth."

My mom appreciated Principal Bailey's candor, but I still wanted to regard my principal as unbiased. Most children would have beamed with pride to be getting a big thumb's up from their principal after doing something wrong, but I still believed hitting Lydia was immoral.

My mom leaned back in her chair and draped her hands off the armrests. She gave me a self-satisfied smile I hoped I did not return.

Principal Bailey folded her hands in her lap and fixed her eyes on my mom. "I have erased the incident from the records of both girls." Principal Bailey shifted her attention to me and continued. "But I will remember what happened today, and if anything like this happens again, I will suspend you for the rest of the year."

I could feel myself sweating under Principal Bailey's watch. She seemed to have eyes that could pierce your mind and call out your thoughts.

My mom nudged me. I lazily turned my head toward her. She was smiling and nodding, but I was still upset.

"Don't you have something you want to tell your principal?" my mom prompted.

"I won't be any more trouble to you, Principal Bailey." I said. Tears flowed down my face. "I'm not proud of what I did. I know Lydia is spoiled, but there's something good in her. Something her parents don't have."

Principal Bailey nodded. "I wouldn't have fought to keep the incident from your permanent record if I had thought you *enjoyed* hitting your friend."

I couldn't stop crying, and Principal Bailey's compliment brought on a fresh wave of tears. My mom tried to grab my hand, but I jerked it away from her grasp.

"You are a lot like Josh," Principal Bailey said. Her voice had changed from its usual business manner to a soothing tone. "He was a peaceful boy, but I think he would have reacted in the same way."

That was funny. I thought my spontaneous outburst was more like something Jerrod would have done.

"You have taken more abuse from Lydia than most people," Mrs. Bailey explained. "By staying close to her, you have suffered for your kindness. I disagree with you on one point, though. Lydia is a Sneed, and she will be self-promoting just like her parents. I hope she changes for her own sake, but her upbringing has already left its mark on her."

I rose out of my seat and pulled a tissue from the box. It felt light and airy, and I wondered if it was strong enough to hold my sadness.

"Take all the time you need, Sydney," Mrs. Bailey said. "Your mom can sit with you for a while in the nurse's station, or you can speak to Mrs. Thomas."

Mrs. Thomas was Pale Woods Academy's guidance counselor. I thought very highly of her, and I didn't want her to be disappointed in me after she learned the reason for my visit.

Mrs. Thomas had always been cheerful when I entered her office. She didn't have much more than regular school drama to deal with, so she maintained a positive attitude. The hardest part of her job was helping children with small grievances and mediating fights. I had already been in her office for grief counseling, and I didn't want to be another problem for her.

I shook my head. "Can I just go to class after I wash my face?"

My mom was stung, and she pulled her arms close to her sides. It hurt her when I didn't want to talk to her.

"I think that will be fine," Principal Bailey said. "I will send an Intra-Message to Ms. Hughes. I think Lydia's going home for the rest of the day."

I tried to treat my mom's wounded ego. "I love you, Mom," I said, putting my hand on the arm of her chair. "Thank you for being so supportive." I hugged my mom, and she received me warmly, but she continued to sit in her seat.

"I know you're busy," I told my mom, "but it means a lot to me that you were here."

My mom's smile returned, and I knew I had bandaged her pride. My mom felt as though Principal Bailey saw her as a caring, concerned parent, and that is what she wanted. It didn't matter what we really did or how my family felt, as long as everyone saw us as a finely tuned unit.

"You know I love you, Syd," my mom said. I hated the nickname, but I never told her.

I left my mom in Mrs. Bailey's office. They would probably talk about my behavior and relate it to my brothers' deaths, but I hadn't hit Lydia because I missed Josh and Jerrod. I had hit Lydia because she had pushed my patience over the edge.

A casual observer would think my punishment was over, but I knew it was only beginning. Lydia would make sure of it.

Chapter Fourteen

I washed my face in the bathroom and glanced in the mirror. I didn't carry any makeup with me except lip gloss, and it was in the classroom. I ran my fingers through my hair and hoped I looked presentable.

I went into a stall and discovered I had started my cycle. I had been spotting off and on for the last six months, so I wasn't surprised.

The academy had an emergency shelf in every stall. I don't know what they kept in the boy's bathroom, but the girl's bathroom was stocked with bandages, disinfectant spray, antibacterial sanitizer, and pads. I had been wearing a pantyliner, so I took one of the school-provided pads from the emergency shelf.

I took my time walking back to class. As an eighth grader, it would be the last year that I could freely roam the downstairs of the academy. Once I was in ninth grade, I could no longer cruise the downstairs hallways without special permission.

I took in the sweaty no-smell that smaller children seem to leave in the places that they populate. I enjoyed the halls that were decorated with masterpieces from small hands.

Voices bombarded me as I approached the door to my classroom. I had to slide down the wall to the floor to keep from falling.

I should have known she was going to use me, one voice said. *When has Lydia cared about anyone but herself?*

This stupid lecture is boring, another voice spoke. *Why do we need to know about the presidents anyway?*

A third voice sighed, *This is going in one ear and out the other. Why do they need to learn about the presidents?*

The thoughts came at me in a whirlwind of speech and emotions. There were other thoughts, too, but they were jumbled and hazy, reflecting various states of consciousness.

I was hearing the people in my classroom. Their words came to me in their natural voices, so I knew I had clearly heard Christian, Donny, and Ms. Hughes's inner feelings.

I placed a conscious block in my mind. I imagined I was building a solid brick wall, and I stacked brick after brick to form an impenetrable barrier. I stopped hearing voices in my head almost immediately.

I hadn't had to block out the thoughts of others since I was five. *Why were people's thoughts charging me now?*

I told myself that it had to be the stress of the day. Maybe I had built a dense wall in my childhood that had stayed intact for almost a decade, and the morning's events had blasted the barrier to pieces.

I was glad I could no longer hear thoughts when I strolled into my classroom. Every eye was on me.

Ms. Hughes nodded toward my seat. She had read Principal Bailey's Intra-Message. I walked to my desk as quickly as my feet would silently tread.

A couple of boys in the back of the room cheered, but Ms. Hughes ended their celebration with a cold stare.

I bent my head over my desk and tried to make myself as small as possible. I heard a few whispers, and I solidified the wall in my mind to keep from hearing my classmate's opinions.

I caught Christian looking at me. I peeked at him, and he gave me a wink. My heart leaped, even though I knew he wasn't suggesting anything romantic. He just wanted me to know that he was on my side.

By the last class of the day, everyone had exhausted spreading the rumor about my disagreement with Lydia. The story had morphed and turned into something that was almost laughable.

On the bus ride home, I listened to what Ella had heard about my little skirmish. She laughed as she told the current rumor, and she put extra emphasis on the parts that were obviously embellished.

"Everyone said that Christian called Lydia by your name," my sister began.

I nodded. That part of the story was true.

"Then they said that Lydia pulled a knife and said that she was going to cut out his cheating tongue."

I laughed at the idea that Lydia would express herself that creatively.

Ella's eyes were full of the story she wanted to share with me. I concentrated on watching her happiness for a few moments. I seldom saw my sister so full of life and wrapped up in the drama of the living.

"They said that you grabbed the knife out of her hand and carved your name on her face," Ella continued.

I looked at Ella skeptically. "I would be going to juvie! How could everyone believe that?"

"I do not know," Ella admitted, "but I really liked the part where Christian gathered you into his arms and carried you out."

"If Christian carried me out of the school, then how did everyone see me all day?"

Ella shook her head in between chuckles. "You two seemed to have a fairy tale romance, almost like that movie Mom used to watch."

I let my sister talk about variations that she'd heard about my deviant behavior for the next ten minutes. By the time I stepped off the bus, I was glad about one thing: I had made my sister popular for a day. Most of the time, Ella sat in the shadows, a pretty, emotionally imbalanced wallflower in our educational backdrop, but today she had been a wellspring of information.

My mom stood at the front door as my sister and I bounced up the steps. She hugged both of us and led us into the kitchen for a snack. My mom hadn't been home long, so Ella and I shared a small, store-bought chocolate cake.

My mom didn't talk about her visit to my school. She swept it under the rug. I wondered if there would ever be a time for an emotional spring cleaning.

The ringing phone interrupted our silence. My mom held up a finger, like she would be back in a minute, and answered the cell phone.

She whispered into the receiver so quietly that I couldn't hear the meat of the conversation. I had finally given up on learning the identity of the caller when my mom shouted, "Okay, Dad, we'll see you in an hour."

I rolled my eyes. My grandpa had learned about the Lydia incident and had called for the full story.

I was finishing my homework when a Unicoi County police cruiser pulled into the driveway. I closed my math book with a slap and opened the front door.

"Let's go for a ride," my grandpa said. I grabbed my coat, shut the door, and slid into the cruiser with my head down and my hands in my pockets.

My mom probably told my grandpa not to talk to me about the incident with Princess Sneed, but he brought it up as soon as my house was out of sight. I asked him about his day, and he ignored me.

"What did you think you were doing?" he scolded.

I knew exactly what he meant. I decided to be straightforward.

"I hit Lydia in the nose because I was deeply insulted," I said proudly. I should have answered more humbly.

"Oh, I'm sorry," my grandpa said with sarcasm dripping off every word. "I didn't know you were *deeply insulted*. Maybe I should go hit that teenager who spilled a drink on me at lunch because I was *deeply insulted*." His hands tightened on the steering wheel when he wasn't using them to put extra emphasis on his words. "And this is going to be a big relief to Ella, because now she can just hit the kids who throw things at her and call her names!" My grandpa stopped for a breath. "Did you think of the ramifications?" He glanced over at me briefly before turning his attention back to the road.

"I just did it," I admitted. "I didn't think. I hit her before I knew I'd done it." I tried to look remorseful.

"Bannon Sneed has been to my department. He tried to file *assault* charges," my grandpa emphasized.

I had thought adults were the only ones who could have charges filed on them. I couldn't think of a way to respond to the new information.

My grandpa seemed satisfied with my reaction. He continued to keep me in one eye and navigate the road with the other eye.

"He threatened my job," my grandpa continued, "which he could never take away, your mother's job, and Ella's position in the school."

"What position?" I didn't know that Ella held a certain status.

"Bannon seems to think that he can get Ella kicked out of Pale Woods," he said. "He thinks that if her mental condition is evaluated, then she will lose her scholarship." My grandfather stole another full glance at me. "I guess you know what would happen to you. You're riding your sister's coattails."

It was true. My brothers and I were invited to join Pale Woods Academy after Ella was accepted. If she were removed from the academy, I would no longer get a scholarship, and my widowed mother couldn't afford the school's steep tuition.

"How much longer do you think we have? Will they let us finish the year?" I asked.

Bannon Sneed could easily have had Ella removed from the halls of the only school she'd known. I didn't want Ella uprooted in the middle of the school year and thrown into a public junior high. *She thought she was teased now!*

"I talked him out of it," my grandpa said. A trace of pride touched his features.

"How?" I asked.

"I reminded him how important it was to have a chief of police in his corner."

I understood. My grandpa had responded with blackmail. He knew some of Bannon Sneed's secrets, and I was suddenly grateful for my grandpa's illegal discretion.

"Bannon agreed he would not file charges on you, and he would leave our family alone," my grandpa relayed. "But I never want you to speak to Lydia again."

I hadn't seen Lydia since her outburst in the school's reception area. I had already decided that I would show polite indifference to her presence when she came back.

"After Lydia's nose heals, she'll be back at school," my grandpa said.

That made sense. Lydia wouldn't want to be seen in any other light than that of a professional model, and her bruised nose would not complement this season's fashions.

"Just stay away from her," my grandpa said with concern. "Lydia Sneed has never been good for you." I nodded my agreement as my grandpa pulled into a local restaurant.

"Now let's celebrate," my grandpa announced. He had almost gotten out of the cruiser when I stopped him.

"What are we celebrating?" I asked.

My grandpa smiled at me like the answer was clear. When I didn't respond, he rolled his eyes and said, "You clocked Lydia Sneed. Bring your right hook and let's get a burger."

Chapter Fifteen

Nothing exciting happened at Pale Woods Academy or at my house until right before the Christmas holidays. I went to school, worked on my homework, and spent the weekends with my grandpa.

Lydia did not return to school in the length of time it would have taken her nose to heal. I heard she had a surgery called rhinoplasty, and she was homeschooled until her features were more aesthetically pleasing. I checked the recovery time for her type of surgery, and Lydia should have been back at school within two weeks. She was absent for the rest of the month of October and the full month of November.

Lydia's absence made the academy much more bearable. I entered the school every morning with a smile and I hopped the steps onto my afternoon bus in a similar disposition.

Christian talked to me frequently, but we never spoke about Lydia. He seemed a little sad, but Donny could always make him smile. My heart still caught in my chest every time Christian said my name, but I never acted as if I cared for him as anything more than a friend.

My mom, Ella, and I had our squabbles, but we kept the guise of a happy family. Ella came out of her room a little more, but it was only to play Jerrod's old video games. Sometimes I couldn't tell if she was planning her next strategy or if she had fallen asleep with her eyes open and the controller in her hand.

My grandpa and I hunted deer when the season opened, and I learned how to field dress. I killed my first buck right before Thanksgiving, and my grandpa had its head stuffed and mounted. It hung on my grandpa's wall. My mom had a soft spot for animals, even though we didn't have a pet, and she wouldn't let it in our house.

I started an internet search for a love interest for my mom. Without her knowledge or permission, I typed her likes and dislikes into matchmaking websites. I received a couple of responses, but none of them seemed promising.

I was perfectly content with my life, and I enjoyed every day as it dawned. Unfortunately, we never know the good times in our life as we are experiencing them, and we are never prepared for the hard times when they show up on our doorstep.

The days turned to weeks, and before I knew it, Christmas break was approaching. I no longer liked Christmas. There were too many bad memories surrounding the holiday, but I was glad for the break in my studies.

No one was more surprised than I when Lydia walked into the classroom two weeks before Christmas break. Christian did a double take, and I almost fell out of my seat when I noticed the beautiful blond who had entered the room.

The girl looked like Lydia, but there was something noticeably different about her. It wasn't anything physical, but the change brushed Lydia's features like the sun.

Lydia's nose job had healed nicely. She looked the same as she had before I had hit her.

Christian stared at me, and I read his expression: *What happened to her?*

I shrugged my shoulders and waited for the verbal abuse I was sure to receive from Princess Sneed. A sick feeling was slowly creeping into my stomach. I wouldn't have eaten breakfast had I known that Lydia had planned to come to school.

The classroom fell into silence, but Lydia continued her morning routine as if it were just another day at the academy. She turned around and held her head a little higher. I tried to face forward, and pretend that I wasn't interested in her, but her padded footsteps stopped at my chair.

"I don't know if you want to talk to me," Lydia said, her tone leaving a sugary-sweet smell in the air, "but I could really use your warm, friendly advice."

I held my breath. I couldn't respond verbally or move my head to show that I had heard her.

Lydia shuffled to her seat. She passed by Christian and patted his shoulder.

"No hard feelings, I hope?" she asked him. Christian shook his head with his mouth open.

Lydia sat in usual seat, and every eye in the room rested on her. Ms. Hughes had moved some students to different seats, and Donny's seat was the one Lydia now occupied. I worried Donny would make a joke when he came back into the room or force Lydia out of her seat, but he walked in and sat at an unoccupied desk in the back of the room.

Donny threw paper balls at Christian to get his attention. When Christian finally grew irritated enough to turn around, Donny threw up his hands and mouthed, *"What is Lydia doing here?"*

Christian glared at his friend and put his index finger to his lips. Donny shrugged and leaned back in his chair.

Our teacher started class, and Lydia didn't interrupt her a single time. Ms. Hughes taught a history lesson, and she discussed the mummification process. She asked Lydia about her family's travels to Africa, and Lydia responded sweetly and concisely. She didn't interject any of her personal opinions.

By lunchtime, I was sure that aliens had abducted the real Lydia and sent back a clone to take her place. I was glad of the change, but I wondered if Lydia had an ulterior motive.

I was prepared to eat at another table or sit behind the garbage cans until lunch was over, but Lydia motioned me over to sit with her at our old lunch table. I hesitated. I would get into a lot of trouble if my family knew that I was talking to Lydia.

I sat down anyway. *Why was I so trusting?*

"I'm very sorry," Lydia said. I expected her to follow the statement with an admission that she had tricked me, but Lydia held my gaze.

"No worries," I said flatly.

"I know I was just terrible to you." She looked over to the football players' table. Christian quickly averted his eyes, but it was obvious he'd been staring. "And I was horrid to Christian," Lydia finished.

I didn't know what else to say, so I ate with my former friend in silence. I struggled to find a topic that would keep our conversation light.

"What did you want to talk to me about?" I finally asked.

Lydia jumped like she'd been spooked, but a spark flicked on in her eyes. She reached into her purse and pulled out a silver locket on a broken, barely visible chain.

"I found this in Mummy's jewelry box while I was—" Lydia paused and considered something, "while I was looking for something."

The locket was old, but it had been polished. I tried to open it without success.

"That's the problem," Lydia said, taking the locket from me. "I can't get it to open. I know that it's special to Mummy because she placed it with the family heirlooms, but I don't know what's inside."

"Why don't you just ask her?" I offered.

"I want to get it fixed for Christmas," Lydia said. Excitement danced in her eyes. "I think it would make Mummy smile."

The only thing that makes Mummy smile is the liquor cabinet, I thought. I said, "I think it's a great idea, but why did you need my advice?"

"I want to find a good shop that will fix it. I need someone to take the locket there and pick it up."

Oh, I got it. Lydia needed me to be her minion. There was no way I was falling for her games again.

"That sounds easy," I said, "but I don't think I'll have time to do it. You should send Beth."

Lydia didn't get angry or issue threats. She burst into tears.

My feelings of sympathy took over instantly. I put my arm around Lydia and held her as sobs shook her body.

Christian walked over to our table and asked, "Do you need any help with her?"

"No," I said quickly and returned to comforting Lydia.

"I know I don't deserve it," Lydia sobbed, "but I really wanted you to forgive me. I thought if you knew I was sincere, then we could be friends again."

"I don't think I can ever be friends like we were," I said.

"Oh no," Lydia said, shaking her head rapidly. "I don't want us to be the way we were. I was just *awful* to you! I know now that I was jealous of you, and I want to have the chance to be your *real* friend."

I might have been the biggest sucker in the world, but I believed Lydia's every word. My heart softened, and I took the necklace out of Lydia's hand.

"I think I know a place that can repair it," I said.

Lydia's tears streamed down her face. I wondered if I had caused her more pain by offering to help her.

"That's what I mean," Lydia said. "You were a *real* friend, and I took advantage of you."

I couldn't argue with Lydia's words. I agreed with her.

I had a vague memory of a trade shop in downtown Erwin that repaired and appraised jewelry. I had gone there with my father and brothers when I was a toddler. Josh had broken one of my mom's earrings, and he asked my father to help him get it fixed without telling our mom. Josh was a good child who rarely got into trouble, so my father had quickly agreed.

As our dad sent our mom away on an erroneous errand, our father piled us into our pink van. Our family referred to it as the "Ta-Ta Van" but our neighbors described it as an eyesore.

Josh held our mom's earring like it was a sacred religious artifact. He kept saying that he was scared he'd drop it because he would lose it forever in the van.

Jerrod told Josh, "Why don't you let me hold it, then?" with a sly smile on his face.

Josh turned a shade lighter than his usual pale and shook his head. Josh gripped the earring so tightly that five minutes later his knuckles were as white as powdered sugar.

The ride to the shop went by quickly. The downtown area was only a couple of blocks away from our house, so Josh didn't have long to fear.

Josh read the name of the shop from the sign as we parked: *Indian Giver*. A couple of years later, I asked Jerrod why the owner had chosen that name for his business.

He thought about it for a moment, because he had always accepted the name without questioning it, and replied, "I think the name had to do with the owner's heavy Native American Cherokee ancestry and some sort of ironic word play."

My father carried me into the building and held me in his arms while the owner shook hands with everyone. He seemed like a sweet man with an easy smile and he talked to my father as if he had known him for a long time.

Josh explained the importance of our mom's earring and the way he had injured it. Josh had been vacuuming our parent's bedroom when he had heard a sharp metal sound, like when an old toaster belches up its contents. Josh had dug through the dirt and fuzz of the dust collector until he discovered an earring he recognized as our mom's. All of our mom's jewelry was special, but our father had given our mom that earring in a set for their recent wedding anniversary.

My young eyes closed as the shop owner and my brother discussed the repair and cost. I woke up in my toddler bed after my nap, and I didn't think about the shop again except fleetingly when I saw my mom wearing the earrings a week later.

Lydia took the locket from me and put it into a small plastic bag. She snapped the top of the bag together to keep the chain from slipping out.

Her face brightened, and she extended her hand to drop the bag into my hand. I reluctantly opened my hand, and Lydia dropped her mother's necklace into it. The locket and chain were light, but I felt an instant heaviness as she placed it in my care.

I rode the bus to my house after school and immediately walked to the shop. Ella had given me a larger plastic bag in which to carry the necklace. I wanted to get the locket out of my possession as soon as possible.

My mom wasn't home from work yet, so I set out for the shop as soon as I got to my house. "Tell Mom I went for a walk," I told Ella.

The distance was short, but I still had plenty of time to worry about getting caught with a Sneed heirloom. I wondered if Lydia was setting me up. *Could she have given me the locket so that I would get caught with it?* The Sneeds would have a case for theft, and I didn't think my grandpa would believe the truth. He would probably be the first person to suggest a tough love boot camp.

I turned onto a street leading out of town, and I spotted the shop. I remembered it because the slogan beneath the shop's name read: *We can fix anything but a broken heart.*

The locket was a broken heart, but I understood the metaphorical meaning. Besides, if this shop could fix a broken heart, I would be dragging my mom behind me.

I took the necklace out of my pocket. The polished silver still shone in the sunlight through the plastic bag.

The warm scent of forgotten treasures filled my nose. Faint echoes of flowers and incense were robbed of their glory in the room of aged valuables.

The bells on the door jingled as it closed behind me. I had been too consumed with my evaluation of the shop to hear them cry my entrance.

A cough as rusty as the items in the store jolted me. I looked to my left and barely made out the man behind the wooden counter.

I'd thought the owner of the shop would be at the back of the store. I imagined I'd walk up to him while he wore a super magnifying glass strapped onto his head and explain my situation.

The man had stepped out of another part of the store. Only a little light had crept in from the outdoors when I had entered the store, but the area beyond the partition that separated the store from the man's private apartment revealed windows with sunlight warming and reflecting off every surface. I wondered if the man's eyes took as long as mine to adjust to the lack of light in his store.

The owner of the shop was as ancient as the objects he sold. Lines created ripples down his face like the reverberations from a stone thrown into a river. His eyes were a piercing pale blue, and he wore a red and blue flannel shirt that had probably started to fade when Richard Nixon ran for president. He seemed proud of his appearance, though. His shirt was clean, and it had been ironed. He stood with a posture that probably cost him a great deal of pain and several evening pain relievers.

He was not the same person who had dealt with my father and brothers. The man who was in the shop that day would have been far younger. I wondered if the store had changed ownership and quickly dismissed the idea. It had probably been the man's son.

"Good evening," he said with a smile. The smile exposed several well-cared for teeth. "I'm Kerry Shelton."

I realized that this man was possibly related to Bryan Shelton, but there were a lot of common names in Erwin. Surnames like Harris, Tipton, Williams, and Shelton accounted for about a third of the town's residents.

I strengthened my guard a little but managed a carefree smile. I took the hand that he offered me, and I shook it the way my grandpa had taught me. I gripped his hand firmly, shook it twice, looked him in the eyes, and said my name.

Mr. Shelton raised his eyebrows, but he didn't comment on my family's past. I respected him for his silence.

I held out the plastic pouch that contained Olivia Sneed's locket. "Could you get this open, Mr. Shelton?"

"My father was Mr. Shelton," he said, "and I'm going to call you Sydney, so I insist you call me Kerry."

I nodded my agreement and waited while he looked at the locket. The chain looked smaller in his old, dry hands as it slid on his fingers. He handled the necklace with care, like he was a doctor examining a sick infant.

The clasp of the heart-shaped locket did not yield its contents to the expert jeweler. Kerry laid it down on the counter and straightened the chain.

"Where did you get it?" he asked.

I couldn't lie to him, but I didn't want to give away Lydia's secrets. "A friend gave it to me to get it fixed for her mother. It's a surprise for Christmas."

He stared into me, trying to peel away any lie in my explanation. After a moment, he seemed satisfied that I was telling him the truth, and his probing eyes left my conscience.

"Let's see if I can get it open, and then we'll discuss a price," he said. He seemed lost in thought for a moment, but a shake of his head dislodged it from his mind. "I just thought I'd seen this locket before."

You probably have, I thought. Kerry would kick me out of his store if he knew he was holding a locket once worn by Olivia Sneed.

"Will Miranda let you come back in a couple of days?" he asked. He had used my mom's name to show that he knew my family and to keep me from trying to cheat him.

"My mom doesn't know that I'm here, but I don't think she'd be against it," I said. I was glad I had told the truth when I saw the grin that spread across Kerry's face. He looked ten years younger when he smiled, even with his sporadic teeth.

"Great!" he said. "I'll see you toward the end of the week."

I had a fleeting thought. "Kerry?"

He had been studying the clasp of the locket intensely, but he gave me his full attention. "Is there something else?"

I had been full of purpose before he turned his eyes on me, but his gaze made me feel shy. I swam through my doubts and asked, "Did you know Bryan Shelton?"

A very strange expression pasted itself to Kerry's face. "If I didn't know your history, I'd swear someone had sent you."

Kerry kept his eyes on me, and I knew I had crossed the line from friendly business to unwelcome visitor. I wished I had just walked out of the door into the cold sunshine.

"I don't understand why everyone talks about him like he's dead," Kerry said. "Bryan's in a state prison serving time for murders he never committed."

I tried to make my face unreadable. I was convinced Kerry's eyes could run through the walls of my mind and gather the information he wanted.

"I'm sure that police chief has filled your head full of the garbage he thinks he knows, but my nephew didn't kill the girls he loved," Kerry continued. "He was a little ill-tempered—he was raised around that—but he loved Nellie and Lily."

"Maybe it was an accident," I offered.

Dark clouds gathered around our conversation, and I was sorry that I'd spoken. The temperature in the room dropped a couple of degrees.

"Bryan was no killer. It was Nellie's woman friend that started his temper." Spit flew from Kerry's mouth as he spoke. The kind businessman from moments ago had been replaced by a rabid badger, ready to attack to prove the innocence of his family.

I thought briefly about the locket that he held. *Would he still have agreed to fix it if he had known Olivia Sneed was the owner?*

"I think it's time for you to leave," Kerry said. His words were steady and coarse.

I tried my best to say something polite and leave, but I could not remember gentle parting words. The bells stormed against the door, and their clanging banged in my ears as I raced from the store.

Chapter Sixteen

I flew out of the store and was two blocks away before I realized I was running. My legs wouldn't stop shaking, and my head buzzed.

The cold air stung my lungs, but I was too upset to breathe deeply through my nose. I tried to pace myself, but I couldn't get my heart or mind to slow down.

My feelings raced around the idea that Bryan Shelton was innocent, but I dismissed those thoughts almost immediately. I had seen him kill his daughter in my dream. It was an accident, but it was an accident caused by his violence.

Nellie had been alive throughout my dream. *How had she died?* There had been people running to help her before my vision ended. *Had they witnessed Bryan kill Nellie?* If there had been witnesses to the murder, then Bryan was rightly convicted.

I started to question myself. *How much did I really believe in my visions?* Just because I was gifted didn't mean that everything I dreamed was true. But somehow, I knew in my gut, where my grandpa told me was a person's best instincts, that the dream about Lily's death and my mom's break-up with Bryan had been visions of the past.

I went home and walked past Ella playing video games on the couch. Impatience burned like a bonfire in the pit of my stomach.

I didn't bother taking off my shoes or coat before I entered the kitchen. My mom was stirring a pot of spaghetti that would probably serve as our lunch and dinner for the next two days.

She turned and smiled at me. Her smile quickly faded when her eyes met mine. I was about to ruin another good mood.

"Did something happen during your walk?" she asked. There was still time for me to salvage my mom's positive disposition, but I was too upset to worry about her feelings.

"How did Bryan kill Nellie?" The words spilled from my mouth.

She stopped stirring noodles and appraised me. She turned off the stove and stomped upstairs, mumbling something about "meddling in her life" and "things best forgotten" as she went.

Why had I been so insensitive? For the past couple of months, I had been looking for my mom's perfect match, and today I was shouting at her about a past in which she hadn't elected to play a part.

I resigned myself to standing outside my mom's bathroom door and begging for her forgiveness. I would forget about Bryan Shelton and let him rot in prison. I needed to concentrate on *my* family and rebuilding our lives.

I shed my coat and kicked off my shoes. I was climbing the first of the steps to my absolution when Ella grabbed my arm. She put her index finger to her lips and quietly led me to our brothers' room.

I felt like I was desecrating a tomb by entering Jerrod and Josh's room. Our mom had left everything the same, except she had placed their last school pictures in opposing picture frames and littered the area around them with artificial black flower petals.

I missed my brothers so much that even the smell of Jerrod's old socks filled my eyes with tears. Ella crossed the room as if she entered it all the time. Not a hint of nostalgia showed in her stride.

Josh had been the last person to use my parent's prehistoric computer, and my mom had not moved it. Ella turned on the monitor, and she located a newspaper article. She stood next to the chair I had last seen occupied by my favorite sibling.

Ella motioned me over and whispered, "It is okay. They are not here." She glanced at the pictures of Josh and Jerrod. "And they would not care anyway."

I hurried over to the computer and sat down in what I still thought of as Josh's chair. Ella tapped the ancient screen, and I read the article she had found.

Erwin Man Sentenced to Life in Prison

By Wendy Williams

Bryan Shelton, accused of killing his wife and child, was sentenced to life in prison without the possibility of parole on Monday. Judge Charlie Freeman delivered the sentence after jurors spent only twenty-two minutes deliberating the facts of the case.

Shelton is being held in the Unicoi County Jail without bond. He will be transferred to a state prison in North Carolina to serve his sentence.

Shelton was taken into custody on April 27, following the drowning deaths of his wife and child. Witnesses were called to the stand to describe the details of the murders...

I lost my place when Ella scrolled down the internet version of a newspaper article. I looked up to voice my disapproval, but my sister nodded her head toward the screen. I followed her gaze and continued to read.

Shelton was arrested shortly after a neighbor found Nellie Shelton and her minor daughter floating lifelessly in the water. The EMS arrived on the scene and pronounced Nellie Shelton dead on arrival. The child's body was not located at the time of his arrest but was discovered by a fisherman in Greene County two weeks later.

The child's body had been attacked by local wildlife but was later identified by doctor and dental records. An autopsy revealed that the toddler had experienced massive head trauma leading to her death.

I couldn't read any more of the sad circumstances surrounding the events that led to Bryan Shelton's imprisonment. I could no longer think about the horrible man that I had believed was innocent.

Ella quietly arranged the computer's shut down sequence while I sat in the chair. I thought we had it bad with our father and his mental illness, but we may have all have been killed, or not have existed, if Bryan Shelton had been our mom's husband.

Ella stopped moving around me. She stared at the closet and tip-toed over to its opening. My sister's every step landed on an article of clothing or an important, discarded item that had belonged to our brothers.

The closet was small with a wooden door, just like the door that opened all the rooms inside the house. The door had been left slightly ajar, and from my position, I could see the arm of an old brown coat, the edge of the sleeve peeking out of the doorway, and a couple of board games on the floor of the closet.

"Ella," I whispered. My sister looked back at me, but it was only to wave her hand for me to be quiet.

"I thought I saw something," Ella said, and chills prickled my skin. When someone who can see the dead says they see something, then you pay attention.

"I thought you said Josh and Jerrod were at peace," I said in a whisper voice.

"They are," she confirmed. "I do not see it now. I must be imagining things."

I doubted her words. My sister often covered up her abilities to make me feel better. Sometimes, she exercised her gift excessively, though, to make me feel guilty for not publicly admitting my endowment.

I slowly rose out of the chair and carefully scripted each step out the door of my brother's room. I hoped my mom was still in her room so that she wouldn't witness my escape into the hallway.

Ella and I crept out of the room without incident. Ella went to our bedroom, but I continued to move forward with my plan for my mom's forgiveness.

I cautiously approached the door to my mom's bathroom. My mom opened the door as I raised my fist to knock, so it looked for a moment as if I had positioned myself to attack her. My mom recoiled before she realized I had planned to use my fist to announce my presence.

"I'm sorry, Mom," I said, before the situation became worse. "I wasn't thinking about the way you must feel about the situation."

My mom's eyes narrowed. "What do you mean?" she asked.

I tried to think back to the things my mom *had* told me about Bryan. I was only supposed to know that she had once dated him, my father knew about him, and that my grandpa rubbed Bryan's good fortune in my father's face.

"Well," I began carefully, "since you have children, it must be hard for you to hear about Nellie and Lily's unfortunate demises."

My mom visibly relaxed. I congratulated myself on my quick thinking.

"I guess I'm still rather sensitive about Bryan," my mom said. "I'd like to tell you I thought of him as a brother, but I didn't."

My mom gave me a confidential smile and led me over to her bed. We sat down together, and she took my hand.

"I probably shouldn't have avoided your questions about Bryan," my mom said. A smile had crept over her features.

"I shouldn't have pressed you for information about him," I said. I wanted to keep my mom in a good mood. I could find another way to get the answers to my questions.

"No, Sydney, I told myself when I was young that I would always be open and honest with my children," my mom said, and I congratulated myself for not laughing in her face. "I hated my father's secretive ways," my mom continued, "but it seems as though I adopted his way of parenting."

My mom's gaze drifted to the floor. She didn't speak for almost a minute, and I worried that her mind had wandered with her eyes, but she shook her head and turned her attention back to me.

"Will you please go get your sister?" my mom asked. "I would like to answer all the questions at one time."

I bounced off my mom's bed and walked to the room next door. My sister had left the door open. Ella was sitting on her daybed, looking out our only window. She seemed like she was in a trance. I sometimes wished that my sister would pick up a book or a magazine, so that it would at least appear as though she was concentrating on something. No wonder her classmates made fun of her. You had to be a special kind of weird if the smart kids bullied you.

Ella's head turned slowly to me. I almost expected her to give me a crazed look or start spewing green vomit, but my sister's angelic blue eyes remained her own. She had known the moment I had entered the room. Her expression did not change as she waited for me to speak.

"Mom wants to talk to us," I said. "She wants you to come to her room."

"I think I will pass if she is doing a two-for-one special on 'The Birds and the Bees' talk," my sister said.

I didn't think our mom would ever have that talk with Ella and me. She probably hoped that the school had taught us everything we needed to know.

I had been so excited when I noticed I was spotting that I couldn't wait to tell my mom that I had started my first menstrual cycle. I watched an episode of a family show when I was in fifth grade where the mother took her daughter out for ice cream after learning that her daughter had started her period. I was full of excitement as I waited for my mom to get home from work, and I told her I had started spotting as soon as she walked through the door.

"You're too small to be holding someone up if they fall," she had scolded. "You're going to get hurt if someone falls on you." She had misunderstood my reference to "spotting."

"No, Mom," I said. I was so happy that I couldn't stop grinning and laughing. "I started my period."

A look of disappointment clouded my mom's face. My enthusiasm dried up instantly, and confusion and embarrassment sucked me into sadness.

"The pads are under the sink," my mom said and walked past me.

I had known she kept the pads under the downstairs bathroom sink since I was four. I fell on the hardwood flooring in our living room one day, and I suffered a long cut from a sharp crack in the wood. I stumbled upon the pads when I was looking for antibacterial spray to disinfect the cut on my index finger.

I opened the plastic covering and looked at the cottony material. I thought the sanitary napkin was a bandage for a really big cut, and it seemed like I was bleeding a lot, so I peeled off the adhesive, and wrapped it around my finger.

I went back to playing with my toys, but it was difficult to move around my bulky new bandage. A gasp startled me into looking up. I turned around and saw Jerrod on the floor holding his stomach.

He was laughing so hard that his face was turning purple, and no sound was coming from his mouth. I watched his body shake, and I wondered about the reason for his silent mirth. Josh stood next to him with his mouth open.

"Where did you get that?" Josh asked, pointing at my bandage. His eyes were wide, and his face was red, but it wasn't from laughing.

It was strange to see two totally separate expressions on the same face. Jerrod kept laughing while Josh stared at me, embarrassed.

"I got it from under the sink," I said. "I had a very bad cut," I added defensively.

Jerrod's body convulsed with a new wave of laughter, but Josh was sympathetic. "Syd, those are Mommy's *special* bandages," he informed me.

My four-year-old mind wrapped easily around Josh's explanation. "So, only Mommy can use them?"

Josh's posture relaxed. Jerrod had finally gotten control of his laughter.

Josh crossed the room and carefully pulled my bandage from my finger. I could see a small drop of bright red blood on the white material.

"Mommy must get very bad cuts," I said.

Jerrod snorted, but Josh remained serious. "One day you will need these bandages, but that won't be for a very, very long time," he said with a wink.

"Don't tell Mom you know about the bandages," Jerrod said, stifling a chuckle, "or where you found them. She would have a cow."

I remembered how much pain my mom had endured when she gave birth to Ella. I had been in the delivery room with her until the doctor had told her it was time to push. I watched my mom scream and cry until a nurse kindly ushered me out of the room and played with me until Ella was born.

Ella had been about as big as a loaf of bread, and my mom had been in agony for hours. A cow was much bigger than Ella's baby body. I imagined a cow ripping out of my mom's stomach.

I promised Jerrod that I wouldn't reveal that I had seen or used one of our mom's "special bandages." Jerrod laughed at me again and ruffled my hair.

He picked me up while Josh disposed of the "special bandage." Jerrod walked me to the window and watched for our mom's car to return from work. She didn't arrive home until long after my brothers had caught me with a sanitary napkin around my finger.

I hadn't thought about my mom's supply of feminine necessities until she responded to my news. I had walked, dispirited, upstairs to my room and quietly shut the door. I had been through a lot of excitement the day I first noticed my spotting, and I needed a nap. Strange things had happened to me all day at school, but I was too excited to think about anything but my mom's displeased response to my entrance into womanhood.

My thoughts about my brothers and the uncomfortable time between my mom and me made me tired. I washed the images away and returned to the present. Besides, reliving the past in my mind was not getting me anywhere.

"Mom *is* doing a sort of two-for-one, but it's to answer the questions I have about Bryan," I told Ella.

"Oh," my sister said and promptly followed me to our mom's room.

Our mom was staring at her carpeted floor when I returned with Ella. She didn't seem to notice our presence until Ella cleared her throat.

She patted a spot on the bed to her right and left, so Ella and I sat down on either side of our remaining parent. Our mom gave us each a one-armed embrace, and we tried to show our interest.

"Sydney has asked me some questions about the man I dated before your father," my mom explained to Ella. Ella nodded, even though she already knew more than our mom was probably going to tell us.

Our mom let out a long sigh and prepared herself to share one of her secrets. I was a little surprised that our mom was going to tell a memory to Ella and me, especially since she spent so much time pretending that the past never happened.

"Bryan and I were kind of thrown together by your grandfather," our mom began. She still seemed to think she was telling us something we didn't know.

"I liked Bryan a lot, and I hoped I could love him one day, but I didn't understand truly connecting with another person until I met your father. Bryan loved me. I know that now, so it was best that I got out of my relationship with him when I did."

I heard sorrowful reflection in my mom's voice. I was intrigued, but Ella kept staring forward at the bathroom door. Talking about feelings made her uncomfortable.

"I ended my relationship with Bryan the day after I met your father," our mom continued. "Bryan didn't want to accept that I would no longer see him, and he and your father fought over me."

My mom smiled. It seemed romantic, but I had felt her emotions in my dream. She had been embarrassed that she hadn't personally broken up with Bryan before she kissed my father, and the fight scared her.

"Your father and I shared a very intense connection, which wasn't so different than the relationship I'd had with Bryan. Your father and I were always together, and I guess I was a little blinded by my newfound love to realize that Bryan was upset about the breakup."

My mom seemed remorseful for a moment. It was hard for her to think back on Bryan's depression after their relationship had ended.

It was probably easy to ignore the sadness my mom saw in her old boyfriend as she explored her new feelings for my father, but as an adult, my mom was ashamed of some of her teenage actions. I didn't want to dive into her thoughts and sort out her regrets.

"Bryan had to endure a certain amount of ridicule from his guy friends," my mom admitted, "but Johnny was a school football star, so most of the people we knew didn't give Bryan too much trouble about losing me to a local hero.

"The girls at our high school threw themselves at Bryan. They thought he was a prime catch because he'd been my boyfriend. Bryan wouldn't date anyone else, though. He told them he was waiting for me to dump 'Mr. Wonderful'."

My mom laughed, and the sound jolted Ella. She smiled at our mom as if she'd been listening attentively.

"The night after your father and I announced our engagement, I was lying in bed, and I heard rocks ping off my window. I knew it was Bryan's way of knocking when he didn't know if my dad was home. My dad was out on a late-night call, so I walked out onto my front porch to talk to Bryan.

"It was early spring, but the night air was still cool. Bryan never seemed to get cold, but he was shaking. I tried to make some small talk, so I asked him about work and school. Bryan didn't respond to my questions. He rushed over to me and placed a ring on my left ring finger—right over the ring your father had just given me!

" 'I should've known that every girl wants to be a bride,' Bryan told me as he held the ring on my hand. I was finally able to remove Bryan's hand and the diamond ring that had belonged to his mother.

"Bryan's proposal opened my eyes to a lot of things. Most importantly, I understood Bryan thought I was using your father to make him jealous. I also realized that he had been working extra hard over the months before our breakup to afford to propose to and marry me."

My mom's story was certainly putting a new spin on my image of Bryan. He was back to being a wrongly accused, hopeless romantic to me. Ella met my star-struck gaze and rolled her eyes.

"Of course," my mom continued, "I told Bryan that I was only interested in marrying your father and he became upset. The dent in your grandfather's left front porch banister was the result of his temper that night."

Okay, that piece of information brought me back to reality. Bryan Shelton had a terrible temper. It seemed strange to me because I only felt a sense of peace from the Bryan Shelton I had seen during my visit to the prison.

"After I married your father, Bryan would see me in town from time to time," my mom said, "but he would barely acknowledge me. I figured it must be hard for him, but I wanted to show my willingness to remain friends.

"I heard Bryan joined the police academy right after my marriage, and he traveled across the country for a couple of years. I think he spent some time driving an eighteen-wheeler for a big distributor.

"Your grandfather told me when Bryan moved back into his childhood home, but I didn't see him for a while. He avoided me like the plague but managed to see my father at least three times a week."

"How long was he gone?" I asked.

My mom raised her eyes to the ceiling and appeared to think about my question. "He was twenty-two when he came back, so almost four years."

My mom's gaze drifted back, and she said, "He must have had some real adventures," and I was reminded of how little of the world she had experienced. My mom had lived in a Tennessee city and visited New York City, but she hadn't even been to all of the states that surrounded the state in which she lived.

"Your brothers and I were walking through the Apple Festival after their seventh birthday, and I ran into Bryan," my mom said, after she was sure I'd finished asking questions. "I was certain that he'd heard about my sons, but he seemed shocked and angry. I remember he said, 'Now this is too much!' and stormed off.

"I read about his marriage to Nellie Riddle about a month later. I thought she was pretty, and they looked happy in their engagement announcement. I felt relieved that he had found someone to share his life with.

"Bryan moved Nellie into his home, and my friends broke their necks trying to be the first to tell me he was working with my father. They shouldn't have bothered. My father had called me about it before the ink was dry on the department's officer transfer form. I was not at all surprised that Bryan had joined the Unicoi County Sheriff's Department. My father had always been Bryan's idol.

"Unfortunately, your grandfather called me every time Bryan was awarded, promoted, or featured in the town newspaper, but your father couldn't do anything right as far as your grandfather was concerned. I heard about Bryan's accomplishments until I wanted to throw up."

My mom put a finger halfway into her mouth and mock-vomited. Ella watched the display with the most interest she'd shown during the conversation, but her eyes wandered off again when our mom grew serious.

"I thought Josh and Jerrod didn't meet Grandpa until they were older," I said.

"They probably don't remember him," my mom replied. "They were young when we had the fight.

"One Thanksgiving," my mom recounted, "I asked your grandfather why he bothered to talk to your father and me if our lives were such disappointments. I told your grandfather that he loved Bryan more than me."

I could imagine my grandpa's outrage at my mom's accusations. He was probably upset, and he would have expressed his hurt the way most proud men do; he would have yelled at her and stormed off.

My mom was recollecting her story much faster. "Your grandfather screamed at me.

"Your father stayed out of it, and your grandfather left without saying he loved me," my mom said. "No matter how mad we were at each other, he'd always tell me he loved me because he hadn't told my mother how he felt about her before she passed away.

"There was a little more to the fight than that," she said, smoothing the wrinkles from her khakis, "but I don't want to talk about it right now. I decided not to talk to my dad until he apologized to me. Your father tried to get us to mend our differences, but your grandfather has had a lot of practice at being stubborn. Our days of estrangement turned into weeks, and the weeks turned into years. I only called a truce because I had to have his help with your brothers. They needed a strong male influence in their lives." My mom nodded as if she were conceding a point. "Your grandfather was always rock solid."

My mom bounced on the bed a little, and she shook Ella out of her reverie. "Maybe this soap opera stuff is a little boring to her," my mom joked. Ella made a token protest and said she was "very interested" in the *Days of Our Mother's Life.*

"I'm supposed to be talking about Bryan, though," my mom said. "Is there anything else you want to know?" She looked from Ella to me.

I didn't hesitate to answer my mom's question with a question. "How much did you know or hear about Nellie and Lily's murders?"

My mom sucked in a deep breath. "Call me crazy, but I thought you were more interested in how I felt about Bryan."

"Do you think he did it?" I pressed.

"Of course she does," Ella spoke. "She has told us how obsessive and violent he was. Have you been listening?"

I prepared myself for a round of sibling rivalry. My mom stopped the situation from escalating.

"I knew he fought a lot with Nellie," she conceded.

Ella and I gave our mom our attention again. She paused to make sure my sister and I were finished bickering.

"Nellie was younger than Bryan," she said. "He was twenty-five when they married, and she had just graduated high school. I think someone told me they met when Bryan picked her brother up for work one day. Nellie's brother had had car trouble or something and needed a ride for a couple of days.

"I got the idea that Nellie was restless. Nellie's family was poor, and she'd never been outside a thirty-mile radius of her home. She wanted to travel, and when Bryan told his stories, Nellie must have thought the tales happened while Bryan served as a police officer in other states. Maybe she thought Bryan had been a state trooper. At any rate, I don't think Nellie had any idea that Bryan intended to stay in Erwin for the rest of his life.

"Nellie had never really been anywhere or had a lot of experiences, but she was very social. I met her at the doctor's office, and she was kind and friendly, even though she knew about the past between her husband and me."

"Why would that matter?" Ella asked. I was reminded that my sister hadn't seen our father's fits of jealous rage.

My mom didn't miss a beat. "Sometimes people are so in love that they don't want to lose what they've got. Bryan and Nellie had a jealous relationship because they loved each other so much."

Ella rolled her eyes. "It sounds like Bryan did not want to lose Nellie to another man, the way he had lost you, and Nellie did not want Bryan to get involved with another woman and whisk that other woman away."

I had to agree with my sister. I might have added that Nellie probably wasn't fully aware of Bryan's obsession with my mom and that Bryan was most likely Nellie's first boyfriend and first love.

"You didn't see the way he loved her," my mom almost whispered. I could hardly hear her over the heat pushing through the vents.

"He loved her to death!" Ella said sarcastically.

My mom shook her head. "We're going backward," my mom said firmly. "I only wanted to explain that we each moved on." My mom sighed and resigned herself to answering my question.

"I was at work when I heard Bryan had killed his family. It was the closest I came to calling your grandfather until the Christmas you met him."

Our mom had our attention again. Ella still looked as though she would rather be staring silently at the walls in our room, but she listened attentively as our mom spoke.

"I felt sick when I heard, and I swore Bryan was innocent, but then I was told there were witnesses."

"I heard Bryan and Nellie were fighting because she wanted to go away with her friend," I mentioned.

My mom didn't like to be interrupted, but she allowed my statement. It seemed she was too emotionally exhausted to chastise me.

"That's true," she said, without explaining her source. "They used to fight about her friend a lot. Bryan was jealous of her, and he thought she was going to talk Nellie into leaving him."

"It kind of sounded like she did," I said.

My mom raised her eyebrows. "What do you mean?"

I was going to have to get better at separating my dreams and visions from reality. "Why would he have killed Nellie if she was going to stay?" I covered.

My mom shrugged her shoulders. "I guess you're right, but I always thought Nellie's death had been an accident. I figured Bryan's temper had just gotten out of hand. I heard he was holding Nellie back from leaving. The problem was that he was holding her in the river.

"If there were witnesses, then why did they watch her murder and do nothing?" Ella asked. Sweat was popping up just over her brows and her voice had an almost hysterical squeak.

Our mom sensed Ella's aggravation. She turned to my sister and placed a hand on her thigh.

"Ella, what's wrong? You don't usually get this upset."

"I do not get upset because I can see the dead, and most of them are okay with being dead!" Ella spat. She jumped off our mom's bed and backed into the hallway. She pointed an accusing finger at my mom and me. "You people want *me* evaluated! *You*," Ella shouted, pointing at me, "have a gift you will not use, even to satisfy your morbid curiosity. And *you*," the finger shot to our mom, "knew what Bryan was capable of, and you let that poor young girl believe his jealousy was just over her. You *knew* she was not aware that you were Bryan's first love!"

Ella flew into our bedroom and slammed the door before her accusations could dissolve in the air around us. The reverberations of sound from the door echoed in my ears.

"I didn't know that she knew," my mom said.

"What and who are you talking about?" I asked.

"The last time your grandfather visited, he told me he thought Ella should be evaluated for schizophrenia," my mom admitted. "He said Ella was smart, withdrawn, and paranoid. He claimed she acted the same way Crazy—" my mom swallowed the word and corrected herself, "—the way Lyle Miller acted in his youth."

"Grandpa didn't even know that Erwin existed when Lyle Miller was a child," I said. I loved my grandpa, but I would not stand behind remarks that had no basis.

My mom glanced away quickly. A secret danced across her thoughts, and I kept talking so I could resist the urge to bounce into my mom's mind and grab it.

"Ella has every right to be angry with us," I conceded.

My mom shook her head. "I told your grandfather that I wasn't going to take Ella to a psychiatrist. A psychiatrist would put her on something to make her act like a zombie."

"So, not much different than she acts now," I pointed out.

My mom was disgusted with my words, but she didn't say anything in Ella's defense.

"I want my children to concentrate on being children," she affirmed. "If Ella wants therapy or medicine, then I will get it for her, but until she asks for help, I refuse to see her as anything but perfectly normal."

I admired my mom's faith in us, but I was afraid she was going to get scared one day. That would be the day that Ella would get help whether she asked for it or not. I knew my mom, and if she couldn't surreptitiously store our differences and wrongdoings in the Family Closet of Secrets, she'd find a way to sweep them under the rug.

Chapter Seventeen

I forgot to pick up Olivia Sneed's locket. I thought of trivial things after my mom's talk, and I enjoyed being a rebellious, superficial teenager.

Lydia and I had to sneak around to hang out together, but somehow that made it more fun. We went bowling in top hats and to the park in bright red bandannas to draw attention away from our faces.

The month and a half Lydia had spent out of school had really seemed to change her. She was much more generous with her feelings and compliments. If I helped her with something, she reciprocated my deed; if she hurt my feelings, Lydia would apologize and admit her mistake.

I waited for the time when her mood would change, and she would go back to her snobby ways. I could sometimes see a trace of the spoiled, rich Lydia when we talked about clothes or other students, but she went out of her way to remain diplomatic.

If I made a comment about a girl's shoes, Lydia would say, "Daddy had my shoes flown from Paris." After she thought for a moment, though, she would add something like, "But her shoes look wonderful on her, and Mummy won't let me out in mine in the rain."

I was ready to form a new opinion of Lydia. I had wanted to open my heart to my *pseudo* friend for so long, and now it looked like I could say anything to my *real* friend.

Lydia and I would use the time between school's dismissal and dinner to talk and hang out together. We ate ice cream floats at a local diner or walked through the library in search of books about obscure topics. Lydia and I took turns walking each other home. One day Lydia would walk into town and to the edge of my property, and the next day I would walk within sight of her home before I turned around and followed a well-worn trail to my house. We had long talks as we wandered home, and I learned a lot about the girl who had been my friend since the second grade.

Our afternoon walks had lasted almost a week when I noticed Lydia seemed a little distant. Usually, it was easy for me to make her laugh, but she seemed lost in a thought that consumed her.

Lydia and I had walked from the academy to a deeply wooded area when she stopped. The sun was out, but the day was cold, and I knew I would get sick if I didn't find a warm place soon.

Lydia guided me to the edge of the woods. The sun still shone its rays on us, and the woods blocked most of the wind.

"I'm so cold, Lydia," I said. I could almost feel the bitter air eating my bones.

"I just don't want to go home," Lydia admitted.

I felt warmth wash over me in the form of excitement. *Maybe Lydia Sneed was ready to open her heart to me.*

I didn't want to ruin the moment. My grandpa had told me once that he sometimes got confessions out of criminals by staying quiet and listening to them talk. I waited for Lydia's confession.

"I spent a lot of time at home after our—" Lydia searched for the right word "—disagreement."

This was definitely a different Lydia. Maybe she wasn't quite the girl I glimpsed beside the river, but she was close.

"My parents fight all the time now," Lydia admitted, "but the house is big enough to escape their arguing. One day, I ran into my father's study to get away from them. I left the door open and looked for a place to be alone. Finding solitude in that house is a joke. The hired help are everywhere, but I knew it would be difficult for someone to find me in my father's study.

"I was going to hide behind my father's thick drapes, but then I noticed that his computer was on. I don't usually pry, but my curiosity got the best of me."

A breeze found its way into our sheltered spot and circled around us momentarily. I jumped in place as I listened, determined to hear the rest of Lydia's story, despite the cold.

"My father has an accountant in the city," Lydia told me, "but he does most of his own bookkeeping on a computer program that he developed. Something like a checkbook register was on the screen. The cursor was flashing on the last entry: Terry Thorpe $20,000.00."

I raised my eyebrows and looked at the ground. I drew a circle in the dirt with my shoe.

"What is it?" she asked.

"I'm sorry," I said, "but your father once spent ten grand on a pair of shoes for you. Forgive me if I don't think the entry is unusual."

"Terry Thorpe was one of Mr. Hernandez's illegitimate sons," Lydia said. She was pleased by my shocked expression. "He went by his mother's maiden name because Mr. Hernandez wouldn't sign his birth certificate."

I understood Lydia's surprise a little better. My family had never had a lot of money, but I would have assumed, if I had seen a large sum of money next to his name in a bank register, that Terry Thorpe was trying to blackmail my father. I guessed Lydia had felt the same way.

"Terry sought out his father after his sixteenth birthday," Lydia continued. "Mr. Hernandez did not deny his paternity, but he told Terry that he was ashamed of him. Terry had been in and out of trouble. He had gone to a juvenile detention center for drugs, and he went on to serve time in prison for selling them. At least that's what the sisters say."

I thought about the two women I'd seen arguing in the kitchen when I went over to Lydia's house. Lydia may have heard a lot of gossip in that kitchen over the years. I would also bet she understood Spanish a little more than she led people to believe.

"I met Terry once when I was little," Lydia recalled. "I was swinging on my play set with my nanny when a red truck pulled up our driveway."

"My nanny was an older lady with roses on her cheeks and an English accent," Lydia reminisced. "She handled me well, but I don't think that I was her first rich kid. When she saw Terry's truck, she stopped swinging and said, 'Hold on, love.'

"The man who got out of the truck was young, he was maybe twenty-five years old. His dark hair and black eyes seemed like a familiar sight to me, and I wasn't scared of him, at first. The young stranger reminded me of a Native American, but his eyes were shaped like the sisters' and he talked like everyone I'd met in the south.

"The man was looking at me in a funny way. I guess my nanny caught him staring at me, because she asked him what he was doing. Terry told her his name, and she asked if he meant to see Mr. Hernandez. Terry laughed and said his business was with my father.

"My father is a busy man," Lydia said, "so he didn't want to entertain Terry. Terry sent my nanny back to my father's office with a manila envelope and, after my father reviewed the contents of the file, Terry was rushed into my father's drawing room.

"My father held meetings in his drawing room. I was almost ten before I realized my father didn't draw in that room," she chuckled a little as she realized her own naivete. "He mostly held meetings with older men who dressed like him.

"My father emerged with Terry two hours later. My father was pale, and he had an expression similar to the one he wore when he saw Mummy's credit card bill.

"Terry was as happy as I am on my birthday. He pinched my nanny on the cheek and skipped out the door before she could swat her hand at him.

"I asked my father about the reason for Terry's visit. My father told me to call Terry 'Young Mr. Thorpe,' but I don't put *mister* in front of a person's name unless they've earned my respect. I nodded my head anyway, and my father looked down the hall where Terry had disappeared.

"That's my new driver," my father said, but I never saw Terry again. I *thought* I saw him a couple of times, but it must have been my imagination.

"Anyway, once I saw his name in the bank register, I got curious about how much and how often my father paid Terry. I entered Terry's name in the search field, and a new sheet came up with just the transactions between my father and Terry Thorpe.

"It looked as though my father paid Terry once a year near Thanksgiving, but something else caught my eye. My father always paid Terry with cash. My father doesn't usually carry more than a thousand dollars with him because he's afraid of being robbed, but the transaction clearly read $20,000 in cash.

"That's a lot of money for driving," Lydia said. She turned her sad blue eyes to me and asked, "Do you think my father's running drugs?"

Lydia meant transporting illegal drugs from one place to another to be sold. I thought of all the income Bannon Sneed could make from the criminal venture.

"Maybe not, but I wouldn't rule it out," I said diplomatically.

"What am I going to do, Sydney?" Lydia cried. "I can't live in a house that's supported with drug money!"

Lydia cried, and I placed my hand on her shoulder. "I bet all your family's money is from your dad's legal business," I said consolingly. "He was probably just giving Terry money to keep him from bothering Mr. Hernandez. You said Mr. Hernandez was your dad's favorite hired hand."

"Yes, he *was* my father's favorite," Lydia said. "But why does my father write Terry a check *every* year?"

"I don't know," I said. "Back child support, maybe?"

Lydia continued to cry. Big tears rolled down her perfect cheeks.

"Can I come live with you?" Lydia asked suddenly. She grabbed my arms and pulled down. "I don't want to live in that house of liars."

Why would a girl who has everything want to come to my little house? We had plenty of room, but my family couldn't afford designer clothes and trips to foreign places.

What would my mom say if I brought Lydia home? I doubted my mom would even let Lydia stay the night.

Lydia's moist eyes were boring into me. I had to find a way to make her feel better.

"I'll ask if you can stay the night, okay?" I found myself saying before my practical side could paste my lips together.

Lydia's tears abated, and she gave me a grateful smile. She led me out of the woods, and we walked the rest of the way to my house.

My mom's car was parked in our driveway. I felt like I was going to faint from all the blood that pounded through my body. I had never been so scared about asking my mom a question.

Fear and gravity worked hard on my legs as I walked up the front steps and into the house. I had told Lydia what to say, or not to say, and how to act, or not to act, but she still looked pale and proud.

"Mom?" I called.

"We're in the kitchen," my mom shouted.

I walked into the kitchen with my head up. I didn't want Lydia to feel like I was ashamed of our rekindled friendship.

I don't know if my mom and Ella's faces reflected shock or horror. My mom was the first one to speak, even though it took her a moment to voice the words coming out of her mouth.

"I thought we already discussed this," my mom said. Her pointed look made me rethink my request, but the thought of Lydia's tears motivated me to chance my mom's anger.

"Lydia and I are friends," I announced. I tried to make it seem as though I never stopped my friendship with Lydia. "I don't want to have to sneak around and hang out with her, but I will."

My mom's eyebrows shot up and down faster than free fall as she processed her outrage and acceptance. It was a long moment before she spoke.

"Lydia," my mom said, and Lydia gave my mom her attention. "I have heard that you've changed. I won't object to your friendship with my daughter unless you revert back to your old ways."

Lydia's voice was soft and small. "I understand, Mrs. Miller."

"I'm glad that's settled," I said. "Can Lydia stay the night?"

My mom's mouth was ready to form a negative response, but she paused. It seemed like she was going down a list of reasons in her head for Lydia not to stay, but in the end, my mom's excuse was lame. "She doesn't have a toothbrush."

Lydia dipped into her designer purse and pulled out a pink toothbrush protector. "Can I call Mummy and let her know that I'm staying?" Lydia asked.

My mom realized that she'd been bested and nodded her head. Lydia pulled out her smartphone and dialed her mother.

I had never really thought about it, but Lydia had never been to my house. I heard her arguing with Olivia Sneed, and I realized Lydia had never stayed overnight at *anyone's* house.

My mom listened to Lydia argue with her mother. I could almost tell what my mom was feeling, so I wasn't surprised when she took Lydia's phone and calmly asked Olivia Sneed about her concerns. I couldn't hear sounds coming from the other end of the conversation, and my mom finally said, "Okay then, it's settled. I will drive Lydia home at three tomorrow afternoon. I will give you my personal number if you think of anything else you would like to say."

Lydia looked at my mom like she was a superhero. "No one ever leaves Mummy speechless."

"There's a first time for everything," my mom said. "Ella and I are going to pick up a pizza. Don't burn down the house while we're gone."

I had never had a sleepover at my house. I didn't know what I was supposed to do. Lydia looked a little uncomfortable, too, so I started by asking the same questions I heard my mom ask when her friends came over.

"Can I get you something to drink?"

Lydia nodded. "Maybe some water?"

I thought about our shivering conversation in the woods. I had started to get cold again now that the excitement of bringing Lydia home had settled.

"How about I fix us some hot cocoa?" I suggested.

Lydia smiled. "That is exactly what I wanted, but I didn't want to ask."

"My mom makes cocoa in a special way," I told Lydia as I pulled down two mugs and the cocoa mix from the cabinets.

My face turned red, and I tried to busy myself with preparing our drinks so that Lydia would not see my embarrassment. I couldn't believe that I was fixing Lydia my mom's homemade cocoa recipe when she had dined in five-star restaurants and had her own personal cooks.

"I can't wait to try your mom's cocoa," Lydia said, possibly reading my embarrassment. "I love to try new things."

I don't know if Lydia had sensed that I was uncomfortable, but she had said the right thing. I smiled as I added sugar, cream, and vanilla to the cocoa mix. I put in a touch of cinnamon and warmed the mugs in the microwave.

I lifted a large bag of campfire marshmallows from the pantry. Lydia's eyes grew large as I added one large marshmallow to each cup. A little liquid from one of the cups spilled over, so I took that one and gave Lydia the mug with the most cocoa.

It is impossible to describe the taste of beautifully made cocoa on a cold day. Visions of snow and icicles turn into dancing snowmen and sleigh rides in your mind as you drink it. The first sip carries heat from your tongue to your toes, slowly warming your soul as it traces a path to your stomach.

I must have had a goofy look on my face as I drank my cocoa, but Lydia's expression mirrored mine. I was surprised by her response.

"Sometimes all the money in the world can't buy homemade goodness," she said.

"You sound like a pie commercial," I teased. We burst into giggles, which ended quickly because we didn't want to spill any of our special winter beverage.

"My mom says cocoa can cure all troubles," I told Lydia. "She hasn't made it a lot, though, since Jerrod's—"

I stopped talking before I said *acceptance.* That would open up too many questions. I had decided to say *passing,* when Lydia placed her hand over mine.

"I've never had anyone close to me pass away," she said.

I was glad she didn't say *die.* It sounded too harsh and brutally final.

"I liked your brothers," Lydia said genuinely. I found it strange that she should feel such strong emotions over Josh and Jerrod when she had only spoken to my brothers a handful of times.

"I miss them," I admitted. I couldn't imagine going through life without their joking and laughter. My house had gotten way too serious, and I couldn't look at Ella for comic relief.

"It's okay to talk about them," Lydia consoled.

I opened my mouth to say something smart, but Lydia's expression stopped me. It was the same look I'd seen on the Lydia by the river. My heart swelled with love for my friend.

"I guess I've been so worried about my mom and my sister that I haven't really thought about how *I'm* going to deal with losing them," I said. I was shocked that I'd told Lydia the way I'd been feeling lately, but she looked sincere, so I continued.

"Josh was my favorite, and Jerrod was okay with that, because Ella was his favorite. Josh was like another parent to me, but Jerrod taught me some of the hardest lessons.

"I loved my brothers so much, and I never thought I would lose them. I used to feel responsible for their deaths, because I saw Josh leave the night he died, but Ella kept me from thinking about that too long."

"You couldn't have known what they planned to do," Lydia said, placing a sympathetic hand over mine. I didn't tell her I had read Josh's mind that night and I knew exactly what he intended to do.

The sound of my mom's key in the lock made me jump. I hadn't even heard her pull into the driveway.

I collected our cocoa mugs and hurried to the sink. I didn't want my mom to see that Lydia and I had drunk cocoa. Hot cocoa made my mom think of Jerrod, and thinking about Jerrod led her to days of depression.

I rinsed out the cups so that any liquid could have been in them. We used the mugs for water and milk, so the sight of the mugs alone would not upset her.

My mom came in the door, and I was blasted by a thought from her. She was balancing the pizza while trying to free her keys from the lock. She was bent over the pizza box, supporting it in between one leg and her stomach. I started to help my mom, but I noticed Ella looked pale.

As I opened my mouth to ask my sister why she seemed upset, she locked eyes with me. I felt like I'd been shot with a laser. I knew I should not ask Ella about her mood as sure as I had read my mom's mind.

I grabbed the pizza box before we'd need to apply the Five-Second Rule. I felt the warm box bottom, and it was too hot for me to hold for long. I raced to the table and put it on a placemat. Lydia had gotten plates and cups out of the cabinets. I was glad she hadn't seen the silent exchange between Ella and me.

My mom poured milk in every glass until she got to Lydia's. "Do you drink milk, dear?"

My mom was wondering if Lydia had a milk allergy. She was probably cursing herself for not picking up a caffeine-free soda.

"I usually drink red wine and mineral water with Italian food," Lydia said.

Everyone was shocked for a moment. Ella even lowered her guard long enough to be astonished over an adolescent's casual admission to drinking alcohol.

"It's only a quarter of a glass with food," she added quickly.

My family slowly came to terms with the level of class difference between the Sneed and the Miller families. Lydia had eaten crepes in Paris, and we hadn't been to a finer restaurant than a local pizza place.

My mom decided to lighten a tense situation. "We have bottled water?" she offered.

Lydia smiled. "That would be wonderful, Mrs. Miller."

My mom pulled a bottle of water out of the refrigerator and handed it to Lydia. I snuck another look at Ella while my mom and Lydia weren't watching.

Not right now, I glimpsed from Ella's mind. She looked away before anyone noticed our thought swap.

The rest of my night went by very quickly. I had never had an overnight guest before, so I tried to fit in all the things I had always wanted to do with a friend. Lydia and I played video games, gave each other makeovers, played Truth-or-Dare, and cried into ice cream as we watched a sappy love story. The craziest thing of all was that it all fell into place naturally. I didn't feel like I was rushing through anything to do another thing on my party list.

Lydia and I tried to include Ella, but she pretended to read a paperback novel. Lydia didn't notice that Ella simply stared at a page without moving her eyes. She was irritated at something. I tried to look into her mind, and I caught the fuzzy shape of a man before

Ella pushed me out. I felt intense burning heat, like Ella was setting me on fire for trying to penetrate her mind.

Lydia and I fell asleep talking about cute movie stars. I was only slightly jealous that she had met most of the actors I thought were attractive.

I woke up the next morning with a feeling that I hadn't even noticed was absent in my life. I had the same feeling when I was four and Ella and I would giggle into our pillows at night. Lydia and I had bonded, and we were finally true friends.

My mom made pancakes, and we gulped them down ravenously. Lydia and I were carrying our plates to the sink when we heard a knock at the door.

My mom turned around sharply. "Are you expecting anyone?" she whispered.

"No," I whispered back. I was used to my mom avoiding uninvited guests. In the past, we had hidden behind furniture in case snooping eyes spotted us through the windows.

Lydia and I stayed still as my mom stealthily made her way into the living room. She slowly moved the curtain aside and relaxed her posture.

"It's just Olivia," my mom announced.

Lydia deflated. I wanted her to stay.

My mom opened the door and Olivia Sneed walked inside. She had on gloves and a fashionable hat. She looked like a full-color movie star in our dull house.

"I'm here for my daughter," Olivia slurred. I was secretly glad that the Sneeds were chauffeured.

"Olivia," my mom said in greeting.

"Miranda, dear, you look so pretty, even after suffering so much." She extended her hand in mock sympathy. It was not intended to be touched.

My mom looked taken aback. I wished Lydia's mother truly had class. She would never have mentioned the death of the men in our house. I could tell by my mom's reaction that days of depression would follow Olivia Sneed's remark.

"Lydia," Olivia Sneed said. Lydia looked at her mother pleadingly, but was answered by, "We need to go."

Lydia surprised everyone by asking, "Can Sydney stay with us?"

Olivia Sneed's eyebrows shot up over her sunglasses. She realized Lydia was serious, and she adopted an uncaring wave.

"If her mother feels it's necessary—"

"My mom feels it is very necessary," I said, jumping up and down. Lydia grabbed my hands, and we jumped together like two excited bunnies.

"Wait a minute," my mom said. Her voice was firm enough to stop our bouncing, but we still had silly smiles pasted to our faces.

My mom looked from Lydia and me to Olivia Sneed. "I still remember what happened the last time I agreed to a sleepover at Lydia's house."

"I promise I'll call you if we fight," I told my mom, but I knew Lydia and I were better friends than I could ever have hoped.

Ten minutes later, I was in the Sneed limousine. Olivia Sneed sat behind the driver facing Lydia and me. She pulled out two mineral waters from a small refrigerator.

I untwisted the cap on my water and watched something like steam float from its opening. I could smell a difference in the water, and I braced myself for a metallic taste. The water was crisp and clean, and it tasted terrible! It was like drinking fresh rainwater as it dripped off a rusty car bumper.

I took two more sips, just to be nice, and told Lydia and her mother that my coughing and sputtering was from drinking the water too quickly. I eased the bottle into my duffle bag when they were looking at a sign announcing the opening of a new jewelry business.

I saw a Christmas display in an open window, and I felt my stomach drop. Lydia noticed the change in me and lifted her eyebrows. A slight shake of her head communicated, *What's wrong?*

I moved Lydia's still beautiful unwashed hair to the side and quickly whispered in her ear. Realization dawned in her features as she understood my dilemma.

"Mummy," Lydia said sweetly. "May we make a small stop before we go home?"

Olivia Sneed tapped impatiently on the tinted, sound-proof glass between her and the chauffeur. The glass slowly rescinded, and a gentleman with a strong, dark moustache responded.

Olivia Sneed looked at Lydia and me for directions, and I explained them the best way I could remember. My father once told my mom that women should never give directions because they couldn't even remember their way home. I assumed every man felt the same as my father.

I must have done a decent job communicating my destination. I made certain that I included buildings and street names. The chauffeur nodded his understanding.

Moments later, Lydia and I left the limo and ran into the shop. My mom would have insisted on accompanying us into the building, but Lydia's mother stayed in the vehicle. The liquor in the mini fridge would be depleted before Lydia and I had finished our business.

I was afraid that Kerry would be angry with me for forgetting to pick up the necklace. I started to second guess bringing Lydia with me. *What if he lectured me about keeping my word in front of her?*

Kerry ambled out of the back room when he heard the bell jingle. Kerry smiled at me, but the smile faltered when he saw Lydia.

Kerry did not introduce himself, and he stood in place, glaring at Lydia. "What gives you the right to come into my shop?"

Bannon Sneed had clawed his way deeply into Erwin's businesses and politics, but he was still an outsider. In the process of gaining his status in the town, he had made a lot of enemies, but I never considered that Lydia would be unwelcome anywhere in Erwin.

Lydia was shocked into silence, but she recovered her composure and said, "I am sorry if my presence upsets you. May I pay for the repair of my mother's locket and leave peacefully?"

Three weeks ago, I would have laughed myself into a coma if I had been told that I would hear those words from Lydia's mouth. I had seen a lot of changes in my friend in the last several weeks.

Kerry seemed to be stunned as well, but he decided Lydia's words were Sneed manipulation, and shrugged them off. "I will not do business with *her*." Kerry addressed me and nodded in Lydia's direction. "The blood in her family is as black as the coal the CSX rail cars carried."

Lydia grabbed my hand and placed something discreetly inside it. I knew it was money, and I covered the trade with my other hand. "I'll be back out in a minute," I said

Lydia turned to Kerry and said, "I am sorry for any pain my family has caused you. I hope I can prove that I am a good person."

Kerry stood firmly on his resolve to keep the Sneeds from his shop. The bells jingled as Lydia exited.

Kerry still had a hard look on his face. "You're only as good as the company you keep," he lectured.

I didn't like the insinuation that I deserved less respect because I was Lydia's friend. I decided to finish my business with Kerry quickly and never return to the shop.

"Where did you get that locket?" Kerry said harshly. "I ought to call the cops to report you, but your grandaddy'd make sure you got out of any charges."

He accused me of stealing the locket, but I assumed it would be a charge issued by the Sneeds. I didn't understand the reason he thought I stole it when Kerry saw Lydia come in with me.

I told Kerry the whole truth. I was hurt that he saw me in such a negative light, and I was determined to salvage some respect for my family. "Lydia wanted the locket fixed as a present for her mother for Christmas. They watch her every move, so she asked me to get it fixed for her. I will call them back in so that you will see I am no thief."

"T.V. has wrecked the minds of the young," Kerry said. I looked up at him with a question in my moist eyes.

"It's so easy for you to lie to me without feeling a bit of remorse, but maybe it's not the T.V. Maybe it's the Sneed's influence."

Anger flowed up from my insides and erupted from my mouth. "Who are you to judge?" I shouted. "Have you eaten at their table or slept in their beds? I don't know what Bannon Sneed did to you, but it's time for you to get over it and start acting like a grownup!"

I was on a roll, so I threw the money in my hand onto the counter. I was shocked to see that Lydia had given me a hundred-dollar bill. Kerry would never believe that it was my money.

"Let me have the necklace, and I don't care what you do with the money," I said. "You shook my hand, and a deal's a deal."

Kerry considered it for a moment. He seemed to be struggling deeply between two courses of action.

"You say you got the necklace from Lydia," Kerry said firmly, but not unkindly.

"Yes."

Kerry scratched his chin. "Where did Lydia get it?"

I decided not to lie. "She found it while she was sneaking through her mother's stuff."

"Of course Olivia Sneed had it," Kerry said, looking off to the side. He turned his fierce eyes back to me. "Did you know what was in the locket?"

"Pictures?" I answered. I regretted my sarcasm when Kerry sighed and shook his head.

He pulled a maroon box from under the counter. Golden designs danced along the borders of the box. He opened it, and the polished silver locket and chain seemed to reflect every light in the room. He lifted the necklace out of its new home and opened the tiny clasp.

"Do you know these people?" he asked. He held the locket where I could clearly make out the photos, but he did not offer it to me.

Two pictures, one for each half of the locket, of a man and woman appeared to be looking at one another from opposing sides of the locket.

The black-and-white image of the woman showed her profile from the neck up. She was on the left side of the locket, looking across her left shoulder. The woman had on a shirt or dress that almost reached her chin. I noticed light hair piled in curls on top of the woman's head. I could tell she had been blonde, even though the photo was black and white. She'd had a sharp nose and lips that were turned upward, but did not smile.

The colorless photograph of the man showed a gentleman looking across his right shoulder. I could see the start of a suit and tie, and his dark hair was combed back. It took me a second to realize that the gentleman in the snapshot resembled a man I had seen while watching an old movie about the South.

I stared at them for a long time. "No," I said.

Kerry studied me for a moment. He closed the locket and dropped it back into the beautiful box. He handed me the box, but he did not let it go when my fingers embraced it.

"Be careful that you aren't being used, girl," Kerry said. "The Millers are a topic of conversation around this town just like the Sneeds. It's just funny to see two people from different worlds runnin' together."

Kerry shook his head slowly while still keeping his eyes on me. I hoped he was reading a strong look on my face.

"You really don't know those people?" Kerry asked. I had a feeling that he would know if I lied. You didn't own a business like his without being able to spot a fabrication.

"No," I said forcefully. I wanted Kerry to understand that I was upset that he hadn't believed my word the first time and I did not intend to answer the same question again.

Kerry let go of the box, but his eyes held mine. "We made a deal, and I will honor it, but you should know something of the history of that necklace before you hand it back to the likes of Olivia Sneed."

I nodded because I couldn't find my voice. Kerry's cold blue eyes had robbed me of any argument.

Kerry straightened his posture as much as his old bones and joints would allow and looked off to the side again. I followed his gaze, but all I could see were old, artificial flower arrangements. The dust was so thick on the flowers that they could have belonged to a jilted bride in a Charles Dickens novel.

"I never knew the people in those pictures. I only knew their daughter. She was what they call a 'change-of-life' baby because her mother was in her fifties when she gave birth to her."

I was listening intently to Olivia Sneed's beginnings. I had heard that her parents had died early in her life, so it made more sense to me because they were so old when they'd had her.

"I'm not sure," Kerry continued, "but you may be getting the wrong idea about the story I'm tellin'." Kerry's eyes studied me.

I found my voice out of the embarrassment of his stare. "Olivia Sneed's parents died. That's why she was sent to live with her aunt in New York. I know the rest of her story," I said proudly.

Kerry didn't seem to understand me at first, but then a look of amusement brightened his features. I wished he liked me. I didn't want this kind man to think of me as a lowly Sneed follower, but I owed some loyalty to the new Lydia.

"You are wrong about the owner of this necklace. Olivia's parents were killed in a car accident." Kerry nodded though his explanation.

I had started to absorb what he was telling me as he continued. "The owner of the necklace has passed on. In fact, the locket was a topic of great concern at her funeral because she never parted from it."

I couldn't imagine having a picture of my dead parents and being buried without it. I'm sure the owner of the locket felt the same way about her treasure as I would have felt about a locket with pictures of my deceased brothers. Suddenly the locket felt heavier in my hands and on my conscience.

My family had always made fun of me for missing obvious things. I would see clues to solving a lead actor's plight in a movie, but I would analyze the separate clues while the rest of my family had put them together to solve the mystery. Maybe that's why I was shocked by Kerry's next words.

"The people in the locket are Nellie Shelton's parents. Even though she didn't wear it to her grave, the last time I saw this chain it was around her neck."

Chapter Eighteen

I kept my hand on the small box with the locket safely inside it as I climbed back into the limo. Lydia looked at me with excited eyes, and Olivia gave an impatient gesture for the driver to move the vehicle.

Lydia surprised me by asking her mother if she would pick up a pizza before going home. Olivia seemed mortified by the idea of eating food she said was prepared by "public hands" and assured Lydia that she would tell the cooks to make a pizza for dinner.

Some of Lydia's excitement evaporated, but she still seemed happy when she whispered, "Did you get it?"

I nodded and tried to pass the bill to her. Kerry had told me he would not take money from the Sneeds, and I didn't insist that the money was mine because I could not lie to Kerry.

Lydia moved her hand to suggest that I could give her the change when we were out of her mother's eyesight, but I didn't think it would matter. Olivia Sneed was two sheets further to the wind than she was when she entered my house.

I wondered how Olivia had gotten the necklace. Kerry had muttered something about Olivia getting anything she wanted. I wondered if the locket had slipped from Nellie's neck and traveled into the hands of someone else. Someone could have picked it up by the river and displayed it in a shop or on the internet. Olivia Sneed was fond of silver, so Bannon Sneed could have purchased it for her, but none of those explanations felt quite right.

"Won't Mummy be so surprised?" Lydia whispered. "Then she can talk to me about the people in the pictures. I'll finally get to learn about my grandparents!"

"Won't your mother tell you about your grandparents?" I asked. The idea that Olivia Sneed would not share her family tree seemed ridiculous.

"I think it hurts her to talk about them," Lydia said.

"Is that why she drinks so much?" I asked and was immediately sorry for it.

Lydia sighed, but she answered my question. "No, I was two or three when she started drinking." Lydia's eyes moved to her mother. Olivia Sneed had placed sunglasses over her eyes, but I could tell she was losing touch with consciousness. Lydia talked slowly and quietly, but her mother wouldn't have heard the conversation if Lydia had been screaming it at her.

"I think it was the stress of coming back to Erwin," Lydia said. "I only have a vague memory of Mummy before she started drinking. She was kind and full of life. You can see a difference in her paintings, too. There are darker colors now."

The limo eased onto the Sneed property as Lydia finished discussing her mother's drinking habits. Olivia Sneed jerked to life as soon as the limo stopped.

"Okay, girls," she said, "it's time to go in and have fun!"

I thought Lydia's mother was going to hang out with us for a while, but she walked upstairs and disappeared as soon as we crossed the threshold. Lydia and I went into the kitchen to make our dinner requests.

Lydia took me around her room, even though I had seen it before, and I faked interest in all her girlie over-priced things. We practiced changing our mood in front of her music board, but we always ended up laughing. Every time Lydia and I laughed, the music board would play "Why Can't We Be Friends?"

Lydia and I stayed in her room a little longer before we were called downstairs for an early dinner. Our mood was lighter and our happiness would have infected any other household.

Lydia and I held hands as we walked to the dining room table. Bannon and Olivia Sneed were already eating, but a cheese pizza sat, unmolested, between two empty place settings.

Olivia drained her wine glass when she saw us. No wonder we were having an early dinner. She would probably pass out before seven o'clock.

I tried to show Lydia's parents the respect they didn't deserve. I was on my best behavior, and I didn't even respond when Bannon Sneed compared my impulsiveness to my brothers' mistakes.

Lydia's parents retired early that evening and didn't bother saying goodnight to Lydia and me. As the moon rose higher, Beth brought in fresh chocolate chip cookies that smelled better than any bakery.

Lydia and I talked into the night, but I could tell something was bothering her. I asked my new Lydia about her mood.

"I didn't tell you everything about Terry Thorpe," Lydia admitted. "I left out a very important part."

"What?" I asked.

"The real reason I started going through my father's records was because I read an article," Lydia said. She twiddled her thumbs. I recognized a very un-Lydia-like thing: She was nervous.

"I read a newspaper clipping my father left on his desk, and it talked about Terry Thorpe. He had been traveling the United States, but he had recently settled in Johnson City and rented a house."

"Okay," I said. I didn't see why Terry Thorpe's activities were newsworthy.

"They found him dead in his house," Lydia said. My blood turned to ice, and my legs felt numb.

"The article said that Terry had hung himself, but I think my father had him killed," Lydia whispered conspiratorially. "I think Terry was going to expose him by telling the cops about the drugs my father had him run."

Now it made more sense why Lydia didn't want to go home. If she had provided me with that nugget of information before her mother showed up at my house, I wouldn't have spent the night with her. I guessed Lydia had known that.

"I'm sorry I brought you here without telling you, but I need your help," Lydia said quickly. She inhaled deeply. "I want you to help me e-mail my father's financial records to the paper that reported Terry Thorpe's death."

"What?" I said, and if Lydia's room hadn't been filled with un-necessary stuff, my voice would have echoed down the hall to her parent's room.

"Everyone knows you are a whiz on the computer, and I need it to look like it didn't come from this house." Lydia pleaded with her eyes.

All the Miller children were computer savvy, especially Ella, but Lydia was the progeny of "Bannon Sneed Technology King". I re-minded Lydia that her father owned a technology company.

"I understand, but I need the best," Lydia said. I knew it took a lot for her to admit, even after her miraculous attitude change, that someone else, especially me, was better than her at anything.

After almost an hour of getting my rebuttals shot down by Lydia's assurances, I finally agreed to help her. I expected to be scared as I walked to the downstairs office, but I felt strangely calm.

No one was awake but Lydia and me. We carefully stepped down the hallway, hearing the snores of the live-in maids, cooks, and groundskeepers.

I assumed Bannon Sneed would lock the door to his office. Apparently, he was not paranoid as I would have been if I were in his position.

"He leaves it open so no one will think he has anything valuable in here," Lydia explained, as if she had read my mind.

We closed the door behind us. I waited for the click of the door-jamb before I flooded the room with light.

It took a moment for my eyes to adjust to the brightness. I had been in the dark for only a couple of minutes, but illusionary shadows darted on the floor, too quick for my eyes to focus on them.

Lydia ran over to her father's computer and turned it on. It was password protected, but Lydia seemed to know the password.

"My father always uses 'money' as his password," Lydia explained. "It's the thing nearest and dearest to him." I wished 'Lydia' was Bannon Sneed's password. Maybe then, Lydia and I would be upstairs eating chocolate and giggling over cute boys.

"Welcome, Supreme Bannon Sneed," a disembodied voice echoed.

Lydia and I jumped, and she reached to turn the volume off on the monitor. I switched off the light, and we waited several minutes before we resumed our mission.

Lydia had already copied and saved all the information she wanted to send in a special file marked: SNEED. She moved out of her father's chair and motioned for me to work.

I went through a series of simple actions. I created a new e-mail account, and I typed up a letter to the editor of the newspaper. I attached Lydia's file and sent it to the e-mail address Lydia provided. I finished by clearing the cache and sent the file to the trash bin on the computer. I permanently deleted all the trash in the recycle bin. I turned off the computer and wiped off the keys and mouse. No one would find our fingerprints.

When I turned to face Lydia, she had her mouth open. She sighed with relief.

"That's why I needed you," she said.

"What are you talking about?" My lack of sleep and fully charged adrenaline had made me irritable.

"You remember to do the things I wouldn't think of doing," she said.

My family would never have complimented me for remembering details. In fact, I was surprised at my thoroughness. I still felt like I was missing one small detail, but I didn't want to risk getting caught.

Lydia and I waited just inside the office door for any sign of life. After we were sure that we were the only people awake, Lydia and I quietly raced to her bedroom.

I thought it would take us forever to fall asleep after the stress of our adventure, but Lydia lost consciousness almost as soon as she placed her head on the pillow. I waited for sleep to enfold me in thoughtlessness, but its anxiety-ending embrace didn't find me.

I kept going over everything Lydia and I had done in Bannon Sneed's office. I thought of every detail. I even slowed down our every action to remember what I knew we had missed.

I finally decided that I was being paranoid. I allowed my racing heart and mind to slow, and I drifted toward numbness. Suddenly, I sprang off Lydia's bed. *I knew what we had forgotten!*

My sudden spring from her bed did not wake Lydia. In fact, she was still in the same sleeping position. I decided I would return to her father's office without her.

I crept down the stairs again and was thankful for the uneventful solo trip to Bannon Sneed's office. My mind was hijacked by paranoia, and my heightened senses would have turned a creak in the floorboards into my capture.

I hurried into Bannon Sneed's office and followed the light of the moon to his desk. I lifted my body to use the edge of my nightshirt to turn the volume back to a position Bannon Sneed would be less likely to question.

I popped out of the office and prepared to sprint back to Lydia's room. A sharp sound startled me, and the voice that followed almost caused me to pass out in the hall.

"Sydney," the voice said.

I was caught! There was no getting around it. Bannon Sneed would drag me back home to my mom, or worse, he would call my grandpa to come get me. Forget a tough-love boot camp, my grandpa would find a disciplinary center and throw me under it!

"Sydney, it's Beth!" the voice whispered.

It took me a moment to process that I wasn't in trouble. My mind kept trying to analyze what she had said. I won my battle to stay conscious, and I walked over to the dark feminine shape.

"What did you forget?" Beth asked. "I watched you and Lydia come down and do something. Was it something about my brother?"

It took me a second to understand, but I quickly wrapped my mind around Beth's questions. Of course Terry Thorpe had been Beth's brother because Mr. Hernandez was her father.

Beth continued when I didn't speak. "Terry was a weasel, but he wouldn't have committed suicide. I think *someone* had Terry killed because he requested more money. I told him not to do it, but he moved back here and made threats. There are certain people you don't threaten."

Requested more money for what? For running drugs? What kind of threats?

I could tell Beth required a response. I nodded my head in the darkness. I didn't trust my voice.

"I think something is about to happen," she continued. The three-dimensional shadow head turned to the side. "I get very strong feelings sometimes, and I've learned to follow them."

Beth pulled a piece of paper from her side. It was slightly bent, but still held its rectangular shape.

"This was her best and only friend," Beth said cryptically. She did not tell me anything else, and my thoughts were still frozen from my fear of being captured.

I mechanically took the piece of paper and realized as Beth turned to walk away that it was not a piece of paper. Beth had given me a picture.

Chapter Nineteen

I looked at the picture more closely. The light over the bathroom sink illuminated the entire room, but I still thought I was missing something.

I had run up the steps to Lydia's room but had quietly entered her room. Tip-toeing to her bathroom, I shut the door before I turned on the light. I had let my eyes adjust to the brightness before I looked at the picture.

Two women embraced and stared into the camera. Their excited faces filled the photograph.

I brought the photograph closer to my face. The place it was taken was unrecognizable, but I could tell the image had been captured when dark black eyeliner and skyscraper bangs were popular.

I recognized one woman immediately. I had met her through the eyes of her adoring toddler. Nellie's beautiful oval face and blonde hair brought out the rest of her plain, yet flawless features. Her eyes seemed to lock with mine from her frozen place in time.

The other woman was harder to place. Half of her head was out of the picture. It looked like her hair had been dyed blond, but her eyebrows were painted on with the darkest liner I'd ever seen. The red eye had not been taken out of the photograph before it was developed, so her eyes could have been green or brown.

So this was Nellie's only friend, I thought. I tucked the picture into the elastic of my sleep pants and opened the door into Lydia's bedroom.

The sun had peeked over the mountain while I was in the bathroom, so Lydia's room had a soft, blue glow. I closed the curtains and climbed back into bed. I removed the picture from the elastic band of my pants and placed it on a pile of my stuff by the bed.

Lydia's bed was so large that we could sleep without touching, but I needed to feel her body heat, so I scooted toward the center of the bed until my back was to Lydia's back. I didn't want to be alone in a place that held so many secrets.

Beth didn't wake us until two o'clock that afternoon. Bannon Sneed had gone into town to meet a client, and Olivia was playing with her wine bottles, so no one but the staff noticed that Lydia and I had slept late.

Beth came into Lydia's room, pulled the curtains open, and left before I could say a word. I looked at the clock and congratulated myself on getting seven hours of sleep.

Lydia stretched and yawned. She looked at me with her beautiful blue eyes, and I was reminded of the movie stars on television that always looked fresh and composed after sleeping.

The rest of the world, especially me, could sleep eight hours and wake up with dragon breath and tangled hair. Lydia's locks looked like they had been smoothed by angels in her sleep. I was amazed and disgusted simultaneously.

Beth came back into the room carrying trays of fruit and toast. Fresh squeezed orange juice left pulpy evidence of its freshness along the sides of the glass pitcher.

Lydia and I ate greedily after Beth placed the food on large silver trays that fit easily over our laps. I had never eaten in my bed, but Lydia must have breakfasted alone in her room many times because she seemed to be used to the location of the meal.

"Your mother will be here by three o'clock," Beth said as she balanced our trays. I jumped off the bed and pulled the door open wider so Beth could get through easily.

I had been thinking of redoing my nails until Beth told me my mom was on her way. I knew it must be close to three, and a quick glance at the clock told me I was right.

I ran around Lydia's room throwing my clothes and makeup into my plastic shopping bag. I stopped when Lydia put her hand on my arm.

I looked at the hand holding my arm. A set of pink handles moved from Lydia's hand to mine. I stared down at the shiny letters that claimed the bag's signature design.

"You're going to need a better bag if we have more sleepovers," Lydia said. She smiled awkwardly, like she was afraid I wouldn't appreciate her gift.

I couldn't find words. I held the bag to my chest and hugged my friend tightly.

My grandpa would have bought me a bag if he'd thought I needed it, but Lydia's gift was much more special. I dumped the things I'd already gathered from the plastic bag into the signature bag.

I hadn't thought of telling Lydia about the picture. My friend's next words were certainly a game-changer, and I didn't know what to do next.

Lydia bent over to pick up my clothes and had instead plucked up the picture Beth had given me hours ago. I opened my mouth to tell Lydia about my early-morning mission, but the words died in my throat.

Lydia scrutinized the picture for a moment. She turned it to the side and looked at me.

"How did you get a picture of Mummy?" she asked.

Lydia waited for an answer. Beth had left the room, and Lydia and I were alone.

I closed the open door and rushed over to Lydia. She looked at me with skepticism for the first time since she'd returned from her chosen suspension.

"Beth gave me that picture last night," I said. I explained my mission to cover all evidence of our presence by readjusting the volume on Bannon Sneed's computer monitor.

Lydia nodded, but she looked unconvinced. "How did Beth get a picture of Mummy?"

"Do you mean *that*," I pointed to the woman I didn't recognize, "is your mother?"

Lydia gave me a look like I was in need of a mental examination. "Of course it is," she said.

"It was before the long years of drinking," Beth said from the door. She had soundlessly opened the door and crept back in as Lydia and I were examining the picture.

"She was once very beautiful," Beth continued. "The drinking destroyed her hair and skin and robbed the brightness from her eyes."

"What were you doing with a picture of Mummy?" Lydia repeated. She seemed unable to move past the most obvious questions.

I didn't hear Beth's answer because my mom appeared in Lydia's doorway. She poked her head around the door and stepped into the room.

"I was waiting patiently, but no one ever told me what was going on," my mom said. I somehow doubted that my mom had been waiting long. She was the opposite of patient, so she probably waited a minute, and then set off in the direction Beth had gone.

"I'm sorry," Beth said to me. "I was here to tell you that your mother had arrived."

I smiled apologetically at Beth. She nodded her understanding, and I was reminded of how tolerant she would have to be in order to work in the House of Sneed.

Beth backed out of Lydia's room, and I picked up the rest of my stuff. I didn't take the picture from Lydia. After all, even though Beth had given the picture to me, it was a picture of Lydia's mother.

I looked at Lydia pointedly. "I'll call you later," I said.

Lydia nodded absentmindedly. I left her standing in her room holding the picture and looking into space.

Chapter Twenty

"Did you have fun?" my mom asked. Her smile indicated she knew something was going on, but she didn't really want to hear about it.

"I had a great time," I told her and settled into my teenage silence.

I ran up to my room as soon as I stepped into my house and sat at the end of Ella's bed. She was off in one of her trances, so I waited for her to notice me.

In less than a minute, Ella asked, "What do you want?"

I took offense at my sister's question and tone. It upset me she was so abrasive after we'd had some time apart.

Despite my injured feelings, I told Ella about my experience at Lydia's house. Her face did not betray the slightest emotion.

"What do you think?" I asked my sister. "Who should I talk to next?"

I loved sharing my experiences with my sister, and even though she was younger than me, I still listened to her advice when I asked her opinion. I felt uneasy about her response, though, like I had missed something crucial in my absence.

My sister rubbed her hands down her thighs to straighten the non-existent wrinkles in her jeans. She appeared irritated, like she'd had to explain something a hundred times to a dense person.

"I cannot believe you cry and moan and complain about mysteries you can solve," Ella said. "In all this time, did it ever occur to you to just READ THEIR MINDS!"

My sister never yelled. When she raised her voice, I was so surprised that I slipped off her bed and onto the floor.

I recovered myself quickly and shouted back, "I'm sorry that my freaky abilities aren't at the front of my mind! I don't make them the primary focus of the day by staring into empty space!" I imitated a wide-eyed, crazy version of one of my sister's trances.

Our screaming match had immediately attracted the attention of my mom, and she ran into the room. She grabbed me and dragged me into the hall. My mom seemed to briefly contemplate separating Ella and me by placing me in my brothers' room, but she quickly reconsidered and yanked me into her room instead.

"Not a word!" she said before slamming the door. My mom repeated her command to Ella before she closed my sister's door. I figured my mom must have heard our screaming and the content of our argument. She may have been right outside our door, knowing that I would talk to Ella about my sleepover with Lydia. My mom probably thought she'd hear about the new technology at the Sneed house, not the new Sneed mystery.

I stared at the walls of my mom's room for almost thirty minutes. I ran over all the minds I could have touched at the Sneed mansion to find my answers and cursed myself for trying to stay normal.

I rolled over on my mom's bed and looked at the other wall. The light outside was fading, and I wondered how long Ella and I would be in "time out." Ella's day was uninterrupted. She could stare at a wall all day, but I wanted to look for some answers to the questions rolling in my mind.

My gaze fell upon the phone on my mom's bedside table. I thought of all the people I could call, and my mind naturally landed on an obvious choice.

I quietly picked up the phone. It made a small beep, and the numbers clicked as I touched them and resounded off the walls of the soundless room. I dialed the numbers under my mom's pillow to muffle the noise.

I faced the wall away from the door so that my voice would be less likely to carry down the hall. I cupped my hand over my mouth and around the bottom of the phone.

My grandpa picked up on the second ring. "Chief Conner Murphy."

"Grandpa," I whispered.

"Why are you talkin' so low?" he demanded.

"I need to ask you something."

"Then speak up," he said. "I can barely hear you."

I could hear the police scanner and papers rustling in the background. My grandpa was at the police station.

"Who found Nellie Shelton after she was killed?" I asked.

The silence on the other end of the line told me that my grandpa was stunned by my question. I was about to repeat myself when my grandpa cleared his throat.

"You need to stay out of that," my grandpa began. "I know you've been talkin' to Lydia again, and I—"

"Will you please do what it seems no one else can do and answer my question?" I spoke a little more loudly than I intended, and I thought I heard the scrape of chair legs against the kitchen tile on the floor beneath me.

There was a brief pause. "Nellie's only friend was Olivia Sneed," my grandpa said. "Olivia was the one—"

"That's enough!" My mom yelled loudly enough for my grandpa to hear her.

My mom opened her mouth again, probably to say, 'Time out means time out,' but I stopped her. I had a lot of pent-up emotion in me, and I was tired of my mom's passive-aggressive parenting. I was upset about so many things that, when I spoke, words relevant to my current predicament were abandoned. I said what was really going on in my home, and it surprised both my mom *and* me.

"Haven't you lived in a house of darkness long enough to realize that there are bigger things than your feelings!" I screamed. I lowered my tone, but my voice still echoed off the walls. "My father and brothers are dead, and you knew they were gifted. Now you're considering throwing Ella to the wolves because she doesn't act like a *normal* child? How could she be normal when the dead harass her at school, in her room, and even in the shower! She's got a talent, too, even if it doesn't fall into what you think a *normal* girl should be like."

My mom tightened her fists at her sides. "You try to hold a family together when all they want to do is fall apart!" she screamed at me.

I didn't plan to back down. I did the one thing I'd been avoiding since preschool. I read my mom's mind.

I responded to the surface thoughts I caught floating in her brain. I didn't want to dig too deeply and risk losing the argument.

"Ella scares you," I began. "She has a power I don't fully understand, but I love her. You're not giving the mental facility the go-ahead to collect her from school. No one will ever forgive you! *Why don't you just go into that room and tell Ella how you feel?*"

I hadn't known my mom was going to admit my sister to the mental institution. My mom had decided while I was at my sleepover. She had caught Ella having a heated discussion with the air.

My mom stood with her head in her hands and cried. She still held the end of a forgotten pen she had been using before she heard me on the phone. It bobbed up and down with her sobs, like it understood and validated my mom's tears.

"Ella's going to be labeled a 'Crazy Miller'," my mom said. Her hands muffled her voice, but I understood every word.

"I'm labeled a 'Crazy Miller' and don't actively use my gift!" I declared.

I had admitted that I had an extra ability, and my mom acted like she hadn't heard me. I guess it was better for her to ignore my last words rather than to realize that both her daughters thought they had extra-sensory capabilities.

"Your grandfather and I thought a nice rest would help Ella get back on track," my mom said. She wiped the tears off her cheeks.

"What do you mean?" I said incredulously. "Ella has *always* been this way. It's just that she's turned from a melancholy child to a despondent preteen. You didn't seem to really worry until she started acting like most teenagers, who sit in their rooms all day. Maybe you'd be less concerned if she were staring at the wall *and* listening for other-worldly messages in radio static."

"I just want to have a *normal* family!" my mom cried.

"You've chosen the wrong men if you wanted the thrill of your week to be the ladies' circle at church," I said. I rolled back over and faced the wall.

My mom stopped crying, and I shifted my head so that I could see her face. I mentally recounted my words and realized my mistake. I had said "men."

"You act like I *chose* Bryan," my mom said. "Your grandfather thrust him on me, and I didn't know how to deal with it. I don't actively seek out people with problems. Besides," she said, narrowing her eyes and cocking her head, "at least the men I dated *liked* me."

That was a low blow. I couldn't believe my mom was referring to the night I had kissed Christian. I guess the gloves were off.

I hadn't thought about Christian for a while, but my mom's words stung me. She wasn't supposed to bring up things to hurt me. She was supposed to act like a caring, considerate mother.

My mom and I looked at each other in silence. I heard a pop outside that sounded like our old metal mailbox had been opened and closed.

"Look," I said, deciding to act mature, "this isn't getting us anywhere. Let's get Ella and have a family meeting. We'll air out all our problems, and maybe we can start acting more like the family you want."

My mom had scrunched up her nose at the idea of talking about things she would rather sweep under the rug, but she seemed to like my idea of acting like a normal family. It looked as if we were ready to have a big discussion.

I knew a couple of things about my gift, even though I tried to deny that I could read minds. One of the most exciting things I'd learned when I was young was that I could tune into a person's mind in the same way I could adjust the station and the volume on a radio. When I was a toddler, I could hear my mom think about Christmas presents and then turn the volume down on her thoughts and listen as my father planned a surprise evening out with my mom.

I turned up the volume of my mom's thoughts. She was trying to decide if she wanted Ella to know that she and Grandpa had been planning to get her mental condition evaluated. My mom didn't want to explain herself, but she finally decided that it was a small price to pay to attempt the appearance of a normal family.

My mom nodded her acceptance of my plan, and I rolled off the bed. I followed my mom to the bedroom I shared with my sister. My mom knocked, but I rolled my eyes and walked into my room.

I looked at Ella's usual spot on the bed, but she wasn't there. A small indention in the bedspread showed Ella had been sitting in the same spot for quite some time. I felt a cool breeze, and my insides froze when I realized that our bedroom window was open.

I ran to the window and looked out. I saw no sign of my sister, but I could see my grandpa's cruiser parked in our driveway. *At least he's here, because we're going to need him to help track down Ella.*

My mom had already made it down the stairs and out the door. My grandpa was inside his cruiser, talking on his police radio, with his door open.

I heard my mom scream, and all the blood ran out of my body and left me cold. I forced myself to stay conscious and on my feet.

I hurried toward my mom's screams and found her on the front lawn over Ella's body. I thought my sister was dead. She was lying at an awkward angle, and my mind immediately calculated the possibility of a fatal twelve-foot fall from our porch awning to the unforgiving ground.

"Don't move her," my grandpa yelled from his cruiser. "She could have broken her neck."

My mom jumped at the sound of my grandpa's voice. She turned her frightened eyes to the sound of his voice, and then she hugged herself and stood over her injured daughter.

I could pick up random thoughts from Ella's mind, so I knew she was alive. She had probably either passed out or she was in the limbo between awakened pain and blissful unconsciousness.

My grandpa ran from his cruiser to my sister. He bent down on one knee and then crouched down next to Ella's mouth. He was listening for her breath. I had a feeling that he had already assessed that Ella was alive before he radioed for help, but he couldn't handle waiting for the ambulance and feeling useless.

"She's still alive," I said.

My grandpa gave me a sympathetic look that said, *Of course you want her to be.* I looked back at him, my explanation frozen on my lips.

"Get away from her!" my mom suddenly shouted at her father. "Everyone I love dies whenever *you* come around."

My mom collapsed after her screaming fit and wailed into her hands. More of our neighbors streamed out of their homes, curious about the commotion.

The ambulance arrived five minutes after my grandpa phoned in the incident. The EMS were a couple of blocks from our house, so I wasn't surprised by the reaction time. I was amazed that they gauged the situation and had my sister on the way to the hospital in less time than it had taken them to drive to our home.

My mom rode in the ambulance with Ella, and my grandpa and I tore down the street in his cruiser. I watched the lights on the ambulance and tried not to think that I could be the only living Miller child.

"Don't worry about Ella," my grandpa said. He looked like he needed to take his own advice. His face was pale, and his knuckles were white from the grip he held on the steering wheel.

"What were you doing at our house?" I asked.

"You hung up on me, Little Lady. I had to make sure you were okay."

I opened my mouth to tell him that my mom had interrupted our call and decided against it. I had never been happier about one of my mom's outbursts. It may have saved my sister's life.

My grandpa followed the ambulance until it pulled up to the emergency room doors. Men and women in scrubs ran out to help carry my sister's stretcher. My mom was whispering rapidly in Ella's ear as she bent over my sister's motionless form. I hoped it was a sign that Ella was conscious.

My grandpa parked his cruiser in the first available space and turned off the motor. He tossed me the keys and flew out of the vehicle.

I had never seen him move so fast. My grandpa was still in great shape, but I had always assumed that his age had slowed him down. I certainly wouldn't bet against my grandpa's physical abilities again.

I looked at the shiny keys in my lap and tried to compose myself. The steady ding of my grandpa's open door reminded me I needed to hurry. What was left of my family was counting on my presence for shared comfort and concern.

Why was Ella trying to fly from the safety of our home? My mind immediately supplied an answer I didn't want to accept. *Ella heard you say that her mother and grandfather were going to have her mentally evaluated.*

I hadn't intentionally read my mom's mind in a long time, and I was not surprised with the results. I ended up hurting the person who encouraged me to use my terrible gift.

Ella had gotten scared and fallen from the roof as a newborn chick tumbles from a nest before it's time to fly. *Why had I thought spilling my mom's thoughts would benefit our situation?*

I got out of my grandpa's cruiser and slammed the door. I ran around the cruiser and toyed briefly with climbing into the driver's seat and driving away.

I closed my grandpa's door and locked the vehicle. I knew running away was not the answer. Look what had happened to my sister when she had tried to escape the madness in her home. It still appealed to me in a way I could not describe.

I walked up the short sidewalk to the automatic door of the hospital. I savored the silence like the last bites of a scrumptious meal. Doctors could be shouting orders to nurses and patients might be screaming their final complaints, but no sound escaped the building and traveled to my ears.

The door slid open for me when it picked up my presence, and I walked into the bustle of the emergency room. Receptionists typed information hastily, and padded feet pushed beds and chairs on wheels down the hall.

I had been to the emergency room a couple of times with my family. My brothers had suffered some broken bones, and I had once had a fever too high to ignore, but I had never noticed the faces of the other people in the waiting room.

Several sad expressions glanced up at me from their chosen places. They had a brief flash of hope, but it quickly disappeared when they realized I was not the nurse who would bring them news about their loved ones.

I took a seat next to the soda and snack machines, away from any other person in the room. I felt and heard a slight buzz from the blinking overhead light.

I pulled my arms close to my body and shivered. Hospitals were usually kept a few degrees cooler than comfortable to help prevent the spread of germs. I criticized myself for forgetting my coat, and then I cursed myself for thinking of my comfort when my sister could be dying.

I had a brief jolt of terror when I realized I had not locked the door. In fact, I didn't think I had even shut the front door. Several neighbors had gathered around our yard to take in the scene. I hoped one of them was nice enough to close our door and watch for intruders.

My grandpa entered the waiting room and scanned the area for me before he realized I was in the far corner. He crossed the room and pulled me up gently, but firmly, from my seat. He wordlessly guided me out of the room and down a brightly lit hallway.

I noticed the antenna on the ceiling. I figured the antenna helped the hospital use electronic communication without interference with life-supporting and monitoring machines.

We walked down another hallway, and my grandpa slowed a little. He stopped outside a closed wooden door.

"Your sister is fine." I heard relief in his voice, but his eyes were still strained. "She broke her arm, but she is refusing to talk to anyone."

He must have assumed that I could get Ella to speak. I had never been able to get my sister to do anything I asked, so I doubted I could get her to talk to me.

My grandpa opened the door, but he did not go into the room with me. I looked back at him questioningly, and he shooed me into the room.

The lights were off, and the soft glow of the moonlight illuminated my sister's bed. My mom was a dark silhouette in the corner.

My mom cried softly in a chair under the television. My sister lay in the bed across from her. A plastic cast that reminded me of a hockey mask held Ella's left arm.

Ella was awake, but she was back in a trance, seeming to stare right through her sobbing mother. Anyone who looked in on the pair would assume that my sister was staring daggers of blame for her condition at her mother.

"Mom," I spoke.

My mom jumped up at the sound of my voice. Her face seemed sweaty in the low light, but it was really wet with tears.

I caressed my mom's mind and found that she blamed herself for Ella's condition. *No surprise there.* It dismayed me to discover that my mom also blamed *me* for my sister's unsuccessful flight from our porch awning.

My mom did not admit that she believed in any of her family's paranormal powers, but her nagging intuition would not let her dismiss the idea entirely. My mom thought that I should have sensed Ella's intentions and stopped my sister before her idea led to her injury. She didn't know that I couldn't have read Ella's thoughts because I had focused my abilities on her.

My mom looked like she wanted to speak, but she could not express herself in words. Finally, she got out of her chair and walked out of the room rapidly.

I calmly sat down in the chair my mom had recently vacated and bravely looked into my sister's stare. Ella showed no sign that she was aware of the change, but I caught a snatch of her thoughts.

"—rid of her, too."

I jolted back from Ella's mind. That was something else. That was not my sister.

A chill overtook me as I realized I was not alone with my sister in her room. Something malevolent had followed Ella in her distress.

It was almost impossible to describe the owner of the thought I had glimpsed. I had felt that it was evil and hopeless with no real shape in the present.

"Ella!" I said sharply. "Get back here now!" I was frightened, and I reacted the way my mom did when she was scared. I got angry.

My sister had not physically moved, but her mind was not in the room. I was terrified, and I should not have crossed the distance to Ella and shaken her so violently, but I felt relieved when her eyes cleared and focused on my face.

"Go away!" Ella said. She tried to push me away with her uninjured hand, but I moved back before she could touch me.

"I'm tired of this crap!" I said. I was still anxious about the voice I had heard through my connection with Ella. It was dark outside, and anything paranormal was exaggerated by my mind once the sun set and the lights were out.

I bravely tried to reach out with my mind, but a wall of trees blocked my efforts. The trees bore a resemblance to the forest surrounding Pale Woods Academy.

"Get out of our minds!" Ella barked.

I retreated from the barrier and glared at my sister. "What do you mean *our* minds?"

"I mean that if I am crazy, I am going to be crazy all the time!" my sister yelled. "I am going to embrace the good things and bad things that come with my gift, and I am going to help people along the way. You attract people to you, Sydney, so it is easy for you. Mother calls you a people pleaser, but you really just read people without knowing you are doing it. You get the living, I get the dead, so do not jump into my mind like you have suddenly earned the right to read my thoughts."

I kept expecting my grandpa or a nurse to run into the room to see about the commotion, but my sister and I were left alone. The ticking clock was the only sound in the room.

I had never thought of our gifts as parallel talents, but Ella had shown me a new perspective. We stared at each other; two sides of the same coin.

"Why did you jump off the roof?" I asked. "You could have sneaked down the steps and out the front door."

My words switched Ella's mood and facial expression. She might not let me read her mind, but I could still read her body language.

Ella looked down at her uninjured arm. An IV pumped fluids into my sister so that she would stay hydrated and medicine would go directly through her body if her arm developed an infection.

"I did not think about that," Ella admitted. "My goal was to get out of the house as fast as I could."

"What then?" I asked. My new line of questions made me feel like the older sister again. "What were you going to do? You didn't have money, clothes, or food."

"I had not thought that far," my sister said irritably.

"Action before thought is *my* strong suit," I told my sister, "and you can't take that from me." I finished with a smile to show that I was joking, but Ella continued to stare at her IV.

"How did you turn it off?" Ella asked.

I didn't pretend like her question confused me. "I didn't embrace my gift like you. I only used it occasionally to help with the family. Once I realized that speaking about our powers was taboo, it was easy to pretend that I was normal. I never wanted to read people's minds anyway."

"Was I supposed to enjoy talking to the dead?" Sarcasm and hurt laced Ella's words.

"People don't flock to me," I said, drawing on my sister's earlier words. "That is total nonsense."

"This is where you lose the discussion," she said. "You do not see it because you are so used to it, but you can talk to people about anything. You catch brief pictures of their thoughts, so you pick up on any conversation in their mind."

My sister was wrong. I was popular at school, and it was easy to talk to people, but I followed the thread of their *verbal* conversations.

"Well, move over psychic mediums, Sydney Miller's on the scene," I joked. "Do you think I could get a spot on a talk show?"

"You think it is silly, but you could really help some people," Ella whispered. "I was thinking you would have to do it quietly, like counseling troubled teens."

"I think I'll set my goals a little higher, like running a business or working in a place like this," I said. I was still trying to get my sister to laugh and needed to lighten the atmosphere after I'd brushed the presence of Ella's unseen visitor.

Ella thought I meant I was focused on making more money. "Oh, I forgot. You want to be rich so you and Christian can live in a big house next to Lydia."

Ella had wounded me, and she knew it. I stopped trying to make her laugh, and I let my sister's depression infect me.

"Your assessment of me is wrong," I said. "Christian doesn't like me. I guess I didn't know what to say or how to look to capture his interest."

It hurt me to admit it, but Christian would never like me. After his breakup with Lydia, he went to great lengths to make sure we were never alone together.

"You do not see *anything.* Have you ever read his mind? Christian does not know what he wants. I could tell he was confused. I think he had honestly planned to ask you out when he took you for the walk, but he chickened out. Lydia figured he would."

My stomach dropped to the floor. "What?" I asked. I could feel an angry smile climb my cheeks. "What did you do, Ella?" I asked through gritted teeth.

Ella became defensive and refused to speak. I was tired, irritable, and crazy with hormones and emotions. I grabbed my sister's broken arm before I could stop myself.

An electric pain shot through me. I backed away from my sister's bed, holding my hand.

What was that?

"Do not touch me!" Ella said vehemently. "He does not like it!"

"*Who*, Ella? *Who* doesn't want me to touch you? *Who* keeps you locked in a world away from happiness? What evil force keeps you from being you?"

Ella seemed to consider telling me everything. I could see that her secrets were making her weary. Finally, she gave up and told me the answer to another question.

"I knew Christian was going to ask you out because he told me he was going to," Ella said. "He said that he thought about you all the time."

I noticed my mouth was open, and I closed it sharply. "Then why didn't he ask me out?"

"Because of me," she admitted. "I told him you had not seen him around other girls, so you would always question his feelings for you. I told him to show you how good he could be to a girlfriend so that you would not lose interest in him."

I felt too betrayed to find words to say to my sister. Ella looked up at me, and I could tell she wanted to say something else. *Oh no, there's more?*

"I called Lydia when you and Christian went for your walk," she continued. "I told her you really liked Christian, but he could not pick between you and her. I made it seem as though Christian was conflicted. Lydia made sure that she grabbed Christian first by sending him a text message about you during the walk. Do not ask me about the contents of the message. I only know that she sent it. She never liked him, but she did not want you to have him. Lydia and I were a lot alike. We were both scared we would lose you to Christian."

I know I should have thought it was sweet, but I was enraged. "So, once again Sydney's the fool! Everyone knows what's going on but me. Well, at least nothing's changed!"

Suddenly I wished that I *was* the only remaining Miller child. I expected to feel bad for my thoughts, but the guilt never came.

"I hope you suffer alone with your deception and manipulations," I shouted at my sister. "You're more like your mother than you think. I'll leave you both alone with only your ghosts and voices to keep you company."

I walked out of the room briskly. I heard Ella make a strangled sound, but I didn't turn back. I hoped she was crying. It would be more of a reaction than I'd seen from her in a long time.

I tore open the door and was surprised to see my grandpa standing on the other side. He fumbled for words, and I broke down. My knees buckled, and he caught me before I landed on the unforgiving floor. I wailed my misery into his chest. I didn't feel my grandpa pick me up, but I knew when I was being carried.

My mom's worried voice joined my surroundings, but I didn't look up. I heard the automatic doors swoosh and felt the pleasant tickle of the chilly night air. My grandpa carried me through the parking lot and sat me down on the trunk of his cruiser.

He looked weary in the street light's illumination. Lines of age and worry caressed his face.

"Sydney," my grandpa said. "I'm tired of all the drama, and I know you are too. Would you like to come live with me for a little while?"

I felt like my grandpa had read my mind. I had every intention of asking him to stay at his house permanently, but he had beaten me to it.

"Yes," I said. Joy was bordering my sadness, like when the sun comes out during a rainstorm.

"We'll go buy you some clothes for school tomorrow," my grandpa said. "We can go to your house and gather your personal effects after you get out of school."

I had to smile at the way my grandpa phrased things. "Personal effects" was a category police officers used to describe the items they took from a criminal before he or she went to jail or from a dead body. The criminal would get his or her *personal effects* when he or she was released, and the family of a deceased relative would receive their loved one's *personal effects* after a body had been positively identified.

I nodded my approval of his plan, and my grandpa picked me up off the trunk. He carried me like a baby to the passenger side, opened my door, and closed it after he gently placed me in the seat.

"What about Mom and Ella?" I asked after my grandpa had started the cruiser.

"They have enough to deal with for now," he said with a wink. "We'll just let them sort it out on their own."

I never questioned whether my mom would agree to my move to my grandpa's house. My grandpa would rob her of every argument if she tried to keep me from living with him.

I took a deep breath of freedom and found a weight had been lifted. I hadn't even realized that I had been carrying a load on my shoulders.

I noticed my grandpa was sitting a little straighter, and a smile traced his lips. He had dealt with my mom and her ghosts for over twenty years. Maybe he felt the same way.

I tried not to feel guilty about embracing my liberty. I was over-joyed that I was going to live with my grandpa, but I felt as though my place was in the hospital with my sister.

I put my hand over the hand my grandpa wasn't using to steer the cruiser, and we drove out of the hospital parking lot. I convinced myself that I was moving into a new phase. I never could have guessed the horror of the next chapter of my life.

Chapter Twenty-One

My head felt light with the news of my move to my grandpa's house. I wanted to tell Lydia and invite her to stay the night over the weekend.

My grandpa gave me my mom's old bedroom, and I took down the rest of her old posters and moved the bed from the far wall to the area next to the window. I imagined that I would feel the morning sun on my face as it rose in the east.

My grandpa knocked on my door as I was preparing for bed. I told him to come in, but he waited for a moment before he eased open the door.

His face registered a look of shock as he noticed the changes I had made, but he quickly shrugged away his surprise and smiled. "It's starting to look good," he said.

I tried to pretend that I didn't notice my grandpa's eyes spot the differences in the room he'd sought to preserve. His eyes wandered to the places I had made the smallest changes.

My grandpa glanced at the posters I had carefully rolled up and placed in the corner behind the door. I was making the room my own, but I wasn't trashing the things that had hung on the walls or littered the floor when my mom had lived with my grandpa. After all, I wasn't heartless. My grandpa could take the items I moved out of the room and store them in the basement.

I could tell that he was relieved. I knew my grandpa used the stuff in my mom's old room as a connection to the past they'd shared.

"Maybe we could go get you some paint this weekend," my grandpa said. He walked over and sat on the bed I now occupied. His weight caused my position on the mattress to shift. "You can do whatever you need to make this room your own."

I knew it took a lot for my grandpa to offer to help me change my mom's room. "We could paint it together," I suggested.

"Well, I have to work all weekend," my grandpa said. I understood how my mom must have felt during her adolescence.

"Have you talked to Mom yet?" I asked.

A strange look danced across my grandpa's face. "I have talked to her," he said flatly. He patted my hand. "She said that she won't stand in your way."

I couldn't help feeling a bubble of joy fill my insides. I tried to keep an impartial expression, but my mouth wouldn't let me maintain my neutrality.

"We are going to have the best times," I said hurriedly. "And we'll be the best of friends."

My grandpa smiled, pulling away most of his wrinkles. I was supposed to be at an age where I was pushing my elders away with both hands. Instead, I considered my grandpa to be one of my closest friends.

My grandpa hugged me, and I was amazed that a rugged, macho police chief could be so gentle and loving. He rocked me slowly back and forth, and I listened to the rhythm of his heartbeat. I fell asleep in his embrace, and I didn't wake until the alarm beside my bed announced the morning.

I was disoriented at first, but I smelled my grandpa's familiar laundry detergent and I remembered the previous day. It seemed crazy that so much had happened in such a short time.

I turned on the light in the bathroom. I noticed a note stuck to the bathroom mirror. *Yep, Grandpa remembered what it was like to live with a teenage girl.*

He had written the note on plain notebook paper and stuck to the mirror with duct tape. I read my grandpa's messy print.

```
Little Lady,

I had to go to work this morning, but I'll be
back to take you to school. Doughnuts are on
the table and juice is in the fridge. All you
need should be in the bathroom.

Love, Grandpa
```

My grandpa had carefully laid out all my beauty products with their labels facing forward. My new outfit was hanging on a rack beside a fresh towel.

I showered and went through the long routine that has been perfected by teenagers since the beginning of time. My grandpa had bought me the least embarrassing outfit I could find at a twenty-four-hour store, and he made the mistake of asking if I needed anything else.

The word *need* has a different meaning for teenagers. Adults *need* food, clothes, and a toothbrush. Teenagers *need* chips and chocolate, outfits with designer tags, and everything from the beauty and hair care section.

My grandpa followed me with the shopping cart as I threw in all the things I felt I needed to have to prepare for school. I didn't give a thought about the backpack at my house, full of necessary school supplies, but I threw makeup, lotion, a straightener, and perfume in the cart.

I paid no attention to the price tags on the items I had my grandpa push to the register. A lady with hair the color of storm clouds forced herself to greet us. The cart was only about halfway full, but the total was more than my mom made at her job in a week.

My grandpa did not say a word about the price of the things I *needed*. After all, he had once raised a teenage girl.

I think the female species gets away with a lot. Most men have a "don't ask, don't tell" policy when they deal with women or girls with whom they are not romantically involved. My grandpa had ensured that, by buying me everything I said I *needed*, he would not be asked to go back out and collect embarrassing feminine products. He, like many other men, would have paid any price for that bit of insurance against humiliation.

I slowly went through the ritual of straightening and curling my hair. Then I painted my face with cosmetics that guaranteed the user would not get unwanted blemishes from the products.

I ate my doughnuts while I read a teen magazine my grandpa had left on the table. He had bought my least favorite brand of juice, but I choked it down. I cared too much about my grandpa's feelings to let him know if I disliked something he got for me.

I heard a horn blow as I was brushing my teeth. I spat out the blue, soapy film into the sink and rinsed my mouth.

I finally realized that I didn't have paper, pencils, or pens. I spotted a pen on the kitchen counter. It was probably the pen my grandpa had used to write the note he stuck to my bathroom mirror. I pushed it into the left front pocket of my jeans and ran out the kitchen door.

My grandpa said that he had to hurry back to the station, so he drove very quickly, leaving my stomach behind at every curve in the road. I walked into the academy within ten minutes of climbing into the cruiser.

I flew into my classroom, carried by the wind of change. I was so high on my new situation that I didn't feel the tension in the air.

Lydia cried in her seat. A dozen girls had crowded around Lydia, hoping to gain her favor by comforting her.

I walked over to my friend's seat without realizing my feet were moving. Lydia looked up at me with tears rolling down her face. Her beautiful blue eyes looked darker against their red-rimmed borders.

"Beth is dead," she said, and a fresh wave of tears consumed her.

The news shocked me into silence. I don't know how long I stood over Lydia as she cried. A slamming locker brought me out of my numbness.

I had only known Beth for a couple of months, but she had seemed so young and full of life. I couldn't imagine a heart attack or an accident blowing out the flame of her existence.

I crouched next to Lydia and rested my head against her side. She turned toward me, and we embraced.

I didn't know I was crying until Lydia let go of me and I stared at a damp spot on her shirtsleeve. My sadness was mirrored in Lydia's face.

Mrs. Hughes pretended to prepare for the next lesson. She was actually giving us time to express our grief.

"Would you like to see the counselor?" Ms. Hughes asked after we had comforted each other for a few minutes. She must have realized that our teenage emotions would not relax.

I would have loved to talk to Mrs. Thomas. I hadn't shared time with her in several months, but Lydia firmly shook her head.

"I'm fine," she said in a small voice. She nodded at me, and I knew I was supposed to go to my desk.

The Millers swept things under the rug, and the Sneeds didn't express their troubles to people they considered beneath them. I was used to pretending that I wasn't drowning in grief, so it was easier for me than it would have been for most girls my age to go to my seat and appear ready to learn.

I painfully got to my feet. My knees were stiff from squatting next to Lydia's seat for so long, and I heard them pop as I stood up. My stiffness went away quickly when I sat.

I could not pay attention to the morning lessons. My eyes kept moving to the cold outdoors. I thought of how Beth's body was now as cold as the falling snow.

Lydia had not told me what caused Beth's death. I went through several scenarios. I thought of the woman I believed was Beth's mother. *Would she regret getting Beth a job that had led to a fatal accident?*

I realized the school day was a complete waste at lunch. I toyed with the idea of calling my grandpa to pick me up, but I was afraid he would think that I was taking advantage of him.

Lydia never said so, but I thought she was just staying at school because she didn't want to be alone. By alone I mean in a house with people she didn't trust.

Lydia and I stared into our full trays and didn't speak until lunch was half over. Lydia finally drew in a deep breath.

"Well, I'm just gonna have to get over it," she said.

I knew she and Beth had gotten closer over the past couple of weeks, so I didn't expect Lydia to turn off her feelings. I watched as Lydia composed herself and placed a forced smile on her face.

Lydia hadn't changed as deeply as I'd thought. She was still completely consumed with her self-image.

I grabbed my tray and moved away from Her Royal Fakeness. I felt a hand close over my arm.

"Please, Sydney," Lydia begged. "If you leave, I *will* lose it."

"Maybe you should give in to your feelings for once," I said unkindly. I shook my head and softened my tone when I saw Lydia's eyes moisten with sadness. "I'm just amazed at how easily you can still write people off," I said.

Lydia appeared confused. "Who am I writing off?"

"You said you would 'have to get over it'," I recounted.

The clouds of confusion lifted from Lydia's face. "I didn't mean Beth," she said. "I was talking to myself. I meant that I would have to get over being the daughter of terrible people."

I had never heard Lydia verbally bash her family. "What do you mean?" I asked.

"My parents have hired people from the Hernandez family for years. When Mr. Hernandez, Beth's father, died, his family didn't pay a dime for the funeral, but Beth died in our home, and my father is refusing to help her family with the funeral costs."

I was shocked because everyone had seemed comfortable with Beth, and they never complained about her performance. *Why had Bannon Sneed refused to help Polly and Sissy?*

I finally asked the question that had been on my mind all morning. "How did she die?"

Lydia took a deep, shaky breath and cast her eyes back on her tray. She removed her hand from my arm, so I made myself more comfortable in the seat next to her.

"She fell on a pair of scissors," Lydia said before she burst into a fresh wave of tears.

I knew my mouth had fallen open, but I couldn't close it. I didn't comfort Lydia as she cried.

Beth had been one of the most careful people I had ever met. She moved slowly and deliberately through the mansion, and it was hard for me to believe that she had made such a careless mistake.

Lydia started sobbing. Her words came out between erratic breaths. Lydia's cries got the attention of the students at the tables around us. I waved my hand angrily at the curious faces and they turned around. I knew they were only pretending not to listen.

"Beth was going down the steps," Lydia explained, "and she tripped and fell down the steps on the scissors she was holding."

I understood the accident a little better now. Beth could have juggled the scissors when she lost her balance and ended up with them facing the wrong way during her fall.

Something still didn't seem right to me. "Why was she carrying scissors in the first place?"

Lydia looked at me like I was the Queen of Dumb Questions. "She was hired to perform any task we asked of her. Who knows what she was doing before her death?"

Lydia was right, but I still couldn't push away my ill feeling. My grandpa had told me to always trust my gut instincts if a situation didn't feel right, but how could I tell Lydia that I didn't trust the circumstances around Beth's death?

Lydia looked up at me with a moist face and tear-soaked eyes. "I was the one who found her. I heard a noise in the night and found her at the bottom of the steps."

"What?" I said. I finally expressed my skepticism. "Beth was carrying scissors in the middle of the night down a dark flight of steps?"

"What are you trying to get at?" Lydia growled. "Everything isn't part of a murder mystery!"

"*Excuse me*," I said, getting a little upset. "Wasn't it you that involved me in the Terry Thorpe thing? He died less than a week ago, and his sister died mysteriously last night. I'm sorry, but I don't think it was in Beth's job description to carry scissors down a flight of steps in the middle of the night."

"My family is a lot of things, but we are not murderers," Lydia said, but there was little force behind her words.

"Okay," I said. "Maybe Beth was going to kill someone with a pair of scissors, but changed her mind, and fell down the steps in a rush to get back to her room. Maybe we could even pin Terry Thorpe's murder on her." I said with disdain.

I realized that my sarcasm was way out of line. My friend had either witnessed the result of an accident or a murder. Either way, Lydia was clearly traumatized and needed my support.

"I'm sorry," I blurted.

"It's okay," Lydia squeaked out. "You haven't said anything I haven't already thought."

"You were the one who found her," I said. I put my arm through Lydia's and nudged her. "*You* will have to decide what you believe."

And you better decide what you believe very soon, I added to myself. My grandpa had told me that witnesses needed to relay the events of an accident or crime as soon as possible after the event because their memories were likely to get clouded or confused by over-analyzing the facts or by other people's opinions.

"I knew Beth," Lydia sobbed. She was choking on almost every word, and even though the lunchroom was loud, people still noticed and turned their heads.

"I don't think Beth would have fallen on a pair of scissors in the middle of the night."

"I don't either," Lydia wailed, and no one camouflaged their stares. The cafeteria monitor looked directly at us, and I tried to put up my hand to let her know not to interfere. She couldn't be happier to return to her previous stance. She didn't want to be involved in Sneed trouble.

"Lydia," I said calmly. I gathered our purses. "We need to go to the counselor and let you cry in peace."

Lydia raised her tear-soaked face from her hands and took in the probing expressions of her classmates. "You're right," she said and wiped her nose with the back of her hand. I wondered if her Sneed family handkerchief was in her purse.

"I'll get everything together and meet you in the bathroom," I told Lydia.

The closest bathroom was on the other side of the cafeteria, next to the entrance. Lydia got up on her feet, but she was shaking. I had to abandon our mess on the table and try to balance Lydia and our purses to the bathroom.

"Can I help?"

I looked over at the last person I'd expected to hear. Christian was standing two feet away with a concerned look. He had his hands held out like he was offering an invisible olive branch.

I was too stressed out to feel much of anything, but my heart did a double beat in surprise. I blinked away my shocked expression and pointed to the mess on our table.

"Would you mind taking our trays and clearing off the table?" I asked.

"Yeah, I'll take care of it," Christian said. I could tell he was worried. "Do you need me to get Donny to help carry her?" he said, pointing at Lydia.

Lydia was still shaking with sobs, but she looked like she could walk.

"No," I said. I gave him a weak, half smile and looked away.

I turned my full attention back to Lydia. "Let's go, okay?"

Lydia hid her face in my hair as we walked to the bathroom. I wondered how much snot she had wiped on the back of her hand and how much of it was getting in my hair.

We made it inside the bathroom, and Lydia slid down the red, white, and blue-tiled wall to the floor. I knelt down at first, but then threw away my feelings about germs, and sat beside my friend. The surface of the glossy walls and floor of the bathroom felt like frozen ice and alternated our patriotic school colors.

I was thankful that the tile was cold. My adrenaline had spiked my temperature, and Lydia's forehead beaded with perspiration.

By the time Lydia had settled into a state of sobbing calm, lunch was over and teachers had sent half of the girls in our class to check on us. I gave each girl who approached us a look that stopped the words in her mouth and answered whatever question she wanted to ask.

I held Lydia in an amazingly comfortable silence. I knew a lot of time was going by, but I didn't care about class. My teenage emotions were in shock, and I felt numb most of the time I sat on the floor, warming the tile with my friend.

Lydia's eyes glazed over. Her energy had seeped out during her crying episode, and she was settling into a dispirited state of numb.

Lydia refused to go to the counselor once we were away from the lunchroom, but someone must have realized Lydia needed to see her, because Ms. Thomas came to us.

I really liked Mrs. Thomas, but I wished she had stayed in her office. Lydia was liable to act rudely since Mrs. Thomas's counseling had been forced upon her.

Mrs. Thomas smiled and tilted her head. I read her mind.

I caught images of kid, who mutilated his body. A well-liked basketball player, with a cheerful complexion, and Most Pictured Boy in the yearbook pulled down his polo sock to show burns and cuts. He put them on the bottoms of his feet so that he could take a shower in the locker room and no one would suspect his crime against his body.

Mrs. Thomas's thoughts flipped to me. I didn't like the way I looked through another person's eyes. The part in my hair was uneven, and my nose seemed too sharp.

She remembered the day I came to her office and spoke to her about my brothers' deaths. I looked a little younger, and I kept picking at my unpainted nails and looking away.

I popped out of her mind as she sat down in front of Lydia and me. Mrs. Thomas had kept some of the weight she had gained from her recent pregnancy, but it helped fill out her features. Her brown eyes seemed more youthful in her full face.

Lydia had turned over a new leaf, but she was still very proud. She quickly cleared her eyes and looked away from Mrs. Thomas.

"I heard that you have had a bad day, Lydia," Mrs. Thomas began. She was trying the safest approach. She wanted Lydia to open up without prying.

"I have had an upsetting day," Lydia said coldly.

Mrs. Thomas seemed to be used to receiving similar responses, so she continued her questioning. "Can you tell me what's bothering you?"

"Sure," Lydia said with a sarcastic note in her voice. "I found a family friend dead at the foot of my family's stairwell with her eyes bulging from their sockets and scissors in her chest."

I caught a stray thought from Lydia. I glimpsed an image of Beth's body. Blood was leaving lipstick kisses on the carpet as it dripped from her torso. I noticed something in the vision I gleaned from Lydia, and I asked her about it.

"You found Beth in her nightgown?"

Lydia didn't seem surprised, and Mrs. Thomas had no way of knowing if Lydia had discussed the particulars of the early morning incident with me.

"Yes," Lydia said. "Beth was in a plain white nightgown that all the domestic women wear to bed."

I was glad that Lydia had stopped calling Beth's family "servants."

Mrs. Thomas seemed genuinely concerned about Lydia. She studied Lydia's expressions and words, but I don't think she evaluated Lydia like she did most of the other students in the school. Lydia always overreacted, but she had a good reason this time.

"I can validate your feelings and I can help you work through your grief," Mrs. Thomas said softly. "Your mother seemed to think it would be best for you to go home today, so she's on her way to pick you up."

"You called Mummy!" Lydia yelled.

If Lydia could have thrown daggers with her eyes, she would have impaled the school counselor. I was honestly surprised that Mrs. Thomas had called Lydia's parents before speaking with Lydia. It went against school procedure, but everyone had to be extra careful when dealing with a member of the Sneed family.

Lydia was still staring at Mrs. Thomas with her mouth open. The threat of her mother's arrival had brought Lydia out of her haze and recharged her with liquid fury.

"When should she be here?" Lydia asked, grabbing her purse and flipping through the contents. She finally fumbled a compact out and removed the lid on a powdered foundation.

Mrs. Thomas attempted to go over the stages of grief with Lydia, but Lydia hopped up and ran to the bathroom mirror. The large, wall-length mirror helped Lydia get a better idea of the way her mother would perceive her.

Lydia stopped covering her despair and looked at me with fire in her eyes. "Call your grandfather!"

It took me a moment to figure out what Lydia meant. I almost responded with, 'Why?' so I was glad that my weary mind had prevented a quick response.

"You can't run from your mother," I said carefully. "Please don't involve my grandpa, because if I call him to pick us up, he will defend you, and your mother will make sure he loses his job."

Lydia pondered my response. She slumped her shoulders and hung her head. "You're right," she admitted.

"Please tell me what has gotten you agitated," Mrs. Thomas said to Lydia.

Lydia's eyebrows almost shot up off her forehead in surprise. She dropped her hands to her sides and took a deep breath that did not relax her body.

I tried to think of an excuse to keep Lydia out of family therapy. An idea popped into my head almost immediately.

"Of course Lydia doesn't want to go home," I directed at Mrs. Thomas. Lydia's head turned toward me sharply. "I wouldn't want to go back to the place where I discovered a dead body. Especially the dead body of a person I cared about."

Mrs. Thomas considered my response to the question she had posed to Lydia. She looked straight into Lydia's eyes and said, "I really wasn't thinking." She shook her head. "I hadn't considered that you'd come to school to get away from the drama at your home."

Oh, she didn't know the half of it.

Lydia didn't speak. I hoped Mrs. Thomas would let her finish the rest of the school day in peace.

"You ladies can come with me to my office," Mrs. Thomas began, getting up and dusting the various bathroom bacteria off her pants. "I'll find a quiet room for you two to talk in, and we'll wait on Mrs. Sneed."

Lydia and I were crestfallen. We fell into line behind Mrs. Thomas. I could see Lydia hanging her usually proud head all the way to the main building.

No one was in the halls, but I heard snatches of thought from several classrooms as we walked past open doors. I allowed myself to tune into other people's minds.

"What is wrong with Lydia?"

"—hope she gets what she deserves."

"She was the one who killed that maid!"

"I wonder if she'll feel vulnerable enough to date me."

I tried not to betray my emotions. Lydia looked at me like she was trying to see into my mind, so I offered a half smile and moved my attention to Mrs. Thomas's feet.

I concentrated on the clicking the golden pumps made on the tile floor. I turned the volume down on the thoughts I was receiving and tried to figure out a way I could help Lydia.

Mrs. Thomas entered the office and waved at the secretary. Mrs. Watson waved back, but she quickly dropped her friendly demeanor when she saw Lydia.

"Your mother and father have been yelling at everyone in the school for the past ten minutes," Mrs. Watson said coldly. "They're with Mrs. Bailey now, and I hope your mother lowers her voice because the principal won't put up with a lot."

Mrs. Watson shooed Lydia toward the principal's office, and I heard hysterical screaming. I should have known Olivia Sneed would have flown down to the school after she heard about her daughter's condition.

Lydia glanced back at me for emotional support, and I gave her a thumbs-up. She produced a weak smile and inched open the door.

Olivia Sneed's screaming ceased for a moment before she directed her anxious voice toward her daughter. I wasn't going to stay and listen.

I walked back to my classroom and tried to concentrate on the last hour of class. Presidential history was not interesting enough to hold my interest, so I began trying to piece together Beth's last moments.

The surge of adrenaline had caused my body to push all of its energy forward, so now that the excitement was over, I couldn't hold my eyes open. My mind carried me to the Sneed mansion, and I could no longer hear Ms. Hughes or the other students.

I heard a noise. I was in Bannon Sneed's office and was startled by the sound. The clock on the desk read twenty minutes after two.

I frantically cut off the computer and all the lights. I eased out of the office and down the hall to the kitchen.

I looked at the rack that held all the steak knives. My gaze moved over their sharp blades and rested on the sharpening stone. A pair of scissors lay beside it. The scissors had been sharpened recently along with all the steak knives.

"Hello?" said a small voice. I looked at the kitchen doorway and saw a small woman in a white nightdress. The hallway light was on, so I knew I had a precious window of time where the woman would not see me before her eyes adjusted to the dark.

I grabbed the scissors as she reached to turn on the light. I quickly crossed the distance between the woman and me. The woman's attention was still directed at the light switch. She may have felt a change in the air, but she didn't hear a sound, as I plunged the scissors into her chest with all my force. I pulled them out and stabbed her again, but I couldn't get them to budge easily.

The woman clutched her chest and screamed. I grabbed a dish towel off the nearby counter and muffled her cries. I held the dishtowel over her mouth and nose to give her an express ticket to eternal darkness.

The woman struggled much longer than I thought she would, but I was patient. I constructed a scenario to tell the police as death closed the door on her soul.

I carried her limp body like a child up the stairs so that any blood that spilled would be caught by her nightshirt and would never make it to the floor.

I stood the woman upright at the top of the stairs and scanned the silent hallway for life. I pulled the dish towel from her face and closed her bulging eyes. Her eyelids reopened like lazy window shades.

The scissors were still lodged in the woman's abdomen. Surprisingly, there wasn't as much blood as I had expected.

I wiped the handle of the scissors with the dish towel and positioned the woman's right hand around the handle. Was she left- or right-handed? I decided it didn't matter.

I turned her body forward, into a standing position, and gently let go of her corpse. The woman tumbled down the steps as easily, and soundlessly, as a stuffed doll, sliding on her face the last couple of stairs. I made sure that she had landed on her stomach\ and went to bed.

Too bad, I thought. She had been a good servant, but she had been nosy. Lydia had already started asking too many questions. She had to have gotten the picture from that prying servant! Oh well, now I wouldn't have to worry about forgotten pictures and blackmailers. Beth and Terry Hernandez were dead.

Chapter Twenty-Two

"**S**ydney!"

Someone had shouted my name, but I was being gently shaken awake. A large warm hand on my shoulder urged me back into the world of conscious thought.

I felt like I was waking up in the middle of a roller coaster ride. My body was numb, and students were chatting and packing their books to go home. My mind adjusted to the noise almost immediately.

I jumped up out of my chair and knocked heads with Christian. He had been trying to revive me, and I had rewarded him with a knock on the head.

I grabbed his shoulders. "Are you okay? I am so sorry!" I said in a rush.

Christian locked eyes with me, and I remembered the swoon I had felt the last time I had gazed into his eyes. We both looked away at the same time, and I felt my face redden. I realized I was still holding Christian's shoulders, and I dropped my hands to my sides.

"It's time to go home," Christian mumbled. "You started crying and said 'Beth'."

My dream came back to me in a rush. I knew that the murder I'd witnessed was not a dream. It was a vision.

I shook my head and gave Christian a wide-eyed stare. I hoped he would drop the subject and get ready to go home.

"What do you know?" Christian asked. His eyes locked with mine and I couldn't find the will to turn away. I had a sudden urge to tell him everything.

"You're gonna miss the bus, Dude," Donny said as he clapped Christian on the back. "You can stare at Sydney from the back of the bus where you usually do."

Christian lowered his eyes and turned the same color as a ripe tomato. He walked away with Donny and didn't bother to tell me goodbye. I silently cursed myself for almost letting him know my secrets, but I couldn't help wondering if he would have thought differently about me if I had revealed the source of my information.

I walked by the office on my way to the bus. Everything seemed calm. The receptionist was stamping envelopes, and a student worker was staring intently at the computer.

I was still consumed with thoughts about my vision when my grandpa placed his arm on my shoulder. I jumped, and the warm, open look he had been wearing dropped into a cautious stare.

"Are you okay, Little Lady?" he asked.

I had forgotten that I no longer lived with my mom. I could see Christian staring up at me from the bus, but when he saw I noticed him, he turned and ran up the bus steps.

I faked a smile that relaxed my grandpa and said, "I'm wonderful. Can we go get my stuff?"

My grandpa brightened again and guided me down the stairs. Some students looked at me as if I were being escorted to jail. They didn't know Chief Murphy was my grandpa.

The ride to my house was short. I hadn't been worried, because I thought my mom would still be at work when my grandpa and I collected my stuff, so I almost lost my breath when I saw my mom's car in the driveway.

I cursed myself for not thinking. Of course she would have taken the day off to be with my sister.

I seemed a little silly to be standing outside the door to my house as my grandpa knocked. I felt like a wayward child for a moment, but I knew that I would always be able to walk straight into the home I was building with my grandpa.

My mom opened the door, and I greeted her with a half-hearted hug. She patted me on the shoulder, but she didn't embrace me.

"You have some mail on the kitchen table. "It sounded like she'd had her spirit jerked out, and that's probably how she felt.

I walked into the kitchen. I could hear my mom and grandpa speaking in murmurs.

An envelope lay on the placemat where I used to eat my meals. I picked up the envelope and rejoined my mom and grandpa.

My mom gave me a traitorous look before she turned her attention back to my grandpa. He seemed to sense my discomfort.

"Gather what you need for now," he said. "We can come back for the rest later."

I understood what he meant. My grandpa didn't want to be here any longer than I did.

I climbed the steps to the room my stuff still occupied and opened the door. My sister pretended to be asleep, but I could hear echoes of her thoughts in my mind.

"I know when you're asleep," I said.

Ella responded by opening her eyes. She stared in my direction. "You sound like the Santa Claus song."

"I may know when you're awake, but I can't bring you presents or Christmas wishes," I replied jokingly.

"I think you would be surprised by my wish," Ella whispered.

I pulled my suitcase off the top shelf of the closet. A puff of dust followed it and I sneezed.

"Bless you," Ella said. Her voice was low and strained.

"Thank you," I replied. I would have said more to her, but my mom called my name.

I peeked outside the door and answered her call.

"You have a phone call," she said. I heard a deadness in her voice that pierced my heart. My mom would never forgive me for leaving her.

I only got phone calls from Lydia and my grandpa, so I knew who had called me. I hesitated before I told my mom, "Thank you."

My mom handed me the phone at the bottom of the stairs. I heard silence on the line. My mom stared at me like she was trying to hear the conversation on the other end of the line.

"Okay, Mom, I've got it."

I walked up the stairs to gain more privacy. I heard voices downstairs, so I assumed my mom was no longer trying to listen.

"Hello?"

"Hey," Lydia said in a tiny voice.

"What's wrong?" I could hear static I associated with a moving call. Lydia was in a car.

"Can I come by your house? I need to talk," she said.

I hadn't gotten the chance to tell Lydia that I had moved into my grandpa's house. Lydia cut in again before I could answer.

"Can I come in? I'm in your driveway," she said.

It was a good thing I had come to my house to pack, because Lydia would have been shocked to find out that I had moved. I wondered if my mom would have told her where to find me.

"Okay, come up to my room."

I heard the line buzz the call's end. I stepped into my room and was almost immediately joined by a frantic Lydia.

Ella didn't try to fake unconsciousness. She moved to sit up, but she could not support her weight.

Ella had fear in her eyes. I had never seen her so scared.

Lydia practically fell into my arms. "I know who killed Beth," she wailed.

"Who is she?" Ella said. I chanced a quick glance at Ella, and she was pointing toward Lydia. My sister's voice was shaking, and there were tears rolling off her cheeks.

"You know who Lydia is," I said harshly.

Ella stared her thoughts into me. It felt as though my brain was being pummeled with images, and I could hear my sister's voice in my head.

She is attached to Lydia, and her body is bloated with death. She cannot talk to me. She keeps throwing her arms around. I do not know why I cannot hear her.

Maybe Beth had followed Lydia since her death. Perhaps Ella could find out if Beth needed to tell us something.

Lydia was babbling something about finding letters about blackmail and pictures of Beth with her brother, Terry.

I could hardly hear Lydia over the blood marching through my head. I began mumbling words that were unintelligible to me, but Ella looked at me as though I had said something profound. I kept uttering, but my mouth moved so fast that my mind couldn't keep up with the sounds. The only thing that broke the commotion was Ella's screaming.

My sister had painfully pulled herself into a sitting position on the bed. I could see the pink cast on her right arm reflecting its bright neon color on her white nightgown and pale skin.

My insane ramblings and Ella's screaming stopped Lydia's hysterics, and Ella pressed herself against the wall as Lydia approached the bed. Lydia looked at me as if to ask, *Why is she so scared of me?* I knew Ella wasn't scared of Lydia, so I shook my head.

At first, I tried to concentrate on Ella's panicked thoughts. She kept turning an image in her mind. I had never seen my sister scared of her connection with the dead, but the picture I was seeing could scare anyone.

My sister used to say that the dead sent the image of the way they last saw themselves. Most of the ghosts Ella saw were peaceful or confused dead folks who chose to roam the earth. Rarely did the specters have unfinished business that left them walking among the living.

I couldn't see the image of the shadow attached to Lydia, but I could feel a malevolent presence. My sister could not control the ghost in her usual way, by calmly listening. The invader seemed to take over my sister's control and force its will upon Ella.

Ella's cries had reached the ears of my mom and grandpa. I could hear heavy footfalls pounding up the stairs.

My mom entered the room out of breath and went straight over to Ella. My grandpa stopped in the doorway, his senses assessing the situation.

"Stay back, Mother," Ella said forcefully.

My mom took a step away, unsure of what to do next. I could only watch the frozen scene. My mind was still connected in some way.

Ella began hitting herself in the face. She screamed, "I do not want it anymore. Please make it go away!"

My mom could not stop Ella from hurting herself. When she grabbed Ella's shoulders, Ella banged her head on the bed. My grandpa tried to help, but he could not reach my sister before she threw her head against the metal bars of her daybed.

Ella's eyes rolled back and fluttered. I caught one thought before Ella's mind collapsed, and I knew it wasn't from my sister: "*—tell you what happened by the river.*"

Chapter Twenty-Three

I don't think the most skilled hypnotist could have gotten me to recount the things that happened immediately after Ella lost consciousness. I could hardly remember walking out onto the front yard after I followed Ella's stretcher outside.

My mom couldn't stop crying, and my grandpa held a firm, protective grip on my shoulder. I was emotionally numb, but I was glad I was standing next to my supportive grandpa.

A strangely familiar young man dressed in an EMT uniform walked over to my grandpa. He held a clipboard in one hand and a pen in the other.

"Were you the responding officer?" he asked.

My grandpa and I shared a puzzled look before we realized he was still dressed in his police uniform. My grandpa thought before he answered.

"I am Chief Conner Murphy, but I was not called to the scene. I reported the incident and requested an ambulance be sent here. I am related to the people in this house."

"What is your relation, sir?" The EMT was a little less formal, but he was still respectful.

"I am her father," my grandpa said, and pointed at my mom. She was still sobbing over Ella's unconscious body. "That makes me the grandfather of this one," he gave my shoulder a squeeze, "and the one on the stretcher."

I was surprised when he made a reference to Ella. The EMT knew her name, but my grandpa had chosen not to associate us with the Miller name.

"Okay, sir, describe what happened."

My grandpa did not speak, so the EMT looked up from his clipboard. He seemed to understand the reason for my grandpa's silence, but the EMT still pressed him for information.

"The young lady is unconscious, and her mother is in hysterics," he began. "I need to get a description of what caused her injury so that I can treat her," the EMT said.

I made a move to speak, but my grandpa stopped me. I felt like I had a good reason to speak. I had witnessed the entire episode.

"The young lady is not well," my grandpa said.

"You mean she is sick?"

"Not exactly," my grandpa said, stroking his naked chin. "She has an untreated mental disorder, and she began hitting herself. She beat her head against the bed when her mother tried to restrain her."

I couldn't believe what I had heard! My grandpa had sold out my sister. It was no secret he questioned Ella's mental stability, but he should not have thrown her to the wolves. His words were sure to get my sister committed.

"Her mother is afraid of losing her," my grandpa continued, "so she has never found her a mental doctor."

The EMT looked up at my grandpa. My grandpa was trying to advocate for Ella's mental health, but he didn't know the proper way to convey his feelings. Mental health issues were a taboo subject when he was growing up, so this was a new area for him.

My grandpa noticed the young man's curious look and felt the need to clarify. His voice was much firmer than I had ever heard it.

"I came from a different area with my daughter." He pointed at my mom. "I don't know what needs to be done, but the young lady needs help." He squeezed my shoulder again.

The EMT was scribbling down information as fast as his hand would move. He smiled at me awkwardly, and I realized he was Tony, Christian's brother, but before I could relate my recognition, my grandpa spoke again.

"If you don't need anything else, I would like to get my granddaughter out of this circus."

"Oh," Tony said, "That may not be possible, sir."

"Why in the world wouldn't I be able to take Sydney home?" my grandpa said.

"Well, her mother would have to approve it," Tony said carefully.

"Then go ask her, so we can get out of here," my grandpa said irritably.

Tony strode over to my mom and talked with her. My mom seemed in a daze, but when he pointed in my direction, her expression turned grim, and she nodded her approval. I looked up at my grandpa just in time to see his eyes staring forcefully in my mom's direction. He was willing her to question his authority over me.

"Run into the house and grab your things, Little Lady," my grandpa said before Tony returned.

I stumbled up the porch steps on numb legs and ran into the door. The house I had once called my home was eerily quiet, and I wondered if the shadow's presence was still lingering.

The constant outside commotion reassured me I was not alone, so I decided to gather my things and leave. I paused at my brothers' room. I toyed with the idea of opening the door, but Ella was right. Josh and Jerrod had moved on and they couldn't offer me any advice.

I registered a sweaty, metallic smell when I walked into my old bedroom. My suitcase was open on the floor where a few outfits had been tossed.

I opened my drawers and emptied them into the large suitcase. I ran into the bathroom and collected my toothbrush, make-up, and straightener. I left the hair dryer and designer hair products for my sister, or my mom, if Ella was committed.

I threw my suitcase onto my bed and sat on it. The air rushed out with a flatulent, and I clicked the clasps securely.

I was on my way out of the bedroom door when I spotted my mail on the floor. I picked up the envelope, folded it, and stuffed it into my pocket. I ran all the way down the steps and out the door.

My grandpa took my suitcase from me and opened the passenger side door of his cruiser. I looked around. Something wasn't right, but I couldn't wrap my traumatized mind around it. I finally stepped into the cruiser and let my grandpa shut the door on all the drama.

I was resting in a warm bath when I thought about the letter. I had stuffed it into my jeans, and I had not remembered it until I was completely relaxed.

I reached out of the tub, balancing the lower half of my body on the edge. I pulled the envelope out of my pants and retreated back into the water.

The warm bath had taken the edge off my nerves. My grandpa had suggested it after he gave me some warm milk. I felt peaceful, and my mind told me it would be too hard to think about cheerless things.

I ripped the top off the envelope and pulled out two sheets of notebook paper. They smelled like lemon cleaner and hopelessness.

I realized who had written the letter almost immediately after I began reading it. It was penned almost perfectly, and the handwriting was beautiful. I unfolded the letter, and my sense of calm was shattered by the time I finished reading it.

```
Dear Sydney,

I wish I had written you sooner, but I couldn't
find the nerve. I didn't put my name or return
address on the envelope because your mother
would have burned it before it got to you.

I guess you have heard about the incident that
led to my stay in prison, but you don't know the
truth. I was wrongly accused and convicted, and
I didn't even have a chance to defend myself.

Without saying too much, I have found a way
to set things right. I lost everything that
mattered to me when my wife and daughter died,
so I never tried to appeal the court's decision.
I decided to devote the rest of my life to
helping criminals rehabilitate, but now I know
I am needed back home.

It was a shock to see you touring the prison
with your grandfather. I suppose you must have
done something bad, or at least it was bad to
him, and he is using the old "tour the place
where you'll go if you keep up your deviant
behavior" approach. Unfortunately, there are
```

some good people in jails and prisons, and there are some bad people who walk the streets beside you every day. Sometimes, bad people can get away with murder, and our justice system doesn't always work.

I knew your grandfather on sight, but I almost mistook you for your mother. Miranda looked just like you when I first met her, even though you must only be about thirteen now.

It hurts me to think about you because I know my daughter would only have been a year or two older than you, and she will never know the joys of going to school or spending time with her family. It also hurts me because you look so much like your mother, and you could have been my daughter.

I don't know if your mother told you about our relationship, but we had a love that was greater than she may want to admit. I hope that one day you will find a man who loves you as deeply as I loved your mother.

Uncle Kerry sent me word of the jewelry you found. I think he told you it was Nellie's necklace.

The discovery of that necklace sparked a fire in a soul that I thought was hardened and frozen. I realized I had a reason for living. I can't explain that feeling, but I couldn't believe the locket was found in the possession of the most hated family in Erwin.

I heard you are friends with their young daughter. Please don't be fooled by them. They can manipulate minds with money and power. I'm afraid you may already be under their spell.

I want to ask you two things: Did I ever hurt your mother? Where was the necklace when you found it?

I guess you must be wondering why I wrote you this letter. I think it is because I don't want you to think badly of me. I *was* wrongly accused of killing my wife and daughter. I hope you will examine the facts before we meet again. It may be sooner than you think.

Please don't be afraid of me. There are other people in town that you need to be afraid of, but *I* will never harm you.

Best wishes,

Bryan Shelton

It could have been a friendly letter out of any grammar book. It was hard to believe it had been sent to me by a convicted murderer.

The date on the post mark said the letter had been mailed over a week ago. Bryan could have escaped and been in Erwin watching us.

I was hit by a sudden realization. Lydia knew who had killed Beth. It had been Bryan Shelton. He had somehow escaped from prison and he killed Beth because she was going to catch him in Bannon Sneed's office. I didn't know if Bryan was in my vision of Beth's death, but it made sense. She had interrupted his plan to hurt the family who put him in prison.

I had witnessed Bryan's actions from a semi-conscious state. *Did that mean Bryan had been at my school while I was having the visions?*

And what about Lydia? Where was Lydia?

I reached back in my mind and found that I couldn't remember seeing Lydia after my mom and grandpa came to Ella's rescue. I tried to piece everything together.

I believed Lydia had come to my house to tell me Bryan had escaped, and he had killed Beth. Ella freaked out, so Lydia left. *Was she running from Bryan?*

Bryan had hated Nellie's friend, and it seemed like Nellie's only friend had been Olivia Sneed. *Was Bryan going to settle his score and "set things right" by killing the Sneed's only daughter?*

I didn't care if Olivia and Bannon Sneed were killed, but I was going to help my friend. I had to start by finding Lydia.

I hopped out of the bath and pulled the plug. My relaxation was sucked down the drain with the rest of the warm water.

I wrapped a towel around myself and darted from the bathroom to my bedroom. I slung clothes out of my suitcase as I searched for a sweater to go with the first pair of jeans I grabbed.

My grandpa had heard the commotion, and I could feel the vibrations from his large feet hurrying down the hall. He stopped short of my room, uncertain whether I was dressed after my bath.

"Sydney?"

My name sounded foreign on his lips. I was used to the way he called me by his special nickname.

I slid on my jeans and wiggled into my sweater.

"Yes?"

"Is everything okay?"

Now this was a conundrum. On one hand, my grandpa was the Chief of Police, and he seemed to be able to pull from unlimited resources. He could probably find Bryan much faster if he knew

Bryan was in the area. On the other hand, he was my grandpa, and he might feel as though he should protect me from everything. I also worried that I could be putting my loving grandfather in danger by setting him out to look for Bryan. *What if Bryan felt betrayed by my grandpa and killed him on sight?*

My thoughts kept rushing at me, but my grandpa was waiting for an answer. I bought myself another minute.

"I'm decent, Grandpa. You can come in."

My grandpa whipped around the doorway and scanned the room. He was looking for anything that could have caused my agitation.

His perfect eyesight fell on the letter on my bed. He could have easily snatched it up, but he respected my privacy.

"Does your sudden need to leave have something to do with that note?" he asked. I guess I should have known he would figure me out when he spotted me in jeans and a sweater instead of in my nightclothes.

I couldn't lie to my grandpa. His strong arms had held me since Iwas a little girl, and his cold, blue eyes had never told a lie to me.

"It's from Bryan," I managed to say before another part of my brain stopped me.

My grandpa's face showed no emotion. It was the calm before the storm.

I should have kept my mouth shut, but I let everything spill out of me like an overturned garbage can. The strangest thing about my confession was that it left me feeling better, as if a load had been lifted from my soul.

My grandpa looked for lies in my story. I wondered if he believed a word I had spoken. His face changed, and he looked puzzled.

"How do you know Bryan has escaped from prison?" he asked.

I started to answer and realized that I had merely guessed at Bryan's fugitive status. I thought the words in his letter meant that he would bust out of his confinement and claim revenge on every-one he felt had betrayed him.

My grandpa understood I was having a hard time answering his question, so he asked me another one. "Why would Bryan go after Lydia, or anyone in the Sneed family? Olivia just recounted what happened to Nellie."

I felt confident about my response to this question. It seemed obvious.

"Olivia was trying to take Nellie and Lily away from him, and that's why he got mad in the first place. He probably blames Olivia for Nellie and Lily's death."

My grandpa seemed to consider something but quickly dismissed it. He steeled his resolve to tell me the truth.

"I don't think you have your story straight," my grandpa told me.

He didn't offer for me to sit down, but I wish he had asked me to sit on the bed. I found myself dizzy by the time my grandpa finished talking.

"I was in the courtroom the day Bryan and Olivia testified," my grandpa began. "I couldn't believe that someone I had been so close to was capable of a crime against nature. It was terrible that Bryan killed his wife, but to kill little Lily showed a terrible—" My grandpa's eyes grew moist, but he blinked away his softer emotions, and continued.

"I read Bryan's statement. I was finished with the boy long before I read his account, but I decided to pay him a visit anyway. Bryan must have misunderstood the reason for my visit because he thought I was on his side when I entered his cell."

My grandpa started pacing. He walked from the bedside table to the small desk. He stepped on the small pink fingernail polish stain every time he turned to pace in my direction. He gestured wildly when he talked about the way he felt toward his former fellow officer and friend, but he lowered his voice and carefully spoke every word he meant in defense of Lily and her mother.

"Bryan said he dropped Lily on a rock and she was bleeding from her head," my grandpa recounted from the report he'd read. "Bryan said that he argued with Nellie for a few minutes before they realized how serious Lily's bleeding had gotten. He said Olivia, Bannon, and their manservant heard the commotion and came to help. Bryan then claimed that he blacked out and woke next to his wife, floating beside him. She was already dead."

"When I saw that lying piece of garbage alive in his cell with hope in his eyes..." my grandpa trailed off, clenching and unclenching his jaws in time with his fists. After he had regained some control over his words, my grandpa said, "He said that he knew I would believe him. Bryan told me that if anyone would believe him, it would be Miranda and me."

My grandpa stopped pacing. He looked at the floor, where a small pink stain marked the only imperfection on the carpet. My grandpa shook his head and resumed pacing.

"I don't know if it was in my head all along or if the mention of my daughter's name started it, but I crushed his hope and his face with my fists. He didn't cry for help, but I was yelling everything I thought about him. I landed two or three punches, but when Bryan didn't defend himself, I spat on him, and walked out.

"I was told that I had given him a broken nose, and he wouldn't be able to hear well out of his left ear again. I wasn't sorry, and I'll tell you, Little Lady," my grandpa said, turning his attention briefly to my face, "I'm glad he'll always wear that scar on his left cheek."

My grandpa raised his left hand, and his police ring caught the light. He seemed mesmerized by it for a moment, but then he turned his attention back to his story and the rate of his steps.

"So what did everyone else say?" I asked, trying to get my grandpa's thoughts away from Bryan and on less anger-invoking people.

"Olivia, Bannon, and the manservant stuck together on their stories. They said they found Bryan and Nellie arguing over the dead body of the child. Olivia said that Bryan picked Lily up and threatened to let the fish eat her dead body before he'd let her go with Olivia Sneed. Nellie was knocked to the side in her struggle to get Lily, and she rushed Bryan. Olivia claimed everything was a blur, but Bryan caught Nellie by the neck and held her down in the water. Olivia realized her friend was about to drown, so she ordered her manservant to help. The manservant picked up a large rock and knocked Bryan over the head with it as Bryan held Nellie under the water. Bryan was knocked out, but they were too late. Nellie had lost too much of her life to come back. Olivia called the police, and Bannon and the manservant searched for Lily's body. The child was swallowed up in the swollen water of the river and she was found a couple of weeks later."

My grandpa had to pause his story. I couldn't see his face, but I knew he was holding back powerful emotions.

"The Sneeds were heartbroken. *They* were the ones who paid for the extensive tests that were done to Lily's decomposed body. An autopsy was not enough for them. Olivia Sneed wanted to believe Lily was alive somewhere and had not floated lifelessly for the two weeks before her body was found. Once it was confirmed that Lily was dead, Olivia threw herself into bringing Bryan Shelton to justice."

My grandpa swallowed audibly and stopped pacing. He faced me and held my hands.

"Bryan's trial was swift, and I'm honored to say that I was there to represent Nellie and Lily," my grandpa said with pride. "Bryan was sentenced to fifteen years in prison, and I asked to drive him there so that I could be sure he made it to the place where he could think about his crime.

"Bryan showed no fear of me during the ride, and we didn't speak. I think he knew that nothing he could say would be met with a kind or understanding response.

"I could still see the evidence of the beating I gave him," my grandpa said proudly. "Bryan's nose was purple, and yellow bruises covered one side of his face.

"I left Bryan Shelton at that prison, and I tried not to think of him again. It didn't help that I couldn't see my grandchildren." He rolled his eyes. "Your mom and I weren't seeing eye-to-eye. I wanted to stay busy, so I threw myself into my work.

"Olivia expected to be seen as a hero because she testified against Bryan at his trial. She walked through town with a smug look until Kerry Shelton, Bryan's uncle, slapped her and called her a liar."

A whole range of questions filtered into my mind. *Where did Olivia see Kerry Shelton? Did she actually have the nerve to enter his shop when he was such a clear supporter of his nephew? Was Kerry Shelton the only person immune from the wrath of Bannon Sneed?*

My grandpa had continued talking, and I had missed some of what he said. Some of my questions may have been answered if I hadn't tuned out, but this was not the type of conversation you asked the other person to repeat.

"That scene was what prompted Olivia to move back to New York," my grandpa was saying. "I suppose you know the rest of the story. She was pregnant with Lydia when she left, and Olivia kept her a secret from this town until Bannon demanded her return. That's why everyone is careful about how they treat Lydia. Bannon Sneed would go after any person who was justly or unjustly cruel to his daughter."

"Wasn't Bannon Sneed mad at Kerry Shelton?" I couldn't help asking.

"Of course he was! Kerry had not only insulted Olivia, but he had actually slapped her!" my grandpa said. "Bannon didn't try to *ruin* Kerry, he tried to *kill* him."

"What?" I shouted. "Why isn't Bannon Sneed sharing a cell with Bryan Shelton?"

"I caught him before it happened," my grandpa explained. "Besides, when has a dirty coward like Bannon Sneed ever gotten the guts to do anything himself?"

I couldn't imagine Bannon Sneed doing anything more than eating and sleeping. I thought about the way he had eaten when I had my doomed sleepover with Lydia. I fought back the image before it made me nauseated.

"I caught his manservant, Hernandez, tampering with Kerry's car. Hernandez had a bomb in his possession. Bannon got his lawyers on it and was able to keep the whole thing quiet. The lawyer plea bargained the offense down to attempted manslaughter.

"I was called in to give a statement, but I wasn't allowed near the court proceedings. I asked to drive him to prison, like I did with Bryan, but Hernandez was transported by a prison guard from North Carolina.

"I was pretty steamed over it, because I thought Bannon would pay the guard to let Hernandez go, but he arrived at the prison just like he was supposed to. I called and talked to a guard I knew at the time. He said Hernandez got there on time and was sitting in his cell."

"Did Bannon Sneed do anything else to Bryan's uncle?" I asked, even though I was pretty sure of the answer.

"Bannon did everything he could legally get away with to destroy Kerry Shelton," my grandpa said. He had calmed down a little, and his voice sounded grave.

"I didn't really care for Kerry Shelton, but I didn't want to see anything bad happen to him. I ran midnight checks on his shop, and I stood up for him at a town meeting. Bannon tried to close Kerry's shop by telling the townspeople that going to a pawnshop was like gambling with your most treasured memories. The town of Erwin was about to vote Kerry out of business when I stood up and reminded them that Kerry had always been fair with them. A normal pawnshop owner would have charged an outrageous amount of interest on a pawned item, but Kerry would sometimes forgive the interest on an item if the customer couldn't afford it. As long as the customer paid back what they owed, Kerry didn't care to break even on a pawn."

I liked Kerry Shelton, even if he thought I was a Sneed minion. He was probably a great guy who stood up for his family at all costs. I thought back to how fairly he had dealt with me, and he had been angry with me when I picked up the locket. He had honored our business arrangement, even though he wanted to keep the locket from returning to the Sneeds.

"Kerry was very thankful," my grandpa reminisced, "but I couldn't even shake his hand. To me, Bryan's uncle still carried the stench of his nephew's crime."

"Why didn't I hear that Mr. Hernandez was in prison?" I asked. "Which inmate was he?" I tried to think back to my visit to the prison. I couldn't recall a man who looked like Beth, Polly, or Sissy.

"You wouldn't have seen him," my grandpa said. He let out a long sigh. I wished he would sit down. The weight of our discussion was starting to make me feel dizzy.

"Instead of admitting that Hernandez was in jail," my grandpa continued, "Bannon was going to tell everyone in town that his manservant was trying to resolve some heart problems. Bannon never shared his lie because Hernandez died of the same medical condition only a week after arriving in prison."

"Had Mr. Hernandez had heart problems before?" I asked.

"I don't think so, Little Lady, but Hernandez had been through a lot in a short time. The guy wasn't a young buck, you know."

I wondered how many of my grandpa's references were derived from his northern upbringing. I imagined most of them were now Southern phrases, since he had lived south of the Mason-Dixon line for a great deal of his life.

My grandpa and I stood together for a long time. I couldn't think of anything else to say, even though I knew I was going to have more questions.

My grandpa was the first to awaken from the silence. "I guess I should call the prison and see if Bryan's in his cell," he said.

He picked up the letter off the bed and looked at me as if to ask my permission to take it. I nodded my approval.

My grandpa's feet padded down his carpeted hallway. I wasn't used to feeling so loved and protected. I knew that my mom and sister loved me, but there was something more comforting in my grandpa's care. I guess I was trying to fill the void my father had left when he decided never to come home again.

I suddenly felt an urge to protect my grandpa. He had dodged bullets and broken up gang fights, but he was getting older, and his reference to Mr. Hernandez's age at the time of his imprisonment worried me. *What if Bryan had used his years in jail to hone his attack and survival skills?*

I hated to think of what I was going to do, but I couldn't let my grandpa walk into a trap. My grandpa had years of rage built up over

Nellie and Lily's deaths, and I knew he would relish the opportunity to rid the world of Bryan Shelton. In fact, he could kill Bryan and be considered a hero.

I heard my grandpa talking to a guard at the prison. He was put on hold so that the guard could ask for permission to share the status of an inmate.

I was glad for the few minutes I had bought myself. My grandpa's phone call gave me time to think and provided a distraction so that I could make a plan to sneak out of my new home.

Chapter Twenty-Four

It was hard for me to cast aside my grandpa's protective arms for the embrace of the cold outdoors. The wind was puffing chilly gusts through the valley and my coat hardly protected me from its icy fingers.

The overcast sky was bloated with clouds that were stacked on each other. They reminded me of an old-fashioned gray quilt.

I regretted jumping out of the window in my bedroom almost as soon as my feet touched the frozen earth. I almost went to the front door and admitted my escape. I couldn't have gotten back into the window without standing on something at least five feet tall, but I ran away from my haven before I lost my resolve.

Lydia had been in her family's limousine when she visited me. I had noticed something strange before my grandpa and I had left my childhood home, but I couldn't fix my mind on what seemed out of place. I realized after reading Bryan's letter that the Sneed limousine was still parked in the driveway when my grandpa and I prepared to leave. I had a funny feeling that at that time the driver had been in the limo waiting for a teenage heiress.

I asked myself where Lydia would go if she couldn't go home. She would come to my house, I had immediately thought. Lydia had tried to come to me, but Ella scared her away. *So where was Lydia now?*

I decided Lydia would follow the ambulance to the hospital. After all, she knew I would eventually check on my sister and Lydia could fake concern for my sister's condition. My mom would be too distracted by the situation to realize that Lydia should be at home with her parents.

I needed a ride to the hospital, but I could think of only one person who would help me. I didn't have any money to negotiate a safe ride, but I felt I could persuade Kerry Shelton to help me if I shared what I remembered of Bryan's letter with him.

I ran through my options several times in the twenty minutes it took me to get to town. It only took a few minutes to drive into Erwin from my grandpa's house, but it took me forever to get to town on foot. My internal debate over the information I'd just learned was the only entertainment I had to keep me from going crazy. I ran for the first ten minutes, but my legs started to feel like jelly, so I could only run in short bursts after I slowed to a brisk walk.

I hoped I was right about the place my friend would go if she had run out of options. I entered Erwin and hoped that my grandpa or one of his deputies would not see me.

Within moments of entering the main street of town, I opened the door to the pawnshop and Christmas bells signaled my arrival. Kerry Shelton came out with a too-wide smile, but his expression dropped into an unhappy scowl when he saw me.

"What do you want?" Kerry asked. I knew my mission was doomed when I realized that Kerry still thought poorly of me.

"I need a ride to the hospital," I said. "My sister is sick."

"Your sister has been *sick* since the day she was born," Kerry retorted. "Besides, you can get a ride from your grandpa or his *law-abiding* officers."

"I don't think you understand," I said. I was trying hard not to respond to the offensive remark he'd made about my grandpa. "I need to talk to someone who understands the full situation."

"What situation?" Kerry said. Those were the first diluted words I'd heard him speak. I wondered what had caused his forthright manner to fade.

"It's okay," a voice said from inside the store. The words were spoken so closely behind me I jumped.

"I'm sorry I startled you," Bryan Shelton said. "I hope you didn't jump because you were scared. I told you I wouldn't hurt you."

I knew my mouth had dropped open, but I couldn't find the power to close it. I mentally congratulated myself on emptying my bladder before I snuck out. Otherwise, warm water would have flowed down my legs.

Bryan Shelton looked the same as he had when I last saw him. Kerry had let his nephew borrow some clothes because the khaki pants and flannel shirt looked foreign on him.

"Are you going to be okay?" Bryan asked. He seemed truly concerned, but I didn't let down my guard.

A large rock fell into my stomach and I wanted to run away. My feet were cemented to the floor and my tongue would not let go of my palate.

Kerry gave an exasperated sigh, and I was broken from my paralysis. I walked up to Bryan and slapped his face.

Bryan's hand immediately went to his cheek. I liked the wounded expression he wore.

"How dare you!" I shouted. "What gives you the right to speak to me? If you think I believe your little story of innocence, then you are sadly mistaken! I hate you, my mom hates you, and my grandpa hates you! Go back to jail and leave us in peace!"

Kerry moved behind the counter, but Bryan held up his hand. "It's okay, Uncle Kerry," he said. "Who knows what people have been telling her."

Kerry relaxed, but he moved to the end of the counter. He cracked his knuckles in what I'm sure he thought was a threatening manner. Kerry was too old and too slow for me to fear.

Bryan Shelton was another story. His arms were as big as my thighs and I had witnessed his uncontrollable temper in my visions. Bryan wore a sweet and sympathetic expression, but I knew his anger could erupt at any moment.

Lydia chose that moment to push the door open. I imagine most of my questions would have been answered if Bryan and I had not been interrupted.

Silence encased the room like a bubble for almost a minute. Bryan dropped to the floor in shock.

I thought I was prepared for anything. I thought I had been through so much in my short life that nothing could surprise me. I was wrong.

Bryan squeaked out one word that changed everything. I can look back on everything that happened and know that moment was the catalyst for the events that followed.

Bryan looked up at Lydia Sneed with hope and desperation and said, "Nellie?"

Chapter Twenty-Five

Lydia had never heard the stories of her mother's best friend. She had studied the picture of her mother and the unfamiliar woman, and she had tried to determine her identity by asking her mother to share the woman's story with her.

Olivia had taken one look at the picture and tears had cascaded down her face. Olivia jumped as if she'd been shot when Lydia tried to comfort her with a soft touch.

Lydia's father had snatched up the photograph and yelled at Lydia for almost half an hour. By the time she was able to get away from Bannon Sneed, Olivia was buried in liquor bottles. Lydia couldn't make out the sounds coming from her mummy. They didn't even sound like words.

I thought of the picture I had seen of Nellie and Olivia. I tried to remember Nellie's smile, hair, and eyes. I was terribly confused and my tired mind could not fully process the truth I now knew.

Bryan looked like he was seeing a ghost. His face was pale and his lips trembled. He made no effort to look away from Lydia or to get off the floor.

Lydia returned the obvious response. "Who's Nellie?"

"Sweet goodness," Kerry said from behind me. My head turned toward his voice and registered the same look on Kerry's face that Bryan wore.

"I told you it was uncanny," Kerry said.

"What's uncanny?" Lydia demanded. She had popped into the store looking for me, but it seemed as if a tower of lies was tumbling to the ground.

I realized that I had been wrong about the choices Lydia would have made after Ella's fit. I brushed her mind and learned what Lydia had done in the last few hours.

Lydia had hidden in the limo and informed the driver to plead ignorance over her whereabouts when the police asked about her. She had looked up my grandpa's address on the internet and was going to wait until the lights went out to get my attention. Lydia gathered the rocks she was going to use to peck at my bedroom window an hour before she saw me jump from my window. My flight from my grandpa's home had confused her, so she ordered her driver to follow me at a distance. I had been too preoccupied to notice that a vehicle had been tailing me. Lydia had been perplexed when she saw me enter Kerry Shelton's shop, so it had taken her a few moments to gather her courage before she ran inside.

"Why didn't I see it when she was growin' up?" Kerry said. I could hear his astonishment.

Lydia was looking defiantly from one person to another. She finally settled on me. "Do you know what they're talking about?"

I thought about my words carefully. "I believe Bryan thinks you look like his dead wife."

"You mean like in that story about the town's big flood?" Lydia asked. "Didn't he murder her?"

"I don't think he did," I said, surprising myself.

"Well, I'm too young to be Nellie Shelton!" Lydia said incredulously.

"I agree," I said slowly, "but you aren't too young to be *Lily* Shelton."

Lily Shelton would have been a year or two older than Lydia Sneed, but I thought the difference in ages could be easily explained. Lydia had always been physically and mentally ahead of her peers, but no one questioned her age because almost every girl in the world looked and acted older than her age.

"What kind of stupid nonsense is this?" Lydia said. I could tell that she was trying to find a good argument against what I'd said, but she wasn't able to find the logic to counter my statement.

"Look," Lydia said, shaking her head, "I followed you here so I could tell you some things I've learned. I thought the craziest thing I would have to deal with is that old man's—" Lydia pointed at Kerry "—resentment toward my family. I didn't realize the shop was visiting the Twilight Zone."

"What is your first memory?" Kerry interjected. He seemed determined to settle the question of Lydia's identity.

Lydia humored him by reflecting, but she spoke in a sarcastic tone. "Well, Old Man, I remember holding hands with Mr. Hernandez, a manservant with more brains than the men in this shop. He gave me a purple rabbit."

"Oh," was all I could squeak out. I had a feeling that the man Lydia thought was Mr. Hernandez was really my grandpa.

"Mr. Hernandez didn't give you that rabbit," Bryan said. He dropped his gaze. "Conner gave it to you."

I could tell Lydia was still puzzled. I didn't think she knew my grandpa's first name, and she showed no sign of accepting the truth everyone else in the room had realized. I was going to explain it to her, but the worst possible thing happened.

My grandpa slung the door open and swung himself inside. I saw him size up the room and its occupants in less than three seconds. He had his service pistol out, and he trained it on Bryan.

"Don't move!" my grandpa shouted. Erwin's Chief of Police held a locked position with both hands on his gun and his feet apart.

Lydia screamed and ran to me. My knees buckled, and we fell to the floor. From my new vantage point, I could see a gun tucked into the back of Bryan's pants. Its handle stuck out of the top of his waistband, and the light reflected off its polished surface.

I never would have guessed that I would have been so easy for my grandpa to find, but he had years of tracking down experienced criminals, so a thirteen-year-old girl was probably simple to locate. Besides, someone could have recognized me before I had gotten to the shop.

My grandpa's eyes moved quickly. "Grandpa," I shouted, "he has a gun!"

I have been over that sentence a million times. I wish I would have stayed quiet because my grandpa may have heard the bells jingle as another person entered the shop. The fact remains that I shouted a statement that I thought would be the most helpful piece of information in the situation, and it caused my grandpa to divert his attention from the scene and focus on me.

Bannon Sneed stepped coolly into the shop, and he wasted no time firing four shots with the gun he held. Lydia was spared a bullet, and I pretended that I had been shot by causing my body to jerk backward onto the floor. I felt the wind of the bullet as it passed my shoulder.

Bryan, Kerry, and my grandpa had all felt the wrath of the gun. Bannon Sneed quickly pulled his daughter to her feet and ushered her out the door. Lydia's ear-piercing screams echoed through the store but were muffled by the time her voice found the night air.

I was reminded of something that my grandpa had said during our earlier conversation. My grandpa believed that Bannon Sneed didn't have the guts to do his own dirty work. I guess the years had changed him.

I stayed motionless in case Bannon Sneed burst back through the door. I heard male grunting and sighing, so I knew the men in the shop were moving.

"Bryan," Kerry whispered. "Are you okay, boy?"

"Yeah," Bryan said. "Were you hit, Lily?"

I raised my head and met Bryan's eyes. "He took Lydia."

Kerry was the first to make it to me. "Where are you hit?"

"I faked it," I said, quickly getting up. "He just missed me." I could see golden glitter in my eyes, and I felt light-headed.

Kerry crawled over to his nephew, holding his side. Bryan had been shot in the arm. It seemed to be causing him a lot of pain. He kept saying, "Hurry, we can still catch them!"

"Hush, boy," Kerry said, investigating Bryan's wound.

"I didn't come all this way just to have her slip through my fingers," Bryan said. His forehead was pressed against his uncle's arm.

"Well, go get her then," Kerry said forcefully. Bryan got up slowly, but he crossed the distance to the door very quickly. He paused for a moment to peer out of the glass before he stepped out into the night.

I crawled over to my grandpa. He had been closest to Bannon when he stepped in and had gotten the worst of his random shots.

My grandpa had fallen on his front side, so I rolled him over to revive him. I screamed when I saw his face.

The movies don't show you what it really is like when a person dies. My grandpa had been shot in the head, and bits of brain, bone, and blood were all over the floor. I looked into my grandpa's dead eyes and knew that there would be no last words of wisdom or a final, tearful farewell. All I had left of my grandpa was what I'd gotten before Bannon Sneed ended his life.

My heart froze, and my blood boiled. I lost most of my conscious thought in my grief, so I don't remember much of what I said or did in the moments that followed.

I couldn't think or feel. My breath seemed caught in my throat, but I didn't realize that it was because I was screaming.

Chapter Twenty-Six

I finally got my emotions under control. I had passed out for a few moments, and when I awoke, I realized I had been mumbling.

I couldn't remember when I stopped screaming, but I knew it had been because I wanted to hear what Kerry was saying. He kept his voice low and steady, even though his words were indistinguishable under my loud cries.

I thought of my grandpa's love and kindness and his belief in all that was just and right. I looked at his arms, sticking out from the coroner's blanket, and I thought of the way those arms had always protected me and held me up on a pedestal.

All the wisdom and love my grandpa could have shared with me was gone, all because Bannon Sneed had tried to kill everyone to protect his lie. *I hated him!*

I was tired, but I wanted to find Lydia. I would kill Bannon Sneed myself. I should still be young enough to stay out of jail, even if I landed in juvie for a couple of years. I would be the model murderer, and the town would throw a party for me when I turned eighteen because I rid the world of a vicious little man.

I didn't bother to inform the police about the details of the murder. They either wouldn't believe me, or they were Bannon Sneed's
puppets.

There were three policemen gathered around my grandpa's body.
I recognized Detective Novack, he seemed to be my grandpa's pro-
tégé, and he was the most upset adult in the room. Two highway
patrolmen were shaken. They had worked with my grandpa for
years, but they were assessing the scene and taking pictures.

I couldn't hear ambulance sirens like I did when Ella had been
hurt, and I assumed it was because the policemen had determined
that my grandpa was beyond help.

They talked in low murmurs. Kerry must have left the shop while
I was passed out on the floor. I couldn't see him.

One of the officers put a blanket over most of my grandpa's body.
Detective Novack took off his hat and placed it over my grandpa's
face. The hat covered my grandpa's eyes, the same eyes that had
trusted me. The same eyes that I had diverted seconds before his
death.

I thought it would be difficult to slip by the policemen with their
sixth senses, but I simply walked out the door. The door did not
jingle when I opened it. Someone had taken the row of bells off the
door.

I looked back through the glass once I was on the other side, but
I had still gone unnoticed. The policemen were trying to stay busy
enough to keep their emotions from spilling over.

"Where do you think you're going?" said a voice behind me.

I jumped as if I'd been shot at again. Kerry Shelton stood against
the wall of his building with a cigarette in his mouth. The bullet had
only grazed him, and he had refused medical treatment.

"I'm going to kill Bannon Sneed," I said simply. I dared Kerry to
challenge my words.

Kerry chuckled and dragged the lighted part of his cigarette across the brick wall. I could hardly see him in the dark.

"Bryan's gonna beat you to it," Kerry said. "Best to come in and let the police call your mother."

"Bryan doesn't know where he's going," I said.

"Oh, and I imagine you do," Kerry chided.

Kerry Shelton was no longer openly hostile toward me. We had been through a lot together.

The realization that my grandpa was gone got my blood pumping again. I placed a stronger guard over my emotions.

I didn't extend the conversation any further. I jumped into a run. It was at least a ten-minute ride to the place where Bannon Sneed was trying to hide his family, and my legs might carry me there within the hour if I took a couple of trails through the woods. I hoped my tired body could propel me forward.

I had been running for less than five minutes when I realized my mistake. My poor, exhausted body could not withstand more than a ten-minute run before it would collapse off the side of the road. I was barely sweating, but my muscles would not allow me to run much farther. It took a conscious effort to put one foot in front of the other.

I heard a car slow behind me. I turned and saw my grandpa's cruiser.

I almost believed my grandpa had caught me. My brain had not had time to fully process my grandpa's passing before I remembered he was dead.

I recognized the figure in the driver's seat. The streetlights cast enough blue-white light on him to make out his tall stature and brown hair. I was too emotionally spent to be surprised when Bryan stumbled out of the cruiser.

Bryan had found a blanket in the cruiser's trunk and had torn it into pieces to wrap around his arm. The bleeding had probably slowed, but the shirt showed evidence of the wound it held.

Bryan was determined to continue running from the authorities, even though a lot of his energy was gone. His face was two shades lighter, and long lines of moisture trailed from his temples down his cheeks.

Tears clouded his vision, and his voice cracked when he spoke. He had more than a flesh wound, and he wouldn't last long without medical attention.

"I'm so sorry," Bryan said.

What was he sorry about? He hadn't killed my grandpa. I had already decided that *I* was to blame for leading my grandpa to the shop and to his death.

"What do you want?" I said harshly. I wasn't scared of Bryan now that I had assessed his condition.

Bryan flinched when he heard my words. He extended a shaky hand. "I didn't want you to get involved, Sydney, and I didn't want your grandfather to get killed."

I believed every word Bryan said, but I wasn't going to forgive him. I couldn't forgive myself.

"You can't run up to the river with your head full of revenge," Bryan said. "I've done it, and look where it got me."

It suddenly hit me. There was still a large possibility that Bryan had murdered Nellie in his rage.

"Where are you going?" he asked.

"Didn't you just say that you thought I was going to the river?" I said innocently.

"I took a guess,' he said. "You are headed in that direction. After all, isn't that where Bannon lives?"

"I'm going after Bannon Sneed," I said carefully. "I think I know where he took Lydia."

"I don't think it's safe for you to be running down a street this time—"

"He killed my grandpa," I cut in.

I had been short and to the point, and Bryan didn't try to come up with reasons for me to go back to his uncle's shop and let the police call my mom. We stood staring at each other.

I started to understand my mom's estrangement from God. I had heard her praying for my dad to come home and for Josh to live through his bullet wound, and for Jerrod to be found alive, but her prayers were not answered. Everyone she loved died, so why invest time in something that wouldn't matter?

I had looked into my grandpa's dead eyes, and I had been there when Josh took his final breath. I cried for my father's return, and I begged for a way to let Jerrod know he could ascend to the heavens. I tried to believe in God, and I said a prayer to Him for guidance. *Should I go with Bryan or should I continue on my own?*

"Look," Bryan said. He was having trouble moving, but it seemed he was getting better instead of worse. "I *swear* I won't hurt you."

Bryan extended his left pinky. He was going to pinky swear. *God had answered my question.*

My family put a lot of faith in the pinky swear. We all used it whenever we wanted to put extra emphasis on the word of another person. My mom said that a promise should always be kept, but our family viewed the pinky swear as an unbreakable contract. I had broken a pinky swear only once, and I had regretted it. I sacrificed the love and trust of my sister so that I could live what appeared to be a normal life. That hadn't turned out too well.

Poor Ella was now in some asylum because she chose to be true to herself. If I had only validated the gift she possessed, then my sister could be free.

It's true that we may have both been ridiculed for our special talents, but we could have faced the world together. In fact, Ella could have helped me hone my skill and we could have helped a lot of people.

I thought of Ella all alone in a padded cell. *But that wasn't right, was it?* Ella was taken by an ambulance to the hospital. The EMTs told my mom that the hospital would run some tests on Ella to make sure an infection from her broken arm had not caused her to have hallucinations. Ella was resting in a sterile bed at the Erwin Hospital.

I quickly constructed a plan. It was a little deceptive, but I thought I could pull it off.

I extended my pinky and curled it firmly around Bryan's finger. I locked eyes with him, and I was momentarily sorry for the ruse I had drummed up. He seemed sincere.

I got into my grandpa's cruiser and closed my door. It was the first time I had ridden in any police cruiser without my grandpa at the wheel. I tried not to think about the happy times my grandpa and I had experienced or the confidences we'd shared. My secrets would lie in a cold grave with him. I felt almost numb, hoping that I was in a vivid dream brought on by the stress of Ella's condition.

I started to tell Bryan that Bannon was in a house near the hospital, but he hurriedly drove in the other direction toward Pale Woods Academy. At first, I thought he might be looking for a place to turn around, but he floored the gas. My teeth vibrated in my mouth as he raced the car over two sets of railroad tracks.

"You *pinky* swore that I could trust you," I said, grabbing the handle above the window for support.

"I said that I would never *hurt* you," Bryan said.

Great, he was being technical.

It was hard for me to stay positioned in my seat. Bryan's crazy driving pulled me from one direction to another as he took curves at a high rate of speed.

"Where are you taking me?" I asked between curves.

"You wanted revenge on Bannon Sneed, so I'll let you watch while I kill him," Bryan said evenly.

I was horrified at the thought of watching as Bryan killed my new nemesis. I was going after revenge, but I hadn't thought about *actually* killing the man. Hearing the words come out of Bryan's mouth made the idea a reality.

Bryan had appeared on the verge of passing out when he held out his pinky to me. After I got into the car, a surge of adrenaline gave him new energy.

I thought about jumping out of the car or grabbing the wheel. The river road was narrow, and both ideas would have probably led to our deaths.

The ride to the Sneed estate was too short. Bryan was barreling up the paved drive before I could come up with a way to stop him.

Several lights were on inside the house, and I tried to think of the rooms which might occupy people. I wondered if the staff were inside or if they were staying somewhere else as they mourned Beth's death.

Bryan shot out of the cruiser and ran up the walk to the porch steps. I slung open the car door and followed him, trying to swallow the acid that had climbed up my throat.

Amazingly, the door was open. A black wreath that had been hanging on the door flew onto the porch. I should have taken its presence as an omen. I stepped over it and into the house.

Bryan and I never made it past the foyer. Bryan turned almost toward the front door with his hands out and his eyes glazed. He seemed to be in shock. His stooped posture and sweaty face made him look sick and deranged.

I followed Bryan's gaze to the floor behind me. In a corner, just inside the door, Olivia Sneed was slumped in a sitting position. Her eyes were frozen in a death stare. Pale purple bruises dotted her neck. I could almost see where fingers had choked the life out of her skinny, frail body.

"I want to go home." I repeated over and over. It finally became a chant to keep me from passing out.

Bryan was the first to gather his wits. "Sydney, we need to leave quickly and quietly," he whispered. I couldn't understand why he was talking so low. Anyone on the property would have heard us screaming up the driveway and barging into the house.

Bryan rubbed the outside doorknob with his shirt. I wondered if his blood had splattered on the shirt and would show up when the police scanned the area for forensic evidence.

"Was this on the ground when we came in?" Bryan had made his way to the front porch and was pointing to the black wreath.

I was afraid my feet wouldn't move. I had heard of feeling frozen in place, and I really didn't trust my mind to direct my body.

The light caught something shiny by Olivia Sneed's body. Against my better judgment, I bent down to investigate.

I recognized the locket almost immediately. The chain was missing, but the locket was lying by one of Olivia's legs.

I grabbed the locket and went out to join Bryan. He had replaced the wreath on the door by pulling the sleeves of his shirt over his hands.

I stuck the locket in the front pocket of my jeans and asked, "What do we do now?"

I thought Bryan might mention calling 911 or going back to his uncle's shop. "Didn't you say you knew where Bannon would take Lydia?"

I nodded, even though I had said I knew where Bannon Sneed would take his *family*. It was a moot point.

Bryan called over his shoulder, "Then I'll go where you point."

I knew that this would be my only chance to contact Ella. I pointed back into Erwin.

"They have a house by the hospital," I lied.

Bryan's jaw clenched, and he jumped back into the cruiser. He was going to be really mad at me when he found out I had misdirected him. I could only hope that a pinky swear meant more to him than it had to me.

Chapter Twenty-Seven

I told Bryan to park in the hospital parking lot so the cruiser would be less conspicuous. Police cruisers were often seen at the hospital.

I was out and running to the automatic doors before Bryan could stop the cruiser. I was secretly happy that he had let me ride up front. The back doors had safety locks that could only be opened from the outside.

I was so nervous and emotionally and physically exhausted that I collapsed on the sidewalk. I hit the cement with a smack, and I could feel red-hot pain in my knees and right elbow.

I was jerked up after a few seconds. Bryan brought me eye level with him. I could feel the heat from his arm as his body sought to fight off the invading bullet and the impending infection.

"Where are you going?" Bryan said. He wasn't angry, but he looked confused. He was still trying to keep his voice down.

"I have to go see Ella!" I shouted.

"Who's Ella?" Bryan asked.

I could see he was truly bewildered. I wondered how he could know about me and not have heard about Ella.

"She's my sister," I said, squirming in his hands.

"Your father never told me you had a sister," Bryan replied. A faraway look carried him back to a memory.

"When did you talk to my father?" I had stopped trying to free myself, but I was still on guard.

Bryan came out of his reverie and said, "He used to write me all the time. He helped me a lot during my sorry excuse of a trial and my first years in prison."

Suddenly things went into place. Kerry had been nice to my father when he brought Jerrod to fix my mom's earring! They were on the same side of a very important issue. My grandpa must have hated my father when he didn't share the same view of Bryan. I had always thought my grandpa's hatred of my father stemmed from the Miller's mental illnesses, and maybe that was the start of it, but my father's support for Bryan could not have warmed my grandpa's feelings toward my father.

Bryan must have analyzed my look and understood what I was feeling. He set me down gently on the sidewalk.

"You can choose to go," he said, "or you can help me. We can help each other. My guess is that she's with him right now."

"Okay," I said, deciding to be honest with Bryan. "I need to talk to my sister first."

"Then I'll do anything that helps you," Bryan said. I saw sincerity in his eyes, and I hoped I wasn't imagining it.

Moments later, we had walked casually through the double doors to the hospital and into the hall. The front entrance to the emergency room was within eyesight of a nurse's station and the reception desk. The side door Bryan and I took emptied us into a hallway where only the nurses could see us from their station. We turned into the hallway because if we peeked, we were sure to be noticed and questioned.

The next hallway led us to a third corridor, where patients were kept overnight. Bryan checked the rooms on the left, and I looked into the rooms on the right.

I was afraid we would be looking in every room. Fortunately, the nurses placed overnight patients in the rooms closest to the emergency room. I had only poked my head into three rooms when Bryan whispered for my attention.

He motioned me over to a closed door with a long slit for the window. I could see my sister on a bed next to a large window to the outside world. She was awake, with a dazed stare, and her hands were strapped to the bed.

I moved to the other side of the door and looked through the window again. This perspective showed my mom slumped in a seat under the television. A book lay open at her feet. It must have slid from her hands as she drifted into sleep.

I tried the door and opened it a crack. It opened soundlessly, and I waved Bryan inside. He waited until I had passed through the doorway before he entered Ella's room.

Bryan seemed mesmerized with my mom. He kept staring at her like she were a beauty queen. I didn't understand his current infatuation. My mom's mouth was open and a string of saliva was dangling from her lips.

Ella jerked out of her daze and turned to me. She raised a finger to her lips, and I nodded my understanding.

I walked toward my sister. I briefly wondered if Bryan was behind me but didn't turn around to find out.

Ella raised her chin to speak to me. She kept her eyes locked on something by the window. I didn't want to know what she saw.

I leaned in to hear my sister's words. Ella spoke softly, but clearly.

"I know how Nellie died."

Well, that was no big surprise. Nellie was drowned in the Nolichucky River.

Ella kept speaking. She was emotionally spent, and her body was paying the price. She was shaky and weak. There were huge circles under her eyes that looked like bruises, and her skin was a couple of shades lighter than the snow-white complexion she usually wore.

"Nellie told you she was drowned," Ella said. "She mentioned the name Terrance."

Ella looked at me pointedly, like it should all be clear to me. I'm sure that I wore a bewildered look.

"You were reading her mind, Sydney," Ella continued. "You read the mind of a ghost, and you sent it to me. I don't know why I couldn't hear Nellie, but she was trying to tell us that Terrance was the one who killed her."

I finally understood that the incoherent rambling I'd expressed before Ella's fit had been unclear to Lydia. Somehow I had translated Nellie's message and sent it to Ella without knowing I had done it.

"Terrance," I said aloud. I heard a rustle behind me, and I noticed Bryan standing next to my mom. He had pulled a pillow off of the foot of Ella's bed and propped my mom's head up with it. My mom was sleeping much more comfortably.

"Terrance," Bryan repeated. He was glowing with rage.

"Terry Thorpe wasn't old enough to have murdered Nellie," I said softly.

Bryan stomped his foot. My mom groaned something in her sleep, but settled back onto her pillow.

"Terry Thorpe was never called Terrance," Bryan said. His fists were clenched, and I worried about his bullet wound again. "Terrance Hernandez was Terry's father."

Something hit me hard on the head. I saw golden glitter as the world lost meaning to me.

Chapter Twenty-Eight

I was mad!

How could she leave? We had been through so much together, and she was going to sneak away while I was working a crisis?

I flew through my house, tearing open the doors. I finally heard laughter outside and ran to the back door.

My heart leaped a little. It always did when I saw my beautiful wife. Her long blond hair caught every ray of the sun, and her face was flawless as a perfected statue.

She had my daughter in her arms, and they were collecting her metal pail. Lily kept her rock collection in the pail. Lily cried, "Why we leave, Mommy!" while she clutched her purple rabbit.

My temper cooled a little, but I still ran out screaming at Nellie. Nellie was screaming back. I picked up Lily with the intention of leaving with her because Nellie wouldn't go anywhere without Lily.

Lily squirmed in my arms as her mother and I elevated our voices. I tried to hold on to her, but even though she weighed less than forty pounds, my little girl concentrated all her weight into one push. She jumped out of my arms and landed squarely on a large rock.

Nellie started screaming that I'd killed her baby. I knelt down to examine the wound. Just to add to the fun of the situation, I heard Olivia Sneed's voice yell, "We'll get you now, Bryan. Now we have proof that you're just a stupid redneck."

I was trying to examine the gash on Lily's head. The gash would need a couple of stitches, but it didn't look like she had a concussion.

To my surprise, Nellie yelled back, "Bryan didn't hurt Lily. It was an accident."

Olivia came closer and lowered her voice to a regular speaking tone. "We talked about this, Nellie. You're in denial. He'll kill your whole family before you really see the light."

I wasn't proud of what I was about to do, and I would probably lose my job. I was being self-destructive. If I were going to lose my family, then what did I have to live for?

I swung my fist toward Olivia's perfectly permed hair. My fist never connected because Hernandez, the Sneed's bodyguard, blocked my blow. I tried to counter his move, but my feet were thrown out from under me. I could hear Olivia Sneed screaming toward the house.

"He tried to kill me!" she yelled.

"Don't hurt him!" my wife screamed. I heard a splash and figured she had been thrown away from defending me.

I tried to get up, but my head told me it was just a dream. The water running down my cheek was warm and...

"Sydney!" Bryan shook me frantically. "You passed out, and I couldn't get you to wake up."

Bryan's eyes held a crazy stare. He really was frightened.

"Can I see your head?" I said groggily. I scooted into a sitting position on the floor and rubbed a spot on my head that had been bruised by the tile.

Bryan was surprised, but I wanted to prove that I had just had another vision. I ran my fingers over a spot next to his right ear. The warm liquid he had felt before losing consciousness in my vision had been his own blood. I located a thin line of scar tissue where I expected.

I looked back at Ella. I had assumed she'd knocked me out when she realized I would need a vision in order to believe Bryan's story and fully trust him, but his hands were held firmly to the plastic bed rails.

"Who hit me on the head?" I asked. I looked from Bryan to Ella.

"You just passed out," Bryan said. "It must be all the stress—"

"There is another presence in this room," Ella said simply and slowly. "I asked it to cause you to lose consciousness."

Bryan scoffed, "I thought you were in here for your broken arm, but you really are Johnny Miller's daughter."

He realized his mistake too late. The temperature in the room cooled, and darkness fell over the already shadowy night.

Bryan was determined to stay a skeptic. He swiveled his head to look around the room at the shapeless cold that had overwhelmed the room. "Am I supposed to clap three times and say I believe in ghosts?"

There was a clap, and Bryan grabbed his cheek. "What the—"

The light of the night returned to the room. Bryan looked at me accusingly, but I was too far away to have landed the punch. He glanced at Ella and my mom to make sure one was still strapped to her bed and the other was asleep.

"Don't make fun of us," I whispered. "We can't help who our father and grandfather were."

Bryan nodded, but he was probably afraid to say anything. I turned to Ella and wished that I could free her.

I bent toward her ear again and whispered, "Thank your friend for the vision. I know the truth and where to go now."

Ella nodded and said, "Do not get yourself or that man killed. Try to save Lydia if you can. She probably still does not know the whole story."

"I don't think any of us knows the *whole* story," I mumbled.

I turned to leave. I cast one more look in my mom's direction. Bryan stood over her. He touched her cheek tenderly. She smiled and sighed in her dream.

I suddenly felt pity for Bryan. He had lost everything he had ever loved, and he'd spent a decade in jail for crimes he didn't commit.

"Do you want to wake her?" I asked. I brushed Ella's mind. Her wall was down. She agreed with me.

"No," Bryan said firmly. "I will have to go back to jail for breaking out, but it should only be for a little while once the murder charges are dropped. I want to remember her contentment when I touched her. I don't want to see her scared or upset at the sight of me. Maybe she can see me the way I see her when I come home for good."

I understood Bryan's feelings. I kissed my mom lightly on the cheek and nodded to Ella.

She nodded back. *Bannon Sneed has ruined so many lives. Do not give him the chance to ruin more,* my sister sent.

I didn't have to send back my intentions. Ella knew that I wasn't going to let Bannon Sneed go unpunished.

Chapter Twenty-Nine

Bryan and I walked out of the hospital without trying to avoid being seen. If anyone caught us now, we would just leave. We had accomplished what we wanted to do.

I tried not to think about my grandpa's cruiser as I stepped into it and closed the door. I couldn't seem to keep my mind off him. *He had been alive only a couple of hours ago!*

After a couple of quiet minutes in the cruiser, I said, "So Bannon killed Olivia."

Bryan nodded his agreement. He knew I wasn't asking a question.

Suddenly my mind was full of questions. They swirled around my brain and popped out of my mouth.

"Why did Bannon kill Nellie? Why didn't anyone recognize Lily when she came back as Lydia? Why didn't Lydia, or Lily, remember herself? Didn't the autopsy confirm that Lily had drowned? Why did Bannon kill Olivia?"

Bryan nodded like he had considered each of my questions before they were voiced. He spoke the answers my tired mind was too exhausted to compute.

"Bannon Sneed didn't want Olivia to go back to the city. It had taken him years to get her back after she left the first time. He probably had Terrance Hernandez kill Nellie. He never liked to get his hands dirty. Lily was gone for a couple of years, so no one would have expected her to be anything more than who Bannon said she was."

Bryan took a deep breath. He must have thought his daughter was dead for years, and he was reluctant to believe that God had given him another chance. I could tell he wasn't giving in to his assumptions yet. Bryan was too afraid to believe that his daughter was alive, and he worried he would suddenly find out that he was wrong.

I brushed his mind and saw visions of Lily the toddler and Lydia the teenager. The resemblance was eerily similar. I also saw Bryan's fear that he had seen characteristics that weren't there or that Bannon would kill Lydia before he had the chance to see the girl who could be Lily again.

After a brief pause, Bryan said, "Lily hit her head on a rock, so she could have had amnesia. Another possibility is that she was almost two at the time, so she may have accepted anything the Sneeds told her. Without Nellie and me around, there was no one to spark her memory. My Uncle Kerry stayed away from that family, and even your grandfather gave them a wide berth. *After* my trial, I mean.

"It wouldn't have been hard to bribe people to overlook certain things about the body that was discovered. The Sneeds could have bought the body from a hospital, or they could have paid the forensic specialist and the prosecutor to present the evidence any way they chose."

Bryan grew grave. "Everyone wanted me convicted."

I took a deep breath. There were still a lot of uncertainties in Bryan's explanation. I was sure there were limits to what the wealthy could do. *The rich can't always get what they want, right?*

Bryan cleared his throat and looked at me before responding my last question. He answered me when he seemed sure that I wasn't upset about the rationalizations he had made about the situation.

"Bannon probably killed his wife because she had a sudden attack of conscience. After all, I heard Olivia's been drinking for the past decade. It was most likely sparked by the death of her best friend. Nellie really was close to Olivia. That's why I still wonder if my wife died accidentally or if she was murdered."

I could answer that question, but I knew I should proceed carefully. I patted Bryan's hand.

"Nellie *was* murdered," I said. I expected Bryan to get upset, but he kept driving calmly. "I'm sorry, but if you think back to your trial, you'll remember that your wife's windpipe was crushed and there were finger marks around her throat. I guess Terrance must have murdered her."

"I'm sorry," Bryan said almost sarcastically. "I wasn't paying too much attention to my murder trial. I knew I would be convicted if the Sneeds wanted me to be, and I was still numb from the grief of losing my family."

I closed my mouth with a pop and looked out the passenger-side window. Bryan's tone—more than his words—had hurt my feelings.

Bryan seemed to understand that he had overreacted, and he reached out to pat my hand. He seemed unsure whether he should touch me, so his hand hovered over mine for a few seconds before he quickly touched the pads of his fingers to my knuckles.

"I'm sorry," Bryan said sincerely. "I have spent a long time around men who don't have feelings, or they don't want to admit that they have feelings."

Bryan's fingers pressed my knuckles firmly before he took his hand away. He returned his hand to the steering wheel, and I noticed it was shaking.

I couldn't see the temper in my mom's first boyfriend that everyone had described. Maybe the years he had spent in jail had softened him.

"That's okay," I said.

We shared a few moments of silence that made Bryan terribly uncomfortable. I let him squirm.

"Where do we go now?" Bryan asked. "By now, Barren Seed probably has Lily on a private jet far away from here."

"I don't think so," I said, and I told Bryan my plan.

Unfortunately, my plan was put on hold. A flash of blue lights cast eerie shadows in the interior of the cruiser.

"I'm not ready to go back to prison," Bryan said firmly.

I could only watch as Bryan pulled over and jumped out. I heard an officer bellow a warning, and two shots were fired in the direction Bryan had run. I secretly hoped the shots had missed.

The woods offered the perfect camouflage, and Bryan was in excellent shape. I sat in the cruiser and waited for the portly officer to attempt to catch him. I was relieved to hear coughing and heaving five minutes later.

The officer radioed the dispatcher and reported that he had engaged Bryan Shelton in the woods, but Bryan had pulled a gun and shot at me. It was a fabricated story, but the officer made it sound like he was a hero for protecting me.

He probably thought I was in shock, so he could embellish his story, but I was not kidnapped like he had assumed. I doubted he had seen Bryan after he entered the woods. Bryan moved quickly for a man who had been shot and had lost a lot of blood.

I sat in the cruiser as the open door dinged, and I took a deep breath. I could smell traces of my grandpa's scent. I tried to memorize the smell, to absorb it, so that I could call on the memory at any time. I finally closed my eyes and let darkness overwhelm me.

Chapter Thirty

My mom was waiting for me at the door of the emergency room. She had departed from Ella's bedside after Detective Novack had arrived to tell her the news of her father's death. My mom had left Detective Novack in charge of looking after my sister until she could collect me and drag me back to Ella's room.

My mom was exhausted, and her red-rimmed eyes made her seem drunk instead of tired and sad. Her grief was stamped onto her face, and her eyes were puffy with tears yet to fall.

My mom seemed relieved to see me, but she grabbed me after she had established that I was physically unhurt. Her fingernails laid tracks on the inside of my arm.

I was firmly pulled along beside my mom. She did not speak until we had almost reached my sister's room.

"What were you thinking?" my mom demanded in a strained whisper. "You knew he would follow you to the ends of the world!"

My mom was talking about my grandpa. Tears cascaded down my cheeks, but no sound passed my lips.

"I honestly don't know what to do with you!" my mom continued. "I hope you're satisfied with the chaos you've created."

Words can hurt more than a physical attack. My heart was sobbing in my chest. My mom's accusations washed over me and threatened to choke the life from my body. I wish she had just hit me. It would have hurt me less.

My mom studied me for a few seconds and finally gave up on getting a response. Her eyes darted from side to side, looking for a better angle to attack. She cut her nails back into my skin and continued to my sister's door.

Right outside my sister's room, my mom said, "Don't embarrass me. Use your manners when you speak to Detective Novack. He was a trusted friend of your grandfather's."

I nodded, and my mom opened Ella's door. Ella was pretending to be asleep. I could hear the hum of her conscious thoughts. Detective Novack was slumped over in the chair my mom had occupied during my earlier visit. He seemed to be praying or reflecting on something, but he quickly rose to his feet when he noticed that my mom and I had entered the room.

The bathroom light was on, and it provided enough light to see without disturbing Ella's false sleep. My eyes adjusted quickly to the low light.

"I'm glad she's okay, Miranda," he said. His voice cracked around my mom's name, and I wondered if he had been crying in my sister's silent room.

"Thank you for staying with Ella, Lewis," my mom said. "I appreciate you coming down and personally telling me about my father's death."

Detective Novack placed his hand on my mom's shoulder. She jumped at the touch, and he pulled his hand back quickly.

"I'm sorry." It was dark in the room, but I could tell that his face had colored.

My mom appeared equally embarrassed. "It's m-my fault," she stammered. "I guess all these unfortunate happenings have me a little on edge."

Detective Novack nodded and extended his hand. My mom shook it, and he expressed his condolences again.

"Thank you," my mom said. "I'm glad he had someone like you close to him."

Detective Novack released my mom's hand and walked toward the door. He patted me on the arm, and I didn't startle at his touch. I could feel his mind searching for the right words to say to me, but I didn't pierce his thoughts past his surface notions. I didn't prolong his struggle.

"Thank you, Detective Novack," I said. "My grandpa really cared for you, and I'm glad his friendship meant so much to you."

Detective Novack's mouth momentarily turned up at the corners. He was grateful for being bailed out of an awkward situation.

He cast one more look at my mom before he left. I was blasted with a thought from him about her. Bryan was not the only man who secretly cared for my mom.

His sadness hung over him like an ominous cloud, but I had no more comfort for him. I had my own pain, and in my life, unhappiness and grief were like a storm that had no end.

Chapter Thirty-One

My mom and I stayed in the hospital for two more days, and when it was time to bring Ella home, I returned to my mom's house as if nothing had happened. My mom didn't mention my change of residence or my grandpa's demise. She was practiced at avoiding topics that would cause animosity.

A missing person's report had been filed for Lydia and Bannon Sneed. Bryan was still at large. I had been making my mom use the little power she held as the former police chief's daughter to secure information about Lydia's whereabouts.

The police had searched Lydia's home, and they had alerted detectives to search the Sneed's summer homes and known vacation spots. No one had located Lydia or Bannon Sneed. It had been over a week since the two of them had been seen, and I worried more with every day that passed.

Detective Novack had been compassionate with me when I gave my official statement, but the new chief of police shook his head when he received it. He refused to believe Bannon Sneed had shot anyone, even though my statement and Kerry Shelton's account of that night matched.

He told his detectives and officers to keep looking for Bryan Shelton. He claimed Kerry was covering up for his nephew and I was too traumatized by my grandpa's death to remember the incident accurately.

I missed the last two days of school before Christmas break. Christian brought my assignments to my house, but we weren't home, so he left my homework and books wrapped in a plastic bag on the porch.

My mom made funeral arrangements for my grandpa while I stayed home and "watched" Ella. I had already decided I wouldn't stop my sister if she wanted to run away again, but she just lay in her bed, staring into the ceiling.

I couldn't say Ella was looking *at* anything. She just stared through whatever her eyes rested on.

My grandpa's funeral was a town event. I thought three hours was a long time to view a corpse, but the viewing went by very quickly.

I stood by the casket with my mom and sister and received hundreds of people who knew and loved my grandpa. I was so upset and distracted that I'm not sure what I said to the sympathetic folks who held my hands and hugged me.

The bullet wound had damaged the front of my grandpa's head, but his service hat covered the entry point, so the casket was open. He was placed in his service uniform and decorated with medals he had earned from his military and civil service. His hands were folded, and his police ring caught the light. Every time I looked at my grandpa my eyes were drawn to the word *Protect* on the ring.

I tried not to study the corpse, but I peered down at the body in the casket. The shell that had once housed my grandpa's spirit looked nothing like he had in life. I could do nothing to change the pale, sunken features, but I wiped away the creamy pink lipstick that had been used to brighten his lips.

After the funeral, my family took showers and went to bed. The image of my grandpa in a cold casket was burned into my mind like the after-image I used to see when I'd look at the sun too long.

The sky was crying the day my grandpa was buried. My mom, my sister, and I left the house in the early morning and didn't return until late that night.

We stood with separate umbrellas at the interment as the icy rain pelted my grandpa's casket. We each laid a red rose on the wooden box that held my grandpa's body, but we didn't cry. He wasn't there to see our grief. I would have felt him the same way I had sensed Jerrod wasn't at peace after his death.

A blonde woman in a green dress approached the casket after my mom, Ella, and I loaded into the funeral home's limousine. There was something in her grief that made her stand out from the other mourners.

Funerals are really for the living. Family and friends bond over the tragic event that took a mutual loved one. Close family and friends form stronger ties and, most times, get closure.

Edna Roberts, Detective Novack's aunt and a stand-in dispatcher for the police department, opened her home to Chief Conner Murphy's family and guests after the interment. My mom was thankful for the gesture. It meant that people wouldn't be walking through our home and staying until late at night.

I became practiced at receiving condolences. My sister wouldn't talk to anyone, and, thankfully, no one approached her.

I didn't mind when people offered their sympathy, but I couldn't help feeling a twinge of anger when they tried to say they had been through the same situation or they knew how I felt. I felt like screaming, *'Wow! You mean you watched the most important person in your life gunned down as if their life was as insignificant as an ant in a field? Well then, we must be kindred spirits!'*

My family and I stayed until the last guest left. My mom and I tried to help with the cleaning, but Mrs. Roberts told us to go home and get some sleep. We went home, but I don't think we slept very much. My mom's thoughts were laced with regret, and I still couldn't get the image of my grandpa's body in the casket out of my head. Ella's mind was closed to me.

Almost all the people in our small town loved and respected my grandpa, but he meant more to me than he did to any of them. I couldn't help feeling like I had loved him the most. I'd been robbed of all the men I loved, and I couldn't even will a tear to trickle from my eyes. Maybe my heart had broken and absorbed all my tears. Maybe I had grown so used to death that it was a part of life, like losing your baby teeth or getting wrinkles. It made you sad, but you knew it was a part of growing up.

I finally fell into a restless sleep. I dreamed I was fishing with my grandpa by the Nolichucky River. He was using a purple rabbit as a lure, and Bryan was bobbing like a fish in the water.

I was so glad to see my grandpa that I reached out to him. I stopped short when he turned to me and I saw his dead eyes.

I woke up screaming, but no one came to me. My mom and Ella were dealing with their own nightmares.

Chapter Thirty-Two

There were four people called to the reading of my grandpa's will. The strange woman I had noticed at my grandpa's interment, Detective Novack, my mom, and me seated ourselves around a large, wooden table and prepared ourselves to hear Chief Connor Murphy's final words.

It had only taken a short time to prepare the reading of the will. It probably helped that my grandpa never bought anything on credit and personally knew the lead lawyer in the firm.

My mom kept throwing daggers with her eyes at the woman sitting opposite us. The woman pretended not to notice my mom's silent animosity.

I could easily penetrate the mysterious woman's mind and find out her involvement with my grandpa, but I wanted to repress my ability again. I blamed myself and my gift for my grandpa's death. I had been punishing myself by refraining from anything that made me feel happy or special since I'd returned home.

I was depressed, and I had barely stayed awake since my grandpa had been murdered. Sleep was my only escape. My mom had been distant with me during the first couple of days I was home, but she became concerned when my sadness remained unchanged.

I wondered if my father had felt like I did. It seemed there was no point to this life. *If everyone who touched your heart died, then why should you bother loving anyone?*

I looked at the woman again and tried to use my common sense to determine who she had been to my grandpa. I absorbed the woman's surface characteristics.

The woman was pretty and smartly dressed. She filled out a royal blue dress that buttoned all the way down the front. Her simple black belt and her small gold chain somehow made the dress's color stand out even more. The woman seemed older than my mom, but not by a lot. Her face had only a few wrinkles, and she wore very little makeup. She had blonde hair, cut in a bob, with red highlights that had faded to a dark shade of pink. Her skin was pale, but she didn't have a trace of freckles, and her eyes were a brilliant green. The perfect amount of color flushed her cheeks, and her pouty lips were painted a pale pink. The only flaws I could see were a few raised, white areas in the bend of her elbow.

I started to introduce myself, but when my mom saw me extend my hand over the table, she froze my words in my mouth by delivering a small, but swift and painful, kick to my shin. I coughed and drew my hand back. I bumped my head on the table as I looked down at my leg to survey the damage.

The woman blinked but continued to eye the lawyers. She seemed to know where she stood with Miranda Miller.

Detective Novack had chosen a chair on the other side of my mom. He was dressed in his police uniform, but he would not be on duty until after he left the reading of the will.

My mom leaned into Detective Novack to hear him whisper a question. My mom's face tensed and her jaw set, but she didn't answer his question, even after he stared at her for several moments.

I was seated across the table from the expertly dressed woman. I was so close to her I could smell her perfume, which probably cost more than my entire wardrobe.

Finally, the lawyers called our attention, and we all turned our faces to them. I could feel my mom's staggered breath on my neck. She was nervous.

One lawyer sat at the head of the table, and the two other lawyers gathered papers and sat on his right and left sides. The lawyer who sat at the head of the table had wire glasses and full, pinkish-red lips. He must have lost a lot of weight recently because the folds of skin on his neck fell forward when he lowered his head to read. He slightly resembled an over-grown human turkey.

The other two lawyers seemed like they were present to do the bidding of Turkey Lawyer. They referred to him on every paper they reviewed, and he would nod or shake his head with an air of importance.

There was a brief introduction, where the lawyers told us how privileged they were to have met my grandpa and handled his business. I translated it to mean, 'We're glad your grandpa gave his money to us so that we could arrange some legal gibberish on paper for an extraordinary fee.'

The woman across from me nodded her head and responded to the lawyers' formalities, but my mom cut her off. She loudly expressed her appreciation and waved for the lawyers to continue with the reading.

The lawyers shuffled some papers, and the meat of my grandpa's will was given to the lawyer at the head of the table. Turkey Lawyer straightened his wiry glasses and spoke in a firm, no-nonsense tone.

"To Miranda Denise Miller, I leave our apartment in New York City and all the money that remained in her trust."

The woman let out a small gasp, and I wondered if she was currently living in that apartment. She had better start looking for another place to stay.

Turkey Neck paused and took a long drink of filtered water. "I assume you didn't empty your trust fund on your twenty-first birthday?" he asked my mom.

My mom shook her head once. She had never told me she had a trust fund. I was almost angry that I had spent years barely getting by and my mom could have swallowed her pride and asked her father for the money to help satisfy her family's needs.

Giblet-Neck continued, "To Sydney Avery Miller, I leave my Erwin home and all of its furnishings, my fishing and hunting equipment, and my life insurance money after the affairs of my estate have been settled."

The other two lawyers looked up from their papers. Turkey Lawyer rolled his eyes just above his glasses. I tried to meet his eyes with a blank expression.

"Young lady," he spoke, "The final amount of money after everything is settled will be in the neighborhood of four hundred thousand dollars. Your grandfather paid a premium on his life insurance that doubled if he was killed in action. He was murdered while on duty, even though his death was brought upon by personal decisions. Your grandpa did not wish to put the insurance money in a trust for you, but he did request that it be kept in an account that you would draw from as needed."

I should have been thinking about purses and designer clothes, but I could only think of Ella. Poor Ella would feel even more alienated once she learned she was not included in our grandpa's will. My mom had told my sister that she was too young to be present at the reading, but Ella was smart. She knew that a person only had to be mentioned in the will to be present at the reading.

Turkey Lawyer had given up on getting a response from me. He turned his attention back to my grandpa's final wishes and cleared his throat.

"Which brings me to Detective Lewis Novack," he said.

I caught a flash from Detective Novack's mind. He was embarrassed about being here, but he was determined to present himself that would have made his Chief of Police proud.

Detective Novack fidgeted in his chair and glanced at my mom before meeting Turkey's eyes. He seemed to draw some strength from the older gentleman, and he relaxed a little.

"There is a personal note included for you," Turkey Neck said.

I felt an icy stab in my heart. *My grandpa had not left a note for me!*

The lawyer took out a piece of yellow legal paper and read my grandpa's handwritten words. I was so disappointed that I had to look at the floor and blink hard to keep my tears in my eyes.

" 'I don't know if you will ever understand how much your companionship meant to me,' " the lawyer read. " 'I hate to get sentimental, but if I'm dead, I guess it won't matter what you say about me around the coffee pot at the station.' "

Detective Novack grinned. His smile attracted the attention of the blonde woman. My mom picked up on the stare and placed her hand over Detective Novack's arm. He seemed surprised, but he did not pull away. I could see my mom's smirk with my head half turned away.

" 'I leave you my old truck.' " the lawyer continued. " 'It may not seem like much to some people, but I know you'll appreciate it, because of the comment you made about it during our first cookout.' "

Detective Novak nodded, and the note was passed to him. I had already decided that I wouldn't voluntarily pillage Detective Novack's thoughts. It was something he understood that was between him and my grandpa.

"And finally," Turkey Lawyer turned his eyes to the blonde woman, "To Amanda Gregory Murphy, I leave the ring you gave back to me on our last evening together. Thank you for your love and support. I always loved you, and you stayed in my heart even though we couldn't be together."

The blonde woman, Amanda, cried. Tears poured through her fingers, and I noticed a plain gold band that circled her left ring finger.

Detective Novack looked like he wanted to console Amanda, but my mom put the tiniest pressure on his hand, and he stayed in his seat. He looked defeated and confused.

One of the minion lawyers walked to Amanda and waited for her to acknowledge his presence. When she looked up, he placed a ring box in her hand.

The high-profile box was covered with black velvet. I could see a white satin interior when Amanda opened the mouth of the box.

It was the most splendid ring I had ever seen. A large, clear diamond adorned the ring's center, and smaller diamonds traced the band. Leaves and vines were intricately engraved around the diamonds on the platinum band.

She put the ring on her left hand, over the gold band, stood up, straightened her dress, and walked out of the office. I watched her walk out without bothering to close my mouth.

"She was always good at leaving," my mom said.

Detective Novack pulled his hand out from under my mom's and returned it to his lap. He wouldn't support my mother's rude comments.

"Grandpa was married?" I asked.

My mom acted like it was common knowledge. She waved away my question.

My mom noticed everyone looking at her, so she answered my question. It was better than explaining her hostility toward my grandpa's widow.

"Your grandpa was *remarried*," she said. Dinosaur bones would be erected as roller coasters before she told me anything more in the presence of strangers.

The lawyers expressed their condolences again and wished us future success. Turkey Lawyer told my mom that he had gotten to know my grandpa and that he was a great man.

My mom and Detective Novack walked into the hall while Turkey Neck gave me the check that made me rich in the eyes of most of my town. I lost my mind briefly before the older lawyer handed me the check and I exploded with questions.

"Why didn't my grandpa write *me* a personal message? Why didn't I know he was married? Why didn't he leave *anything* for Ella? Why did he have to die and leave me alone with all these crazy people?"

I hadn't meant to go so far. I had started talking in a normal tone, and Turkey Lawyer had raised his eyebrows slightly, but then my questions started to really upset me, and I couldn't stop my emotions. My feeling spurted up like an erupting volcano, and I was helpless to stop them.

My mom and Detective Novack ran back into the room when they heard my raised voice, and were just in time to see my full emotional breakdown. My mom tried to comfort me, but when I realized she was managing the situation instead of consoling me, I pushed her away with both hands. I was tired of covering family drama.

Turkey Lawyer's chair squeaked as he rose from it. He hitched up his pants and bent down over me.

"Little Lady," he spoke. My tears dried up instantly, and my sobs were caught in my throat. *Had my grandpa told his lawyer friend the pet name he had called me?*

I looked up into Turkey Neck's face and tried to remember the name he had given when we shook hands. I responded with, "Yes, sir," instead of taking the risk of calling him by the wrong surname.

The kind lawyer waved my mom and Detective Novack out of the room. My mom left reluctantly, but not because she was worried about me. She was curious about what Turkey Lawyer would say.

"I knew your grandfather well," the kind lawyer began. "He loved you, and he would never have wanted to worry you with his past life."

The lawyer made it seem like my grandpa had been reincarnated. I guess I could validate his use of the phrase because it seemed as though my family had been whole in another lifetime.

"I was told to watch over you and offer advice," he continued. "You weren't given a personal note because your grandfather trusted you would know his wishes."

The lawyer swallowed hard. He sat down on the chair beside me with some effort.

"I shouldn't have to tell you that you need to share that money with Ella. Your grandpa felt as if her mental condition was too unstable to leave her anything, and your mother's too impulsive to be her benefactor, so your grandpa gave you the money to put into an account. You and your sister should not have to worry about finances if you invest the money and use it prudently."

I understood my grandpa's wishes, but I still wanted something more from him. I would have given anything to have heard a comforting word written or recorded by my grandpa. His voice was the most soothing sound I had ever known.

It is unfortunate that you don't know you're having the best time of your life until it's over. The average man who relived his "glory days" on a football field did not think he was living the best days of his life as he sat in a hot history room taking a test before a big game, and I didn't know that all the men who made my life worth living would be jerked away from me before I was barely a teenager.

Chapter Thirty-Three

I left the law office and fell into pace behind my mom and Detective Novack. He tried to make arrangements to pick up my grandpa's truck.

"Would you mind picking me up and driving me to your father's house?" Detective Novack asked my mom.

My mom weighed his question. She was thinking about how dangerous it could be to leave Ella alone again. I caught a few disturbing images of my house on fire or flooded before I backed out of my mom's mind.

Detective Novack thought it had something to do with him. "I'll buy you dinner," he offered with a winning smile.

My mom laughed indulgingly. "I'm sure that would be fun, but I have two girls to look after. Their grandfather, my father, just passed away."

Detective Novack's face colored. "I'm very sorry, ma'am. I wasn't thinking of your loss."

"I know you meant well," my mom said. Her mood had deflated a little when she realized she had embarrassed him. "Maybe I could take you next week," she added. "If you don't mind waiting that long."

"No, ma'am," Detective Novack said. He wiped a layer of nervous perspiration off his forehead in the icy air. "I will wait for you." He realized the way his words sounded, and quickly added, "You could bring the girls, too. We could all go to dinner, or lunch, if you prefer."

My mom reflected on his words. It was possible that she was considering his request.

"We'll see," she said and gave him a half-smile.

I was surprised to feel sad for him. He seemed disappointed and embarrassed.

I made sure Detective Novack was out of earshot before I asked, "Why won't you date a nice-looking man that's interested in you?"

My mom looked in the direction he had gone. He had already climbed into his cruiser, so he couldn't have heard my words.

"This is not a subject I wish to discuss with my teenage daughter," she said. My mom started the car and waved at Detective Novack as we passed him in the parking lot. He had been waiting for us to leave, and he immediately pulled out behind my mom's car and followed us down Main Street.

"*Who* are you going to discuss it with?" I asked. I was being brave because I wasn't sure about my mom's mood. She could be pleased and amused by the situation, or she could be upset and uncomfortable. I didn't want to trouble my mom. She still had the power to make my life miserable.

My mom seemed to struggle to find the name of a friend. "I can talk with Debbie if I need advice on relationships," she said finally. A self-satisfied smile appeared on her lips.

"You mean the same Debbie you haven't spoken to in four years?" I reminded her. I was treading on dangerous ground.

My mom's eyes were locked on the road. I glanced in my side mirror and noticed Detective Novack's cruiser still following us. He would never know the sacrifice I was making for him.

"Do you want to go deposit your money?" my mom asked.

"No, I want you to answer the question."

"Good luck."

"Why?" I whined. "He's a *nice* man. What would it hurt to go out with him? If it doesn't look like it's working, I could fake an allergic reaction."

A genuine laugh spurted from my mom's mouth. She stifled the aftershocks with her hand.

"Is this important to you because your grandfather liked him or because you actually think Detective Novack and I are compatible?"

It was an honest question, and it deserved an honest answer. I hadn't really thought about why I was applying so much pressure on my mom. Maybe it was because of the look of disappointment I saw on Detective Novack's face.

"Both," I decided.

My mom turned on her right signal and pulled into a car wash. Detective Novack pulled in behind us.

Cold air rolled into the car as the window descended into the door. My mom motioned Detective Novack to her car.

He slid out of his cruiser and walked to my mom's open window. He opened his mouth to speak, but my mom spoke before his voice could hit the chilly air.

"When does your shift end today?" she asked.

"Seven o'clock, ma'am," he replied. "I'm working a different shift so I could be there for the reading."

My mom continued to stare at him. How could anyone look at another person when they were asking them out? I admired my mom's confidence, but I guessed she knew Detective Novack would agree to anything she asked. He had bumbled through asking her on a date only moments ago.

"Would you like to ride around tonight and look at Christmas lights with us?" my mom asked.

Detective Novack bent his knees until he was squatting beside my mom's car. He ran his fingers down his clean-shaven chin.

"It's supposed to snow tonight," he said thoughtfully, looking at my mom's vehicle. "I have a four-wheel drive, though. I could pick you up at eight."

"Will Sydney and Ella have plenty of room in your truck?" my mom asked.

"Of course," he said. "I have an extended cab, so they should have room to stretch their legs."

He looked over my mom to smile at me. I smiled back and gave him a thumbs up. Now he knew the reason for my mom's change of heart.

"I'll see you then," my mom said in a smooth voice I wasn't used to hearing. *Was she flirting with him?*

Detective Novack didn't break my mom's stare until an ambulance siren penetrated the winter breeze. He looked behind him, gave my mom an apologetic look, and ran to his cruiser.

My mom's face was robbed of its fleeting joy. She put the car in reverse and quietly drove home.

I was afraid to ask her why she seemed upset. I watched her jaw clench and unclench. Finally, my mom expressed her anger in our driveway.

I was poised to get out of the car when she said, "That's why I didn't want to date Bryan!"

My mom's sudden outburst shocked me, but I wanted to remain cool. If I lashed out at her, she would cancel her date, and I would never be able to talk her into seeing someone.

"I liked Bryan!" my mom shouted. "He was fun and caring and extremely devoted to me. I could have lived with Bryan forever and not worried about anything."

I hoped my mom was getting to a point because I knew Ella was watching. She was deciding if she was the cause of the argument my mom and I seemed to be having in the car.

"I knew what he would become," my mom said. Her eyes searched me for understanding. I had no idea what she was talking about.

"I knew Bryan was going to follow in my father's footsteps," my mom reflected. "The day Bryan told me he was going to train at the police academy, I decided we were over."

I was starting to understand. My mom had been left alone for years while my grandpa was on police duty. It had to be hard for her.

My mom's eyes were moist with tears, and her face was red. I leaned in to hug her, but she backed herself against the door. It was almost as if she had a force field that resisted affection.

My mom saw she had hurt my feelings, so she patted my hand and continued her story. I crossed my arms and stared straight out the windshield.

"I tried to break up with him when he told me he planned to become a police officer," she recounted. "I told Bryan that we needed to see other people, and he blew up. In his mind, he was making a long-term career choice that would help us with a steady income and benefits. He thought I would be proud of his choice because of my father's position."

I could almost see Bryan's cheerful face as he explained his long-term goals to my mom. He had thought about marriage and children with my mom. *Would I still have been me if Bryan had been my father?*

"I tried to explain to him I was tired of being alone," my mom said. Her resistance still wound me, and I wanted to ignore her. I wished

I could step out of the car and forget that I had an emotionally dried-up parent, but I wanted to hear about her relationship with Bryan too badly.

"Sure, the money and benefits would have provided a secure future," my mom was saying, "but where would he be for holidays and special events? When I was a girl, my father could never attend my dance recitals or field trips. I was left at home all night sometimes with only the sounds of the drug dealers making transactions and gunshots. I didn't want to step back into that life as an adult.

"My mother would cry every Christmas over a bottle of wine she had hoped to share with my father," my mom said. She always wore a strange expression when she talked about her mother. "He was always called into work during the holidays."

I hadn't heard a lot about my grandmother. I absorbed the information and cataloged it.

My mom didn't like to talk about her mother because it always made her sad. Up to this point, I had only heard about my grandma from my father and grandfather.

"Bryan was unable to understand that I didn't want to end up like my mother," my mom said. "He didn't seem to realize that I had ended our relationship in my heart. We still talked, and it appeared that we were dating, but I knew I would never marry Bryan. Unfortunately, Bryan didn't realize how serious I was until he saw your father in my driveway."

My mom didn't know that I had first-hand experience of the scene she was about to describe. I tried the obvious question.

"What does that have to do with Detective Novack?"

My mom looked at me like I was a rare form of idiot. "He's a police officer. Did you see the way he chased after that ambulance?"

"That's his job," I said. "He was on duty. I'm sure he wasn't supposed to be making a date on the job."

My point seemed to throw my mom for a second. She quickly recovered.

"He didn't even say goodbye. He ran after that ambulance so fast that he was a blur. Do you think that our date will matter to him if he's filling out a police report?"

"But Mom," I challenged, "what would you have him do? What if it was you, me, or Ella in that ambulance? Wouldn't you want a dedicated officer to respond to the call?"

My mom got out of the car without answering. I had hit a sore spot with her, but I didn't know if it was something I had overlooked, or if it had to do with the myriad of secrets my mom stored in her heart.

I got out of the car and shut my door. It echoed softly against the silent winter day.

I spent the rest of the day successfully avoiding my mom. I saw her at dinner, but I didn't speak to her. She didn't ask me about my favorite part of the day, but she might have refrained from that because of Ella's response to her question.

"Do you have anything to share today?" my mom had asked my sister over dinner.

"I could share my misery," Ella said, "but *you* have shared enough of that with your family."

My mom stared at Ella for a long moment with her fork positioned between her plate and her mouth. I hoped the fork wouldn't be used as a weapon.

My mom dropped her fork and carried it to the sink on her plate. She noisily cleaned her plate and let the garbage disposal suck the remainder of her food into the drain. She marched down the hall and up the stairs with her nose in the air.

"Why are you being so hostile toward Mom?" I asked.

"Amanda called," Ella said accusingly.

I raised my eyebrows. "So what?"

"She wants to give Mother her mother's ring back," Ella explained.

I was shocked. "So the ring wasn't even Amanda's?" I had forgotten to bombard my mom with questions about Amanda after we left the lawyer's office. I was too busy trying to set her up with Detective Novack.

"You must be slow," Ella said. She gave an exasperated sigh that I often heard from members of my family. My mom would roll her eyes and say, 'Book smarts don't equal common sense,' when she answered a question she thought had an obvious answer.

Ella didn't use a condescending tone, but she spoke slowly. "The ring was Grandmother's, but Grandfather gave it to Amanda when he asked her to marry him. Mother was upset about the marriage in the first place, and the ring added to her anger and jealousy. Amanda returned the ring when she decided she could no longer live with Mother and Grandfather. Mother was satisfied that Grandmother's ring was hers until she saw it handed over to Amanda today."

"But why wouldn't Mom want Amanda to have the ring?" I asked. I thought about all the information Ella had related. I was still overwhelmed by what I had found out about my grandpa at the lawyer's office.

"I will let Mother tell you that story when she is ready," Ella said. "I have already been informed."

"Mom told you?" I yelled at my sister. I could hear the marching soldiers that indicated blood was racing through my ears.

Ella looked away. "It was not Mother," she said simply.

My anger disappeared as quickly as it had surfaced. "I'm sorry," I told Ella. My sister must have had a very enlightening conversation with our step-grandmother.

I left my sister shaking her head over her plate. I understood more than Ella thought I did, but it wasn't worth the argument we'd have as I tried to explain myself.

Chapter Thirty-Four

My mom had seemed doubtful that Detective Novack would honor their date, but she didn't act like it. She took an hour-long shower, and I heard her makeup containers sliding along the bathroom counter. When I went into her room, I noticed at least fifteen outfits on her bed. I took a moment to look at each of the choices, and I placed the best outfit, a maroon blouse with a pair of light-colored jeans, in the front.

I wanted to ask her if she'd made the daily call to find out if there were any leads on Lydia. I approached her open bathroom door and knocked on the frame.

My mom was straightening her hair when I opened the bathroom door. The room was humid and smelled sweeter than usual. My mom was wearing the perfume she saved for special occasions. I smiled to myself. This date was important to her.

"What do you need, Syd?" my mom asked after scrunching her nose disapprovingly at my unchanged appearance. "You're wearing that?"

I laughed. "What do you *want* me to wear?"

She rolled her eyes. "Anything but the same thing he saw you in the last time we talked."

"You mean when I saw him earlier today?" My playful tone was not appreciated, and my mom turned back to the mirror.

"You could wear that pretty purple sweater suit that your—"

My mom stopped before she said my "grandfather." She had frozen in the process of moving her straightener down a lock of hair, and steam was pouring from the strand.

"—that looks so good on you," she finally finished. Her straightener continued along her already sleek and smooth locks.

Whatever amusement I had been having disappeared when my mom had almost mentioned my grandpa. I wondered if talking about him had suddenly become taboo, since he had passed away. I voiced the question I had come in to ask.

"Have you called about Lydia?"

"I called the station before we went to the reading," my mom said. "I'm sorry I didn't tell you, but I had a lot of things on my mind."

I waved for my mom to go on. I knew there wasn't anything of great importance to be relayed or my mom would have told me before we'd left the house.

"The police still have no idea about Lydia and Bannon's whereabouts, but they think they know where Bryan is."

I was suddenly anxious. "They aren't going to arrest him, are they?"

My mom sensed my concern, so she spoke in a softer tone. "I can't lie to you, dear, the police will eventually have to arrest him. It's their job. But I think they will overlook the place he's believed to be hiding until Bannon and Lydia are found."

"Where do the police think Bryan is hiding?" I asked.

My mom studied me for a moment and finished straightening the last piece of her hair. She crossed her arms and leaned against the sink.

"Bryan told you he used to write your father letters while he was in jail, didn't he?"

I nodded. It wasn't really a question. I had told my mom about my conversation with Bryan several hours after it had taken place.

"Bryan and your father were closer than I would have liked," my mom continued. "I never read the letters they exchanged, but I think your father was trying to help Bryan with his appeal process."

"Dad was going to get Bryan acquitted?" I asked.

"No, but he wanted to move Bryan to a better facility. Bryan had a hard time with the other inmates, and he had hidden through two prison riots. I guess your father felt like Bryan deserved better."

"What does this have to do with where Bryan's hiding?" I asked.

The doorbell jolted my mother and me out of our conversation and back to the present. My mom's eyes swelled with panic as she realized her date had not been broken.

"Go get the door! And stall him!" she said, shooing me out of her bathroom and slamming the door.

Ella was standing in the doorway to our room. "Why is Detective Novack here in regular clothes? Is someone else dead?"

In all the excitement, my mom and I had forgotten to tell Ella about the date. I quickly tried to explain as Ella's face stretched wide with horror.

I gave Ella a condensed version of the events leading up to the date. "Mom needs to date, and Detective Novack asked her out," I explained. "I talked her into it, so we're going to see Christmas lights in his truck. Mom was afraid he'd break the date, but he's here, so be nice and act normal."

I don't know what kind of response I expected from Ella, but it wasn't the one she gave me. My sister's eyes were wide and unhappy.

"There will be repercussions," she said solemnly.

I shook my head and ran for the door. "I don't have time for your brand of silliness. Just be cool and don't say anything weird."

I bounded down the steps, but I stopped short of the door. I peeked through the living room curtains, even though I knew Detective Novack was on my porch. He was waiting to be recognized and waved at me. The harsh porch light showered him, but his glow was not from its illumination.

Detective Novack had spent just as much time on his appearance as my mom. He had on shiny black boots, brand new faded jeans, and a white button-up shirt that looked like it had been starched to stand straight up.

He must have been in his late thirties or early forties, but his hair showed no signs of leaving him. My grandpa's hairline remained consistent, but I had noticed that all the other policemen I'd seen without their caps had thinning or receding hairlines. The top part of his hair was thicker and faded down his head to his neck. It was amazingly blond and thick in the front. His hair was delicately spiked, but it was not over-glossed with product.

I pointed my finger at him, and he gave me another unsure wave of his hand. I quickly opened the door and invited him into our living room.

I noticed a strong male scent, but it wasn't an unpleasant smell. I could almost distinguish between Detective Novack's aftershave and cologne.

He seemed uncomfortable in the house and looked around nervously. I wondered if he was scanning his surroundings for other exits.

"Where's your mother and sister?" he asked.

"My mom's finishing a grueling transformation, and my sister is planning sabotage."

"Sabotage of what?" he asked.

"Your date, the local government, the world," I replied.

He didn't even crack a smile.

I was getting uncomfortable when I heard a rustle at the top of the steps. I glanced up the steps and almost ran into my mom.

She had worn the outfit I had placed on top of her other choices. Her auburn hair shone brightly against the maroon shirt.

My mom had stayed dangerously thin since Ella had been born, so she easily moved in her skinny jeans. I really noticed my mom's form, but maybe that was because I had to raise my efforts to keep out the buzzing of Detective Novack's brain when she walked into the room.

"You look wonderful," he said.

"Thank you, Lewis," my mom said easily. She didn't comment on his appearance.

"Are you ready?" he asked.

"Sure," my mom said, "just let me collect my youngest." My mom turned at the edge of the steps and called, "Ella!"

Ella walked down the steps slowly, and she was wearing a scowl when she entered the living room. My mom and I pretended not to notice her expression, but Detective Novack picked up on it immediately.

"Hello, Detective," Ella said without looking at him.

"Hello, Ella," Detective Novack replied evenly. "Are you ready to go see the Christmas lights?"

"I loved looking at them with my *father*," Ella said. She focused her eyes on her mother.

What? I thought. The notion was echoed from the minds of my mom and Detective Novack. Ella had never even met our father.

"Hey," Detective Novack began. He looked from Ella to me. "I am not here to replace your father. I *liked* him, but I *never* wanted to *be* him. I *want* to take your mother out to see the Christmas lights, and honestly, I *want* to take her on more dates after that. I don't know where it will lead, but I would like to find out."

"That was a very diplomatic way of putting things," I said encouragingly. Detective Novack smiled at me with his ultra-white teeth.

"Yes, just like a practiced politician," Ella mumbled.

"What was that?" my mom asked.

"I said, 'We should go before the snow starts,' " Ella lied. She yanked her coat off the coat rack by the door.

Detective Novack took my mom's coat from her arms and held it out for her to slip inside. He surprised me by plucking my coat from the rack and placing me inside it. He noticed my shocked expression.

"Ladies should be treated like ladies," Detective Novack said. "I will always be a gentleman when I am allowed to be," he continued, looking pointedly at Ella.

My sister stuck her nose far enough in the air to warrant a cautionary look from our mother. Ella returned her nose to a downward direction.

Detective Novack opened the front door for us, and I walked out into the crisp night air. Ella followed me, and we stood shivering as our mom turned off the lights and locked the front door.

She had brought a thermos and some plastic cups with her. A bag of marshmallows stuck out from under her arm.

Ella reluctantly climbed into the backseat of Detective Novack's truck. Luckily, there was enough room for me to sit on the other side of the cab. Ella could have barely touched me if she had extended her fingers to maximum lengths.

"Everyone secured?" Detective Novack asked. He turned his head so that he could see me, but Ella was still beyond his range of sight. I gave him a thumbs up and smiled. He smiled back gratefully and turned the ignition.

We drove through Erwin and Unicoi for two hours looking at Christmas decorations. Detective Novack took us up streets I didn't even know existed, and he, my mom, and I sang Christmas carols almost the entire time. He would pull slowly by a festive house, and I would 'Ooo' and 'Awww' at the appropriate moments.

My mom passed out hot chocolate and marshmallows during the ride. The marshmallows were small and white, like the snow falling on the road. She gave each person in the truck seven marshmallows at a time, but I was the only one who noticed the attention she gave to the number. Seven had been her favorite number since my father left. I think it had to do with the members of her family, the number of children she had carried plus she and my father.

I let a marshmallow slowly dissolve in my mouth with a little of the cocoa. The mixture I swallowed was creamy and warm.

"Is anyone hungry?" Detective Novack asked after we had seen dozens of decorated homes.

Everyone was silent, but my mom looked at her date with a smile. No one in our house had eaten their dinner. Ella's outburst had caused our appetites to vanish.

"Well, I have one more trick up my sleeve this evening," Detective Novack said.

Ella opened her mouth to make a snide comment, but I shot her a murderous look. *Please don't ruin the happiness.*

Ella glanced at our mom as she laughed and closed her mouth. My sister contented herself with staring out the window.

Detective Novack directed his truck off the Main Street and down a road that would lead you to North Carolina if you followed it for a quarter of an hour. My mom had taken my brothers, Ella, and me to a swimming area on this road. The park was called Rock Creek Park, and the water was colder than a sunless winter day in the Arctic.

The day we had gone swimming had been sweltering, and we were all sweaty and irritable. Josh, Jerrod, Ella, and I were packed into my mom's small car. Josh had lost a *Paper, Rock, Scissors* game and had gotten stuck in the back with Ella and me. I was extra hot because I was positioned between a sweaty teenage boy and an unforgiving car seat. The only reason we had agreed to ride in my mom's box of heat was because my mom promised our destination was to the coldest water she had ever touched.

My mom did not use the air conditioning in her small vehicle. She preferred to feel a cool breeze rolling through her car. Unfortunately, the temperature outside was so hot, that the air was almost as suffocating as being squeezed between a hard car seat and the bones of a growing adolescent.

My brothers argued over the winner of another *Paper, Rock, Scissors* game. Josh was the victor, but Jerrod complained that Josh had sent him a thought to confuse him. Josh stated his side with a straight face, but smiled to himself when he looked out the window.

The loser of the game had to keep an eye on Ella and me for the first part of the outing. My mom seemed perfectly capable of watching her two- and four-year-old girls, but her mind still drifted off when she thought of her husband.

My mom pulled her car onto a heavily wooded road and slowly drove through the park. The trees made a nice canopy against the sun, and the air coming through the windows was much cooler.

My mom had hardly parked the car before Jerrod bolted out of the car and ran for the water. The dings of his open passenger door could barely be heard over the water in the swimming hole and the splashing and laughter of other water-lovers.

My brothers were unaware of the water's temperature, and Jerrod ran for its cooling embrace without hearing my mom's cautionary shouts. He jumped into the water off a large rock and was out of the liquidy cold only seconds after touching its icy surface.

Jerrod came back to the car covered in chill bumps, and coughing cold water out of his mouth. My mom and brother seemed satisfied that Jerrod had learned his lesson and simply ignored his complaints about the freezing water.

He plucked Ella from my mom's arms, and he helped me out of the car. I slipped on some of the water that had dripped from his body onto the metal on the car's step plate, but Jerrod pulled upward on my hand, so that I wouldn't cut myself on the gravel parking lot.

I looked up at my brother gratefully, and he looked down at me with a smile. Jerrod wasn't my favorite brother, but my heart was full of love and devotion when I thought of his face.

"I'll always be here to catch you," he said. His kind blue eyes warmed his words.

I pulled myself out of my memories before my heart shattered. Ella had been staring at me with concern.

I realized tears had created two moist tracks down my face. I turned toward the window and casually rubbed a hand over my cheeks.

The truck moved down a road beside the trees that formed the barrier of Rock Creek Park. He turned left onto the first driveway.

Detective Novack pulled to a stop in front of a large white brick home with green shutters. It had lights strung down the driveway, around the trees, and under the eaves of the house. It glowed like a beacon.

"Welcome to my humble abode," he said grandly.

The house and grounds were anything but humble, and I wondered how he afforded the light bill, let alone the mortgage, of a house this size.

Detective Novack pulled the keys out of the ignition, grabbed his cell phone from the console, and hopped out of his door. He walked carefully through the snow to open my mom's door. It had started snowing more heavily as we had ridden up the road.

My mom accepted Detective Novack's hand as she stepped from the truck. He helped me out of my door, but my sister ignored his kind gesture.

Instead of acting upset over Ella's actions, he turned a brighter smile to my mom and me. His smile was contagious, and I found myself grinning along with my mom.

Detective Novack unlocked the door to his enormous house, and we walked into the foyer. I was instantly warmed by ashy-scented heat.

A fire burned in a large room to the left. It lit the room well enough to show a bearskin rug on the floor and enough stuffed wild game to make a taxidermist's dream.

A grand wooden staircase in front of me led to the rooms upstairs. He led us to the room on the right, a large, globally decorated dining area. Tapestries and painting of maps adorned the walls, and flags from several countries were sewn together in an interesting pattern on the curtains, napkins, and tablecloths.

Detective Novack pulled out a chair for each of his guests and disappeared down the hall. We were left without words to marvel at the detail in the room.

Aside from the material objects, the room appeared extravagant. The chandelier had polished golden arches that held light bulbs covered with painted glass. The walls were concrete, and the paint on them was so thick that I wondered if Detective Novack would ever have to paint them again.

He returned with a silver tray and four china cups. The tray held a punch bowl filled with a creamy liquid.

"Please be careful," Detective Novack said. "It's still pretty warm."

A silver ladle lay against the bowl. My mom used it to fill the four cups with the creamy substance.

Detective Novack jumped out of his chair. "I'll be right back," he said and jogged down the hall.

"What is this stuff?" I asked my mom.

My mom rolled her eyes. "Syd, don't tell me you don't recognize homemade eggnog?"

"Do I have to drink this concoction?" Ella asked.

My mom rounded on Ella so quickly that it looked like she teleported from one position to another. Ella jumped when my mom's index finger came within an inch of her face.

"You will drink every drop," my mom began through clenched teeth. "You will tell Detective Novack that it is the best eggnog you have ever tasted. You will thank him for his kindness. If you embarrass me one more time tonight, I will sit next to you every second of the day tomorrow and distract you every time you stare into space."

Most parents threaten their children with the restriction of television or video games. Other parents take away the right to visit with neighborhood friends or play organized sports. My mom was suspending Ella's right to be alone in her room with her thoughts, and who knows what else.

My mom knew her children well, and Ella pasted an ersatz smile on her face as soon as Detective Novack entered the dining area. I looked at my cup of eggnog so that my expression would not give away the tension the room had recently held.

He seemed to be an intelligent man. I could tell by the way he slowed his pace upon entering the room that he could feel that something had transpired in his absence, but he was wise enough not to comment on it directly.

He had returned with a container of cinnamon and a small silver spoon. He asked Ella if he could sprinkle some of the spice into her cup, and she nodded. I noticed my mom's head turn slightly, and Ella added her appreciation for his generosity.

Detective Novack rested in a chair by my mom and added a small spoonful of cinnamon to his eggnog. He did not stir it.

Ella and I had lived in a large family. We had learned that you got to the table quickly so that you could get food on your plate, but you didn't dare eat until everyone was ready. We had waited patiently with our cups of eggnog before us until Detective Novack raised his cup for a toast.

Everyone raised their cups. I was a little shaky. I hadn't eaten well all day, and I was feeling weak. I really hoped there was some food in my future.

"I feel very lucky to have you ladies in my home during the Christmas season," he began. "I know that we have experienced many sad losses in our lives, but my Christmas wish is that our futures will be as bright as the star that shone over Jesus in the manger."

Detective Novack didn't know that my mom always insisted that her children make a Christmas wish. She stared at him like he had looked into her soul. I secretly hoped my mom would take his toast as a sign to trust him with her heart.

We all raised our cups a little higher and clinked them together. I waited until our host brought his cup to his lips before I sampled my drink. It was creamy and warm. I could taste vanilla and cinnamon, but I did not taste egg.

Ella started coughing and sputtering. She had not liked the eggnog, but she knew she could not tell Detective Novack anything negative about his recipe.

"You didn't like it," he said with an encouraging smile.

"No, Detective Novack," Ella said, under the steady gaze of our mom. "It was wonderful. I was just so choked up by your toast that it went down the wrong way."

He laughed. My mom seemed horrified by his reaction to her daughter's words.

"First of all," he began, wiping moisture away from his eyes, "you should call me Lewis in my house."

He looked at my mom for approval. She smiled briefly and nodded. My mom wasn't pleased about dropping formalities, but she wouldn't argue with her date in his home.

Lewis turned his attention back to Ella. "Second of all, if you don't like something, just tell me; I won't make you eat or drink anything you don't want."

Lewis decided that he had said enough for now. He picked up Ella's cup and asked if he could get her some milk.

"Please." She seemed happy that she could respond without calling our host by his first name. I had already decided I would use Lewis's name several times before we left his home.

My mom stared at Ella silently until Lewis walked in with another silver tray full of sugar cookies. The cookies were homemade. He must have prepared them and cut them out before he picked us up and then cooked them as we enjoyed the eggnog.

The cookies were in different shapes and sprinkled with either red or green sugar crystals. Christmas stockings, stars, Santa hats, and sleighs were piled on the large serving tray.

"Please, dig in," Lewis said after he realized we were waiting for him to begin eating.

I enjoyed a warm Santa hat with red sprinkles, and my sister dunked a red-sprinkled star into her milk. My mom took the cookie Lewis handed her, but she broke it into pieces over her eggnog instead of biting into it. She didn't want to get a red or green sugar crystal stuck in her front teeth.

The cookies were hot, and the eggnog was warm, and before I knew it, my eyes were heavy. I relaxed my mind and drifted to sleep in my chair.

Give them back, thief! I heard clearly. The voice had muffled the soft chatter between the two adults.

I jerked to attention and looked around the room. Everyone had noticed my startled expression. My mom and Lewis were looking at me with concern, and Ella was trying to ignore my reaction by dunking another cookie in her milk. Her eyes were rimmed with fear.

My mind had snapped shut as soon as I had heard the voice. I knew I could hear it again if I wanted, but I was content to stay blissfully ignorant of its presence. Besides, the icy darkness enveloped my surroundings and threatened to reach into my mind at any moment.

"I'm fine," I told my mom and Lewis. "I just fell asleep and jerked myself awake."

My mom looked skeptical, but Lewis was nodding his head.

"I do that all the time," he said. "I'll start to go to sleep, and my legs will jump or start running, and I'll wake up."

I smiled at Lewis. He seemed so innocent and naïve. He had no idea about the lies that were swirling around him.

Stop thinking that way, Ella sent to me. It was a sharp thought that pierced the center of my brain like an ice pick. She would have had to have used a lot of energy for me to hear a thought when my defenses were up.

I stared at my sister and narrowed my focus on her, in case she had anything else she wished to tell me. Ella could tell that I was ready for a confidential conversation.

She knows you heard her, Ella sent. *Be careful, or she will follow you around, trying to get through again.*

I listened to Ella's thoughts and shut my mind. Our exchange had lasted only moments, but Lewis had stopped talking to my mom. His mouth hung open. He could tell my sister and I had shared something.

"Body language," my mom said with a forced laugh. "They communicate with their eyes, or whatever, but it's not funny when they seem to be conspiring against me."

Lewis joined her laughter, but he seemed unconvinced. Still, I had never been more grateful for one of my mom's lies.

Chapter Thirty-Five

I watched Ella closely to see if she communicated with any more dead people, but she just ate cookies and stared at the wall. My mom and Lewis talked about current events, and Lewis was very animated as he discussed a serial killer who could be in the area.

"If I were there, I would wait for him, night and day, in Chestoa, where they find the bodies," he said. "I would wait until he dropped off another body, and I would shoot him in the head."

I had not heard the entire conversation, but I had heard enough to upset me. My mom was nodding politely, but something didn't sit right with me.

"Why wouldn't you want to find him *before* he committed another murder?"

Lewis had been getting closer to my mom's chair, but he backed away and met my eyes.

"Sydney, the guy we're talking about, is sick. From what we understand, he keeps young women locked up for days. He seems to almost drown them several times before he finally strangles them with a leather belt. Another girl is already missing by the time he drops off the body of his latest victim. If an officer waited in Chestoa, where the killer *always* drops the bodies, and shot him in the head—" he seemed to remember he was talking to minors "—or arrested him, the killer could not return home to torture another young woman. It might take a couple of hours, but the police department could locate the killer's name and address from his driver's license or the registration on the car he drove."

"But why don't the police try to stop him from abducting another woman?" I asked. I could not give up. I had read that men and women who were kidnapped were never the same again, even though they were glad to be alive.

"It's not easy to stake out thousands of blonde women in their late twenties," Lewis said. He seemed satisfied that he had avoided another round of my questions.

I settled back into my chair while Lewis continued his conversation with my mom. She stopped him before he could tell her how he would handle our country's debt problem.

"Lewis," she started, "I have enjoyed our conversation and your hospitality, but I'm afraid my girls are going to drift to sleep in these chairs."

Lewis looked at Ella and me with surprise. He jumped out of his chair and began fishing keys out of his front pocket.

"I am so sorry," Lewis said. He was looking in my direction, but I think he meant it for all of us. "I don't get company very often, and I guess I got a little carried away."

I got out of my chair and felt something bump me. I almost fell over onto the table, but I caught myself.

Lewis, Ella, and my mom looked at me. Their faces wore a mixture of confusion and concern.

"My legs were asleep," I said. The lie flowed easily from my lips, and the adults in the room believed my fabrication.

I tried to get Ella to tell me about what she saw in Lewis's house once we were in the truck. It rolled easily over the snow that was already accumulated on the roads.

"What did you see?" I whispered.

Don't talk about it now, Ella hissed inside my head.

When we finally reached the security of our own home, Ella and I left our mom and Lewis to make plans for another date. Ella bounded up the steps, and I took long strides to follow her. Instead of running to our bedroom, my sister pushed me into the bathroom.

"It's time for your shower," Ella said. I took the suggestion to heart, and I peeled off my clothes.

Ella ran a warm shower for me, and I stepped into it quickly. The air in the bathroom was too cool on my bare skin, and I broke out in goose bumps immediately.

Ella made me stay under running water for half an hour. Every time I would complain, she would tell me, "Be quiet." At least my sister gradually adjusted the temperature of the water so that I had hot water for my entire shower.

"Okay," Ella said finally, "you can get out."

I turned off the water and took the towel she offered me. I dried off and wrapped the pink fluffy towel around my hair like a turban to keep it from dripping onto the floor.

I pulled on my pajamas behind our closed bedroom door. The feeling of flannel warmth covered parts of my body I hadn't realized were cold. I could still hear Detective Novack talking to my mom.

I waited for Ella to speak. I knew she would explain things to me when she thought it was safe.

"You had a hitchhiker," Ella said as if those were words I was used to hearing.

"Pardon me? What do you mean?"

"The spirit you heard attached herself to you," my sister said simply. "You almost lost her in the snow, but you detached her completely in the shower. The detective is still here, so she should follow him back to his house."

I thought I understood. The bump I had felt was a spirit connecting to me. *But how had I almost lost the spirit in the snow?*

I almost asked Ella the question that had rolled to the surface of my mind, but I shook my head. "This is ridiculous."

"Maybe it is," Ella said simply, "but the spirit knew you could hear her. She wanted to possess you."

"Possess me?" I screeched. "How did I go from having a hitchhiker to being demonically possessed?"

My sister let out one of the few genuine laughs I've heard her release. She held her stomach and muffled her laughter in her bedspread.

"You were not going to be *demonically* possessed," she said when she regained her composure. "The ghost was going to direct you. You would have been aware of what you were doing, but the spirit would have made you feel like making certain choices."

"If it's that easy, then why isn't the whole world possessed?" I asked.

"The ghost has to find a host with an open mind and a soluble spirit. That was why I was so glad that you had learned to put up a barrier between you and the voices you heard."

I threw up my hands. "That's news to me," I said. "The last time I checked, you were still sulking about my public denial of my gift."

Ella smiled sadly. "I meant that you had put up a block against the voices you heard. You could still hear them if you chose, but it seemed you could tune into whomever you wanted to hear. The voices did not seem to invade your conscious mind."

I decided not to respond to Ella's rebuttal. I thought about my schizophrenic paternal grandfather. Maybe the voices he'd heard weren't what the doctors thought they were. *Was it possible that Crazy Lyle Miller was hearing voices beyond the grave?*

"So where is she now?" I asked, referring to my phantom hitchhiker. "Is she loose in the house since she followed us here?"

"No," Ella said.

I was really confused, but I had not lived in the same world that Ella had chosen to reside. I shrugged my shoulders to show my indifference, but I was secretly thankful that my sister could recognize ethereal beings and protect her family from ghostly hauntings and spiritual possessions.

We climbed into our beds, but I could not sleep after Ella turned off the lights. I lay in my bed and thought about what the spiritual hitchhiker had wanted.

"Do not upset yourself," Ella said.

I was pretty certain that my sister could not read minds, but sometimes she said things that made me feel like she could hear my thoughts. "I still can't shake how easy it was for that thing to latch onto me," I admitted.

Ella let out a sigh. "Detective Novack thinks he lives alone, but he is surrounded by voices he cannot hear and people he cannot see," she said. "There were a lot of angry spirits in the house, but only one was strong enough to breach your psychic shields."

I stayed quiet and let Ella speak. I didn't want to make a comment that would keep her from telling me the things she had witnessed at Detective Novack's house.

"I could feel the presence of spirits as soon as we turned onto Detective Novack's driveway," Ella continued. Her voice lacked emotion and inflection. "The spirits rushed the door as when it opened, just like dogs welcoming their master after being left in a lifeless house all day.

"Detective Novack was going to guide us left, into his sitting room, but a spirit from the fire exerted its influence. He turned away from the room and led us into the dining room."

Ella stopped for a moment. I was still digesting "the spirit from the fire" when she spoke again.

"I could tell you were drawn to that room," Ella said about the sitting room. "Detective Novack never uses that area, but he tells himself that it is because the stuffed remnants of the live animals cause him distress."

There was more to the story, but I didn't press Ella for the details. She usually avoided talking about malicious spirits.

"Detective Novack kept us waiting in the dining room for a long time," Ella continued. "I saw no spirits when we entered the room, but I watched ten or twelve once-living people saunter into the room before he returned with the eggnog." I could almost see Ella scrunch up her nose at the thought of Lewis's eggnog.

"Mother tried to warn us against bad behavior, but it was all I could do to remain calm in the presence of all the dead. I concentrated so hard on her words I could not tell you a single thing she said."

I remembered Ella's frightened face. I hadn't realized that it was fear over almost a dozen spirits.

"I will not repeat the words they shouted in the presence of Detective Novack," Ella said.

"I heard one say, 'Give them back, thief!' " I told my sister.

"We are straying from the subject." I could hear her adjusting her body in the dark to make it easier for me to hear her. "You can read minds," Ella said. "I think you can read energy too, because spirits are just energy."

I opened my mouth to ask a question, but my sister cleared her throat. She had heard the front door close.

Our mom's padded feet crossed the hall after a few minutes of silence. She eased open our door, and Ella and I faked an open-mouthed sleep that must have put our mom at ease. Ella started talking again as soon as the door to our mom's bedroom closed.

My mom had left the door to our bedroom cracked. The open door made me feel more vulnerable, but I was too tired and warm to get up and close it.

"Spiritual energy is recycled as long as a person feels incomplete or is taken by surprise by death," Ella continued.

"So reincarnation *is* possible," I gasped. My voice betrayed my amazement.

"No, it is not like that," Ella sighed. "It takes energy to animate our earthly bodies. I believe that our essence, or soul, returns to our creator, but the energy that was used to animate us either returns to a great energy pool or creates a shape from its last host. These spirits haunt the living, trying to accomplish something."

My silence betrayed my bewilderment. I was too tired to process everything Ella had said, but I briefly wondered how the energy that animated a body could feel dissatisfied if the soul that guided the body had departed. I supposed that the soul could leave an emotional signature on the energy.

"Another way to look at it," my sister explained, "is that science has proven that the human body weighs less at the time of death than it did while it was living."

"What a great way to lose weight," I joked.

"The difference in mass is measured in grams, not pounds," Ella said testily. "And mass can neither be created nor destroyed."

I stopped laughing in my blanket and guided my eyes to my sister's bed. My pupils had adjusted to the dark, but I could only see a dark shadow in the shape of my sister on her bed.

"*Anyway,*" my sister continued, "some people think the disappearance of the weight proves that there is a soul."

"Wait," I said. "Couldn't the extra grams have been air in the lungs or tension the body holds while it's in a living state?"

"Nothing that I have read has been one hundred percent conclusive, but I believe the missing mass is the soul that returns to the creator and the energy that is recycled." Ella cleared her throat and adjusted her pillow.

I was getting tired and irritable, so I backed out of a conversation that was sure to lead to an argument. I wanted to find out more about the spirit that had attached to me.

"What did that spirit want with me?" I asked.

"I already told you," Ella said. I could tell she was getting annoyed. "She wanted to possess you so that she could try to ruin Detective Novack's life."

My sister was agitated, so I remained quiet. I stayed up for another hour, trying to remember the feelings I had experienced. I was trying to find some way to know that I had picked up a "hitchhiker" so that I could keep from ever becoming possessed.

I was almost asleep when I heard my mom's voice. I thought she might be praying before bed, but my mom had been estranged from God since my father left.

I slid out of bed and tip-toed across the floor. My bed was closest to the door, so I walked a few steps and moved into the hallway. My mom's voice was louder in the hall, but I dropped down beside a crack in my mom's door to hear her voice more clearly.

I thought she had finished speaking when I finally heard her giggle. My mom hadn't giggled in years. I peeked carefully through the crack in the door, and I saw my mom was on the phone.

"Yes, Bryan, I know you fought for me," she whispered. "But I needed you to be there for me. You couldn't do that if you were a police officer."

Bryan? Why was my mom talking to him?

"I'm serious," my mom was saying, "you better not tell the police that I kept your secrets. I would go to jail, and where would the girls go?"

I had not thought about that. *Where would Ella and I go if something happened to our mom?* I shook the disconcerting thought out of my head.

I was too amazed and curious to give my mom privacy, so I stayed on the hall floor with my ear pressed to the cracked door. It was exciting at first, because I thought I would learn more about my mom's relationship with Bryan, but my mom's side of the conversation was superficial. I was almost bored of listening to middle-age nostalgia when my mom's voice rose in distress.

"What do you mean, someone's breaking in?" my mom shouted. "Is it the police? Did you turn on the lights in your house?"

The line must have lost connection because my mom stared at her phone as the light from the call blinked off. A brush of my mom's mind gave me a mixture of frantic thoughts. I rested my head on my knees and tried to separate them.

How did they find him?

What did he do to get caught?

How can I call the sheriff's department to ask about Bryan when I not supposed to know that he's been apprehended?

What if there's a tap on my phone that I didn't know about?

I heard my mom go through a range of emotions before she finally settled into her bed. I guess she had decided that anything else she did might incriminate her.

I crawled into my room and settled my body on my firm mattress. I didn't risk making more noise by lifting my covers over myself.

I thought I would be awake all night running through the day's events in my head, but I fell asleep almost immediately. I faced the door I had closed on my way back to the safety of my warm blankets and felt my eyelids pull over my eyes.

I stand by the fact that so much can happen in a day. That morning I had been barely middle class, with a perpetually grieving mom and a strange, but gifted, sister. After the day's events, I was a wealthy teenager surrounded by a bunch of crazy people and ghosts. Well, I guess the only thing that really changed was my wealth.

Chapter Thirty-Six

Christmas came without fanfare. I had never felt less like celebrating. I moped around the house all day and tried to think of inexpensive, yet thoughtful, gifts I could give my mom and Ella.

My grandpa had taken me Christmas shopping for the last couple of years. We had also bought my mom's birthday presents, since her birthday fell on Christmas Day.

I tried to shake the thought of my grandpa's merriment during the holiday season out of my mind. I had to concentrate on the living.

My mom fixed a traditional Southern Christmas dinner with ham, mashed potatoes, sweet potato pie, green bean casserole, macaroni and cheese, and biscuits. She said it was okay to talk about Christmas, but she told Ella and me she would make our next birthdays extra special if we would forget her birthday. My sister and I lowered our heads and sighed.

"We'll do whatever you want, Mom," I said. I felt like I was the spokesperson for the children now that I was the eldest living child.

My mom nodded and returned to her meal. She had mentioned Christmas, but I still felt like my family was neglecting Jesus's birthday. I decided to cut my mom some slack. Ella and I could say a special prayer to Jesus in our room after dinner.

An hour after dinner, I heard the doorbell ring. I came bounding down the steps as my mom opened the door.

"Merry Christmas, Miller family!" Detective Novack boomed cheerfully.

Detective Novack stood on our front porch with snow on his boots and a red bag thrown casually over his shoulder. He hadn't recently showered, but he had taken the time to change out of his uniform. His khakis and red shirt were speckled with precipitation.

I was immediately infected with his happiness. I bounced off the landing and let him pull me into a hug. The embrace was casual and natural. I applauded myself again for setting up my mom with him.

My mom and I ushered him inside the house. He kicked his boots against door plate before he stepped inside. Snow flew from the bottoms of his shoes and scattered across the porch.

Detective Novack's face fell slightly when the atmosphere in the house reached out to him. He shook his head quickly, and his face brightened again. He seemed determined to stay positive.

He hugged my mom and pushed himself into the living room. He gleefully readjusted the red sack over his shoulder.

"Where's your tree?" he asked, looking around before returning his eyes to my mom.

Detective Novack didn't know that my mom was playing Scrooge. Our tree was in the garage, wrapped in last year's plastic.

"I didn't put one up this year," my mom admitted. She held her elbows in her hands nervously.

He stared at my mom for a long moment. He tried to keep his cheerful expression, but his smile faltered.

"No matter," he said finally. "I'll put them on the couch." He turned to me. "Go get your sister and tell her it's present time."

My mom apologized for not having a present for him as I walked upstairs. She talked quickly around her apology.

"I didn't bring these presents to get anything," he said. "I just wanted to brighten your family's holiday. I could *never* replace the family you and your girls have lost, but I can still be a friend."

I hoped my mom had hugged Detective Novack. His heart was bigger than my house.

I walked into my room and nudged Ella with the back of my hand. She had been sitting on the end of her bed, staring at a bare place on the wall. I felt an electric shock, like the one you get from dragging your feet across the carpet in the winter.

"What the heck was that?" I asked, rubbing my hand.

"What do you mean?" Ella asked. I didn't pursue the subject because my sister would deny anything I said.

"Detective Novack brought presents," I told her. "We're supposed to open them now."

"He is really trying hard," Ella said. She focused her eyes back on the same spot on the wall.

I turned defensive. "Don't ruin this, Ella. You can sit and ignore him, but don't you dare make him feel upset or uncomfortable."

"He is not a good match for Mother," she stated simply.

"That's not for you to decide," I said. I turned on my heel and skipped back downstairs.

I was proud of myself for dealing with my sister. I was convinced that no one could argue with my mature reasoning. I was so high on my cloud of maturity that I didn't process the scene in my living room for almost a full minute.

I stepped onto the landing and opened my mouth to say something festive, but the words were sucked back down my throat. Detective Novack was kissing my mom in my living room. He held the back of her head tenderly in one hand while the other hand was around her back at the waist, pulling her closer to him. They broke apart as soon as they noticed me.

"Why'd you creep up on us?" my mom demanded.

I shrugged and stomped my feet on the landing. The padded carpet hardly let a sound echo off the walls. "I didn't know that I had to make a lot of noise when I walked from one room to the next," I defended.

My mom stopped glaring at me, so I guess I had proven my point. Besides, she probably didn't want to admit that she had been too wrapped up in kissing Detective Novack to hear any sounds in the house.

My mom was embarrassed, but he was smiling like he'd won the lottery. He took my hand and helped me sit down on the couch.

I tried to act normal after the scene I had witnessed. I'd never seen my mom kiss anyone besides my father.

Detective Novack handed me two packages. One package was wrapped in metallic green paper, with a red bow, and the other package was the size of a ring box and was covered in red paper with dancing Santas.

"Wait for Ella to open hers," he said and winked at me. He moved next to my mom, but he didn't touch her. My mom still colored from her suitor's proximity.

I thought I should try to extend some hospitality to Detective Novack. After all, he was spending a holiday with my family, and he had brought gifts for everyone.

"Could I get you something to drink?" I asked, getting up from my place on the couch.

"Oh, no," he said. He crossed the room to place a gentle hand on my shoulder. He applied enough pressure to insist that I remain seated.

My mom had flown to the kitchen after my suggestion, and Detective Novack's eyebrows shot up when he noticed her absence.

Ella entered the living room at the same time he was walking out of the living room to retrieve my mom. They ran into each other.

"Ow!" Detective Novak said. He brushed his hand down his front like he was dusting debris off of himself. I was reminded of the shock I had felt when I had touched my sister. Maybe he had felt a similar shock.

"Detective Novak," Ella said in greeting. She nodded and took a seat next to me on the couch.

"Ella," he returned. He thought about his next words carefully. "I'm sorry I ran into you."

"It is of no concern to me," my sister said, staring forward. "I felt nothing."

"Look at the presents Detective Novack gave me," I said, feigning happiness and excitement.

Ella turned to me, and his face fell. I wondered if he regretted visiting our family.

I narrowed my eyes at Ella and said, "Wasn't it so nice of Detective Novack to bring us presents?"

"He is trying too hard," my sister said. She put her nose in the air.

My mouth fell open, and heat rushed to my face. If you could die of embarrassment, I would have been buried that night.

He pretended not to hear us. He bent over his sack and pulled out the remaining gifts.

He quietly placed two packages on the table next to Ella. The lamplight danced over the metallic green paper.

One of my sister's gifts was obviously a book. Four sharp corners gave away the mystery of the present. Ella's other gift was contained in a small box similar to mine.

"Thank you, Detective Novack," Ella said. I was worried that my sister wouldn't show appreciation for her gifts. I let out a low sigh of relief.

"You're welcome, Ella," he said. Most of his merriment had been drained. "It's Christmas. Would you ladies please call me Lewis?"

I nodded, and Ella pretended something had gotten her attention through the window. I doubted that my sister had seen anything through the small gap in the curtains, but I didn't call her out for ignoring Lewis's request.

My mom carried in a tray full of wafers and hot cocoa. The tray was old and battered. It had been Josh's television tray. I could see E.T. painted on the face of the tray.

"You didn't have to do this, Miranda," Detective Novack said. He bent down to kiss her, but my mom dodged the kiss by pretending that she was placing the tray on the coffee table.

"I have a little something for you, too," he told my mom. She gave him an indulging smile and sat down on the loveseat opposite Ella and me.

Detective Novack sat directly beside my mom, almost on top of her, and placed one small box in my mom's hands. It was wrapped in gold paper.

"Well," he said, "are you guys going to open your presents?"

My mom and I directed our attention to Ella. In our house, the youngest child opened his or her presents first.

Ella tore into the paper covering the book. She held up the hardcover for everyone to see. The title was *Harris Hodge: Playing Chess with the Dead*.

I felt like a ball of lead fell into my stomach, but I tried to play it cool. My mom shifted uncomfortably.

"Thank you, Lewis," Ella said. I thought I heard a touch of sincerity in her voice. Whatever my sister was feeling was closed to me.

What was Lewis Novak trying to do? I was sure that he had heard the rumors about Ella from people in the town or from my grandpa, but why did he choose to encourage my sister's behavior? He was trying to win Ella's favor.

Ella opened her other present. She held up a beautiful pair of gold earrings. Tiny dancing stars dangled from the post and reflected all the light in the room.

"They are lovely." She seemed mesmerized by her sparkling earrings. It surprised me that my sister liked them. She had never expressed an interest in jewelry.

My mom's attention shifted to me. I tore open my packages and laid them on my lap. The two white boxes did not betray their contents. I opted to open the box that contained the larger gift. In my excitement, I tore the box.

A purple and green dreamcatcher lay on snow-white tissue paper. I held it up a couple of inches from my face. My eyes crossed as I studied the intricately woven threads.

"It's a dream catcher," Detective Novak said. I fought an urge to roll my eyes at him. Dreamcatchers were sold in stores and craft shops everywhere, but, I had to admit, my gift seemed customized somehow.

"Thank you, Lewis," I said. I twirled it around for everyone to see.

"Native Americans thought that dream catchers would filter their dreams," he explained. "The bad dreams would get caught in the web and the good dreams would pass through to the dreamer."

"Thank you," I said again. I sucked back an exasperated sigh.

I popped open the ring-sized box, and a pair of gold earrings jumped into my lap. I picked them up and held them to the light.

Each earring had three dancing ballerinas hanging from a golden ball. The ballerinas were poised in a frozen pirouette.

It was my turn to be caught in the beauty of jewelry. I took out my earrings so that I could wear my gift.

"I'm glad you like them," Detective Novack said. "They were my mother's."

I stopped in the process of removing my other earring. *He had given me a dead woman's jewelry!*

"Thank you," I repeated. Now I understood why my sister had put her earrings back into the box.

Thankfully, he turned toward my mom. I took the opportunity to slide the ballerina earrings into the box.

Ella smirked. I glared at her.

My mom obediently turned her present over and ran her fingernail under the tape. She didn't rip through the wrapping paper.

My mom carefully removed the wrapping without a tear and opened the small box. She looked at the box for what seemed like forever, and a tear ran down her cheek.

"Mom?" I said. I rose from my spot on the couch and peered over her. My eyes watered.

Lewis was obviously a fan of gold. He had given my mom a gold charm bracelet lined with rubies. There were six charms. Five of the charms bore the name of one of each of my mom's children. The last charm on the bracelet was blank.

"Did it belong to your mother, too?" Ella asked. My mom shot eye daggers at my sister.

"No," Detective Novak said, wading through my sister's sarcasm. He fidgeted and ran his hand through his hair. "I bought the bracelet from a man in town."

I figured he had gotten my mom's gift from Kerry Shelton. I wondered how Kerry was feeling and decided to check on him before Christmas break ended.

"I had the charms made special," he said. "I hope you like them."

"I love them," my mom said quickly and firmly. She shot a look at Ella that challenged her daughter to say anything to the contrary.

"Like I said before," Ella said. "He is trying too hard."

The yelling and embarrassment that followed are easy to imagine. My mom told Ella that she was "an ungrateful brat", and my sister said my mom was a "harlot." Neither person was justified in their allegations, but their voices escalated until I thought Lewis would have to write a citation for violating the noise ordinance.

Lewis stood up and watched the scene unfold in front of him. He started to say something to try to end the argument, decided against it, reached for his coat, decided against it, and threw up his hands.

I took charge of the situation. I grabbed his coat, led him to the door, expressed my family's appreciation for his generosity and understanding, and shut the door in his face.

My mom and sister were still yelling at each other. I picked up the first thing I saw, a vase, and smashed it on the floor.

My mom and Ella stopped fighting and turned to me. My mom's gaze drifted slowly to the broken vase.

I narrowed my eyes and silently dared my mom or my sister to say a word against my actions. I was so angry that sweat had beaded on my face and was rolling down my neck in rivers.

I was upset, frustrated, and embarrassed. I said the first words that sprang to my mind, and I never regretted saying them.

"I hate you." I spoke the words calmly and firmly, locked eyes briefly with each of the remaining members of my family, and walked upstairs.

I didn't hear a word as I climbed the stairs and walked down the hall. I don't know if the sounds from downstairs could have been loud enough to be heard over the blood marching through my ears.

I stopped short of the room I shared with Ella and doubled back to my brothers' room. I opened the door and an adolescent boy smell of sweaty socks and oily machinery ran into me. I closed the door behind myself.

I didn't need to turn on the light to find the place I most desired to be in the room. I climbed a short ladder and rolled onto Josh's bed. I buried my head in his pillow, taking in all that remained of my favorite brother, and cried. I cried so hard and so long that I thought eternity would pass before my tears dried up and the ache in my soul was soothed.

Unfortunately, I had more tears to cry over many other things, and I couldn't hide from life by staying in my dead brother's bed. At least I was able to fall asleep in Josh's old room and have a few moments of peace before another cloud of sadness settled over me.

Chapter Thirty-Seven

I still thought I was dreaming. I pinched myself half a dozen times to reassure myself that I was riding with Bryan.

I had been sleeping peacefully in my brother's bed when my mind picked up on some frantic thoughts. I tried to mentally bat them away, but they insisted on penetrating my mind.

What am I going to do?

How do I get to her?

What can I do to make her believe me?

I knew the tone of Bryan's thoughts. Experiencing his memories had left a signature of his thought process burned into my mind.

I got out of the warm bed and I smoothed the wrinkles out of yesterday's clothes. They still had the fresh smell of inactivity.

I plodded down the steps and quietly opened the door. I reached for my coat and slid it on as I peered off the porch.

Bryan was parked on the other side of the street in an old blue truck with rust replacing the areas where paint had once been. He looked surprised to see me, but did not convey his shock through his actions.

I walked around the truck and got into the passenger seat. He started the truck and noisily slid it into gear. Bryan kept looking at me, but we didn't speak until we could no longer be seen from the windows of my house.

"You already know what's going on," he said. It was not a question.

I decided to be honest. "I read your mind."

I waited for his inevitable skepticism, but Bryan simply nodded. "Your father had a touch of that."

"Wait," Bryan said, waving a hand in front of his face. "How much else do you know?"

I wanted to trust him. Besides, no one would take his word against mine if he mentioned my extra sensory ability.

I turned the volume up on Bryan's thoughts. I plucked information from his mind as easily as I picked out marshmallows from my cereal.

"I *know* that this was once your father's truck," I regurgitated. "I know you spent some time trying to get it to start, but someone must have kept it maintained while you were in prison. I know that you've been hiding in an old dumbwaiter at your old house. I know the police did not know the dumbwaiter existed, so they did not find you when they searched your house."

Bryan's eyes grew larger with every sentence I said. He kept his attention on the road, but his knuckles turned white.

"You want my mom to run away with you when you leave the area," I continued. I surprised myself. I hadn't used my gift this extensively in a long time. "You wish there was a way for her to go without Ella and me."

Bryan was starting to sweat. *Let him drown in it.*

"Lydia and Bannon have been hiding in your house for a day." I swallowed hard. I narrowed my eyes and swatted the back of Bryan's head. "You watched her get verbally abused, and you snuck out instead of untying her hands!"

The last words I spoke weighed on me. I said things as I picked them up from Bryan's consciousness.

"How could you watch Lydia get hurt now that you know she's your daughter?" I shouted. "How could you use me and want me to disappear from my mom's life at the same time?" I tried to keep my face expressionless, but I couldn't hide my anger.

"It's not that easy." He jerked up his shirtsleeve and showed me a bandage.

I felt a wave of hostility from Bryan. I braced myself for his fear to take form in his words.

Bryan hit the steering wheel with the palm of his right hand. He looked at me, prepared to yell something, thought better of it, and returned his attention to the road.

"Get out of my head!" he said. His eyes were on the road, but I knew his rage was directed at me. "I don't want you and Ella to disappear, I just wanted Miranda and me to be back to the way we were!" he yelled. My mom's old boyfriend switched gears. "Who says I could have rescued Lily? I may have gotten us both killed. Bannon hid in a closet with Lily when your mom came to the house today. I couldn't come out or call to Miranda or Bannon would know that I was in the house. Your mother left in tears. She thought I'd been secretly arrested."

I hadn't gotten used to the idea that Lydia was really Bryan's daughter, Lily. I had been referring to her as Lydia because that was the name I had always called her.

"If you don't want me to read any more of your thoughts, then tell me why you came to my house," I challenged. I raised my eyebrows in an attempt to look indifferent.

There was a long silence before Bryan finally said, "I told you that your father and I exchanged letters?"

I nodded my head and turned up the heat. The cab of the truck was freezing.

"I learned a lot about your family before—"

I'm sure Bryan was going to say, 'before your dad lost it,' or, 'before your father killed himself,' but he stopped himself before the words spilled from his mouth. I should have been happy that Bryan didn't want to upset me, but I would have preferred a straightforward approach.

"I'll just say that your father was very intelligent and reliable until the last few years of his life," Bryan continued. "I could tell he was getting sick when he wrote me about things he was seeing in the woods where he worked. The spaces between his letters became longer, and the content was less friendly."

My mom had called my father a logger when people asked about his profession. I never remembered my father talking or thinking about anything supernatural surrounding his job, but I had muted the volume of my gift at an early age.

"Wait a second," I said. "How long did my father write to you?"

I had heard that my father had written Bryan a couple of letters, but Bryan made it seem as though my father had corresponded a lot with him. *Why wouldn't any member of my family have talked about the letters?*

I was so upset and confused that I gave up trying to understand my father's motive for having written my mom's past boyfriend. I should have wanted to hear every memory Bryan had of my father, but I found it was easier to keep my father *and* his memories buried. I was turning into my mother's daughter.

"What did you want when you pulled up next to my house?" I asked. I was tired of trying to decipher the meaning out of people's coded words.

Bryan seemed offended. "I wanted someone I could trust to help me free Lily."

"And you thought I would be perfect for the job since my father had been sympathetic to your cause?" I asked.

"I suppose that is exactly what I thought," Bryan admitted. "And you are Lily's friend," he continued. "And I thought you might have a touch of whatever the Miller's are rumored to have."

I hoped Bryan was referring to the Miller's extra sensory gifts and not the Miller supposed mental craziness. I appreciated his honesty.

"What's the plan?" I asked.

"I want to distract Bannon outside while you run in and untie Lily," Bryan said.

I liked the plan because it was simple, and it kept me away from Bannon Sneed. I decided I would rather be locked inside Bryan's prison than be in Bannon Sneed's presence.

"Why didn't you just phone in an anonymous tip?" I asked. "The police could have surprised Bannon and removed Lydia from the house."

"That's just it," Bryan said. "I don't want to get the police involved."

I finally understood the part of the plan Bryan wasn't telling me. He was going to kidnap Lydia and go on the run with her.

"You can't expect Lydia to understand all of this and willingly leave with you on the spot," I told him. "She has a life here, and even if it's been turned upside down, Lydia still needs to have something constant in her life."

"I am constant," Bryan said, without asking me how I had figured out his agenda. "I couldn't help that I was wrongfully jailed and told that my entire family was dead!"

"I know you were not treated fairly."

Bryan snorted.

"Going on the run with your teenage daughter is not the answer. Did you ever think about how Lydia must feel?" I pleaded. I wanted to make Bryan see things from Lydia's perspective. She was probably already emotionally damaged beyond repair.

Bryan was ingesting my words. He still looked straight at the road, but I could tell that I had his attention.

"Lydia became Lily in a flash," I continued. "She found out her parents were frauds and her real mother was dead. I'm sure she now realizes that Bannon is the cause of the deaths of both of her mothers."

Bryan looked at me harshly when I referred to Olivia as Lydia's mother, but I wasn't completely sure about Olivia's part in the drama. She had known something, because she had tried to slowly drink herself into forgetfulness, but had her husband disillusioned her? Had Olivia known all the circumstances? Had she tried to stop Bannon Sneed's madness? Is that why she was murdered?

I tried not to dwell on the dead. I turned my thoughts back to my kidnapped friend.

"Who knows what Lydia's had to endure in the past week since Bannon's hidden her from the authorities? It's not exactly every day teenaged conflict," I finished.

"I understand that," Bryan said, but he was light years from comprehending the emotions of a teenage girl in crisis. "I just know that I'll be put back in prison, even if Bannon confesses to Nellie's murder and DNA confirms Lily is my daughter."

Bryan looked me squarely in the eyes. "I will not go back to prison."

I couldn't think of anything else to say to Bryan, so I kept quiet. We passed Pale Woods Academy, and Bryan sighed heavily.

"Is there something on your mind?" I asked.

"Why don't you tell me?" he asked. "You're the one who's been reading my thoughts like a paperback novel."

"You told me to stay out of your head, so I respected your request," I said. It wasn't necessarily true.

"Well, you didn't get that from your mother," Bryan said. "If she could have read my thoughts, she would have written all of them down and used them against me. I guess you're not as stubborn as her."

I wasn't going to encourage his verbal bashing of my mom, so I turned toward the passenger side window. We rode in silence a few moments.

"I was just curious about Lily," Bryan finally said. "Was she happy? Did she have a lot of friends? Did she share Nellie's love of the river?"

I looked at Bryan and noticed just how old and pale he was. He must have lost a lot of blood from the bullet wound and he hadn't been able to eat well. Bryan may have worked out every muscle in prison, but he was beginning to look weak and unwell.

"Did you remove the bullet?" I asked.

"I took care of it," Bryan said gruffly. "I lost a lot of blood, but I have been pouring peroxide into the hole the bullet left and I've been eating foods with a lot of iron."

"What food?" I challenged.

"You know," Bryan said, "bread and peanut butter."

Bryan needed medical attention. I was afraid he was pushing himself to stay free, and I worried his wound had become contaminated. Maybe he was running a high fever from the infection. I hoped not, because I had heard that people who ran high fevers hallucinated. All I needed was for Bryan to freak out and begin thinking that he saw little pink elephants.

We pulled up to the property that still belonged to Bryan and killed the motor. He left the headlights on so that we could see around the house. I wondered if that horrible little man would notice the lights.

Bryan told me to stay in the car, so I followed a few steps behind him. He didn't realize I was behind him until he was already on the front porch.

"I thought I told you to stay in the car," he whispered harshly.

"How am I supposed to know if something's happened to you?" I explained. "I figured that instead of worrying and waiting, I would just follow you now. If you get hurt or killed at least I'll know so that I won't be a sitting duck for Bannon Sneed if he comes out."

Bryan thought about my convoluted logic. He crossed his arms and I could see tattoos going vertically down the outside of his forearms. The tattoo on the left arm spelled out *Nellie* and the one on his right arm read *Lily*. The names were inked in Old English letters and there were a small set of angel wings above Lily's name.

I suddenly felt very sorry for Bryan. He only had memories of the dead to keep him company after my father stopped writing to him.

Bryan noticed my gaze and quickly dropped his arms. The action caused swift pain to the hole the bullet had left in his skin and muscle tissue. Bryan covered the bandage on his arm and bent over in pain. He recovered his posture and his face did not betray the tenderness in his appendage.

I recalculated Bryan's odds against Bannon Sneed. Bryan had suffered an injury that would need medical attention soon. It amazed me that Bryan had lived as long as he had when he was losing blood every day and he could not eat or rest enough to help repair his wound. Bryan would probably require a blood transfusion and a lot of antibiotics in order to recover, and I still didn't think he'd be able to recuperate quickly.

"Go back to the truck!" Bryan almost shouted at me. "Your mother has suffered enough pain and death. Bannon has already made it clear he will shoot you and anyone else who gets in his way!"

Bryan's words moved me. His outburst almost made him seem like a toddler having a tantrum, but at least he cared about my welfare.

"She loves the river," I told him in my softest voice.

"What?" Bryan said before he realized I was talking about Lydia.

"She used to get in trouble for going down to the river," I said. "She collected strangely shaped rocks she hid from her par—I mean those people." I jerk my finger in the direction of the Sneed home. It was almost like she was a different person when she stood beside the water."

Bryan eyed the ground. I could feel his emotions swell, but he didn't let them pour out of his body.

"You still shouldn't go," he said. "I would feel terrible if something happened to you."

"Then why did you bring me here?"

I had decided that I would argue with Bryan until he saw my point. In the end, Bryan would probably have had to carry me kicking and punching to his father's old truck and locked me in the cab. I opened my mouth to voice another protest, but I heard a strong splash.

I easily dodged Bryan and ran around the outside of the house and into the backyard. The grounds had been mowed, but teenagers knew no one lived in the house, so I almost tripped over a couple of old blankets and beer bottles. Bryan became tangled in one blankets, and put some distance between him and me.

One light had been turned on in the back of the house. I assumed it was a kitchen light because my kitchen was located in the same place at my house. The light lit up a square patch of grass that seemed dark green in spite of the harsh elements.

An outside security light revealed most of the backyard and illuminated a short trail to the Nolichucky River. I saw the form of a crouched figure at the end of the trail. I made out Bannon Sneed's silhouette in the half-light of the night.

Bannon Sneed had no problem holding Lydia down in the water. It seemed the splash I'd heard was one of her last attempts to fight the man she'd known as her father.

I tried to sneak up on him, but he heard my approach and whirled around. I could see my friend's body floating lifelessly in the water.

Lydia's nose and mouth were submerged, but the rest of the front part of her body floated on the surface of the river. He was merely holding her in place to make sure the water washed away any of the life she once possessed.

I assaulted his mind. I raced through his memories and I was consumed with feelings of loneliness, guilt, anger, and despair.

I saw him as a child. He was beaten until his face was almost unrecognizable. He couldn't remember more of his own father than the liquor on his breath and his unmerciful fists.

I saw his memories of a younger and more beautiful Olivia. I felt his happiness at wedding her, but he was secretly scared of losing her. He kept his wife close to him to keep an eye on her. Olivia was the reason he felt he had to kill Lydia. He didn't understand that he had murdered his wife, and he thought Olivia would leave him because she would see him as an unfit father.

He kept one hand on Lily's pale white neck and reached for his gun with the other. Lydia wasn't fighting anymore, but his hands were cold and wet from the water, and the gun slid away from him.

I snapped out of his mind, but I still held my link to his surface thoughts. I ran for him, almost slipping on the wet trail. He watched me lunge. He let go of Lily's neck and made a dive for the gun. His fingers wrapped around the cold, metal handle and he raised the gun to my face.

I have never been more frightened in my life. I could see the gun that was going to end my life, and I knew I could not be saved.

I jumped back into Bannon Sneed's mind, past his intention to kill me, and bathed in all the information I could glean in the last short seconds of my life.

I buzzed through his brain to the time when Olivia was making preparations to leave with Nellie. He was afraid that he would never see Olivia again. She was going back to New York, and Olivia's Aunt Lonnie, who had never liked him, would convince her to stay. He was sure that Olivia would agree because Nellie, her best friend, would be with her. He would be left to suffer his loneliness in the mansion he'd built for his wife.

He was weeping outside in the rain when he heard Bryan and Nellie arguing echo off the rocks in the mountains. He had wiped his eyes and had gotten the attention of his wife and Terrance.

Terrance Hernandez was Bannon Sneed's most trusted companion. He had not left him since his father had hired him. Bannon Sneed rewarded loyalty and faithfulness, so Terrance's entire family was invited to work at the Sneed mansion. He had also helped Terrance out of some tight spots, like covering up his infidelities.

He, Terrance, and Olivia ran across the street and around the Shelton's house. Bryan and Nellie were yelling by the river.

Olivia looked on helplessly while He tried to assess the best way to work the situation to his benefit. Terrance stood silently still, waiting for his order.

Bryan was bent over his daughter, Lily. It seemed the child had been injured, but Bryan did not act as though Lily was seriously hurt.

The couple kept fighting and Olivia looked at him with desperation in her eyes. She wanted to help her friend badly, but she was too weak to interfere. He took the initiative.

"Take out the redneck," he ordered Terrance. Terrance nodded and walked casually over to the fighting duo.

Terrance bent over, picked up a large rock, and bounced it in his hand. After Terrance was satisfied with its size and weight, he calculated his next move.

Bryan never knew that Terrance was planning a death blow from less than a foot behind him. He had not meant for Terrance to kill Bryan, but he was not dissatisfied with the result.

Bryan yelled and shook his fist in the air. Terrance wound up, like he was going to throw a fastball, and hit Bryan squarely in the head with the rock.

Bryan stopped yelling and fell to the rocky shore. He landed in an unnatural heap.

Olivia ran into the Shelton's house, crying and screaming. Nellie hit Terrance's massive chest and yelled over the raging river.

Terrance looked up at Bannon and suddenly it dawned on him he had the power to make his wife stay. He communicated his intentions to Terrance by locking and holding the manservant's eyes. Bannon Sneed nodded his head once.

The two men had spent a lot of time together, and even though they were not friends, they understood each other very well. Terrance communicated his understanding by lifting young Nellie up by her long, fragile neck.

Nellie's screams were cut short and the rushing river muffled the splashing as Nellie fought for her life. Her attempt was futile. Terrance held her down in her beloved river until she stopped moving and breathing. He let Nellie go and the "River of Death" rolled her lifeless body between two large rocks.

Terrance lifted Lily off the rock and carried her to him. The toddler's head bobbed, but her torso was curled between his arms.

He examined the child. She was alive and breathing, but she had a large cut on the side of her head, just beyond her hairline. Lily would need a couple of stitches, but she would be fine.

Terrance followed him inside the house with Lily still in his arms. He turned sideways to walk through the doorway behind his employer.

Olivia had collapsed in a corner by the refrigerator. Bannon could smell sweat and tears as he bent down to talk to his wife.

Olivia looked up at his approach and noticed Lily in Terrance's arms. She looked questioningly from him to Lily.

"Are you ready to be a mother?" he said. Olivia appeared even more puzzled.

"Lily is going to need a mother. Bryan has killed Nellie," he lied and Olivia's face contorted. She let out a wail of pain he had heard only one other time, after her miscarriage.

He shook his wife. *"Do you want Lydia's first memories of you to be in this state?"* He had made up the name spontaneously by combining Lily's and Olivia's names. *"There will be plenty of time for tears later, but now you have to hold it together."*

"But what about Kerry?" Olivia asked. *"He will fight for her and he'll win. No amount of your money can keep her family from getting custody of her."*

Olivia's sadness had plugged her nose, and she sounded like she had a cold. Her hair was matted to her head with sweat.

"I have a plan that will keep Lily away from Kerry or Bryan if he happens to get away with murdering his wife," he said. *If he even survives the gash he just got from the river rock,* he thought.

He put extra emphasis on the idea that Bryan could get away with murdering his wife by adding, *"You know he has friends in high places."*

He was referencing Bryan's relationship with the Chief of Police. Olivia's tired mind only worried that her friend's murder would go unavenged and Lily would be subjected to Bryan's wrath once he was freed.

Olivia's face suddenly cleared, and her eyes found her husband. Bannon had always trusted Olivia, so he believed every word she said.

"I will do whatever it takes to put Bryan behind bars and keep Lily safe," she said. Olivia cleared her throat. *"I mean, I'll do anything to keep* Lydia *safe."*

Bannon pulled his wife into his arms and related his plan. Bannon, Master Manipulator and Sordid Schemer, had won again.

Chapter Thirty-Eight

Bannon Sneed's recollections flashed before me with the speed of a bullet and with lightning emotion. Most of my energy was zapped away, and I found that I no longer wanted to touch the man at whom I had flung myself.

I heard two shots fired, and their echoes off the mountains brought me back to my own mind. I had landed on Bannon Sneed and heard a crack as my weight drove his head back. I guessed that his head had connected with a large rock.

I tried to untangle myself from his body as soon as I landed on him. I could smell his orange-scented cologne and his sweat and deception. All those smells clung to his body and could never be washed away.

I had heard the shots, but I felt no pain. My energy slowly ebbed away.

"Help my daughter!" a voice screamed in my head. I didn't have to see the ghost to know it was Nellie. Bannon Sneed seemed to be unconscious beneath me. I crawled over his body and blindly reached out. I found a branch that had floated to the edge of the river. The same branch had kept the river from swallowing Lydia.

My friend looked peaceful, but she was pale and blue. I hoped that the water had caused the coloration and not the lack of oxygen.

Reviving Lydia was a lost cause before I dragged her to the shore. Her life had flitted away before I had reached her.

"Nellie?" Bryan said.

I turned around, expecting to see a ghost, but Bryan was looking at me. *I looked nothing like Nellie!*

Bryan's wound had reopened and leaked his life's blood to a point that could be fatal. He was hallucinating. I played along so that I could get him to take action, even if it meant that he would die trying to save Lydia.

"Save Lydia," I begged, but Bryan didn't hear me. He was looking past me. *Was everyone going crazy?*

I tilted Lydia's head back and opened her mouth. I gave her a few short breaths and pumped her chest. I was trying to do CPR the way our school's P.E. coach had taught us. I doubted my efforts were helping the situation, but I kept going.

Bryan passed me. On his way around me, he looked down at his daughter and said, "She's dead."

Bryan showed no emotion about his lost child. He said the words almost casually, as if he were observing the remains of a dead animal on the side of the road.

I felt helpless. I couldn't convince Bryan to help me with Lydia and I couldn't get my friend to breathe.

I heard another gunshot. It rang in my ears like the community fireworks display on Independence Day.

The shot was fired behind me. I could feel a difference in Bryan's thought pattern. He went from confused to scared and hurt.

Bannon Sneed had propped himself up on his left shoulder. He wore a grimace of pain, but he steadied his gun to take the next shot.

I was in the middle of delivering pumps to Lydia's chest. I knew I had to take cover quickly, so I pushed off Lydia's chest and dove to the ground. The bullet meant for me sprinted through the air.

The last push I gave Lydia's lungs had released her from death's fingers. She began coughing and gagging on the water that had been released from her lungs.

I worried he would try to shoot Lydia, but he had passed out. He was used to air conditioning and pedicures. The pain of a concussion was too much for him.

I crawled to where Lydia was crying and clutching her throat. I looked at Bryan's body lying on the ground and decided I would help him later. I thought he really might be dead, but I didn't care. *How could he have stood by so casually while Bannon drowned his daughter and shot at me?* Honorable men protected women and children.

"It was my fault," a voice echoed in my head. *"I got his attention when I—"*

I blocked out the voice of Nellie's ghost. I had read enough minds to last me a lifetime.

After a couple of moments, I was able to get Lydia to her feet. She could hardly stand; her legs kept shaking from her terrifying experience.

I helped my friend hobble into the house in unsteady movements. I let go of Lydia long enough to open the screen door that led to the kitchen.

Once Lydia got inside the house, she shielded her eyes from the overhead light, and lunged for the first chair she could touch at the kitchen table. She held her hand like a visor over her eyes and blinked hard when she looked up at me.

Lydia tried to speak several times, but the words never made it past her throat. I didn't have to read her mind; confusion and despair were emotions I could understand.

My eyes adjusted to the light quickly, and I briefly scanned the kitchen. The room was a mess. A fine sheet of dirt covered every-thing, and objects littered the floor. It looked like someone had emptied every drawer and most of the cabinets in the kitchen. In fact, some drawers appeared to have been thrown against the walls. They lay broken and useless on the floor.

I noticed an ancient landline phone beside the refrigerator. Its color matched the light blue checked country décor on the walls and counters.

I lifted the phone from its cradle. I was praying for a dial tone, but I became concerned about removing the hold of the base after the receiver was not easily moved. I pushed the receiver upward, and I felt it release.

I did not hear the dial tone echo. The receiver was as silent as the night.

I locked eyes with Lydia and followed her gaze to one of the only drawers that remained intact. I slid open the drawer and discovered that its only contents were a passport and a cell phone. It was password protected, but Lydia had once told me Bannon's most prized possession. I pressed the numbers that correlated with the word *money* and pressed the phone icon. My fingers stopped dialing midway through the number. I had been dialing my grandpa's cell phone. He could no longer be reached where he had gone.

Lydia dropped her chin on the table. She stared at me without seeing me. I erased the number and dialed the police station.

"Sheriff's Office," the dispatcher answered. I knew her voice, even though it was hoarse. She was either still upset over my grandpa's death or she'd smoked too many cigarettes in her life.

I recognized the dispatcher's voice, but I did not remember her name. She was in her mid-forties, mildly attractive, with bot-tle-blond hair and too-tight khaki pants. My mom had once hinted that she and my grandpa had once "had a thing". I assumed that meant that the dispatcher had a romantic relationship with my grandpa.

"Sally?" I heard an officer say. The name he called the dispatcher seemed right, so I tried it.

"Is this Sally?" I asked.

"Sydney!" Sally said. I heard her muffled words as she placed her hand over her mouthpiece. "It's her!" she told someone excitedly.

Sally readjusted the mouthpiece and said, "We were so worried! Where are you, child?"

They were worried? Had my mom already discovered that I was not in my bed?

I told Sally I was at Bryan Shelton's old house, and she surprised me by reading an address. I asked Lydia if the address was correct, but she was still staring into space.

"Could you ask a police officer and an ambulance to come?" I said.

"Of course, child," Sally said. "Detective Novack is on his way."

I assumed Sally had been speaking to Detective Novack when she covered her mouthpiece. I was surprised that he was at the station again. Whatever the reason, I was glad he had taken a personal interest in finding and helping me.

I spoke with Sally for a few moments before I hung up on her. She had wanted me to talk with her until help arrived, but I was becoming increasingly concerned about Lydia. She was starting to remind me of my sister when Ella was deeply entranced.

I slowly approached Lydia and pulled out the chair beside her. The scraping chair made on the linoleum and the rushing water from the river were the only sounds in the house.

I laid my head down and looked into Lydia's eyes. She didn't respond.

I touched her shoulder, and Lydia's head popped up. I was afraid she was going to fall out of her chair, so I sat up in case I needed to reduce the impact of her fall.

A tear leaked out of her eye. I hoped no more would follow it until help arrived. My mom was the queen of non-emotion, so I hadn't learned the best way to handle a person in need of emotional support, and I wouldn't know how to handle her if Lydia broke down.

I was surprised and relieved when Lydia straightened herself in her chair. I saw a different side of her than I had ever experienced.

"Lydia?" I asked.

"Please don't call me that anymore," she said. She acted as though we were having a simple conversation at an ice cream social. "I am Lily Shelton."

Lily had been through a lot in the past couple of weeks, but I wasn't going to press her for the details. In fact, I doubted I wanted to know what had happened to her since I had last seen her.

Lily had obviously been subjected to Bannon Sneed's cruel and deteriorating mind. I wondered how much he had told her, and if any of his words were true.

"My mummy, even though she was a co-conspirator to evil doings, taught me several valuable lessons," Lily said.

I had been worried that Lily would break down and I wouldn't be able to help her pick up her scattered emotions. I became more frightened of Lily's lack of emotion. She had wiped any readable expression from her face, and I was too afraid to penetrate my friend's fragile mind.

"Do you think your grandfather would welcome back his Little Lily?" Lily said, surprising me out of my rationalization.

I hadn't felt like I was walking a sensitive tightrope, but the mention of my grandpa's name sent me falling into an emotional abyss. I broke into hysterical crying. Through my sobs I managed to choke out, "He would have loved to know you, Lily, but Bannon Sneed killed him the night he kidnapped you."

I let my body fall from my chair, and I hit the floor hard when I landed. Lily's arms were immediately around me. I was disappointed in myself for crying. I should be able to hold myself together in the face of grief. After all, I hadn't cried at the funeral or the interment, but I was not like my mom and Lily. My mourning began at that moment, and my heart turned sour and bitter.

I could hear the sirens, and I knew the EMT's needed to focus on Lily. I tried to dry my eyes, but the tears kept pouring down my cheeks.

"Do you know how I got through this past week?" Lily asked.

The question was so unexpected that I was able to push some of my emotions aside. My tears slowed to a trickle as I directed my attention to Lily.

"After I watched my Mummy die," Lily began, "and when my so-called *father* dragged me over here to drown me, I thought about the best way I could die with dignity." Lily practically spat out the word *father*, but her eyes still didn't betray a hint of emotion.

I waited for her to continue. I could feel Lily's heart racing, but her breathing was slow and rhythmic. I settled onto her shoulder and let my friend rock me.

Lily was silent for a moment and then pulled her face around to meet my eyes. "I thought of what you would do if you were in my situation," she said.

Lily's words startled me. *Why would she want to be like me?*

Lily settled back into holding and rocking me. She answered my unspoken question.

"I thought I would be okay if I could carry myself the way you did when everyone circulated rumors about the men in your family," Lily said. "I thought of all the times you took Ella's hand and walked her into the school as people around you threw jeering remarks. I did not cry in front of the monster that extravagantly clothed and fed me for most of my childhood. I walked slowly and quietly to what I thought would be my doom. I fought for my life, because I wanted to live, but I did not cry out. I wanted to inflict as much pain on him as possible, and I managed to kick him pretty hard in the face. I guess he regrets those karate lessons now."

I turned and looked at my friend's face. Lily wore a sheepish expression. A smile tugged at the corners of her mouth.

I laughed despite the gravity of the situation. Once I started laughing, Lily joined me, and we held our stomachs and rolled on the floor.

I'm sure Detective Novack thought Lily and I were hysterical, and we probably weren't sane at the moment he looked in on us from the back door. His first glimpse of us was through the screen door at the back of the house. I'm not sure what he expected to see, but I bet he didn't think he would look into the house and see Lily and me hugging and laughing.

Chapter Thirty-Nine

My mom was waiting for me at the hospital when the ambulance carrying Lily and me arrived. Detective Novack had followed the ambulance to the hospital. He had left several officers and another ambulance in charge of the scene.

I wanted to tell my mom, 'See? Aren't you glad Detective Novack is dedicated to his job?' but I let it go. My mom looked horrible. Her hair was slightly damp with perspiration, and her eyes were red-rimmed and full of emotion.

I hugged my mom and cried on her for a long time. I had been through more than my body could handle, and my reserve supply of adrenaline had been sucked dry. I cried myself to sleep with the bustle of the hospital moving into a faraway land.

"Sydney," I heard. I opened my eyes, and a jolt of fear and guilt ran through me.

I had fallen asleep without checking on Lily! She probably thought I was a horrible friend. What if they had already moved her to another home?

My mom was out of the room, and Detective Novack was resting in an uncomfortable position in a chair next to my hospital bed. Ella was watching him from the foot of my bed. *Why was my sister looking so hard at him?*

"Ella?" I whispered.

Ella glanced at me and back to Detective Novack. "Everyone has ghosts," she said, "but some people could run a haunted house in their mind."

I made a mental note *never* to read Detective Novack's mind. I didn't want to even brush his thoughts and risk lowering my opinion of him or picking up another spiritual hitchhiker.

I was no longer tired, but my muscles cried out in pain when I tried to remove myself from the thin, sterile hospital sheets. It seemed as though Ella and my mom had slept awkwardly in a chair that was only slightly larger than the one Detective Novack occupied.

"I figured out why Nellie could not speak to me," Ella said. Her voice was only slightly louder than the steady breathing of the sleeping officer in the room.

I surprised myself by saying, "She was bound to the water." I lifted forward so that my sister could straighten and fluff my pillow. "I thought about it after you washed my ghostly follower down our shower drain."

Ella glanced around the room. Her eyes stopped in a couple of places, but I didn't see anything and wanted to keep it that way.

"You are opening your mind a little more every day," Ella admitted, "but a lot of your developing spiritual connectedness has come about because of tragic events."

Ella's eyes were glazed with moisture, but I knew she wouldn't cry. I waited for her to either praise me some more or condemn me for my past refusal to exercise my talent openly.

"It is a little more complicated than that," my sister said, speaking more about Nellie's ghost, "but she certainly feels avenged."

I was thankful that Ella hadn't made me promise to actively tell people about my gift. I was willing to learn more from my sister, but I wasn't ready to be a traveling freak show.

An idea suddenly came to me. It seemed like an extreme oversight that I hadn't asked my sister in the last week.

"Has Grandpa visited you?" I asked.

Ella looked down at her hands. I immediately regretted asking my question. My sister may have psychic abilities, but she had just lost her grandpa, too, and she really didn't need me to question her.

"I have not seen his spirit," she said. "Grandfather must have passed on after his death." Ella spoke the words miserably.

Ella was frustrated and disappointed. She wanted to prove to our grandpa that she wasn't crazy, but our grandpa had not given her the chance, in life or death.

"Maybe you'll still see him," I said sympathetically. "Jerrod's ghost didn't appear until after Josh's funeral."

Ella gave me an indulging smile. She noticed I was looking nervously out the door.

"Go find Lydia," she said.

I quietly slipped out of the hospital sheets and moved through the room silently, forgetting to correct my sister. She had not heard about Lily's name change.

I had been changed into a hospital gown, but my mom had put a housecoat around me. It had probably been the same one she had been wearing when she met Detective Novack and me at the hospital's entrance. I didn't look vogue but at least my rear end would be concealed.

I found Lily two rooms down the hall on the right. An officer was sitting in a chair beside her. He was alert and jumped quickly to his feet when he saw me snake my head into the room.

The officer recognized me and motioned me into the room. He extended his hand, and I shook it the way my grandpa had taught me.

"It was a pleasure to work beside your grandfather, ma'am," he said. "He honored his position, and we will miss him."

My eyes went to the gold nameplate that was on the officer's pocket. "Thank you, Officer Riddle," I said. I had practiced the same sentiment many times during my grandpa's funeral. "My grandfather was a good man, and I will try to honor his memory by practicing the lessons he taught me."

Officer Riddle seemed satisfied with my response, and he sat down. I put my hands into the pockets of my mom's housecoat. I knew I'd repeat that exchange many times in my life. Almost everyone in our small southeastern community had loved and respected my grandpa.

A sharp poke in my finger commanded my attention, and I fished out the silver locket. My mom must have cleaned out the pockets of my jeans and placed the locket in the pocket of her housecoat. I corrected myself. Ella had most likely been the one who had put the locket in a place where I would find it.

Lily smiled sadly at me from her bed. She had taken a shower, and she rested in a hospital nightgown. Her sadness had not dimmed the radiance of her loveliness. I no longer envied my friend. I could look at her and appreciate her beauty without coveting her wealth and position.

I reached out to Lily with the locket in my hand. Lily's face contorted into a grimace, but she held back her tears. She plucked the silver locket out of my palm and closed her hand over the locket without opening it.

Officer Riddle looked at the commercials aired on the silent television. He didn't damage my opinion of him by asking what we had exchanged.

Chapter Forty

I glanced around the courtroom. The size and grandeur of the room amazed me. The height of the door misrepresented the dimensions of the criminal court area. The polished wood could have been lacquered only hours ago, and I was close enough to the judge's bench to smell the leather of his seat.

I was grateful that the judge had asked Lily to appear in a closed-court setting for the arraignment. She would never have been able to live in Erwin if she had given her testimony in open court.

Unfortunately, Lily would eventually be called as a witness in another courtroom. The Unicoi County Courthouse was not properly staffed to handle a case of this magnitude.

I looked behind us and thought I saw Bryan for a moment, and then I realized it was Bryan's uncle, Kerry. He gave me a reassuring thumbs up.

The court had awarded Kerry Shelton temporary custody of his great-niece only hours after her life had almost ended in the Nolichucky River. Years had fallen from his face in the last couple of weeks. Taking care of another person had strengthened his resolve for living.

Lily had humbled herself since the horrible night she spent by the river. It was almost as if Lydia Sneed and Lily Shelton were two separate people, or at least two different personalities. Lydia Sneed would have mocked Kerry's attempts to please her and outright laughed at his gifts. Lily Shelton giggled at all of her Uncle Kerry's corny jokes and wrote him a short note on a napkin on his mirror every day to thank him for his kindness to her.

Bryan Shelton was apprehended beside the river, and he had been taken to the hospital in Johnson City. He had minor surgery to repair some of the damage from the gunshot wound he had received, and IV antibiotics kept his infection from the wound from becoming worse. He was released into police custody after he was deemed fit enough to be discharged from the hospital.

Kerry had talked to a lawyer for Bryan, but it would still be some time before Bryan was released from prison. The lawyer hoped Bryan would be released after the murder charges were officially dropped, and he could argue the escape charges down to the time Bryan had already served, but the prosecutor from the original case was not rushing the issue.

Detective Novack had taken Lily to see her father once in the hospital. Lily had been quiet about the visit, and I did not press her.

Kerry was not the father Lily wanted, but he was the guardian she needed. He showed her pictures of her past relations and told Lily stories about her mother and father. Most of the stories made her want to cry, but Lily's tears stayed behind her eyes.

I was afraid to ask my friend about the terrible week she had spent with Bannon's deteriorating mind. She started to tell me about it a couple of times, but she wouldn't let herself cry.

A glint of metal caught my eye when I turned back around. Kerry had given Lily a small braided silver chain to wear around her neck.

Lily's locket had slipped easily onto the chain, and now I never saw Lily without the necklace.

A handful of people in the courtroom were told to stand as the Honorable Judge Howell entered the courtroom. He waved an agitated hand that indicated he wanted everyone to be seated. He seemed tired of courtroom formalities and wanted to get straight to business.

"Miss Shelton," the judge said.

A DNA test had been performed, and it was proven that Bryan Shelton was Lily's father. Her name had been restored without fanfare.

The judge's eyes were kind, and his countenance softened when he addressed Lily. "I'm going to need you to explain to me what happened after Bannon Sneed took you out of Kerry Shelton's pawnshop," Judge Howell said.

I was outraged that my friend had to relive her horrible experience aloud. This morning Lily, her lawyer, and me had been informed that the police documents that held the statements Lily and I had made on the night of the incident were missing. My friend and I would have to make our statements again for the judge.

A court reporter had been typing busily under the judge's stand. Her fingernails made tiny clicks on the keys.

Lily took a deep breath. The courtroom was so silent that I could have heard Lily fill her lungs in the back of the room.

"Take your time, young lady," the judge said. We watched Lily's face drain of the little color it had held since she'd entered the courthouse.

I listened as Lily explained her side of the happenings on that cold December night. I held my friend's hand and put my arm around her shoulders during parts of the events that seemed too hard for her to tell.

Lily held all the people in the courtroom engrossed in her description of the weeks with Bannon Sneed's failing sanity. Everyone leaned forward as she described watching the man she thought was her father strangle his wife.

"She tried to save me," Lily spoke of Olivia Sneed. "She was very intoxicated when Bannon pushed me through the house."

Lily wouldn't call Olivia Sneed anything besides a pronoun, like "she" or "her", but she had started calling Bannon Sneed by his first name. No one contradicted her.

Lily continued. "Bannon ran into his office and threw some papers around. He was looking for something that he couldn't find. I still thought he was my father, so I thought Bannon was looking for our passports to take us away. After all, I thought I had just witnessed the murder of four people."

I tried not to let my emotions shake my composure. My grandpa had been the only murder in Kerry's shop.

"Will you tell us the names of those four people for the record?" the prosecutor asked gently.

The prosecutor, Janie Williams, was a young woman who was very aggressive when it came to justice. She had explained the types of questions Lily could expect and prepared her for the overwhelming emotional tension in the courtroom.

"I watched Bannon Sneed shoot Chief Conner Murphy in his head, but I couldn't tell where the rest of the shots were fired. I guess my brain registered a shot for each person in the room. I thought he had killed the man I later learned weas my real father, Bryan Shelton, my friend, Sydney Miller, and Kerry Shelton, the man who owned the pawnshop."

Prosecutor Williams grimaced when Lily said "guess". Lily had been warned not to make ambiguous statements. Prosecutor

Williams had stressed to Lily that her words should be firm because a defense attorney would challenge her memory.

Lily spoke for a few moments before an officer approached the judge with a sheet of paper. The judge read the official-looking document and kicked his bench.

Everyone in the courtroom was startled. The judge lifted his gavel and spoke roughly to us.

"It *appears* as if we have to adjourn for half an hour. The defendant will be joining us," Judge Howell said, and then shouted at the back door of the courtroom, "*as is his right.*"

The judge banged his gavel and shot out of his chair. The door banged shut after he left the courtroom.

Lily and I exchanged a look that spoke our concern and fear without words. Lily grabbed her locket, and I prayed for my friend. She would now be forced to face the man who had almost murdered her.

Chapter Forty-One

Most of the time, life is not fair. I tell people I accept that storm clouds sometimes follow good people while the sun seems to shine on evil wrongdoers, but I really just want to live in a make-believe world where everyone is considerate and just.

Half an hour after Judge Howell had called a recess, the door behind the judge's bench opened and a bailiff stepped into the courtroom. A man dressed in a tailored suit with un-exercised dimples on his left and right cheeks followed him.

I don't think I will ever understand why Bannon Sneed's life was spared when good people like my grandpa were destined to wink out of existence.

His worst injury had been a concussion that healed quickly. I knew I should not wish ill on others, but I had secretly hoped that the dent in his skull would kill him in his sleep.

I narrowed my eyes and focused all my hate on Bannon Sneed. I concentrated so hard on him that blood marched in my ears and my body turned cold, but he merely sat in a comfortable leather chair.

Lily and Kerry had told me he was still a powerful man, even behind bars. He had won the right to intimidate Lily while she reaffirmed her statement.

Bannon Sneed had a sly grin on his face that I knew scared Lily. A week ago he had sent a young thug to threaten Lily and Kerry.

Kerry opened his shop one morning, and a young man ran through the shop, tearing items off the shelves and spraying red paint from a can. Kerry was so shocked by the thug's actions that he didn't respond to the destruction for almost a minute.

Kerry shouted for the man to get out of the store. The thug stood five feet away, even when Kerry pulled out a large firearm.

Kerry was unable to intimidate him, but the man left after delivering a message. Kerry told me he had said, 'If you want to live, you'll move and forget all the things that happened by the river.'

Kerry was worried for his niece, but the incident just strengthened Lily's resolve.

"I will testify if it kills me," she said firmly. I don't think she intended the pun.

"Please continue, Miss Shelton," Prosecutor Williams said. Everyone was angered by Bannon's presence, but he sat with a self-satisfied smile on his face.

Lily remembered her place in the account of events. She went on to describe Olivia Sneed's murder.

"Bannon held my wrist the entire time, and I was too scared and confused to know that he was the reason for the situation," Lily continued. She willed her focus on the prosecutor and away from the man she had known as her father. "She came into Bannon's study and tried to knock him out with a frying pan. It always works in the movies, but..."

Lily trailed off. She had a distant look in her eyes.

"I'm sorry, Miss Shelton," Prosecutor Williams interrupted, "but, for the record, the female you are referring to was the woman you once believed was your mother, Olivia Sneed."

Lily swallowed hard and thought of the best way to answer the question. "Yes, it is one and the same."

I was glad that Lily had found a way to satisfy the court without going against a promise she had made to herself. Lily didn't hold Olivia Sneed accountable for the death of her biological mother, but she knew Olivia was not blameless, and my friend did not want to honor the woman she had known as her mother by saying Olivia's name or title.

"Bannon was shocked that she had hit him," Lily continued, "but he recovered quickly and head-butted her. He gathered me under his arm and strode to the front door."

The rest of the courtroom listened intently to Lily's account of the events. I had tuned out my friend's voice after I saw the look in her eyes. I preferred a first-hand viewing of the events.

I had gotten better at scanning people's minds since my experience by the river. I no longer needed to be asleep to glance at a person's memory, but I still needed that person's focus to be on the memory for me to view a particular recollection.

I felt myself slip through the fabric of time. I knew that everyone around me would see a young woman staring intently at her friend, but my consciousness was actually at the Sneed mansion in mid-December.

"What did you do, Bannon?" Olivia Sneed yelled. *She had her hands on her hips.*

"Nothing you need to concern yourself with!" he said in a calm voice. *"Go back to your bottle."*

"You didn't hurt anyone, right?" Olivia said. *She advanced a couple of steps. "Surely you're not that heartless!"*

"I don't know who you think you were sleeping beside all these years, but you can't run a town with a clean conscience." He held up his left hand. "Sometimes you gotta get your hands dirty."

It was strange to see Olivia without a haughty air about her. It seemed she only let her social guard down around her immediate family.

"Believe me," Olivia whispered, "I've been drowning my conscience for years.

"Please, Bannon," Olivia pleaded, "don't destroy our family. Let's go back to the city. You can pay people to keep us safe, and we can go back to the way we were before we came to this town."

Lydia's vision shifted to Bannon Sneed. He seemed to be absorbing his wife's words. He slowly shook his head from side to side.

"No, Liv, I've got business to take care of here. Besides, I was small potatoes in New York, but everyone fears and respects me in Erwin."

"No one respects you," *Olivia said quietly. She lowered her head and looked at the floor.*

"Fear equals respect," *Bannon told her and lifted her chin. He gazed into her face.* "You used to be such a beautiful woman."

"What are you going to do?" *Olivia asked. She looked at her husband with eyes that would have been intoxicating if she had been sober.*

"You know what I have to do," *Bannon said.* "You can help me tie up loose ends," *he held up Lydia's hand,* "or you can go back to your bottle." *Bannon laughed.* "Maybe you'll both drown tonight, just in different ways."

Olivia's tears poured down her cheeks. She looked down at Lydia, and sobs shook her frail, alcohol-aged body.

Suddenly, Olivia grabbed for Lydia. She freed her enough for Lydia to unhook herself from hi hold. Olivia reached for Lydia's hand, and once they touched, the two ran for the front door.

"What are you going to do, Olivia?" *Bannon mocked.* "How successful was it the last time you ran away?"

Olivia turned around. Lydia could almost touch the front door.

"I never got the chance!" Olivia screamed at Bannon. "You made sure of that. Why did you want to stay?" Olivia demanded. "There were so many crazy things happening."

Bannon stepped slowly toward them. Lydia pulled Mummy's arm, but Olivia wasn't finished talking.

"You saw what happened to Nellie! The curse is real!" Olivia screamed. Bannon continued his advance.

"I'm tired of playing around," Bannon finally spoke. "If we're punished, then so be it. We went into it knowing that we could be haunted for the rest of our lives."

Lydia was confused by their words. What had Bannon and Olivia Sneed done that would haunt them?

Bannon had reached the spot where Olivia and Lydia had stopped. He spoke softly. Lydia could hear the rage beneath Bannon's calm demeanor, but Olivia seemed enchanted by his every word.

"Don't you see, Olivia?" he reached out and stroked a piece of hair behind her ear. "We weren't meant to have a child. That's why you lost our baby and you stole this one."

"Don't you talk like that in front of her!" Olivia screamed.

Lydia was still in the doorway. She didn't feel her body fall onto the floor with a thump. Bannon and Olivia Sneed were lost in their argument. They didn't see Lydia's horrified realization.

"Where are you going?" he asked gently. His hand had moved from Olivia's hair to her shoulder.

Lydia tugged on Mummy's arm. Mummy did not respond to her frantic pulls.

"We are going to the city," Olivia said resolutely. "Whatever it is will have a hard time finding us—if it ever does." Olivia grabbed his hand. "Come with us! Please! Leave this place and never come back. I remember the way you used to be. You were never withdrawn and depressed in New York."

"I was miserable in New York!" he bellowed at her. "The only thing I won over in the city was your attention." He looked over Olivia's emancipated form. "But who would want you now?"

Olivia moved back a step like she'd been slapped. She wiped her face clean of any emotion and turned away from her husband. Lydia sighed with relief. Maybe Mummy would move closer to the door.

"Do you know who murdered your precious friend?" Bannon asked, a smile caressing his lips.

Olivia turned around, and Lydia watched Bannon move in toward her. He put his left foot between Olivia's feet and placed his hands at his sides. Lydia could tell he was ready to pounce on Mummy at any moment, but Olivia Sneed never guessed Bannon's intention.

"I know you stood by and let it happen, but you didn't do it," Olivia said. She lowered her gaze and shook her head.

The evil grin Lydia had known was just beneath Bannon's calm demeanor uncovered itself. "I may not have strangled the life out of Nellie, but I ordered her murder."

Olivia looked confused, but she wasn't angry. "You told Bryan to kill Nellie?"

He smiled into his middle-aged wife's still naïve eyes. "No, but I told Terrance to kill your friend and dispose of her body. It turned out it was a blessing that he didn't throw her further out into the river. Nellie's body ended up floating upside down beside her unconscious husband."

The alcohol seemed to have clouded Olivia's ability to think things through. She swayed in the doorway, trying to understand why her husband's words should upset her.

He threw up his hands. "Nellie was taking you away. I saw my opportunity to end her influence over you, and I had Terrance strangle her to death."

"So you lied to me?" Olivia asked innocently. The incident had happened many years ago, so Olivia seemed more upset about her husband's betrayal than her friend's murder.

"Yes," Bannon said, grabbing Olivia's arms and laughed into her face. "I had your friend murdered and then I told you it was Bryan who did it. You sent an innocent man to prison!"

Olivia's face crumbled, and her cheeks reflected the rivers of moisture from her eyes. He took advantage of his wife's emotions to grab Lydia and begin dragging her out the door.

"Where are you going with my baby?" Olivia demanded. She had turned off her tears and stood with her hands on her hips.

Lydia looked from one to the other. Olivia was weak after years of alcoholism. She might have weighed ninety pounds, and she didn't look healthy. On the other hand, Bannon's new exercise routine had gotten him in better physical condition. He was a long way from six-pack abs, but his skin was firm from the muscles beneath it.

"I'm going to the river to finish what I started twelve years ago," he said simply.

It didn't take long for Olivia to process his statement. Unfortunately, most people can see the scripted response of a drunkard moments before that person physically responds.

"No!" Olivia yelled and hurled herself at her husband.

Bannon stepped easily into his wife's crazed embrace and placed his hands around her neck. Olivia realized she had been bested, but she thought Bannon would not actually risk hurting her too badly. It was only as she neared unconsciousness that she feared for her life.

Lydia understood his murderous state of mind well before Olivia realized that her husband's hands were serious. Lydia was the first to register the malicious grin that had always been lurking under his poker face.

Lydia scanned the foyer for anyone or anything that would help her. Two long-handled umbrellas stood in a rack near the door. A heavy coat rack had fallen at some point, and a few of its many arms were broken on the floor.

Lydia's gaze fell upon a bronze pot near the coat rack. It was empty, but Lydia could hardly lift it when she finally reached it.

She could hear Mummy's choking sounds. He was laughing and looking intently into his wife's dying eyes.

"I never realized it before," he said. He almost sounded like he was having a conversation with a friend over dinner. "You will always be mine." Lydia could see his smirk. "I had you during the best years of your life."

Olivia was turning a strange blueish-gray color. She tried to close her eyes, but they continued to bulge from their sockets.

He was so delusional and enraged that he couldn't even feel Olivia scratching and kicking him. Lydia aimed the pot over her Bannon's head. She couldn't lift it too high or wait to position it perfectly, so the pot crashed down on his head before Lydia was ready.

Bannon swayed for a second, but he kept his grip on Mummy's neck. Mummy looked into Lydia's eyes and tried to communicate her last words, but Lydia couldn't read her mind. In the end, Lydia believed Mummy was telling her she was sorry and that she loved her. Lydia could name two mean or embarrassing things Mummy had done for every good thing, but she tried to push the good memories to the front of her mind. Lydia nodded her head at Mummy during Olivia Sneed's final seconds. Lydia hoped she had communicated her love and forgiveness, but who lives to tell the true thoughts of the dying as they pass out of their bodily restraints?

As Olivia Sneed winked out of existence, Lydia felt a change wash over her. She wasn't sure about the lies that had been told, but she knew that Bryan and Nellie Shelton had been her parents. When the *last of Mummy's life trickled out of her, Lydia Sneed decided she was Lily Shelton.*

Lily watched life exit the body of Lydia's Mummy. Olivia Sneed had been a snotty alcoholic, but she hadn't deserved to die while the breath was chased out of her by the man who promised to love and protect her. Olivia's dead eyes remained perfectly fixed on her husband until he lowered her to the ground in a sitting position in the corner behind the door.

Lily understood that her chance to run had slipped away. She bolted toward the free air, but Bannon grabbed her arm and tucked her close to his side. Her face and hair dangled inches from the ground.

Lily noticed a small silver object by Mummy's lifeless hand. She knew it was the locket, but when she tried to grab it, her captor tore out of the door and across the grounds. Lily kept reaching, but she was jerked out the door, and she lost sight of the little silver locket.

Lily experienced a time where she remembered mostly darkness. She could feel her wrists bound to a wooden chair, and she only regained consciousness long enough for Bannon to stick her with another needle.

All Lily could remember about her surroundings was that the curtains were brown, and they were always pulled against the light. Lily recalled being fed and taken to the bathroom, but she was bound and gagged after every meal.

Lily had no idea how much time had passed between Olivia Sneed's murder and the moment she regained consciousness in front of Bannon Sneed's mansion. She had not noticed the world around her for some time and she had not felt the motion of the car ride.

Lily jolted into conscious thought as she was dragged out of the backseat by her upper arms. She remembered feeling weak, and there was a tingling sensation in her wrists, but she could process the world around her more clearly.

Lily didn't know if she was dizzy or if she felt that way because she was getting dragged across the grounds of her former home. She could tell that it was late at night, but her body barely registered the cold air.

Bannon carried Lily around her waist under one of his arms. She could feel his fingers dig into her ribs.

Bannon stopped once at the road to look both ways. He stepped on Lily's hair when he began walking again, and she cried out. He dug his fingers deeply between her ribs to reward her cry.

Lily sobbed, but she was not loud enough to disturb Bannon. He walked straight over to the old house and kicked in the front door. It gave easily against Bannon's force.

Lily looked around and tried not to think of the way she used to dream up princes and princesses within these walls. She felt sick that she had loved and trusted the people who had murdered her real mother and stolen her like a coveted object.

A calming touch spread over Lily's neck and back. She had been more aware of the presence since her phone call with Ella.

Lily had answered a phone call on the last day she attended school and heard Ella's voice. Ella had frightened Lily when she said that Nellie was following her, so Lily hung up on her.

Lily tried to write off the warning as part of Ella's strangeness, but she had to admit that she had felt an otherworldly presence since she was a young girl. She decided to confide her worries to Sydney.

Actually, Lily had done some digging through her father's papers, and she had learned a lot about a couple named Bryan and Nellie Shelton. Lily just didn't want to admit the validity of the documents she'd found. If the papers were real, then her life had been a lie, and she'd never be the same.

Lily could feel Bannon's fingers poking between her ribs, but she didn't want to cry out again. She decided to think of something else. Lily turned her thoughts to a time when she was still Lydia and she'd just moved with her mummy to the small town of Erwin.

A week after the party that announced young Lydia Sneed's arrival, Lydia went swimming in the river that sparkled in the sun. Mummy paid for swimming lessons in New York, and she didn't fear the water. To her, the Nolichucky River was just a large, rocky pool.

Lydia had been used to Mummy's undivided attention since her memories began. Mummy had taken her running and swimming every day at their in-home track and indoor pool.

Mummy had been giving her attention to the man who said he was Lydia's father since they moved to this town. Lydia felt lonely, and she missed Mummy, so she decided to do something the two of them had often done together.

Lydia had seen the river from her bedroom window. The sun glinted off the water and almost hurt her eyes, but Lydia was drawn to it.

Lydia didn't bother putting on a bathing suit or telling anyone where she was going. The servants were busy preparing dinner, and no one saw the young, blonde child slip out the door.

Lydia breathed in the fresh crisp air. It almost hurt her nose to breathe. She couldn't hear a car horn or a person.

Lydia walked across the grounds and stopped at the road. There wasn't a crosswalk or a crossing sign, but Lydia knew to look both ways for vehicles before she crossed the road.

Lydia could hear her feet padding across the asphalt. It was a sound she had never heard. The streets of New York were always loud with traffic and people.

The river was talking rapidly as Lydia approached it. She watched it move across rocks and small life wiggled and rushed in what her mummy had called "The River of Death."

Lydia kicked off her shoes and stepped into the water. It was cold, but Lydia had felt colder temperatures in the city.

Lydia noticed a small house near the river where she stood. It seemed to be cared for, but she didn't think anyone lived there. The curtains were drawn on a sunny day, and several stones were upraised on the trail to the river.

Lydia closed her eyes and thought of who might live there. Maybe the house was a secret location for princes and princesses who had to hide from the evil in their kingdoms. Maybe it was the only place they could rest.

Lydia imagined the royal runaways arrived through the fireplace, like the people in a book series she liked about witches and wizards, and exchanged pleasantries while they danced until dawn. As the sun rose, the noble children would close the curtains and shut their eyes on the light of the day. Lydia resolved to swim quietly, so that the princes and princesses could rest peacefully.

Lydia slipped into the water. The river's temperature was about the same as the air that reached her sixteenth-floor window in the city's winter. Lydia's clothes weighed her down, but she pushed forward in the water with her arm strokes.

The rushing water and mountain air filled her senses. Lydia was so consumed with tranquility, that she didn't hear a shrill scream and frantic shouts echoing from her new home.

Lydia's serenity was interrupted by a splash. She looked back at the shore and spotted her father's manservant swimming out in the water. Mummy was on the shore screaming, and a police car had rolled to a stop on the road.

Mummy had gone into a hysterical fit and convinced Mr. Hernandez to swim out and "rescue" her, even though Lydia had only been twenty feet from the river bank. Lydia let Mr. Hernandez's strong arms guide her back to the shore.

Mummy was at the edge of the water, and she gathered Lydia close to her, and made Lydia promise never to swim in the river. Lydia had agreed because she wanted to please Mummy.

"Is everything okay here?" a familiar voice echoed down the river bank.

Mummy hugged Lydia close and whispered, "Don't talk to or look at this man or he will take you away from me."

Lydia couldn't imagine a worse punishment than being forced away from Mummy, so she buried her head in Mummy's chest and kept still and quiet.

"Are you okay, Little Lady?" the familiar voice asked.

Lydia threw out one of her tiny hands, but she did not move any other part of her body. She had seen Mummy tell the servants everything was okay this way when they were eating.

Mummy told the man something about her daughter's shyness. The man finally got back into his car and drove away.

Lydia disentangled herself from Mummy's arms and noticed that Mummy had been sweating. Mummy ran to Mr. Hernandez and whispered to him while gesticulating wildly.

Lydia understood she needed to stay close to Mummy, so she took large steps until she reached Mr. Hernandez and Mummy. She studied Mr. Hernandez's massive hands until Mummy finally took notice of her.

"I'll talk to you more about this later," Mummy said sharply and turned toward the grounds.

Mr. Hernandez nodded at Mummy's back and followed her. Lydia watched her feet as she ambled over the river rocks to the bank. The small stones picked at her bare feet, but Lydia didn't mind. The small pricks of pain she felt helped to remind her that she had had a moment of freedom in the river. She could still hear whispering its way into town.

Lydia was leaving the riverside when she felt a hand on her back. The pressure of the touch was warm and comforting, but she couldn't tell from where it had originated. Mummy and Mr. Hernandez were walking in front of her, and Lydia could not see any other people by the river. Lydia decided she had imagined the touch, but she felt warmer and more complete.

Lydia grew used to the touch. It was almost like a tight pair of jeans that irritated you until your body got used to them. Lydia felt the touch for a couple of days, but then she became accustomed to its presence, and she only noticed its absence because the warmth she usually felt on her back was gone.

Lily felt the same warm touch caress her back as Bannon threw her into the kitchen. Lily was too weak to get up or talk, so she lay on the floor and waited for the next round of abuse.

Bannon threw drawers open in the kitchen. Yellowed straw wrappers and plastic kitchen utensils fell all around Lily.

Her captor had placed Lily on the floor at his feet. Lily thought she could get away, but when she tried to get up and run, she felt a strong pull at her scalp. Bannon had placed his foot on her hair. Lily thought she could do without some of her hair, but she was afraid the pressure on her scalp might be too great to pull away from Bannon's reach before he stopped her escape.

"Where is it?" Bannon yelled. He took out the drawer and dumped its contents on the floor. He threw a drawer against the wall in his frustration, and the drawer busted into a plethora of wooden pieces.

Lily tested her voice. A scratchy grumble rumbled her throat, but she knew a scream was not possible. Bannon realized Lily was attempting to voice her location, and he jerked her into a sitting position on a wooden kitchen chair.

Lily cried out from the pain in her scalp, but the sound was only a little better than a whisper. Her throat was raw and dry.

Bannon looked into Lily's horrified eyes.

"I ran out of liquid calm for you, but we're going to play a game," he said. Anyone who heard Bannon's words and tone of voice would assume he was really suggesting a fun activity.

Lily saw the cruel smile return to Bannon's lips. She felt sickness in her stomach that was totally unrelated to the dizziness in her head.

"We're gonna play quiet mouth," Bannon said. He looked like an overjoyed adult who realized that he made a toddler-sized child very happy.

"I'm gonna take a little nap, and you're gonna sit in this chair and shut your mouth!"

Bannon had begun his sentence calmly, but when he described what he meant for Lily to do, he ended his statement sharply. Lily tried to keep her features calm and relaxed.

A sharp sound that seemed to echo through the walls of the house caused Bannon to jerk to attention. He waited a full moment before dismissing the sound as an animal or a creak in the dilapidated house.

Bannon unbound her wrists, but Lily couldn't feel her arms. They hung like heavy, unmovable weights at her sides.

Bannon retied Lily's wrists to the arms of the chair. She grimaced when she felt the tingling that signaled the return of blood to her appendages.

She fell asleep soon after Bannon retied her bonds, and she woke as the morning light was creeping through a crack in the curtains. She thought she heard a noise inside the wall, but she assumed it was a nesting opossum or mouse.

Lily heard a woman knock and call out. She couldn't fight through her pain to remember the owner of the familiar voice. The woman came into the house, but Bannon hid Lily with him in a closet while the woman searched the house.

The woman went into every room of the house, but she didn't check the closets or the pantry. The woman kept yelling for Bryan Shelton, but Lily couldn't recall why the name was important to her.

Later that night, Lily was awakened from one of her dozes by Bannon's frantic movements. She saw shapes dance across the ceiling from the headlights of a car.

"I didn't want to do this so soon," Bannon said as he untied Lily's wrists, "but people just can't mind their business."

Lily cried out when Bannon pulled her up by her hair and her right arm. Bannon dragged her through the kitchen and out the back door. Lily realized she was living the last moments of her life.

Lily didn't fight the man who used to be her father as her body thumped the ground. He was taking her to the river, and Lily knew he intended to drown her.

Bannon lifted Lily up to meet his eyes. "I thought you would make her happy. You should have shared the same grave with your mother!"

Lily met Bannon's eyes and did not prepare a response. She tried to wipe her face of emotion.

Bannon nodded knowingly. "Oh, you're scared. But look on the bright side," he said, and Lily smelled the decay and bitterness on his breath. "You'll finally get to meet your mother."

Lily gathered all her energy and head-butted him. She spat in his face, even though her eyes were spinning and her nose felt numb. Before Bannon could recover, Lily kicked him.

Bannon strengthened his hold on her and threw her into the water. His hands found Lily's neck, and he pressed on her windpipe. She felt a sharp pain near the base of her neck, and Lily kicked him one last time before she blacked out for a moment. She returned to the world, hearing voices and feeling less pressure around her throat.

I backed out of Lily's mind as coolly as I had entered it. I had so gently brushed my friend's thoughts that I doubted Lily knew I had been there.

I thought Nellie had meant to kill Olivia, but she had been trying to warn Ella and me that Bannon planned to kill his wife. I had believed Olivia's murder had not been premeditated, but Bannon had probably harbored ill feelings toward his wife since she had first planned to leave him. *What was wrong with Bryan and Barron? Their wives wanted to visit the city, not go on a lifetime vacation?*

Lily finished her statement, and the judge asked the prosecutor and Bannon Sneed's defense attorney to approach the bench. She relaxed her posture and let out a heavy sigh.

I hugged my friend as she returned to the seat beside me, and I felt her sobs rattle her small frame. Tears threatened to run away from my eyes, but I blinked hard several times. I had to be strong for Lily.

Life can be unfair at times, and no one can see that better than an adolescent. As a child, I had always thought the adults in my life would keep away all the wrong-doers, but as I held Lily, I realized that life plays its cruelest jokes on children. Most times, though, they are just too young to realize it.

Chapter Forty-Two

I turned the key in the lock and stepped inside. A warm pine scent greeted me with a vanilla undertone. I had burned vanilla candles weeks ago, while I soaked in the bath.

I promised myself that I wouldn't give my emotions time to catch up with me, but when I took in the smell of the home my grandpa had wanted to share with me, I felt a sharp pain in my heart. Our home would have smelled like pine wood and vanilla.

I felt the warm press of a hand, and I jumped. I rounded on Ella before I realized it was my sister.

Ella's spirit was completely broken. Her neon pink cast was the only bright thing about her.

I had vouched for Ella at the hospital, and with our mom, but the doctor who had seen Ella after her fall demanded that my sister be mentally evaluated. Ella had been seen and pronounced competent by a couple of psychiatrists, but she had still resigned herself to being placed on medication or put into a mental institution.

I had cried and told Ella to fake her mental health. Most people, even the crazy ones, would have been offended by my request, but Ella simply nodded her head. She had walked quietly behind our mom to the psychiatric wing.

I was surprised when Ella had come back out of the wing, skipping behind our mom. I enjoyed the effervescent Ella for several hours before bed. In our room, Ella told me how she had fooled two psychiatrists in order to keep her promise to me. I didn't realize I had made her promise me anything.

The night of her mental exam, Ella admitted she thought she would be evaluated again within the year. Her sanity had already been examined, and she wasn't going to change her strange ways, so it would be only a matter of time before her mental ability was questioned again.

The house returned to my family's version of normal the day after Ella's mental appraisal. I continued to spread joy through our dismal house as Ella sat on the edge of her bed in a trance. A slightly strengthened bond between my sister and me was the only difference.

Several days later, I realized that I would have to visit my grandpa's home and make sure the house was winterized. My mom drove me out to the house that was titled in my name while she chatted with Detective Lewis Novack in the front of the car.

I left my mom, Ella, and Lewis by the truck my grandpa had left to him. I had forgotten that my mom and Ella were waiting for me to finish my business inside the house.

"I did not mean to scare you," Ella said quietly. Her voice relayed the stress and pain she'd endured.

I put my arm around my sister. I felt her shoulders tense, but I didn't release or loosen my hold.

"I'm glad you came in," I said. "Having you here will give me the strength to do what I need to do."

My first stop was my grandpa's spare room. I picked up the only item of importance and stuffed it in my plastic garbage bag. The ears of the purple rabbit poked out of the bag.

Lily and I were still close friends, and I knew she would appreciate the return of her rabbit. She was outwardly happy, but there was a sadness just beneath her façade. I felt like the purple rabbit would bring out a genuine smile.

I dwelt on the visions I had experienced during the last couple of months. *What had Olivia Sneed meant when she mentioned a curse? What was the it she had been so afraid of?*

I spent several minutes in my room, throwing clothes and accessories into my bag. I moved quickly, knowing I could sort out my things when I returned home.

I was lucky that my mom had let me come home. There had been a lot of tension in our house after Bannon Sneed's arrest. My mom was stressed out about Ella and me, and she was still grieving over her father, husband, and sons. She yelled at me and picked fights, so I stayed with Lily and Kerry until the court date. Kerry finally brought up the subject that had danced across everyone's mind.

"When are you going home?" he asked me over dinner one night.

Lily was two days away from giving a closed statement in court. She had asked me to stay with her at first, but when no one called looking for me, Kerry got concerned.

I thought he was worried partly because he knew that I had unsettled business with my family, but I'm sure he was also concerned because people could think he was taking advantage of young, vulnerable girls.

"I don't know that I have a home," I answered. I was not afraid to be honest with Kerry and Lily. I knew my words would not be repeated.

"Your mother really isn't as stubborn as she seems," Kerry said. He opened his hands over the table. "I love having you here, Sydney, but you need your family now. Lily and I can be there for you through anything, but there's nothing like the bond shared through blood."

Kerry sighed. He looked at Lily, and something passed between them.

"Ella is getting worse," Lily said. "The doctors gave her sanity a pass, but Ella is…"

I thought I understood. "This is less for my good than for hers."

"You are the eldest child," Kerry said firmly. "You have a responsibility to your family, and you really must take care of your sister."

"You are your brother's keeper," I muttered under my breath.

They looked at me questioningly. Until then, I didn't realize I had spoken aloud.

I had watched Kerry go through the Shelton line with Lily, so I knew he had been the oldest of six children. Lily was lucky that she was an only child.

I struggled to find the perfect response to Kerry's statement. In the end, I merely said, "Yes, sir."

Lily and I had returned to school after the winter break, so Kerry drove me to my mom's house after school the day after Lily and I made our appearance in court. I had hoped Lily would go with me, but her uncle gave her a look that told her to stay in place. At least they stayed in the driveway as I approached the front steps. I could run and jump into the car if things got crazy.

I had never felt so apprehensive about approaching the house where I had grown up. *Was this house really my home, or did that feeling leave when my brothers' spirits left the earth?*

"Coming," my mom yelled. I saw her lift aside the living room curtains quickly. I imagined her shock at my presence and her cautious footsteps as she approached the door.

I heard the bolts and latches turn, and soon my mom and I were standing face-to-face on opposite sides of the doorway. We stood looking at each other for a moment, and then my mom surprised me by squeezing me into an embrace.

"I wondered which one of us would make the first move," I choked out.

"You made the first move by coming here," my mom said through her tears. "I was too proud to ask you to come home, but when I saw you here on the doorstep, I couldn't imagine another moment without my Sydney."

I was going to have to hand it to Kerry. He was smarter than he let people think. Maybe he would be okay raising a teenage girl after all.

"What are you going to do about the rest of Grandpa's things?" Ella asked, interrupting my reverie.

I knew that my sister was simply curious. She didn't care about material possessions.

"I guess I'll straighten everything out over the summer," I told her.

Ella nodded and went to the bathroom to collect my toiletries. I thought about the last time I had been in the house. *Why hadn't I shared my thoughts with my grandpa before I left?* He could still be alive if not for my rash behavior.

All of a sudden, it was all too much for me. I could smell my grandpa and see the possessions that had been dear to him, but I would never see him again. I would never go on a road trip with him, or go fishing or hunting, or even share a meal with the man who had meant more to me than I could have ever guessed.

I had never realized that my grandpa had been my father. There are people who would argue that he had been a father *figure*, but I had to disagree. My grandpa had taught me right from wrong, cared for and loved me unconditionally, and he hadn't made the choice to leave me. Chief Conner Murphy had been my father, and I didn't care about titles and formalities.

I hadn't noticed the tears coursing down my legs or the aches in my body from my continuous sobbing until Ella's feet came into view. I had been sitting on the floor, and my crying fit had attracted my sister's attention. I kept my eyes fixed on her feet.

"Why are you crying?" Ella asked.

It was a simple question, but for some reason, it was the worst thing my sister could have asked me. I think I would have responded more cordially to her if she had said, 'Why does your breath smell like rotting sewage?'

I jumped up and came within inches of my sister's body. I pointed my finger down into her face, and all the garbage in the world came out of my mouth.

I still don't remember all the horrible things I said to Ella, but I can recall downing her mental state, criticizing her inability to control her gift, and accusing her of a lack of conscience. My sister never so much as blinked an eye while I yelled at her. She stood calmly in place and listened to my insults.

I must have been angry that Ella did not become upset over my offenses, and I did something that I swore I would never do. I'm sure it burned a bridge between my sister and me that I will never be able to rebuild.

I remembered looking into Ella's crystal blue eyes and realizing that I was being cruel. My sister had not hurt me in any way, and I was berating her for things she couldn't control. I was ashamed of myself, but instead of apologizing, I made matters worse.

"There is just *nothing* good about you," I shouted at my sister. "I bet that's why Dad and Grandpa haven't contacted you since they've passed. They couldn't stand to be around you in life, so why would they want to see you now?"

I hadn't seen the note in my sister's hand, but I watched it fall to the floor after Ella calmly turned and walked away from me. My actions dumbfounded me, and all I could do was fall to the floor.

I picked up the note and read my grandpa's writing. Ella had probably wanted to share something with me about our grandpa, but I had ruined any confidential moments we would share for a long time. Possibly ever.

I clutched the note to my chest and cried. Tears ran down my upturned face like water, and no one rushed to my side to comfort me.

"Why did you have to go?" I said to the memory of my grandpa over and over. I think I screamed it at one point, but I was having a fit, so I can't be sure of anything.

Once I calmed down enough to know that it was getting harder for my mom to explain the length of time I'd spent in the house, I decided I should leave. I would take the things I had thrown into the bags, and I would come back periodically to finish going through my grandpa's possessions.

A loud thump jolted me into reality. *Was I sure that I was alone? Had Ella really left the house when she walked away from me?*

I tried to place the source of the noise, and I decided it must have come from my grandpa's bedroom. I walked across the hall carefully and eased open the door.

The smell of pine and cologne was heaviest in his room. The warmth of the air in the closed room would have been oppressive to some people, but it was just right for me.

I walked around the room, but I couldn't see anything that would have made a noise like the one I had heard. Pictures were still standing in their frames, and the clock and the lamp by the bed had not moved.

I decided that my grief-stricken mind had imagined the noise, and I turned around. Another noise stopped me before I could touch the door to my grandpa's room. It sounded like it was right behind me, and against my better judgment I turned around.

I don't know what I expected, but I was relieved when I saw nothing more than the contents the room had held when I first entered it. But that wasn't quite right.

The closet door was open. *Had it been open when I scanned the room?*

On the floor in front of my grandpa's closet was a small blue box. I had been sure that the door to the closet had been closed when I first entered the room, but I was willing to give my mind some leeway.

I dropped to my knees in front of the box and picked it up. It was heavier than I thought it would be, so I had to use quite a bit of strength to turn the box to investigate it.

The box may have been a shoebox at one time, but it was for a brand of shoes I didn't recognize. An almost alien-like insignia, a circle with two tribal lines, was branded onto the top of the box.

The box was duct taped shut, but I knew where my grandpa kept his knives. I opened his bedside table drawer and picked up the first knife that touched my fingers. It was already open. Its blue handle rested easily in my hand.

I slid the knife along where I hoped the box's top separated from its bottom, carefully cutting away from myself. I cut along three sides and stopped. I was too eager to see its contents to free the remaining side.

I opened the box and was assaulted by the smell of the woods. In fact, the box smelled like you could step inside it and magically transport into the forest.

There were pictures on top, but I placed them aside and investigated the rest of the box. I found a couple of letters, a map, and a strange metal object.

The only description I could have given the object was that it was metallic and gray. I picked it up to my eyes. It was definitely the heaviest item in the box.

Once I was satisfied that I had seen all the contents of the box, I turned my attention back to the letters and pictures. I picked up the letter at the top of the pile and read.

Amanda,

I really miss you. I wake up every morning and hope to see you smiling next to me, but you're never there. What can I do to make you see I love you and I want to spend the rest of my life with you?

I know you're worried about Miranda, but she'll come around eventually. I agree, we shouldn't have hidden our relationship from her, but we didn't know that we were falling in love until it had already happened.

Please come home to me. I need you, and I love you.

Your loving husband,
Conner

There were a dozen letters like the first, and I had almost given up looking through them when I stumbled across a sheet of paper that made me stop. The letter was typed, but the paper was yellow, and it looked like it had been read many times. My blood ran cold when I saw the name of the sender.

Conner,

You may not believe me, but it's started again. I don't know who woke it up, but the curse is back. I tell my wife I'm going to look for work, but I search the woods for it. I've tried going

back to the place I think it rests, but I haven't been able to destroy it.

My family says that I'm going crazy, and I am seeing things I'm not sure are there. I think my boys can see it, too.

Please come help me before I go crazy. You know what it did last time. It picked off most of our parents before it stopped. I don't think it did stop. I think it was just waiting for us to develop relationships with other people, so it would have more people to destroy.

Please come back. I'm scared for my boys and my wife.

Your friend,

Lyle Miller

I glanced over the pictures again. I saw a couple of baby pictures that must have been of my mom, two wedding pictures of my grandpa and Amanda, and a few other, older photographs.

I had never met my paternal grandfather, and I assumed my grandpa had never met him, but it seemed my father's father had known my mom's family. One of the older pictures was of my grandparents holding hands by a lake, but the rest of the pictures were of young boys. The boys had been pictured playing in the river, just outside the woods, and helping another young boy wax a shiny new truck.

I didn't want to admit that the boys and the truck looked familiar. I had ridden in the same truck with Bryan only a month ago. I had to steady my shaking hand to read the back of the last picture. A woman's plain script documented the photograph so that it could be used as a keepsake: *Lyle, Timmy, Jimmy, and Conner help Richie wax his birthday present.*

I let the picture fall to the floor. My mind tried to wrap around the truth the pictures and letters revealed, but I couldn't fully analyze it. My grandpa hadn't approached Ella after his death, but he had found a way to communicate with me from beyond the grave. I only hoped I could understand the contents in the box before "it" was could cause more harm.

Epilogue

*"Y*ou know she has to die," he told her.

Ella tried to turn away, but his voice followed her. Finally, she stared straight forward, hoping that she could block out his voice by meditating.

"I will wait," she heard him say. *"You have to come back eventually."*

"What do you want me to say?" Ella asked angrily. She investigated the face that had haunted her for years and realized that he was right. She was bound to him as surely as a person in her family bound himself or herself by a pinky swear.

"Your family has more secrets than I do," he said.

"You have no secrets," Ella asserted. She crossed her arms and looked away. "You are dead."

Ella felt a chill envelope her that she associated with his anger. She jabbed her elbows down and around, but she couldn't break free of the hold. Her breath left her as a compression pressed her chest. A moment later she was released.

"Not too bad for a dead *person,"* he said triumphantly. He had settled back into a talkative mood.

Ella decided not to test him. He had brought her to the brink of death many times, but he never got her to bend to his will unless he threatened the ones she loved. He had caused events to unfold that had led to her grandfather's death the last time Ella had tested his patience. Ella wanted to believe her grandfather would have been shot anyway, but the timing was too coincidental.

"*It is almost time,*" he said.

Ella nodded. A promise had been made and, unfortunately, it was almost time for him to collect.

THE END

Did you enjoy the book?

If you liked the story, please consider leaving a review on Amazon, Goodreads, and/or BookBub. Your review can help me a lot, even if you write, "I liked it!"

Thank you so much for reading my book. I hope you enjoyed Pinky Swear!

About the Author

Courtnee Turner Hoyle is the author of the award-winning My Brother's Keeper. She also crafted the characters in Solomon's Tears, Hollis's Hobby, and the Amazon best-seller, Finding Emma. Courtnee lives with her children on her own hill of mystery in Northeast Tennessee. She earned two undergraduate degrees and a Master of Arts in Teaching from East Tennessee State University, and she enjoys reading, writing, and any reasonable music. She helps people travel all over the world, and she's delighted companies pay her to live vicariously through her clients' travel. Otherwise, Courtnee spends her days in comfortable chaos, avoiding sweet tea, chocolate, and unannounced visitors. If you're lucky enough to find her on Facebook, you should tell her your opinion of her work.

Also by Courtnee

Pale Woods Mystery Series
My Brother's Keeper
Book One
Courtnee Turner Hoyle

Seventeen-year-old Jerrod Miller has struggled with the guilt of his actions for an event that took place almost a year ago. His friends have abandoned him, his family ignores him, and he lost his best friend. To make matters worse, he was unable to access records that may have revealed his father's whereabouts. His sister, Ella, guides Jerrod as he tries to learn and accept secrets his family has tried to hide. However, a sinister spirit may be influencing Ella's actions, and it has an agenda of its own.

Also by Courtnee

Finding Emma
It's About Time Series
Book One

What if the only anchor to your identity was a tattoo with a name?

David Winsome answers the door to a beautiful woman who can't remember how she ended up on the hill near his family's home. The woman assumes the name on her tattoo, Emma, and blends into the community while questions about her past plague her.

Why is the town familiar, even though no one seems to know her? And why does she feel an intimate attraction to David, even though she just met him?

As Emma accepts her new life and begins a loving relationship with David, a person who claims to know her enters her life. Does this person hold the key to Emma's past, or is there a mystery much deeper than Emma's identity?

Someone has manipulated the events in his favor, and he has a much larger plan in mind.

Where Will You Go?

A re you thinking about a trip to Disney or Orlando Studios?

Do you want to sail away on a cruise ship?

I can help!

Destination Companies pay me to help you, so you won't pay extra for my travel services.

I can:

- help plan and book your travel, accommodations, and tickets

- order special event tickets

- manage any hiccups

- arrange travel insurance

- make hard-to-get dining reservations

I will:

- send emails with tips and tricks customized to your travel and destination

- monitor deals to grab the best prices for you

- keep my eye on the destination's weather and crowd calen-
  dars

- answer questions quickly

Courtnee's Magical Vacations
turnerco6@yahoo.com

Chapter 50